Tim

Time's Eye

ARTHUR C. CLARKE
AND
STEPHEN BAXTER

The right of Arthur C. Clarke and Stephen Baxter
to be identified as the authors of this work has
been asserted by them in accordance with the
Copyright, Designs and Patents Act 1988.

First published in Great Britain in 2004 by

Gollancz
An imprint of the Orion Publishing Group
Orion House, 5 Upper St Martin's Lane,
London WC2H 9EA

This mass-market paperback edition first published in 2005
by Gollancz

A CIP catalogue record for this book is available
from the British Library

ISBN 0 575 07647 X

Typeset at The Spartan Press Ltd,
Lymington, Hants

Printed in Great Britain by
Clays Ltd, St Ives plc

www.orionbooks.co.uk

Authors' Note

This book, and the series which it opens, neither follows nor precedes the books of the earlier *Odyssey*, but is at right angles to them: not a sequel or prequel, but an 'orthoquel', taking similar premises in a different direction.

The quotation from Rudyard Kipling's 'Cities and Thrones and Powers', from *Puck of Pook's Hill* (1906), is used by kind permission of A.P. Watt Ltd, on behalf of the National Trust for Places of Historical Interest or Natural Beauty.

Cities and Thrones and Powers
Stand in Time's eye,
Almost as long as flowers,
Which daily die:
But, as new buds put forth
To glad new men,
Out of the spent and unconsidered Earth
The Cities rise again.

— Rudyard Kipling

Time's Eye

PART ONE

DISCONTINUITY

CHAPTER 1
SEEKER

For thirty million years the planet had cooled and dried, until, in the north, ice sheets gouged at the continents. The belt of forest that had once stretched across Africa and Eurasia, nearly continuous from the Atlantic coast to the Far East, had broken into dwindling pockets. The creatures who had once inhabited that timeless green had been forced to adapt, or move.

Seeker's kind had done both.

Her infant clinging to her chest, Seeker crouched in the shadows at the fringe of the scrap of forest. Her deep eyes, under their bony hood of brow, peered out into brightness. The land beyond the forest was a plain, drenched in light and heat. It was a place of terrible simplicity, where death came swiftly. But it was a place of opportunity. This place would one day be the border country between Pakistan and Afghanistan, called by some the Northwest Frontier.

Today, not far from the ragged fringe of the forest, an antelope carcass lay on the ground. The animal was not long dead – its wounds still oozed sticky blood – but the lions had already eaten their fill, and the other scavengers of the plain, the hyenas and the birds, had yet to discover it.

Seeker stood upright, unfolding her long legs, and peered around.

Seeker was an ape. Her body, thickly covered with dense black hair, was little more than a metre tall. Carrying little fat, her skin was slack. Her face was pulled forward into a muzzle, and her limbs were relics of an arboreal past: she had long arms, short legs. She looked very like a chimpanzee, in fact, but the split of her kind from those cousins of the deeper forest already lay some three million years in the past.

3

Seeker stood comfortably upright, a true biped, her hips and pelvis more human than any chimp's.

Seeker's kind were scavengers, and not particularly effective ones. But they had advantages that no other animal in the world possessed. Cocooned in the unchanging forest, no chimp would ever make a tool as complex as the crude but laboriously crafted axe Seeker held in her fingers. And there was something in her eyes, a spark, beyond any other ape.

There was no sign of immediate danger. She stepped boldly out into the sun, her child clinging to her chest. One by one, timidly, walking upright or knuckle-walking, the rest of the troop followed her.

The infant squealed and pinched her mother's fur painfully. Seeker's kind had no names – these creatures' language was still little more sophisticated than the songs of birds – but since she had been born this baby, Seeker's second, had been ferociously strong in the way she clung on to her mother, and Seeker thought of her as something like 'Grasper'.

Burdened by the child, Seeker was among the last of the troop to reach the fallen antelope, and the others were already hacking with their chipped stones at the cartilage and skin which connected the animal's limbs to its body. This butchery was a way to get a fast return of meat; the limbs could be hauled quickly back to the relative safety of the forest, and consumed at leisure. Seeker joined in the work with a will. The harsh sunlight was uncomfortable, though. It would be another million years before Seeker's remote descendants, much more human in form, could stay out in the light, in bodies able to sweat and store moisture in fatty reserves, bodies like spacesuits built to survive the savannah.

The shrinking of the world forest had been a catastrophe for the apes that had once inhabited it. Already the evolutionary zenith of this great family of animals lay deep in the past. But some had adapted. Seeker's kind still needed the forest's shade, still crept into tree-top nests each night, but by day they would dart out into the open to exploit easy scavenging opportunities like this. It was a hazardous way to make a living, but it was better than starving. As the forest fragmented further, more *edge* became available, and the living space for fringe-dwellers actually expanded. And as they scuttled perilously between two worlds, the blind scalpels of variation and selection shaped these desperate apes.

Now there was a concerted yapping, a patter of swift paws on the ground. Hyenas had belatedly scented the blood of the antelope, and were approaching in a great cloud of dust.

The upright apes had hacked off only three of the antelope's limbs. But there was no more time. Clutching her child to her chest, Seeker raced after her troop towards the cool ancestral dark of the forest.

That night, as Seeker lay in her tree-top nest of folded branches, something woke her. Grasper, curled up beside her mother, snored softly.

There was something in the air, a faint scent in her nostrils, that tasted of change.

Seeker was an animal fully dependent on the ecology in which she was embedded, and she was very sensitive to change. But there was more than an animal's sensibility in her: as she peered at the stars with eyes still adapted for narrow forest spaces, she felt an inchoate curiosity.

If she had needed a name, it might have been Seeker.

It was that spark of curiosity, a kind of dim ancestor of wanderlust, that had guided her kind so far out of Africa. As the Ice Ages bit, the remnant forest pockets dwindled further or vanished. To survive, the forest-fringe apes would rush across the hazard of the open plain to a new forest clump, the imagined safety of a new home. Even those who survived would rarely make more than one such journey in a lifetime, a single odyssey of a kilometre or so. But some did survive, and flourish; and some of their children passed on further.

In this way, as thousands of generations ticked by, the forest-fringe apes had slowly diffused out of Africa, reaching as far as Central Asia, and crossing the Gibraltar land bridge into Spain. It was a forward echo of more purposeful migrations in the future. But the apes were always sparse, and left few traces; no human palaeontologist would ever suspect they had come so far out of Africa as this place, north-west India, or that they had gone further still.

And now, as Seeker peered up at the sky, a single star slid across her field of view, slow, steady, purposeful as a cat. It was bright enough to cast a shadow, she saw. Wonder and fear warred in her. She raised a hand, but the sliding star was beyond the reach of her fingers.

This far into the night, India was deep in the shadow of Earth. But where the surface of the turning planet was bathed in sunlight, there was a shimmering – rippling colour, brown and blue and green, flickering in patches like tiny doors opening. The tide of subtle changes washed around the planet like a second terminator.

The world shivered around Seeker, and she clutched her child close.

In the morning, the troop was agitated. The air was cooler today, somehow sharper, and laden with a tang a human might have called electric. The light was strange, bright and washed-out. Even here, in the depths of the forest, a breeze stirred, rustling the leaves of the trees. Something was different, something had changed, and the animals were disturbed.

Boldly Seeker walked into the breeze. Grasper, chattering, knuckle-walked after her.

Seeker reached the edge of the forest. On a plain already bright with morning, nothing stirred. Seeker peered around, a faint spark of puzzlement lodging in her mind. Her forest-adapted mind was poor at analysing landscapes, but it seemed to her that the land was *different*. Surely there had been more green yesterday; surely there had been forest scraps in the lee of those worn hills, and surely water had run along that arid gully. But it was difficult to be sure. Her memories, always incoherent, were already fading.

But there was an object in the sky.

It was not a bird, for it did not move or fly, and not a cloud, for it was hard and definite and round. And it shone, almost as bright as the sun itself.

Drawn, she walked out of the forest's shadows and into the open.

She walked back and forth, underneath the thing, inspecting it. It was about the size of her head, and it swam with light – or rather the light of the sun rippled from it, as it would flash from the surface of a stream. It had no smell. It was like a piece of fruit, hanging from a branch – and yet there was no tree. Four billion years of adaptation to Earth's unvarying gravity field had instilled in her the instinct that nothing so small and hard could hover unsupported in the air: this was something new, and therefore to be feared. But it did not fall on her or attack her in any way.

She craned up on tiptoes, peering at the sphere. She saw two eyes gazing back at her.

She grunted and dropped to the ground. But the floating sphere did not react, and when she looked up again she understood. The sphere was returning her reflection, though twisted and distorted; the eyes had been her own, just as she had seen them before in the smooth surface of still water. Of all Earth's animals only her kind could have recognised herself in such a reflection, for only her kind had any true sense of self. But it seemed to her, dimly, that by holding such an image the floating sphere was looking at her just as she looked at it, as if it was a vast Eye itself.

She reached up, but even on tiptoe, with her long tree-climbers' arms extended, she could not reach it. With more time, it might have occurred to her to find something to stand on to reach the sphere, a rock or a heap of branches.

But Grasper screamed.

Seeker fell to all fours and was knuckle-running before she had even realised it. When she saw what was happening to her child she was terrified.

Two creatures stood over Grasper. They were like apes, but they were upright and tall. They had bright red torsos, as if their bodies were soaked in blood, and their faces were flat and hairless. *And they had Grasper.* They had dropped something, like lianas or vines, over the infant. Grasper struggled, yelled and bit, but the two tall creatures easily held down the lianas to trap her.

Seeker leapt, screaming, her teeth bared.

One of the red-breasted creatures saw her. His eyes widened with shock. He brought around a stick, and whirled it through the air. Something impossibly hard slammed against the side of her head. Seeker was heavy and fast enough that her momentum brought her crashing into the creature, knocking him to the ground. But her head was full of stars, her mouth full of the taste of blood.

To the east a blanket of black, boiling cloud erupted out of the horizon. There was a remote rumble of thunder, and lightning flared.

CHAPTER 2
LITTLE BIRD

At the moment of Discontinuity, Bisesa Dutt was in the air.

From her position in the back of the helicopter cockpit, Bisesa's visibility was limited – which was ironic, since the whole point of the mission was her observation of the ground. But as the Little Bird rose, and her view opened up, she could see the base's neat rows of prefabricated hangars, all lined up with the spurious regularity of the military mind. This UN base had been here for three decades already, and these 'temporary' structures had acquired a certain shabby grandeur, and the dirt roads that led away across the plain were hard-packed.

As the Bird swooped higher, the base blurred to a smear of whitewash and camouflage canvas, lost in the huge palm of the land. The ground was desolate, with here and there a splash of grey-green where a stand of trees or scrubby grass struggled for life. But in the distance mountains shouldered over the horizon, white-topped, magnificent.

The Bird lurched sideways, and Bisesa was thrown against the curving wall.

Casey Othic, the prime pilot, hauled on his stick, and soon the flight levelled out again, with the Bird swooping a little lower over the rock-strewn ground. He turned and grinned at Bisesa. 'Sorry about that. Gusts like that sure weren't in the forecasts. But what do those double domes know? You okay back there?'

His voice was overloud in Bisesa's headset. 'I feel like I'm on the back shelf of a Corvette.'

His grin widened, showing perfect teeth. 'No need to shout. I can hear you on the radio.' He tapped his helmet. '*Ra-di-o*. You have those in the Brit army yet?'

In the seat beside Casey, Abdikadir Omar, the backup pilot, glanced at the American, shaking his head disapprovingly.

The Little Bird was a bubble-front observation chopper. It was derived from an attack helicopter that had been flying since the end of the twentieth century. In this calmer year of 2037, this Bird was dedicated to more peaceful tasks: observation, search and rescue. Its bubble cockpit had been expanded to take a crew of three, the two pilots up front and Bisesa crammed on her bench in the back.

Casey flew his veteran machine casually, one-handed. Casey Othic's rank was Chief Warrant Officer, and he had been seconded from the US Air and Space Force to this UN detachment. He was a squat, bulky man. His helmet was UN sky blue, but he had adorned it with a strictly non-regulation Stars and Stripes, an animated flag rippling in a simulated breeze. His HUD, his heads-up display, was a thick visor that covered most of his face above the nose, black to Bisesa's view, so that she could only see his broad, chomping jaw.

'I can tell you're checking me out, despite that stupid visor,' Bisesa said laconically.

Abdikadir, a handsome Pashtun, glanced back and grinned. 'Spend enough time around apes like Casey and you'll get used to it.'

Casey said, 'I'm the perfect gentleman.' He leaned a bit so he could see her name tag. '*Bisesa Dutt.* What's that, a Pakistani name?'

'Indian.'

'So you're from India? But your accent is – what, Australian?'

She suppressed a sigh; Americans never recognised regional accents. 'I'm a Mancunian. From Manchester, England. I'm British – third generation.'

Casey started to talk like Cary Grant. 'Welcome aboard, Lady Dutt.'

Abdikadir punched Casey's arm. 'Man, you're such a cliché, you just go from one stereotype to another. Bisesa, this is your first mission?'

'Second,' said Bisesa.

'I've flown with this asshole a dozen times and he's always the same, whoever's in the back. Don't let him bug you.'

'He doesn't,' she said equably. 'He's just bored.'

Casey laughed coarsely. 'It is kind of dull here at Clavius Base. But you ought to be at home, Lady Dutt, out here on the Northwest Frontier. We'll have to see if we can find you some fuzzy-wuzzies to pick off with your elephant gun.'

Abdikadir grinned at Bisesa. 'What can you expect from a jock Christian?'

'And you're a beak-nosed mujahedin,' Casey growled back.

Abdikadir seemed to sense alarm in Bisesa's expression. 'Oh, don't worry. I really am a mujahedin, or was, and he really is a jock. We're the best of friends, really. We're both Oikumens. But don't tell anybody—'

They ran into turbulence, quite suddenly. It was as if the chopper just dropped a few metres through a hole in the air. The pilots became attentive to their instruments, and fell silent.

With the same nominal rank as Casey, Abdikadir, an Afghan citizen, was a Pashtun, a native of the area. Bisesa had got to know him a little, in her short time at the post. He had a strong, open face, a proud nose that might have been called Roman, and he wore a fringe of beard. His eyes were a surprising blue, and his hair a kind of strawberry blond. He said he inherited his colouring from the armies of Alexander the Great, which had once passed this way. A gentle man, approachable and civilised, he accepted his place in the informal pecking order here: although he was prized as one of the few Pashtuns to have come over to the UN's side, as an Afghan he had to defer to the Americans, and he spent a lot more time co-piloting than piloting. The other British troops called him 'Ginger'.

The ride continued. It wasn't comfortable. The Bird was elderly: the cabin reeked of engine oil and hydraulic fluid, every metal surface was scuffed with use, and there was actually duct tape holding together splits on the cover of Bisesa's inadequately padded bench. And the noise of the rotors, just metres above her head, was shattering, despite

11

her heavily padded helmet. But then, she thought, it had always been the way that governments spent more on war than peace.

When he heard the chopper approach, Moallim knew what he had to do.

Most of the adult villagers ran to ensure their stashes of weaponry and hemp were hidden. But Moallim had different ideas. He picked up his gear, and ran to the foxhole he had dug weeks ago, in preparation for a day like this.

Within seconds he was lying against the wall of the hole with the RPG tube at his shoulder. The hole had taken hours to dig, before it was deep enough for him to get his body out of the way of the back blast, and to get the elevation he needed with the RPG. But when he was in the hole and had pulled a little dirt and loose vegetation over his body, he was really quite well hidden. The grenade launcher was an antique, actually a relic of the Russian invasion of Afghanistan in the 1980s, but, well maintained and cleaned, it still worked, was still lethal. As long as the chopper came close enough to his position, he would surely succeed.

Moallim was fifteen years old.

He had been just four when he had first encountered the helicopters of the West. They had come at night, a pack of them. They flew very low over your head, black on black, like angry black crows. Their noise hammered at your ears while their wind plucked at you and tore at your clothing. Market stalls were blown over, cattle and goats were terrified, and tin roofs were torn right off the houses. Moallim heard, though he did not see it for himself, that one woman's infant was torn right out of her arms and sent whirling up into the air, never to come down again.

And then the shooting had started.

Later, more choppers had come, dropping leaflets which explained the 'purpose' of the raid: there had been an increase in arms smuggling in the area, there was some suspicion of uranium shipments passing through the village, and so on. The 'necessary' strike had been 'surgical', applying

12

'minimum force'. The leaflets had been torn up, and used to wipe arses. Everybody hated the helicopters, for their remoteness and arrogance. At four, Moallim did not have a word to describe how he felt.

And still the choppers came. The latest UN helicopters were supposed to be here to enforce peace, but everybody knew that this was somebody else's peace, and these 'surveillance' ships carried plenty of weaponry.

These problems had a single solution, so Moallim had been taught.

The elders had trained Moallim to handle the rocket-propelled grenade launcher. It was always hard to hit a moving target. So the detonators had been replaced with timing devices, so that they would explode in mid-air. As long as you fired close enough, you didn't even need a hit to bring down an aircraft – especially a chopper, and especially if you aimed for the tail rotor, which was its most vulnerable element.

RPG launchers were big and bulky and obvious. They were difficult to handle, awkward to lift and aim – and you were finished if you showed yourself aiming one from the open or a rooftop. So you hid away, and let the chopper come to you. If they came this way the chopper crew, trained to avoid buildings for fear of traps, would see nothing more than a bit of pipe sticking out of the ground. Perhaps they would assume it was just a broken drain, from one of the many failed 'humanitarian' schemes imposed on the area over the decades. Flying over open ground they would think they were safe. Moallim smiled.

The sky ahead looked odd to Bisesa. Clouds, thick and black, were boiling up out of nowhere and gathering into a dense band that striped along the horizon, masking the mountains. Even the sky looked somehow washed-out.

Discreetly she dug her phone out of a pocket of her flight suit. Holding it nestling in her hand, she whispered to it, 'I don't recall storm formations in the weather forecasts.'

'Neither do I,' said the phone. It was tuned to the civilian broadcast nets; now its little screen began to cycle through the hundreds of channels washing invisibly over this bit of the Earth, seeking updated forecasts.

The date was 8 June 2037. Or so Bisesa believed. The chopper flew on.

CHAPTER 3

EVIL EYE

The first hint Josh White had of the strange events unfolding in the world was a rude awakening: a rough hand on his shoulder, an excitable clamour, a wide face looming over him.

'I say, Josh – wake up, man! You won't believe it – it's quite the thing – if it isn't the Russians I'll eat your puttees—'

It was Ruddy, of course. The young journalist's shirt was unbuttoned and he wore no jacket; he looked as if he had just got out of bed himself. But his broad face, dominated by that great brow, was flecked with sweat, and his eyes, made small by his thick gig-lamp spectacles, danced and gleamed.

Josh, blinking, sat up. Sunlight was streaming into the room through the open window. It was late afternoon; he had been napping for an hour. 'Giggers, what on earth can be so vital it deprives me of my shut-eye? Especially after last night . . . Let me wash my face first!'

Ruddy backed off. 'All right. But ten minutes, Josh. You won't forgive yourself if you miss this. Ten minutes!' And he bustled out of the room.

Josh, bowing to the inevitable, pulled himself out of bed and moved sleepily around the room.

Like Ruddy, Josh was a journalist, a special correspondent of the *Boston Globe*, sent to file colour reports from the Northwest Frontier, this remote corner of the British Empire – remote, yes, but possibly crucial for Europe's future, and so of interest even in Massachusetts. The room was just a cramped little hole in a corner of the fort, and he had to share it with Ruddy, thanks to whom it was cluttered with clothes, half-emptied trunks, books, papers, and a little fold-away desk on which Ruddy penned his despatches for the

Civil and Military Gazette, his newspaper in Lahore. At that, though, Josh knew he was lucky to have a room at all; most of the troops stationed here at Jamrud, European and Indian alike, spent their nights in tents.

Unlike the soldiers Josh had a perfect right to an afternoon nap, if he needed it. But now he could hear that something unusual was indeed afoot: raised voices, running feet. Not a military action, surely, not another raid by the rebellious Pashtuns, or he would have heard gunfire by now. What, then?

Josh found a bowl of clean warm water, with his shaving kit set out beside it. He washed his face and neck, peering at a rather bleary face in the scrap of mirror fixed to the wall. He was small-featured, with what he thought of as a pug nose, and this afternoon the bags under his eyes weren't doing his looks any good at all. Actually Josh's head hadn't been too sore this morning, but then to survive the long nights in the Mess he'd learned to stick to beer. Ruddy, on the other hand, had indulged his occasional passion for opium – but the hours Ruddy had spent sucking on the hookah seemed to leave no after-effects on his nineteen-year-old constitution. Josh, feeling like a war veteran at the age of twenty-three, envied him.

The shaving water had been set out unobtrusively by Noor Ali, Ruddy's bearer. It was a level of service Bostonian Josh found uncomfortable: when Ruddy was sleeping off his worst binges, Noor Ali was expected to shave him in bed, even asleep! And Josh found it hard to stomach the whippings Ruddy found it necessary to administer from time to time. But Ruddy was an 'Anglo-Indian', born in Bombay. This was Ruddy's country, Josh reminded himself; Josh was here to report, not to judge. And anyhow, he admitted guiltily, it was good to wake up to warm water and a mug or two of hot tea.

He dried himself off and dressed quickly. He took one last glance in the mirror, and finger-combed his mop of unruly black hair. As an afterthought he slipped his revolver into his belt. Then he made for the door.

It was the afternoon of 24 March 1885. Or so Josh still believed.

Inside the fort there was a great deal of excitement. Across the deeply shadowed square soldiers rushed to the gate. Josh joined the cheerful crowd.

Many of the British stationed here at Jamrud were of the 72nd Highlanders, and though some were dressed informally in loose, knee-length native trousers, others wore their khaki jackets and red trews. But white faces were rare; Gurkhas and Sikhs outnumbered British by three to one. Anyhow, this afternoon Europeans and sepoys alike pushed and bustled to get out of the fort. These men, stationed in this desolate place far from their families for months on end, would give anything for a 'do', a bit of novelty to break up the monotony. But on the way to the gate Josh noticed Captain Grove, the fort's commander, making his way across the square with a very worried expression on his face.

As he emerged into the low afternoon sunlight outside the fort Josh was briefly dazzled. The air had a dry chill, and he found himself shivering. The sky was eggshell blue and empty of cloud, but close to the western horizon, he saw, there was a band of darkness, like a storm front. Such turbulent weather was unusual for the time of year.

This was the Northwest Frontier, the place where India met Asia. For the imperial British, this great corridor, running from south-west to north-east between the Indus to the south and the mountain ranges to the north, was the natural boundary of their Indian dominion – but it was a raw and bleeding edge, and on its stability depended the security of the most precious province of the British Empire. And the fort of Jamrud was stuck slap in the middle of it.

The fort itself was a sprawling place, with a curtain of heavy stone walls and broad corner watchtowers. Outside the walls, conical tents had been set up in rows, military neat. Jamrud had originally been built by the Sikhs, who had long governed here and mounted their own wars against the Afghans; by now it was thoroughly British.

17

Today it wasn't the destiny of empires that was on anybody's mind. The soldiers streamed out over the heavily trampled patch of earth that served as the fort's parade ground, heading for a spot perhaps a hundred yards from the gate. There, Josh could see what looked like a pawnbroker's ball hovering in the air. It was silvered, and glinted brightly in the sunlight. A crowd of perhaps fifty troopers, orderlies and non-combatants had gathered under that mysterious sphere, a mob in various states of informal dress.

In the middle of it all, of course, was Ruddy. Even now he was taking command of the situation, stalking back and forth beneath the hovering ball, peering up at it through his gig-lamp spectacles and scratching his chin as if he were as sage as Newton. Ruddy was short, no more than five feet six, and somewhat squat, perhaps a little podgy. He had a broad face, a defiant moustache and over bristling eyebrows a wide slab of a forehead already exposed by a receding tide of hair. *Bristling* – yes, thought Josh with a kind of exasperated fondness, bristling was the word for Ruddy. With his stiff if vigorous bearing, he looked thirty-nine, not nineteen. But he had an unsightly red blemish on his cheek, his 'Lahore sore', that he thought had come from an ant bite, but which would respond to no treatment.

The soldiers sometimes mocked Ruddy for his self-importance and pomposity – no fighting man had much time for non-combatants anyhow. But at the same time they were fond of him; in his dispatches to the *CMG*, and in his barrack-room tales, Ruddy loaned these 'Tommies', far from Home, a rough eloquence they lacked themselves.

Josh pushed his way through the crowd to Ruddy. 'I can't see what's so strange about this floating fellow. A conjuring trick?'

Ruddy grunted. 'More likely some trickery by the Tsar. A new type of heliograph, perhaps.'

They were joined by Cecil de Morgan, the factor. 'If it's *jadoo*, I'd like to know the secret of the magic. Here – you.' He approached one of the sepoys. 'Your cricket bat – may I borrow it? . . .' He got hold of the bat and waved it through

18

the air. He passed it under and around the floating ball. 'You see? There's really no possibility of anything holding it up – no invisible wire or glass rod, however contorted.'

The sepoys were less amused. '*Asli nahin! Fareib!*'

Ruddy muttered, 'Some are saying this is an Eye, an Evil Eye. Perhaps we need a *nuzzoo-watto* to avert its baleful gaze.'

Josh placed a hand on his shoulder. 'My friend, I think you've imbibed more of India than you care to admit. It's probably a balloon, filled with hot air. Nothing more exciting than that.'

But Ruddy was distracted by a worried-looking junior officer who came shoving through the crowd, evidently searching for somebody. Ruddy hurried over to speak with him.

'A balloon, you say?' de Morgan said to Josh. 'Then how does it hold so still in the breeze? And watch this!' He swung the cricket bat over his head like an axe, and slammed it against the floating sphere. There was a resounding smash, and to Josh's astonishment the bat just bounced off the sphere, which remained as immovable as if it was set in rock. De Morgan held up the bat, and Josh saw it had splintered. 'Hurt my blooming fingers! Now tell me, sir, have you ever seen such a thing?'

'Not I,' Josh admitted. 'But if there's a way to make a profit out of it, Morgan, I'm sure you're the man.'

'*De* Morgan, Joshua.' De Morgan was a factor, who made a handsome living from supplying Jamrud and other forts of the Frontier. Aged about thirty, he was a tall, oleaginous sort of man. Even here, miles from the nearest town, he wore a new khaki suit dyed a delicate olive green, a sky-blue tie, and a pith helmet as white as snow. He was a type, Josh was learning, who was attracted to the fringe of civilisation, where there were fat profits to be made and a certain slackness to the enforcement of the law. The officers disapproved of him and his like, but de Morgan kept himself popular enough with his supplies of beer and tobacco for the men, even prostitutes when possible, and occasional bags of hashish for the officers – and for Ruddy too.

Despite de Morgan's stunt, the show seemed to be over. As the sphere didn't move or spin, or open up, or fire bullets, the audience appeared to be getting bored. Besides, some of them were shivering in this unseasonably cold afternoon, as that wind from the north continued to blow. One or two drifted back to the fort, and the party began to break up.

But now there was shouting from the edge of the group: something else unusual had turned up. De Morgan, his nostrils flaring, once more on the scent of opportunity, ran off that way.

Ruddy plucked at Josh's shoulder. 'Enough of these magic tricks,' he said. 'We should get back – we're soon going to have a lot of work, I fear!'

'What do you mean?'

'I just had a word with Brown, who spoke to Townshend, who overheard something Harley was saying . . .' Captain Harley was the fort's Political Officer, reporting to the Political Agency of the Khyber, the arm of the province's administration intended to deal diplomatically with the chiefs and khans of the Pashtun and Afghan tribes. Not for the first time Josh envied Ruddy his links among Jamrud's junior officers. 'Our communications have gone down,' said Ruddy breathlessly.

Josh frowned. 'What do you mean – has the telegraph wire been cut again?' When the link to Peshawar was broken it was tricky to file copy; Josh's editor in far-away Boston was unsympathetic to the delays caused by horseback delivery to the town.

But Ruddy said, 'Not just that. The heliographs too. We haven't seen so much as a flicker of light from the stations to the north and west since dawn. According to Brown, Captain Grove is sending out patrols. Whatever has happened must be widespread and coordinated.'

The heliographs were simple portable signalling devices, just mirrors on foldaway tripods. A series of heliograph communication posts had been set up all around the hills between Jamrud and the Khyber, as well as back towards

Peshawar. So that was why Captain Grove had been looking so concerned, back in the fort.

Ruddy said, 'Out there in the field, perhaps a hundred British throats have been slit in the night by Pashtun savages – or the Amir's assassins – or, worse yet, by the Russian puppet masters themselves!' But even as he described this gruesome possibility, Ruddy's eyes, behind their thick panes of glass, were alive.

'You relish the coming of war as only a non-combatant would,' Josh said.

Ruddy said defensively, 'If the time came I would stand my corner. But in the meantime words are my bullets – as they are for you, Joshua, so don't you lecture me.' His vital good humour broke through again. 'It's exciting, eh? You can't deny that. At least something is happening! Come on, let's get to work!' And he turned and ran back towards the fort.

Josh made to follow. He thought he heard a flapping sound, like the wings of some great bird. He looked back. But then the wind shifted a little and the strange sound dissipated.

Some of the troopers were still playing with the Eye. One man clambered on the shoulders of another, grabbed on to the Eye with both hands, and hung there, all his weight suspended by the Eye. Laughing, the trooper let himself drop to the ground.

Back in their shared room, Ruddy made immediately for his desk, dragged a pile of paper towards him, took the top off a bottle of ink, and began to write.

Josh watched him. 'What are you going to say?'

'I'll know in a moment.' He wrote even as he spoke. He was an untidy worker, a Turkish cigarette lodged in his mouth as was his habit, and droplets of ink sprayed around him; Josh had learned where to store his own stuff out of his way. But he couldn't help but admire Ruddy's fluency.

Listlessly Josh lay on his bed, his hands locked behind his neck. Unlike Ruddy, *he* had to get his thoughts in order before he could write a word.

The Frontier was strategically vital for the British, as it had been for previous conquerors. To the north and west of this place lay Afghanistan, centred on the Hindu Kush. Through the passes of the Kush had once marched the armies of Alexander and the hordes of Genghis Khan and Tamburlaine, all drawn by the mystery and wealth of India to the south. Jamrud itself occupied a key position, lying on the line of the Khyber pass, between Kabul and Peshawar.

But the province itself was more than a mere corridor for foreign soldiery. It had its own people, who regarded this land as their own: the Pashtuns, a warrior race, fierce, proud and cunning. The Pashtuns – whom Ruddy called Pathans – were devout Muslims, and bound by their own code of honour, called the *pakhtunwali*. The Pashtuns were splintered into tribes and clans, but that very splintering gave them a robust kind of fluidity. No matter how heavy a defeat was inflicted on one tribe or another, still more would melt out of the mountains with their old-fashioned long-barrelled rifles, their *jezails*. Josh had met a few Pashtuns, prisoners taken by the British. Josh had thought them the most alien people he had ever encountered. Among the British soldiers there was a certain wary respect for them, though. Some of the Highlanders even said the *pakhtunwali* wasn't so different from their own clannish code of honour.

Over the centuries many invading armies had come to grief on the Frontier, which one imperial administrator had called 'that prickly and untrimmed hedge'. Even now, the authority of the mighty British Empire extended not much further than the roads; elsewhere the law derived only from the tribe and the gun.

And today the Frontier was again a cockpit of international intrigue. Once more an envious empire had its hungry eyes on India: this time the Tsar's Russia. Britain's interests were very clear. On no account must Russia, or a Russian-backed Persia, be allowed to establish itself in Afghanistan. To this end, for decades the British had been trying to ensure that Afghanistan was ruled by an amir well disposed to British interests – or, failing that, it had been prepared to wage war on Afghanistan itself. The slow-burning confrontation seemed to be coming to the boil, at last. This very month the Russians had been steadily inching forward through Turkestan, and were now approaching Pandjeh, the last oasis before the Afghan frontier, an obscure caravanserai that was suddenly the subject of the world's attention.

Josh found this international chess game rather dismaying. Because of simple geographic logic this was a place where great empires brushed against each other, and, for all the Pashtuns' defiance, that terrible friction crushed the people unlucky enough to be born here. He sometimes wondered if it would be this way in the future, if this blighted place was destined for ever to be an arena of war – and what unimaginable treasures men might fight over here.

'Or perhaps one day,' he had said once to Ruddy, 'men will put aside war as a growing child sets aside the toys of his nursery.'

But Ruddy snorted through his moustache. 'Pah! And do what? Play cricket all day? Josh, men will always go to war, because men will always be men, and war will always be *fun*.' Josh was naïve, a blinkered American far from home, who needed to have 'the youth burned out of him', said nineteen-year-old Ruddy.

After less than half an hour Ruddy had finished his vignette. He sat back, gazing out of the window at the reddening light, short-sighted eyes locked on vistas Josh couldn't share.

'Ruddy, if it is serious trouble – do you think we'll be sent back to Peshawar?'

Ruddy snorted. 'I should hope not! This is what we're here for.' He read from his manuscript. '"Think of it! Far away, beyond the Hindu Kush, they are on the move – in their green coats or grey, marching beneath the double eagle of the Tsar. Soon they will come striding down the Khyber Pass. But to the south more columns will mass, men from Dublin and Delhi, Calcutta and Colchester, drawn together in common discipline and purpose, ready to give their lives for the Widow of Windsor . . ." The batsmen are on the pavilion steps, the umpires are ready, the bails are set on the stumps.

23

And here we are right on the boundary rope! What do you think of that – eh, Josh?'

'You really can be annoying, Ruddy.'

But before Ruddy could respond, Cecil de Morgan burst in. The factor was red-faced, panting, and his clothes were dusty. 'You must come, you chaps – oh, come and see what they've found!'

With a sigh Josh clambered off his bed. Would there be no end to the strangeness of this day?

It was a chimpanzee: that was Josh's first thought. A chimpanzee, caught in a bit of camouflage netting, lying passively on the floor. A smaller bundle nearby contained another animal, perhaps an infant. The captive animals had been brought back to the camp on poles stuck through the netting. A couple of sepoys were unwrapping the larger bundle.

De Morgan was here, hovering, as if staking a claim. 'They caught it to the north – a couple of privates on patrol – only a mile or so away.'

'It's just a chimp,' Josh said.

Ruddy was pulling at his moustache. 'But I've never heard of a chimp in this part of the world. Do they have a zoo in Kabul?'

'This is from no zoo,' de Morgan panted. 'And it's no chimpanzee. Careful, lads . . .'

The sepoys got the net off the animal. Its fur was soaked with its own blood. It was curled into a ball, its legs drawn up to its chest and its long arms wrapped over its head. The men held sticks which they wielded like clubs, and Josh saw weals on the animal's back.

The animal seemed to realise that the netting had been taken away. It lowered its hands, and with a sudden, fluid movement it rolled and came up to a squatting position, its knuckles resting lightly on the ground. The men backed off warily, and the animal peered at them.

'It's a female, by God,' Ruddy breathed.

De Morgan pointed to a sepoy. 'Make it stand up.'

Reluctantly the sepoy, a burly man, came forward. He

24

reached out with his stick and prodded at the creature's rump. She growled and snapped her large teeth. But the sepoy kept at it. At last, with grace – and a certain dignity, Josh thought – the creature unfolded her legs, and stood *upright*.

Josh heard Ruddy gasp.

She had the body of a chimp, there was no doubt about that, with slack dugs and swollen pudenda and pink buttocks; her limbs had an ape's proportions too. But she stood straight on long legs, which articulated from her pelvis, Josh saw clearly, like any human's.

'My God,' Ruddy said. 'She is like a caricature of a woman – a monstrosity!'

'Not a monstrosity,' Josh said. 'Half human, half ape – I have read that the new biologists talk of such things, of the creatures that lie between *us* and the animals.'

'You see?' De Morgan was glancing from one to another of them with greed and calculation. 'Have you ever, ever seen anything like this?' He walked around the creature.

The burly sepoy said, his accent thick, 'Have a care, Sahib. She's only four feet high but she can scratch and kick, I can tell you.'

'Not an ape, but a *man-ape* . . . We have to get her back to Peshawar, then to Bombay, and to England. Think what a sensation she will be in the zoos! Or perhaps even the theatres . . . Nothing like this – even in Africa! Quite the sensation.'

The smaller animal, still in its netting, seemed to wake. It rolled and mumbled, its voice feeble. Immediately the female reacted, as if she had not realised the little one was here. She leapt towards the infant, reaching.

The sepoys clubbed her at once. She whirled and kicked, but she was battered to the ground.

Ruddy waded into the mêlée, eyebrows bristling. 'For God's sake, don't strike her like that! Can't you see? She's a *mother*. And look in her eyes – look! Won't that expression haunt you for ever? . . .' But still the man-ape struggled, still the sepoys threw their clubs at her, still de Morgan yelled, fearful of his treasure escaping – or, worse, being killed.

Josh was the first to hear the clattering noise. He turned to the east, to see clouds of dust thrown into the air. 'There it is again – I heard it before . . .'

Ruddy, distracted by the violence, muttered, 'What the devil now?'

CHAPTER 4

RPG

Casey called, 'We're nearly on station. Going to low cap.'

The chopper dropped like a high-speed elevator. Despite all her training, Bisesa's stomach clenched.

They were passing close to a village now. Trees, rusty tin roofs, cars, heaps of tyres fled through her field of view. The chopper tilted and began circling anti-clockwise. 'Low cap' meant a sweeping surveillance circle. But given the way Bisesa was crammed on to her little bench, she could now see nothing but sky. More irony, she thought. She sighed, and checked over the small control panel fixed to the wall beside her. Sensors, from cameras to Geigers, heat sensors, radars and even chemico-sensitive 'noses', were trained on the ground from a pod suspended under the chopper's body.

The Bird was embedded in the world-spanning communications infrastructure of a modern army. Somewhere above Bisesa's head was a big C2 chopper – C2 for command-and-control – but that was only the tip of a huge inverted pyramid of technology, including high-flying surveillance drones, reconnaissance and patrol planes, even photographic and radar satellites, all their electronic senses focused on this region. The data streams Bisesa gathered were analysed in real time by smart systems on board the Bird and on the higher-level vehicles, and in operations control back at the base. Any anomalies would quickly be flagged back to Bisesa for her confirmation by the link she maintained with her control, separate from the pilots' link to the air commander via the command net.

It was all very sophisticated, but, like the piloting of the chopper itself, the data-gathering side of the mission was mostly automated. With low cap locked in the mission quickly settled down to routine, and the pilots' bored banter resumed.

Bisesa knew how they felt. She had been trained as a CCT, a Combat Control Technician, a specialist on coordinating ground-to-air communications during a conflict. Her basic mission was to be dropped into dangerous places and to direct pinpoint air and missile strikes from the ground. She had never yet needed to use that training in anger. Her skills made her ideal for this kind of observational role, but she couldn't forget that it wasn't what she was trained for.

She had only been attached to this forward UN observation and peacekeeping post for a week, but it seemed a lot longer. The troops were lodged in barracks that had been converted from aircraft hangars. High, bare, always stinking of jet fuel and oil, too hot during the day and too cold during the night, there was something crushing about those soulless boxes of corrugated metal and plastic. No wonder its occupants mockingly called it Clavius, after the big multinational outpost on the Moon.

The troops had a regime of daily PT, and had to pull guard duty, equipment maintenance and other mundane details. But that was not enough to fill their time, or satisfy their needs. In their echoing hangars they would play volleyball or table tennis, and there were schools running apparently endless games of poker and rummy. And, though the ratio of women to men was about fifty-fifty, the place was a raging sexual hotbed. Some of the men seemed to be running a competition to achieve a climax in the most unusual or difficult situation possible – such as 'knocking one out' when hanging from a parachute harness.

In such an atmosphere, no wonder that men like Casey Othic went slightly crazy, she thought.

Bisesa herself kept out of the fray. She could cope with the likes of Casey easily enough – even now, the British army was hardly a haven of sexual equality and decorum. She had even deflected the polite interest of Abdikadir. After all, *she* had her daughter: Myra, eight years old, a quiet, serious, very loving little girl, thousands of klicks away under the care of a nanny in Bisesa's London flat. Bisesa wasn't interested in games or complicated sexual politics to keep herself sane; she had Myra to do that for her.

Anyhow the importance of the mission here kept her motivated.

In the year 2037, the border region between Pakistan and Afghanistan was a centre of tension, as it had been for centuries. For one thing the place was a focus of the continuing worldwide stand-off between Christianity and Islam. To the relief of everybody but the hotheads and agitators on both sides, the final 'war of civilisations' had never quite come to pass. But still, in a place like this, where troops from mostly Christian nations policed a mostly Muslim area, there was always somebody ready to call a crusade, or a jihad.

There were lethal local tensions too. The stand-off between India and Pakistan had not been eased by the war of 2020 which had resulted in the nuclear destruction of the city of Lahore, even though the parties involved, and their international backers, had pulled back from the brink of more widespread devastation. And added to that complicated mix, of course, were the passions, aspirations and plight of the local people: the proud Pashtuns who, although they had been drawn into the civilised discourse of the world, still clung to their traditions, and would still defend their homeland to the last drop of blood.

In addition to such ancient disputes, now there was oil, which kept the rest of the world drawn into this combustible place. Although the long-term possibilities offered by cold fusion, the most promising of the new technologies, were startling, its industrial-scale practicality was still unproven – and the world's store of rich hydrocarbons continued to be burned as fast as they could be dug out of the ground. So, where once the British Empire and Tsarist Russia had faced each other here over the wealth of India, now the United States, China, the African Alliance, and the Eurasian Union, all crucially dependent on the oil reserves of Central Asia, were locked in a tense, mutually dependent stand-off.

The UN's mission here was to keep the peace by surveillance and policing. The area was said to be the most heavily scrutinised of any territory on Earth. The peacekeeping mission was an imperfect, heavy-handed regime that, Bisesa sometimes thought, created as much tension and resentment as it resolved. But it worked after its fashion, and had done so for decades. Perhaps it was the best mere human beings, and the complicated, flawed but enduring political lash-up of the UN, could do.

Everybody at Clavius knew the importance of the job. But there were few things more boring for a young soldier than peacekeeping.

Suddenly the ride got a lot more bumpy. Bisesa felt her pulse rate rise; maybe this mission wasn't quite so routine after all.

As the chopper continued to circle, despite the turbulence, Casey and Abdikadir were both working, both talking at once. Abdikadir was trying to raise the base. 'Alpha Four Three, this is Primo Five One, over. Alpha Four Three . . .' Casey was swearing, something to do with losing the positioning satellite contact, and Bisesa surmised he was flying the chopper by hand through the unexpected turbulence.

'Ouch,' said her phone plaintively.

She raised it to her face. 'What's wrong with you?'

'I lost signal.' Its screen showed various diagnostics. 'It never happened to me before,' it said. 'It feels – odd.'

Abdikadir glanced back at her. 'Our comms is on the fritz too. We have lost the command net.'

Belatedly Bisesa checked her own gear. She had lost contact with her own command centre, both uplink and downlink. 'Looks like we lost the intel net too.'

'So,' Abdikadir said. 'Military and civilian networks, both out.'

'What do you think – electric storm?'

Casey growled, 'Not according to what those assholes in meteorology predicted. Anyhow, I've flown in storms, and none of them had an effect like this.'

'Then what could it be?'

For a couple of seconds they were all silent. This was, after all, an area where a nuclear weapon had been used in anger only a couple of hundred kilometres away, and the centre of a city had been turned to a plain of melted glass. Communications knocked out – winds out of nowhere: it was hard not to assume the worst.

'At the very least,' Abdikadir said, 'we have to assume this is jamming.'

'*Ow*,' said the phone insistently.

She cradled the phone, concerned. She had had it since she was a child: it was a standard UN issue, supplied free to every twelve-year-old on the planet, in that creaky old organisation's most significant effort to date to unite the world with communications. Most people dumped these uncool government-issue gadgets, but Bisesa had understood the motive behind the gift, and had always kept hers. She couldn't help but think of it as a friend. 'Take it easy,' Bisesa told it now. 'My mother told me that when she was young phones lost their signal all the time.'

'It's okay for you to talk,' the phone said. '*I've* been lobotomised.'

Abdikadir grimaced. 'How do you put up with that? I always turn off the sentience circuits. So irritating.'

Bisesa shrugged. 'I know. But that way you lose half the diagnostic functionality.'

'And you lose a friend for life,' the phone pointed out.

Abdikadir snorted. 'Just don't start feeling sorry for it. Phones are like Catholic mothers – connoisseurs of guilt.'

The chopper buffeted again. The Bird tipped and flew level, over bare ground; they sailed away from the village. 'I'm out of low cap,' Casey called. 'Too damn difficult to hold.'

Abdikadir enjoyed a grin of triumph. 'Nice to know we're exploring the outer limits of your competence, Case.'

'Shove it up your ass,' Casey growled. 'This wind's coming from every which way. And look at the fluctuations in our groundspeed – hey. *What's that?*' He pointed out of the bubble window at the ground.

Bisesa leaned forward and peered. Loose vegetation was being scattered by the rotors' downdraught, revealing something on the ground. She made out a human figure in a hole, holding something – a long black tube – *a weapon*.

They all shouted at once.

And the sun shifted, like a dipping searchlight, distracting her.

The chopper had stopped its orbiting and was heading directly towards him, its bubble face dipped slightly, its tail raised. Moallim grinned and tightened his grasp on the RPG. But his heart was thumping, he found, his fingers slippery with sweat, and the dust was getting into his eyes, making him blink. This would be the first important act of his life. If he brought down the chopper he would be an immediate hero, and everybody would applaud him, the fighting men, his mother. And there was a certain girl . . . He must not think of that now, for he still had to do the deed.

But now he could see *people* inside the ugly bubble cockpit of the helicopter. The reality of it suddenly shocked him. Was he really about to snuff out human lives, like squashing bugs?

The chopper surged over his position, and its downdraught, a mighty punch of air, scattered his flimsy cover. All choices had vanished, save one: he must not hesitate, lest he be killed before he carry out his duty.

Laughing, he launched the grenade.

Abdikadir shouted, 'RPG! RPG!' Casey hauled on the stick. Bisesa saw a flash, and a smoke trail stitching through the air towards them.

There was a jolting impact, as if the chopper had run over an invisible speed bump in the sky. Suddenly the cabin noise rose to a roar, and from some split in the hull the wind poured in.

'Shit,' Casey shouted. 'That took a piece out of the tail rotor.'

When Bisesa looked back that way she could see a tangle of metal, and a fine mist where oil was being lost through a ruptured pipe. The rotor itself was still working, and the chopper flew on. But everything had changed in that instant; battered by the wind and the noise she felt exposed, horribly vulnerable.

Casey said, 'Everything nominal, except oil pressure. And we lost part of our gear box back there.'

'We can run without oil for a while,' Abdikadir said.

'That's what the manual says. But we're going to have to turn this Bird if we want to get home again.' Casey worked his stick experimentally, as if testing the tolerance of the wounded aircraft; the Bird shuddered and bucked.

'Tell me what's going on,' Bisesa muttered.

'It was an RPG,' Abdikadir said. 'Come on, Bisesa, you've attended the briefings. Every day is kill-the-Americans day here.'

'I don't mean the RPG. I mean *that*.' She pointed out of the window, west the way they were headed, at a reddening, setting sun.

'It's just the sun,' Casey said, evidently finding it hard to focus on anything outside the cockpit. Then: '*Oh*.'

When they had taken off, surely no more than thirty minutes ago, the sun was high. And now—

'Tell me I've been asleep for six hours,' Casey said. 'Tell me I'm dreaming.'

Bisesa's phone said, 'I'm still out of touch. And I'm scared.'

Bisesa laughed humourlessly. 'You're tougher than I am, you little bastard.' She pulled down the zipper on the front of her flight suit and tucked the phone into a deep pocket.

'Here goes nothing,' Casey said. He started the turn.

The engine screamed.

The tube's sudden heat burned his flesh, and hot smoke billowed around his head, making him choke. But he heard the fizz of the grenade as it looped away through the air. When the grenade exploded, shrapnel and bits of metal sang through the air, and he cowered, hiding his face.

When he looked up he saw that the chopper flew on away from the village, but it was trailing thick black smoke from its tail section.

Moallim stood up and roared, wiping dirt from his face, punching the air with his fist. He turned and looked back towards the east, to the village, for surely the people would have seen his grenade launch, seen the damage to the chopper. Surely they would be running to greet him.

But nobody was coming, not even his mother. *He couldn't even see the village*, though he had been not a hundred metres from its western boundary, and he had clearly been able to see its crude rooftops and slanting walls, the children and goats wandering among the houses. Now it was gone, and the rocky plain ran to the horizon, as if the village had been scraped clean off the earth. Moallim was alone, alone with his scratched foxhole, his smoking RPG, and the great smoke column slowly dispersing above his head.

Alone on this huge plain.

Somewhere an animal roared. It was a low growl, like some immense piece of machinery. Whimpering, shocked, Moallim clambered back into his hole in the ground.

The turn was too much for the damaged rotor. The airframe vibrated around Bisesa, and there was a high-pitched whine as the dry gear shafts started to seize up.

It couldn't have been more than a minute since the RPG had hit, she thought.

'You'll have to put her down,' Abdikadir said urgently.

'Sure,' said Casey. 'Like where? Abdi, out here even the sweet little old ladies carry big knives to cut off your balls.'

Bisesa pointed over their shoulders. 'What's that?' There was a structure of stone and beaten earth, no more than a couple of kilometres ahead. It was hard to make out in the glare of that anomalous sun. 'It looks like a fortress.'

'Not one of ours,' Abdikadir said.

Now the chopper was passing over people – scattered, running people, some in bright red coats. Bisesa was close enough to see their mouths were round with shock.

'You're the intel expert,' Casey snapped at Bisesa. 'Who the hell?'

'I truly have no idea,' Bisesa murmured.

There was a stunningly loud bang. The Bird pitched forward and began to spin. The tail rotor assembly had disintegrated. With the rotor's weight vanished from its rear, the airframe tipped forward, and with the tail rotor gone there was nothing to stop the aircraft spinning around its main rotor spindle. Though Casey jammed his pedals to the floor, the spinning continued – and accelerated, and kept on, until Bisesa was braced against the wall of the cockpit, and yellow earth and blue-white sky whirled past the bubble windows, blurring.

Something came rising up over a low hillock. Josh saw whirling metal, blades like swords wielded by an invisible dervish. Beneath it was a bubble of glass, and rails of some kind below that. It was a machine, a whirling, clattering, dust-raising machine, of a kind he had never seen before. And it *continued to rise*, lifting into the air until its lower rails were far above the ground, ten or twenty feet. Its tail trailed black smoke.

'My giddy aunt,' breathed Ruddy. 'I was right – the Russians – the blessed Russians! . . .'

The flying machine suddenly plummeted towards the ground.

'Let's go,' called Josh, already running.

Casey and Abdikadir worked the main engine's power levers, struggling to raise their arms against the spin's centrifugal force. They got the engine shut down, the chopper's spin abruptly slowed. But without power the chopper fell freely.

The ground exploded at Bisesa, bits of rock and scrubby vegetation expanding in unwelcome detail, casting long shadows in the light of that too-low sun. She wondered which bit of unprepossessing dirt was to be her grave. But the pilots did something right. In the last instant the bubble tipped up, and came almost level. Bisesa knew how important that was; it meant they might walk away from this.

The last thing she saw was a man running towards the stricken Bird, aiming some kind of rifle.

The chopper slammed into the ground.

CHAPTER 5

SOYUZ

For Kolya the Discontinuity was subtle. It began with a lost signal, uncertain sightings, a silent stranding.

The time for the Soyuz ferry ship to detach from the Space Station had arrived. The last handshakes were exchanged, the heavy double hatches were closed, and though Soyuz remained physically attached to the Station, Kolya had already left the orbiting shack where he had spent another three months of his life. Now there was only the short journey home, a mere four hundred kilometres down through the air to the surface of the Earth, where he would be reunited with his young family.

Kolya's full name was Anatole Konstantinovich Krivalapov. He was forty-one years old, and this tour of duty on the International Space Station had been his fourth.

Kolya, Musa and Sable, the crew of the ferry, clambered down through the living compartment of the Soyuz, making for the descent module. They were clumsy in their thick orange spacesuits, their pockets crammed with the souvenirs they intended to keep from the ground crews. The living compartment was to be jettisoned during re-entry and would burn up in Earth's atmosphere, and so was full of junk to be removed from the ISS. This included such items as medical waste and worn-out underwear. Sable Jones, the one American in the crew of three, led the way, and complained loudly in her coarse southern-USA English, 'Jeez, what's in here, Cossack jockstraps?'

Musa, the Soyuz commander, gave Kolya a silent look.

The descent compartment was a cramped little hut, filled by their three couches. Sable had been trained up on the ship's systems, but she was the nearest thing to a passenger on this hop back to Earth. So she was first into the cabin, where she scrambled into the right-hand couch. Kolya followed, clambering down into the left-hand couch. During this descent he would serve as the spacecraft's engineer, hence his allocation of seat. The compartment was so small that even as he headed for the furthest point of the cabin he brushed past Sable's legs, and she glared at him.

And now Musa came plummeting down, a bright orange missile, helmet in hand. He was a bulky man anyhow, made more so by the layers of his suit. The couches were so crammed together that when the three of them were at rest their lower legs would be pressed against one another's, and as Musa awkwardly tried to strap himself in, he shoved Kolya and Sable this way and that.

Sable's reactions were predictable. 'Where did they make this thing, a tractor factory?'

It was a moment Musa had been waiting for. 'Sable, I have listened to your mouth flapping for the last three months, and as you were commander there I could do nothing about it. But on this Soyuz I, Musa Khiromanovich Ivanov, am commander. And until the hatch breaks open and we are hauled out by the ground crew, you, madam, will – what is the English phrase? *Shut the fuck up.*'

Sable's face was like stone. Musa was a tough veteran of fifty who had served as Station commander himself, and had even been to the Moon, though not to command the multinational base there. They all knew that his admonishment of Sable would have been listened to by their comrades on the Station and, crucially, by the ground controllers.

Sable said through gritted teeth, 'You'll pay for that, Musa.'

Musa just grinned and turned away.

The descent compartment was cluttered. It contained the spacecraft's main controls, as well as all the equipment that would be needed during the return to Earth: parachutes, flotation bags, survival gear, emergency rations. Its walls were lined with elasticated tags and Velcro patches, and were covered by material to be returned from the Station, including blood and stool samples from the biomed program, and

38

cuttings Kolya himself had made from the pea plants and fruit trees he had been attempting to grow. All this stuff crowded in from the hull, reducing the space available for human beings even further.

But amid the clutter there was a window, to Kolya's left-hand side. Through it he glimpsed the blackness of space, a slice of sky-bright Earth, and the struts and micrometeorite-dinged walls of the Station itself, shining brightly in the raw sunlight. The Soyuz, still docked to the Station, was carried by the bigger craft's ponderous rotation, and shadows slid across Kolya's view.

Musa worked them through the pre-separation checklist, talking to the ground and to the crew in the Station. Kolya had little to do: his most important item was a pressure test of his spacesuit. This was a Russian ship, and unlike the pilot-oriented American engineering tradition, most of the systems were automated. Sable continued to grumble as she reached for various controls, which were situated around the capsule at all positions and angles. Some of them were so awkward to reach, veteran cosmonauts learned, it was better to poke at them with a wooden stick. But Kolya took a perverse pride in the ship's low-tech, utilitarian design.

The Soyuz was like a green pepperpot, with lacy solar-cell wings stuck on the side of its cylindrical body. Seen from the windows of the Space Station the Soyuz, bathed in the brilliant sunlight of space, had looked like an ungainly insect: compared to the new American spaceplanes it was a clumsy old bird indeed. But the Soyuz was a venerable craft. It had been born in the Cold War age of Apollo, and had actually been intended to make journeys to the Moon. Remarkably, Soyuz craft had been flying twice as long as Kolya himself had been alive. Now, of course, in 2037, people had returned to the Moon – Russians among them this time! But there was no room on such exotic journeys for the Soyuz; for these faithful workhorses there was only the plod to and from the battered ISS, whose few scientific purposes had long been superseded by the lunar projects, and whose glamour had been stolen by the Mars missions –

and yet which remained in orbit, kept aloft by political inertia and pride.

The moment came for the Soyuz at last to undock from the Station. Kolya heard a few subtle bumps and bangs, and the faintest of nudges, and a small sadness burst in his heart. But as an independent spacecraft the Soyuz's call sign that day was Stereo, and Kolya was comforted by Musa's patient calls to the ground: 'Stereo One, this is Stereo One . . .'

There were still three hours to go before the descent was scheduled to begin, and the crew were now set to inspecting the exterior of the Station. Musa activated a program in the ship's computer, and the Soyuz, firing its thrusters, began a series of straight-line jaunts around the Station. Each thruster burst sounded as if somebody had slammed a sledgehammer against the hull, and Kolya could see exhaust products jetting away from the little nozzles, fountains of crystals flying off in geometrically perfect straight lines. Earth and Station wheeled around him in a slow ballet. But Kolya had little time to admire the view; he and Sable, sitting by the windows, photographed the station manually, as a backup to the automated pods mounted on the Soyuz's exterior. It was an awkward job as each of them wore heavy spacesuit gloves.

Each thruster manoeuvre took the Soyuz a little further from the Station. At last the line-of-sight radio contact began to break down, and as a farewell the Station crew played them some music. As the Strauss waltz swirled tinnily under the hiss and pop of static, Kolya indulged in a little more nostalgic sadness. Kolya had grown to love the Station. He had learned to sense the great ark's subtle rotations, and the vibrations when its big solar arrays realigned, and the rattles and bangs of the complicated ventilation system. After so long aboard, he had more deeply embedded feelings about the Station than any home he'd lived in. After all, what other home actually keeps you alive, minute by minute?

The music cut off.

Musa was frowning. 'Stereo One, I am Stereo One. Ground, I am Stereo One. Come in, I am Stereo One . . .'

Sable said, 'Hey, Kol. Can you see Station? It should have come back into view on my side by now.'

'No,' said Kolya, looking through his window. There was no sign of the Station.

'Maybe it went into shadow,' Sable said.

'I don't think so.' The Soyuz had actually been leading the Station into Earth's shadow. 'And anyhow, we would see its lights.' He felt oddly uneasy.

Musa snapped, 'Will you two be quiet? We lost the uplink from the ground.' He pressed the control pads before him. 'I've run diagnostic checks, and have tried the backups. Stereo One, Stereo One . . .'

Sable closed her eyes. 'Tell me you potato farmers haven't fouled up again.'

'Shut up,' Musa said menacingly. And he continued to call, over and over, while Sable and Kolya listened in silence.

The ship's slow rotation was now giving Kolya a direct view of Earth's immense face. They were flying over India, he saw, and towards a sunset: the shadows from the creases of mountain ranges to the north of the subcontinent were long. But there seemed to be changes on the surface of Earth, dapples, like the play of sunlight on the floor of a turbulent lake.

CHAPTER 6

ENCOUNTER

Josh and Ruddy reached the downed machine with the first group of soldiers. The privates had rifles, and they warily circled the machine, mouths open, eyes wide. None of the party had seen anything like it before.

Inside a big blown-glass cabin there were three people: two men in seats in the front, and a woman in the back. They watched, hands held high, as the armed soldiers circled them. They cautiously removed their bright blue helmets. The woman and one of the men appeared to be Indian, and the other man was white. Josh could see how the latter grimaced in pain.

Considering how hard it had landed – and that it was fragile enough to have flown in the air in the first place – the machine seemed remarkably intact. The big glass shell that dominated the front end was starred here and there but was unbroken, and the blades were still attached to a rotary hub, not folded or snapped off. But the tail section, an affair of open pipework and tubing, had been reduced to a stump. There was a hissing noise, as if some gasket had broken, and a pungent oil leaked on to the stony ground. It was evident that this mechanical bird would fly no more.

Josh hissed to Ruddy, 'I don't recognise those blue helmets. What army is this? Russian?'

'Perhaps. But see that the injured one has a Stars and Stripes stencilled on his helmet!'

Suddenly a trigger was cocked.

'Don't shoot! Don't shoot . . .' It was the woman. She leaned forward from her perch in the back of the sphere to try to shield the wounded pilot.

A soldier – Josh recognised him as Batson, a Newcastle

lad, one of the more level-headed of the privates – was pointing his rifle at the woman's head. He called, 'You speak English?'

'I am English.'

Batson's eyebrows raised. But he said carefully, 'Then tell your chum to put his hands where I can see them. *Jildi!*'

The woman urged, 'Do it, Casey. That gun might be an antique, but it's a loaded antique.'

The pilot, 'Casey', reluctantly complied. His left hand came up from under a panel of instruments holding some sort of gadget.

Batson advanced. 'Is that a weapon? Give it to me now.'

Casey shifted in his seat, winced, and evidently decided he wasn't going anywhere. He held out his weapon to Batson, butt first. 'Have you rubes ever seen one of these? It's what we call a skinny-popper. An MP-93, a nine-millimetre submachine gun. German make . . .'

'Germans,' hissed Ruddy. 'I knew it.'

'Be careful, or you'll stitch your own damn head off.' Casey's accent was undoubtedly American, but it sounded coarse to Josh, like a New York City slum dweller's, while the woman sounded British, but with a flat, unfamiliar intonation to her voice.

From her seat the woman bent over Casey. 'I think your tibia is broken,' she said. 'Crushed under the seat . . . I'd sue the manufacturer if I were you.'

'Up your ass, your majesty,' Casey said through gritted teeth.

The woman said now, 'Can I get out of here?'

Batson nodded. He set the 'submachine gun' on the ground, where it gleamed, fascinating, baffling, and stood back, beckoning her. Batson was doing a good job, Josh thought; he kept the three intruders covered with his own weapon, and continually checked the troops around him to make sure all angles were monitored.

The woman had a tough time clambering out of the couch behind the two front seats, but at last she stood on the rocky ground. The second pilot, the Indian, climbed out too. He had the complexion of a sepoy but pale blue eyes and start-ling blond hair. All the machine's crew wore clothing so bulky it masked their forms, making them seem inhuman, and wiry gadgets clung to their faces. 'I guess it could have been worse,' the woman said. 'I wasn't expecting to walk away from this crash.'

The other replied, 'I guess Casey won't be, for a time. But these Birds are designed for worst-case hard landings. Look, the sensor pod crumpled and absorbed a lot of the shock. The pilot seats are mounted on shock absorbers too, as is your bench. I think the spin sent Casey's seat tipping to the left, and that was what did for his leg – he was unlucky—'

Batson interrupted. 'Enough of your *bukkin'*. Who's in charge?'

The woman glanced at the others and shrugged. 'I'm the ranker. This is Chief Warrant Officer Abdikadir Omar; in the chopper you see Chief Warrant Officer Casey Othic. I'm Lieutenant Bisesa Dutt. British Army, on assignment to United Nations special forces operating out of—'

Ruddy laughed. 'By Allah. A lieutenant in the British Army! And she's a babu!'

Bisesa Dutt turned and glared at him. To his credit, Josh thought, Ruddy blushed under his Lahore sore. Josh knew that 'babu' was a contemptuous Anglo-Indian term for those educated Indians who aspired to senior positions in the dominion's administration.

Bisesa said, 'We need to get Casey out of there. Do you have doctors?' She was putting on a show of strength, Josh thought, admirable given she had just come through an extraordinary crash and was being held at gunpoint. But he sensed a deeper fear.

Batson turned to one of the privates. 'McKnight, run and fetch Captain Grove.'

'Right-oh.' The private, short and stocky, turned and ran barefoot over the broken ground.

Ruddy nudged Josh. 'Come, Joshua, we need to be involved!' He hurried forward. 'Ma'am, please – let us help.'

Bisesa studied Ruddy, his broad forehead crusted with dust,

44

his beetling eyebrows, his defiant moustache. She was taller than him and she looked down on him with contempt, Josh thought – though with an odd puzzlement, a kind of recognition. She said, 'You? You'll come to the aid of a mere babu?'

Josh stepped forward, his most charming grin fixed in place. 'You mustn't mind Ruddy, ma'am. These expatriates have their eccentricities, and the soldiers are too busy holding out their guns at you. Come, let's get on with it.' And he strode towards the 'chopper', rolling up his sleeves.

Abdikadir beckoned to Ruddy and Josh. 'Help me lift him out.' With Abdikadir supporting from the far side, Ruddy got hold of Casey's back, while Josh, cautiously, got his arms under his legs. Another man produced a blanket from somewhere and laid it on the ground. Abdikadir gave them a lead: 'One, two, three, *up*.' Casey screamed when they raised him off his seat, and again when Josh allowed his damaged leg to brush the frame of the 'chopper'. But in seconds they had Casey out and set on his side on the blanket.

Breathing hard, Josh studied Abdikadir. He was a big man, made bulkier by his uniform, his blue eyes striking. 'You're Indian?'

'Afghan,' Abdikadir said evenly. He watched Josh's startled reaction. 'Actually I'm a Pashtun. I take it you don't have too many of us in your army.'

'Not exactly,' Josh said. 'But then it isn't my army.' Abdikadir said nothing more, but Josh had the sense that he knew, or had guessed, more about this strange situation than anybody else.

Private McKnight came running back, breathless. He said to Bisesa and Abdikadir, 'Captain Grove wants to see the two of you in his office.'

Batson nodded. 'Move.'

'No,' Casey grunted from his blanket. 'Don't leave the ship. You know the drill, Abdi. Wipe the damn memory. We don't know who these people are.'

'These *people*,' Batson said menacingly, 'have big guns that are pointing at you. *Choop* and *chel*.'

Bisesa and Abdikadir seemed confused by Batson's mixture of strong Geordie with bits of Frontier argot, but his meaning was clear enough: *shut up and move*. 'I don't think we have a choice right now, Casey,' Bisesa said.

'And you, chum,' Batson said to Casey, 'are heading for the infirmary.' Josh saw Casey was trying to conceal his alarm at this prospect.

Bisesa turned to go with McKnight, escorted by a few more armed privates. 'We'll come find you as soon as we can, Casey.'

'Yes,' Abdikadir called. 'Don't let them saw anything off in the meantime.'

'Ha ha, you prick,' Casey growled.

Ruddy muttered, 'It seems that soldiers' humour is universal, no matter where they come from.'

Josh and Ruddy tried to tag along with Bisesa and Abdikadir, but Batson politely but firmly turned them away.

CHAPTER 7

CAPTAIN GROVE

Bisesa and Abdikadir were walked to the fort they had glimpsed from the air. It turned out to be a box-shaped enclosure surrounded by stout stone walls, with round watchtowers in each corner. It was a substantial base, and evidently well maintained.

'But it's not on any map I ever saw,' Bisesa said tensely. Abdikadir didn't reply.

The walls were manned by soldiers in red coats or khaki jackets. Some even wore kilts. The soldiers all seemed short, wiry, and many had bad teeth and skin infections; they wore kit that was heavily patched and worn. Native or otherwise, the soldiers all stared with open curiosity at Bisesa and Abdikadir – and, regarding Bisesa, with undisguised sexual speculation.

'No women here,' Abdikadir murmured. 'Don't let it bother you.'

'I wasn't.' Too much had happened to her today, she told herself, for her to allow a few leering troopers in pith helmets and kilts to worry her. But the truth was her stomach churned; it was never good for a woman to be captured.

The heavy gates were open, and carts drawn by mules passed through. What looked like a stripped-down artillery piece was carried on the back of a couple more mules. The mules were driven by Indian troopers, what Bisesa heard the white soldiers call 'sepoys'.

Inside the fort there was an air of bustle and orderly activity. But, Bisesa thought, what was more remarkable than what was here was what was *lacking*, such as any kind of motor vehicle, radio antenna or satellite dish.

They were taken into the main central building, and led to

a kind of anteroom. Here McKnight issued a blunt order: 'Strip.' His sergeant major, he said, wasn't about to let them into the Captain's hallowed presence without a thorough check of what was concealed under their bulky flight suits.

Bisesa forced a grin. 'I think you just want to take a peek at my butt.' She was gratified by the look of genuine shock on McKnight's face. Then she started to peel off her layers, starting with her boots.

Under her flight suit she wore a load-bearing harness. Into its pockets she had crammed a canteen of water, maps, a set of night-vision goggles, a couple of packs of chewing gum, a small plastic first aid pack, other survival rations and gear – and her phone, which had the sense to keep itself inert. She crammed her useless wraparound microphone into an outside pocket. Off came shirt and trousers. They were both allowed to stop when they got down to the dirt-brown T-shirts and shorts.

They were unarmed, save for a bayonet knife Abdikadir carried strapped under his harness. He handed this over to McKnight with some reluctance. McKnight picked up the night goggles and peered through them, evidently baffled. Their little plastic boxes of kit were snapped open and rummaged through.

Then they were allowed to dress again, and were given back most of their gear – but not the knife, and not, Bisesa noted with amusement, her chewing gum.

After that, to Bisesa's astonishment, Captain Grove, the commanding officer, kept them waiting.

The two of them sat side by side in his office, on a hard wooden bench. A single private stood guard at the door, rifle ready. The Captain's room had a certain comfort, even elegance. The walls were whitewashed, the floor wooden; there was rush matting on the floor, and what looked like a Kashmiri rug hanging on one wall. This was obviously the office of a working professional. On a big wooden desk there were piles of papers and cardboard folders, and a nib pen standing in an ink pot. There were some personal touches, like a polo ball set on the desk, and a big old grandfather clock that ticked mournfully. But there was no electric light; only oil lamps supplemented the fading glow from the single small window.

Bisesa felt compelled to whisper, 'It's like a museum. Where are the softscreens, the radios, the phones? There's nothing here but paper.'

Abdikadir said, 'And yet they ran an empire, with paper.'

She stared at him. '*They*? Where do you think we are?'

'Jamrud,' he said without hesitation. 'A fortress – nineteenth century – built by the Sikhs, maintained by the British.'

'You've been here?'

'I've seen pictures. I've studied the history – it's my region, after all. But the books show it as a ruin.'

Bisesa frowned, unable to grasp that. 'Well, it isn't a ruin now.'

'Their kit,' murmured Abdikadir. 'Did you notice? Puttees and Sam Browne belts. And their weapons – those rifles were single-shot breech-loading Martini-Henrys and Sniders. *Seriously* out of date. That stuff hasn't been used since the British were here in the nineteenth century, and even they moved over to Lee Metfords, Gatlings and Maxims as soon as they were available.'

'When was that?'

Abdikadir shrugged. 'I'm not sure. Eighteen nineties, I think.'

'*Eighteen nineties*?'

'Have you tried your survival radio?' They both carried tracking beacons sewn into their harnesses, as well as miniaturised survival radio transceivers, thankfully undetected during McKnight's inspection.

'No joy. The phone's still out of touch too. No more signal than when we were in the air.' She shivered slightly. 'Nobody knows where we are, or where we came down. Or even if we're alive.' It wasn't just the crash that spooked her, she knew. It was the feeling of being *out of contact*, cut off from the warmly interconnected world in which she had been immersed since the moment of her birth. For a citizen of the twenty-first century it was a unique, disorienting feeling of isolation.

Abdikadir's hand slipped over hers, and she was grateful for the warm human connection. He said, 'They'll start search-and-retrieve operations soon. That crashed Bird is a big marker. Although it's getting dark outside.'

Somehow she had forgotten that bit of strangeness. 'It's too early to get dark.'

'Yes. I don't know about you but I feel a little jet-lagged . . .'

Captain Grove bustled in, accompanied by an orderly, and they stood up. Grove was a short, slightly overweight, stressed-looking officer of perhaps forty, in a light khaki uniform. Bisesa noted dust on his boots and puttees: he was a man who put his job before appearances, she thought. But he sported an immense walrus moustache, the largest facial growth Bisesa had seen outside a wrestling ring.

Grove stood before them, hands on hips, glaring at them. 'Batson told me your names, and what you claim are your ranks.' His accent was clipped, oddly out of date, like the British officer class in a World War Two movie. 'And I've been to see that machine of yours.'

Bisesa said, 'We were on a peaceful reconnaissance mission.'

Grove raised a greying eyebrow. 'I've seen your weapons. Some "reconnaissance"!'

Abdikadir shrugged. 'Nevertheless, we're telling you the truth.'

Grove said, 'I suggest we get down to business. Let me tell you first that your man is being taken care of as well as we can.'

'Thank you,' Bisesa said stiffly.

'Now, who are you, and what are you doing at my fort?'

Bisesa narrowed her eyes. 'We don't have to tell you anything but name, rank, serial number . . .' She faltered to a halt as Grove looked baffled.

Abdikadir said gently, 'I'm not sure if our conventions of war apply here, Bisesa. And besides I have the feeling that this situation is so strange that it may be best for all of us if we are open with each other.' He was eyeing Grove challengingly.

Grove nodded curtly. He sat behind his desk, and absently waved them to sit on their bench. He said, 'Suppose I put aside for the moment the most likely possibility, which is that you are some sort of spies for Russia or her allies, sent on some destabilisation mission. Perhaps you even engineered the loss of contact we are suffering . . . As I say, let's put that aside. You say you're on secondment from the British Army. You're here to keep the peace. Well, so am I, I suppose. Tell me how flapping about in that whirling contraption achieves that.' He was brisk, but visibly uncertain.

Bisesa took a deep breath. Briefly she sketched the geopolitical situation: the stand-off of the great powers over the region's oil, the complex local tensions. Grove seemed to follow this, even if most of it seemed unfamiliar, and at times he showed great surprise. 'Russia an *ally*, you say? . . .'

'Let me tell you how *I* see the situation here. We're at a point of tension all right – but the tension is between Britain and Russia. My job is to help defend the frontier of the Empire, and then the security of the Raj. About all I recognised from your little speech was the trouble you have with the Pashtuns. No offence,' he said to Abdikadir.

Bisesa found this impossible to take in. She was reduced to repeating his words. 'The *Raj*? The *Empire*?'

'It seems,' Grove said, 'we are here to wage different wars, Lieutenant Dutt.'

But Abdikadir was nodding. 'Captain Grove, you have had trouble with your communications in the last few hours?'

Grove paused, evidently deciding what to tell him. 'Very well – yes. We lost both the telegraph link, and the heliograph stations from about noon. Haven't heard a peep since, and we still don't know what's going on. And you?'

Abdikadir sighed. 'The time scale is a little different. We lost our radio communications just before the crash – a few hours ago.'

'*Radio*? . . . Never mind,' Grove said, waving a hand. 'So we have similar problems, you in your flying roundabout, me in my fortress. And what do you suppose caused this?'

Bisesa said in a rush, 'A hot war.' She had been brooding on this possibility since the crash; despite the terror of those moments, and the shock of what had followed, she hadn't been able to get it out of her head. She said to Abdikadir, 'An electromagnetic pulse – what else could knock out both civilian and military comms, simultaneously? The strange lights we saw in the sky – the weather, the sudden winds—'

'But we saw no contrails,' Abdikadir said calmly. 'Come to think of it, I haven't noticed a single contrail since the crash.'

'Once again,' Grove said with irritation, 'I have not the first idea what you're talking about.'

'I mean,' Bisesa said, 'I fear a nuclear war has broken out. And that's what's stranded us all. It's happened before in this area, after all. It's only seventeen years since Lahore was destroyed by the Indian strike.'

Grove stared at her. 'Destroyed, you say?'

She frowned. 'Utterly. You must know it was.'

Grove stood, went to the door, and gave an order to the private waiting there. After a couple of minutes the bustling young civilian called 'Ruddy' came to the door, slightly breathless, evidently summoned by Grove. The other civilian, the young man called Josh who had helped Abdikadir get Casey out of the downed chopper, came pushing his way into the room too.

Grove raised his eyebrows. 'I should have expected you to sneak in, Mr White. But you have your job to do, I suppose. You!' Peremptorily he pointed at Ruddy. 'When were you last in Lahore?'

Ruddy thought briefly. 'Three, four weeks ago, I believe.'

'Can you describe the place as you saw it then?'

Ruddy seemed puzzled by the request, but he complied: 'An old walled city – two hundred thousand and odd Punjabis, and a few thousand Europeans and mixed race – lots of Mughal monuments. Since the Mutiny it's become a centre of administration, as well as the platform for military expeditions to see off the Russki threat. I don't know what you want me to tell you, sir.'

'Just this. Has Lahore been destroyed? Was it, in fact, devastated seventeen years ago?'

Ruddy guffawed. 'Scarcely. My father worked there. He built a house on the Mozang Road!'

Grove snapped at Bisesa, 'Why are you lying?'

Foolishly Bisesa felt like crying. *Why won't you believe me?* She turned to Abdikadir. He had fallen silent; he was gazing out of the window at the reddening sun. 'Abdi? Back me up here.'

Abdikadir said to her softly, 'You don't see the pattern yet.'

'What pattern?'

He closed his eyes. 'I don't blame you. I don't want to see it myself.' He faced the British. 'You know, Captain, the strangest thing of all that happened today was the sun.' He described the sudden shift of the sun across the sky. 'One minute noon, the next late afternoon. As if the machinery of time had come off its cogs.' He glanced at the grandfather clock; its faded face showed the time was a little before seven o'clock. He asked Grove, 'Is that correct?'

'Nearly, I suppose. I check it every morning.'

Abdikadir lifted his wrist and glanced at his watch. 'And yet I show only fifteen twenty-seven – half past three in the afternoon. Bisesa, do you agree?'

She checked. 'Yes.'

Ruddy frowned. He strode over to Abdikadir and took his wrist. 'I've never seen a watch like this. It's certainly not a Waterbury! It has numbers, not hands. There isn't even a dial. And the numbers melt one into the other!'

'It's a digital watch,' Abdikadir said mildly.

'And what is this?' Ruddy called out the numbers. 'Eight, six, two thousand and thirty-seven.'

'That is the date,' Abdikadir said.

Ruddy frowned, working it out. 'Two thousand and thirty-seven. A date in the twenty-first century?'

'Yes.'

Ruddy strode over to Grove's desk and rummaged in a heap of papers there. 'Forgive me, Captain.' Even the formidable Grove seemed out of his depth; he raised his hands helplessly. Ruddy extracted a newspaper. 'A couple of days old, but it will do.' He held it up for Bisesa and Abdikadir to see; it was a thin rag called the *Civil and Military Gazette*. 'Can you see the date?'

It was a date in March, 1885. There was a long, frozen silence.

Grove said briskly, 'Do you know, I think we could all do with a cup of tea.'

'No!' The other young man – Josh White – seemed very agitated. 'I'm sorry sir, but it all makes sense now, I think it does – oh, it fits, it fits!'

'Calm yourself,' Grove said sternly. 'What are you jabbering about?'

'The man-ape,' White said. 'Never mind cups of tea – we must show them the man-ape!'

So, with Bisesa and Abdikadir still under armed guard, they all trooped out of the fort.

They came to a kind of encampment a hundred metres or so from the fortress wall. Here a conical tent of netting had been erected. A group of soldiers stood casually around, smoking foul-smelling cigarettes. Lean, grimy, the backs of their necks shaven, the troops gazed at Abdikadir and Bisesa with the usual mixture of curiosity and lust.

Something was moving inside the netting, Bisesa saw – something alive, an animal perhaps – but the setting sun had touched the horizon, and the light was too low, the shadows too long for her to make it out.

At White's command, the netting was pulled back. Bisesa had been expecting to see a supporting pole. Instead, a silvery sphere, apparently floating unsupported in the air, had provided the tent's apex. None of the locals gave the sphere a second glance. Abdikadir stepped forward, squinted at his reflection in the floating sphere, and passed his hand underneath it. There was nothing holding the sphere up.

'You know,' he said, 'on any other day this would seem unusual.'

Bisesa's gaze was drawn to the floating anomaly, to her own distorted face reflected in its surface. *This is the key*, she thought, the notion bursting without warning into her mind.

Josh touched her arm. 'Bisesa, are you all right?'

Bisesa was distracted by his accent, which sounded to her ears JFK-Bostonian, but his face seemed to show genuine concern. She laughed without humour. 'In the circumstances, I think I'm doing pretty well.'

'You're missing the show.' He meant the creatures on the ground, and she tried to focus.

At first Bisesa thought they were chimps, but of light, almost gracile build. Bonobos, perhaps. One was small, the other larger; the big one cradled the little one. At a gesture from Grove, two squaddies stepped forward and pulled the baby away, grabbed the mother's wrists and ankles, and stretched her out on the ground. The creature kicked and spat.

The 'chimp' was a biped.

'Holy shit,' Bisesa murmured. 'Do you think that's an australopithecine?'

'A Lucy, yes,' Abdikadir murmured. 'But the pithecines have been extinct for – what? A million years?'

'Is it possible a band of them have somehow survived in the wild, in the mountains maybe?'

He looked at her, his eyes wells of darkness. 'You don't believe that.'

'No, I don't.'

'You see?' White shouted excitedly. 'You see the man-ape? What is this but another . . . *time-slip*?'

Bisesa stepped forward, and peered into the haunting eyes of the older pithecine. She was straining to reach the child, she saw. 'I wonder what she's thinking.'

Abdikadir grunted. ' "There goes the neighbourhood." '

CHAPTER 8

ON ORBIT

After hours of fruitless calling, Musa sat back in his couch.

The three cosmonauts lay side by side, like huge orange bugs in their spacesuits. For once the cosiness of the Soyuz capsule, the way they were pressed against each other, was comforting rather than confining.

'I don't understand it,' Musa said.

'You said that already,' Sable murmured.

There was a grim silence. Since the moment they had lost contact, the atmosphere between them had been explosive.

After three months of living in such close quarters, Kolya had come to understand Sable, he thought. Aged forty, Sable came from a poor New Orleans family with a complicated genetic history. Some of the Russians who had served with her admired the strength of character which had taken her so far: even now, in NASA's Astronaut Office, to be anything other than male and WASP was a disadvantage. Other cosmonauts, less charitable, joked about how launch weight manifests had to be recalculated if Sable was on board, on account of the immense chip she carried on her shoulder. Most agreed that if she had been Russian she would never have passed the psychological tests required for every cosmonaut to prove suitable for space duty.

During the three-month tour on Station, Kolya himself had gotten on fairly well with Sable, perhaps because they were opposite types. Kolya was a serving Air Force officer, and he had a young family in Moscow. To him, spaceflight was an adventure, but what drove him were loyalty to his family and duty to his country, and he was content to let his career develop where it would. Kolya recognised a fierce, burning ambition in Sable, which would not be satisfied, surely, until she had reached the pinnacles of her profession: command of Clavius Base, or perhaps even a seat on a Mars flight. Perhaps Sable had seen Kolya as no threat to her own glittering progress.

But he had learned to be wary of her. And now, in this awkward, frightening situation, he waited for her to explode.

Musa clapped his gloved hands together, taking command. 'I think it is obvious we won't be proceeding to re-entry just yet. We should not worry. In the olden days Soviet craft would only have contact with their ground controllers for twenty minutes of every ninety-minute orbit, and so the Soyuz was designed to function independently.'

'Maybe the fault isn't with us,' Sable said. 'What if it's on the ground?'

Musa scoffed, 'What fault could possibly take out a whole chain of ground stations?'

'A war,' said Kolya.

Musa said firmly, 'Such speculation is useless. In time, whatever the fault, the ground will re-establish contact, and we will return to our flight plan. All we have to do is wait. But in the meantime we have work to do.' He rummaged under his seat for a copy of the on-orbit checklist.

He was right, Kolya realised; the little ship wouldn't run itself, and if it was to be stuck up here in orbit for one more revolution – or two, or three? – its crew would have to help it function. Was the compartment's pressure appropriate, was the mixture of gases correct? Was the ship rotating properly as it followed the great curve of its orbit, so that its solar panels tracked the sun? All these things had to be ensured.

Soon the three of them had settled into a familiar, and somehow reassuring, routine of checks – as if, after all, they were in control of their destiny, Kolya thought.

But the fact was that everything had changed, and it couldn't be ignored.

The Soyuz was floating into the shadow of the planet again. Kolya peered through his window, looking for the orange-yellow glow of cities, hoping for reassurance. But the land was dark.

CHAPTER 9

PARADOX

Josh was intrigued by this woman from the future – if that was what she was! Bisesa's face was handsome and well proportioned, if not beautiful, her nose strong and her jaw square; but her eyes were clear, her cut-short hair lustrous. She had a strength about her, even physically, that he had seen in no woman before: faced with this unprecedented situation, she was confident, if edgy with fatigue.

As the evening wore on, he took to following her around, puppy-like.

It had been a long day – the longest of Bisesa's life, she said, even if she had lost a few hours – and Captain Grove's advice that the newcomers should be allowed to eat and rest seemed wise. But they insisted they had work to do before resting. Abdikadir wanted to check on Casey, the other pilot. And he wanted to return to the machine they called their 'Little Bird'. 'I have to erase the memory banks of the electronic gear,' he said. 'There's sensitive data in there, especially the avionics . . .' Josh was entranced by this talk of intelligent machines, and he imagined the air full of invisible telegraph wires, transmitting mysterious and important messages hither and yon.

Grove was inclined to allow the request. 'I can't see how we can be harmed by allowing the destruction of what I don't understand anyhow,' he said dryly. 'And besides – you say it is your duty, Warrant Officer. I respect that. Time and space may flow like toffee, but duty endures.'

For her part Bisesa wanted to retrace the track her helicopter had taken, she said, before the crash. 'We were shot down. I think that was just *after* we noticed the sun dancing around the sky. So – you see? If we've somehow come through some, some *barrier in time*, then whoever shot at us must be on this side too . . .'

Grove thought this jaunt would be better left until morning, for he could see Bisesa's fatigue as well as Josh could. But Bisesa didn't want to stop moving, not yet, as if to stop would be to accept the extraordinary reality of the situation. So Grove approved the mission. Josh's respect for the man's judgement and compassion grew; Grove understood what was going on here no better than anybody else, but he was clearly trying to deal with the simple human needs of the people who had, literally, fallen out of the sky into his domain.

A field party was drawn together: Bisesa, with Josh and Ruddy, both of whom insisted on accompanying her, and a small squad of privates under the nominal command of the Geordie private Batson, who, it seemed, might have impressed Grove enough that day to earn a promotion.

By the time they set out from the fort the dark was gathering. The soldiers carried oil lamps and burning torches. They walked directly east from the site of the chopper's crash. Bisesa had estimated the distance at no more than a mile.

The lights of the fort receded, and the Frontier dusk opened up around them, huge and empty. But Josh could see thick black mounds of cloud on every horizon.

He hurried beside Bisesa. 'If it is true—'

'What?'

'This business of slipping through time, you, and the man-ape creatures. How do you think it can have happened?'

'I've no idea. And I'm not sure if I'd rather be a castaway in time or a victim of a nuclear war. Anyhow,' she said briskly, 'how do you know *you're* not the castaway?'

Josh quailed. 'I never thought of that. You know, I can scarcely believe I am even holding this conversation! If you had told me this morning that before I slept this night I would see a flying machine powerful enough to carry people inside it – and that those people would, and plausibly too, claim to be from a future a century and a half hence – I would have thought you were insane!'

'But if it's true,' Ruddy said insistently, jogging alongside them – never very fit, he was panting a little – 'if it's true, there's so much you know, so much you could tell us! For *our* future is *your* past.'

She shook her head. 'I've seen too many movies. Have you never heard of the chronology protection conjecture?'

Josh was baffled, as was Ruddy.

Bisesa said, 'I guess you don't even know what a movie is, let alone know *Terminator* . . . Look, some people think that if you go back in time and change something, so that the future you came from can't exist any more, you could cause a huge catastrophe.'

'I don't understand,' Josh confessed.

'Suppose I told you where my great-great-great-grand-mother lives, right now, in 1885. Then you go out, find her, and shoot her.'

'Why would I do that?'

'Never mind! But if you did, I would never be born – and so I could never come back to tell you about my grandmother and you'd never shoot her. In which case—'

'It's a paradox of logic,' Ruddy breathed. 'How delightful! But if we promise not to molest your grandmother, can you tell us *nothing* of ourselves?'

Josh scoffed, 'How would she ever have heard of *us*, Ruddy?'

Ruddy looked thoughtful. 'I have the feeling that she *has*, you know – heard of *me* at any rate. A chap knows when he's been recognised!'

But Bisesa would say no more.

As the last daylight seeped away, and the stars receded to infinity above them, the little party grew closer together, the soldiers' bantering talk subdued, their lanterns held high. They were walking into strangeness, thought Josh. It wasn't just that they couldn't know *who* lay out there, or *where* they were going. They couldn't even be sure *when* they would find themselves . . . He thought they all seemed relieved when they passed a low hill and the rising Moon, a quarter full, shed a cold light on the rocky plain. But the air was strange, turbulent, and the Moon's face an odd yellow-orange.

'Here,' said Bisesa suddenly. She had stopped before a scraping in the ground. Stepping closer, Josh saw that the earth was fresh and moist, as if recently dug.

'It's a foxhole,' Ruddy said. He hopped down into the hole, and brandished a length of pipe, like a bit of drainpipe. 'And is this the fearsome weapon that shot you out of the sky?'

'That's the RPG launcher, yes.' She peered east. 'There was a village just over there. A hundred metres, no more.' The soldiers held up their lanterns. There was no village to be seen, nothing but the rocky plain that seemed to stretch to the horizon. 'Perhaps there is a boundary near here,' Bisesa breathed. 'A boundary in time. What a strange thought. What is happening to us? . . .' She lifted her face to the Moon. 'Oh. Clavius is gone.'

Josh was at her side. 'Clavius?'

'Clavius Base.' She pointed. 'Built into a big old crater in the southern highlands.'

Josh stared. 'You have cities *on the Moon*?'

She smiled. 'I wouldn't call it a city. But you can see its light, like a captured star, the only one in the circle of the crescent Moon. Now it's gone. That isn't even my *Moon*. There is a crew on Mars, and a second on the way – or there was. I wonder what's become of them . . .'

There was a grunt of disgust. One of the soldiers had been rooting at the bottom of the foxhole, and now emerged with what looked like a piece of meat, still dripping blood. The stink was sharp.

'A human arm,' Ruddy said flatly. He turned away and vomited.

Josh said, 'It looks to me like the work of a great cat. It seems that whoever attacked you did not live long to enjoy his triumph.'

'I suppose he was as lost as I am.'

'Yes. I apologise for Ruddy. He doesn't have a very strong stomach for such sights.'

'No. And he never will.'

Josh looked at her; her eyes were full of moonlight, her expression empty. 'What do you mean?'

'He was right. I do know who he is. You're Rudyard Kipling, aren't you? Rudyard bloody Kipling. My God, what a day.'

Ruddy didn't respond. He was hunched over, still retching, and bile stained his chin.

At that moment the ground trembled, hard enough to raise little clouds of dust everywhere, like invisible footfalls. And rain began to fall, from thick black clouds that came racing across the Moon's empty face.

Time's Eye

PART TWO

CASTAWAYS IN TIME

CHAPTER 10

GEOMETRY

For Bisesa the first morning was the worst.

She suspected that some combination of adrenalin and shock had kept her going through the day of what they were starting to call the Discontinuity. But that night, in the room given to them by Grove, a hastily converted storeroom, she had slept badly on her thin down-stuffed mattress. By the next morning, when she had reluctantly woken up to find herself *still here*, she had come crashing down from her adrenalin high, and felt inconsolable. The second night, at Abdi's insistence, desperate for sleep, she cracked her survival gear. She donned earplugs and eye shades, swallowed a Halcyon tablet – what Casey called a 'Blue Bomber' – and slept for ten hours.

But as the days passed, Bisesa, Abdikadir and Casey were still stuck here in the Jamrud Fort. They had no contact on any of their military wavelengths, Bisesa's phone muttered about its continuing cauterisation, no SAR teams came flapping out of the UN base in response to their patiently bleeping beacons – there was no medevac for Casey. And there was not a single contrail to be seen in the sky, not one.

She spent most of her time missing Myra, her daughter. She didn't even want to confront those feelings, as if acknowledging them would make her separation from Myra real. She longed to have something to do – anything to stop her thinking.

Meanwhile life went on.

After the first couple of days, when it was obvious the Bird crew had no hostile intent, the British troops' close military scrutiny of them was relaxed a little, though Bisesa suspected Captain Grove was too wary a commander not to keep a

65

weather eye on them. They certainly weren't allowed anywhere near the small stash of twenty-first-century pistols, submachine guns, flares and the like that had been extracted from the Bird. But she thought it probably helped these nineteenth-century British accept them that Casey was a white American and that both Bisesa and Abdi could be regarded as belonging to 'allied' races. If the Bird's crew had been Russian, German or Chinese, say – and there were plenty of such troops in Clavius – there might have been more hostility.

But when she thought about it Bisesa was astonished even to be considering such issues, culture clashes spanning the nineteenth and twenty-first centuries. The whole business was surreal; she felt as if she was walking around in a bubble. And she was continually amazed how easily everyone else accepted their situation, the blunt, apparently undeniable reality of the time-slips, across a hundred and fifty years in her case, perhaps across *a million years* or more for the wretched pithecine and her infant in their net cage.

Abdikadir said, 'I don't think the British understand this at all, and maybe we understand too well. When H.G. Wells published *The Time Machine* in 1895 – ten years ahead in this time zone! – he had to spend twenty or thirty pages explaining what a time machine does. Not how it works, you see, but just what it *is*. For us there has been a process of acculturation. After a century of science fiction you and I are thoroughly accustomed to the idea of time travel, and can immediately accept its implications – strange though the experience is to actually live through.'

'But that doesn't apply to these Victorian-age Brits. To them a Model T Ford would be a fabulous vehicle from the future.'

'Sure. I think for them the time-slips and their implications are simply beyond their imaginations . . . But if H.G. Wells was here – did he ever visit India? – of all thinkers, his mind might explode with the implications of what is happening . . .'

None of this rationalisation seemed to help Bisesa. Maybe

the truth was that Abdikadir and everybody else felt just as peculiar as she did, but they were better at hiding it.

Ruddy, though, sympathised with her disorientation. He told her he was occasionally afflicted by hallucinations.

'When I was a child, stranded in an unhappy foster home in England, I once began to punch a tree. Odd behaviour I grant you, but nobody understood that I was trying to see if it was my grandmother! More recently in Lahore I came down with a fever that may have been malaria, and since then, on occasion, my "blue devils" have returned. So I know how it is to be plagued by the unreal.' As he spoke to her he leaned forward, intent, his eyes distorted by the thick spectacles Josh called 'gig-lamps'. 'But you are real enough for me. I'll tell you what to do about it – work!' He held up stubby fingers stained black with ink. 'Sixteen hours a day I put in sometimes. Work, the best bulwark for reality . . .'

So it went, a therapy session on the nature of reality with nineteen-year-old Rudyard Kipling. She walked away more dazed than before it had begun.

As time passed and both parties, the Victorian-age British and Bisesa's crew, continued to lack communications with their respective outside worlds, Grove grew very concerned.

There were very practical reasons for this; the stores here at the fort would not last long. But Grove was also disconnected from the vast apparatus of the imperial administration, which Bisesa glimpsed in the rapid talk of Ruddy and Josh. Even on the civilian side there were local Commissioners, with staffs of Deputies and Assistants, who reported to a Lieutenant Governor, who reported to a Viceroy, who reported to a Secretary of State, who reported, at last, to the Empress herself, Queen Victoria in far-off London. The British were encouraged to think of themselves as locked into a unified social structure. Wherever you served you were a soldier of the Queen, part of her global empire. For Grove to be isolated from this was as disturbing, Bisesa saw, as it was for her to be cut off from the global telecommunications nets of the twenty-first century.

So Grove began to send out scouting patrols, particularly using his sowars, his Indian cavalry troopers, who seemed able to cover impressive distances quickly. They reached Peshawar, where the local army cantonment and military command centre should have been found – but Peshawar was gone. There was no evidence of destruction, not even of the hideous erasing of a nuclear blast which Bisesa had trained the British to recognise. There was only bare rock, a river bank, scrubby vegetation, and the spoor of creatures that might have been lions: it was as if Peshawar had never existed at all. It was a similar story, the sowar scouts reported, when they went out to find Clavius, Bisesa's UN encampment. Not a trace, not even of destruction.

So Grove determined to explore further: down the valley of the Indus, deep into India – and to the north.

Meanwhile Casey, still pretty much immobilised, likewise took on the challenge of making contact with the rest of the world. With the help of a couple of privates from a signals corps assigned by Grove, he scavenged comms gear from the fallen Bird, and improvised a sending and receiving station in a small room in the fort. But no matter how long he spent calling into the dark, there was no reply.

Abdikadir, meanwhile, had his own projects, which concerned the peculiar floating sphere. Bisesa was envious that both Casey and Abdi quickly found useful work to occupy their time, as if they somehow fit in better than she did.

On the fourth morning, Bisesa emerged from the fort to find Abdikadir standing on a stool, holding a battered tin bucket up in the air. Casey and Cecil de Morgan sat on fold-out camp chairs, their faces bathed in the morning sun as they watched the show. Casey waved at Bisesa. 'Hey, Bis! Come see the cabaret.' Though de Morgan immediately offered her his chair, Bisesa sat in the dirt beside Casey. She didn't like de Morgan, and she wasn't about to give him any kind of leverage over her, however trivial.

Abdikadir's bucket was full of water, so it must have been heavy. Nevertheless he propped it on his shoulder one-handed, and marked the water's level with a chinagraph pencil. Then he lowered the bucket, and revealed the floating sphere, the Evil Eye, with water running off its surface; Abdi made sure he caught every drop. The tent containing the two 'man-apes' had been set up a few dozen yards away, with some kind of pole at its centre.

Casey snickered. 'He's been dunking that damn thing for half an hour already.'

'Why, Abdi?'

'I'm measuring its volume,' Abdikadir murmured. 'And I'm repeating it for accuracy. It's called science. Thanks for your support.' And he lifted the bucket up around the sphere again.

Bisesa said to Casey, 'I thought the surgeon-captain said you shouldn't get out of bed.'

Casey blew a raspberry, and thrust his heavily bandaged leg out in front of him. 'Ah, bull. It was a clean break and they set it well.' Though without anaesthetic, Bisesa knew. 'I don't like sitting around with my thumb up my ass.'

'And you, Mr de Morgan,' Bisesa said. 'What's your interest in this?'

The factor spread his hands. 'I am a businessman, ma'am. That's why I'm here in the first place. And I am constantly on the look-out for new opportunities. Naturally I am intrigued by your downed flying machine! I accept that both you and Captain Grove want to keep that particular item under wraps. But *this*, this floating orb of perfection, is neither yours nor Grove's, and, in these days of strangeness, how strange it remains, though we have quickly become accustomed to it! There it floats, supported by nothing we can see. No matter how hard you hit it – even with bullets, and that's been tried, somewhat perilously given the ricochets – you can neither knock a chip out of its perfect surface, nor even move it from its station by so much as a fraction of an inch. Who made it? What holds it up? What lies inside it?'

'And how much is it worth?' Casey growled.

De Morgan laughed easily. 'You can't blame a man for trying.'

Josh had told Bisesa something of de Morgan's background.

His family were failed aristocracy, who could trace their ancestry back to William the Conqueror's first assault on England, more than eight hundred years before, and had carved a rich estate out of the defeated Saxon kingdoms. In the intervening centuries a 'trait of greed and foolishness that transcends the generations', in de Morgan's own disarming words, had left the family penniless, though still with a kind of race memory of wealth and power. Ruddy said that in his experience the Raj was plagued by 'chancers' like de Morgan. As far as Bisesa was concerned there was nothing to be trusted in de Morgan's slicked-back black hair, and his darting, questing eyes.

Abdikadir clambered down from his stool. Dark, serious, focused, he switched his watch to calculator mode, and punched in the numbers he had recorded.

'So, Brainiac,' Casey called mockingly, 'tell us what you've learned.'

Abdikadir settled to the dirt before Bisesa. 'The Eye resists our probing, but there are things to measure nonetheless. First of all, the Eye is surrounded by a magnetic anomaly. I checked that with a compass from my survival kit.'

Casey grunted. 'My compass has been haywire since we hit the dirt.'

Abdikadir shook his head. 'It's true you can't find magnetic north; something peculiar seems to be happening to Earth's magnetic field. But there's nothing wrong with our compasses themselves.' He glanced up at the Eye. 'The flux lines around that thing are packed together. A diagram of it would look like a knot in a piece of wood.'

'How come?'

'I've no idea.'

Bisesa leaned forward. 'What else, Abdi?'

'I've been doing some high school geometry.' He grinned. 'Dipping the thing in water was the only way I could think of to measure its volume – seeing how the water level in the bucket goes up and down.'

'*Eureka*!' de Morgan cried playfully. 'Sir, you are the Archimedes *de nos jours* . . .'

Abdikadir ignored him. 'I took a dozen measurements, hoping to drive down the errors, but it still won't be too hot. I can't think of a way of getting the surface area at all. But my measurements of the radius and circumference are pretty good, I think.' He held up a jury-rigged set of callipers. 'I adapted a laser sight from the chopper . . .'

'I don't get it,' said Casey. 'It's just a sphere. If you know the radius you can work out the rest from all those formulae. The surface area is, what, four times pi times the radius squared . . .'

'You can work that out if you make the assumption that this sphere is like every other sphere you've encountered before,' Abdi said mildly. 'But here it is floating in the air, like nothing I've ever seen. I didn't want to make any assumptions about it; I wanted to check everything I could.'

Bisesa nodded. 'And you found – ?'

'For a start, it is a perfect sphere.' He glanced up again. 'And I mean *perfect*, within the tolerances even of my laser measurements, in every axis I tried. Even in 2037 we couldn't shape any material to such a fantastic degree of precision.'

De Morgan nodded soberly. 'An almost arrogant display of geometrical perfection.'

'Yes. But that's just the start.' Abdikadir held up his watch so Bisesa could see its tiny screen. 'Your high school geometry, Casey. The ratio of a circle's circumference to its diameter is . . . ?'

'Pi,' rumbled Casey. 'Even a jock Christian knows that much.'

'Well, not in this case. The ratio for the Eye is *three*. Not about three, or a bit more than three – three, to laser precision. My error bars are so small it's quite impossible that the ratio is actually pi, as it ought to be. Your formulae don't work after all, you see, Casey. I get the same number for "pi" from the volume. Although of course my reliability is way down; you can't compare a laser with a bucket of dusty water.'

Bisesa stood and walked around the Eye, peering up at it. She continued to have an uneasy sense about it. 'That's

71

impossible. Pi is pi. The number is embedded in the structure of our universe.'

'*Our* universe, yes,' Abdikadir said.

'What do you mean?'

Abdikadir shrugged. 'It seems that this sphere – though it is evidently *here* – is not quite of our universe. We seem to have stumbled into anomalies in time, Bisesa. Perhaps this is an anomaly in space.'

'If that's so,' Casey rumbled, 'who or what caused it? And what are we supposed to do about it?'

There was, of course, no answer.

Captain Grove came bustling up. 'Sorry to trouble you, Lieutenant,' he said to Bisesa. 'You'll remember the scouting patrols I've been sending out – one of the sowars has reported something rather odd, to the north of here.'

'"Odd",' Casey said. 'God love your British understatement!'

Grove was unperturbed. 'You might be able to make more of it than any of my chaps . . . I wondered if you fancied a short excursion?'

CHAPTER 11
STRANDED IN SPACE

'Hey, asshole, I need the john.' That was Sable, of course, yelling up from the descent compartment, welcoming Kolya to another day.

He had been dreaming of home, of Nadia and the boys. Hanging in his sleeping bag like a bat from a fruit tree, with only the dim red glow of low-power emergency lights around him, it took him a few moments to realise where he was. *Oh. I am still here.* Still in this half-derelict spacecraft, endlessly circling an unresponsive Earth. For a moment he floated, clinging to the last remnants of sleep.

He was in the living compartment, along with their space-suits and other unnecessary gear, and surrounded by the junk from the Station that they still carried with them – they could hardly open the hatch to throw it out. His sleeping up here gave them all a little more space, or, to put it another way, stopped three stir-crazy cosmonauts from killing each other. But it was scarcely comfortable. He could still smell the rotting discarded underwear, the 'Cossack jockstraps', as Sable had put it.

He groaned, squirmed, and pulled himself out of his sleeping bag. He made his way to the little toilet, opened it out from the wall, and activated the pumps that would draw his waste out into the emptiness of space. When they had realised they were going to be stuck on orbit, they had had to dig out this lavatory from under the heaps of garbage; their journey home had been meant to last only a few hours, and toilet breaks hadn't been scheduled. This morning it took him a while to finish. He was dehydrated, and his urine was thick, almost painfully acidic, as if reluctant to leave his body.

Wearing only his longjohn underwear he found himself shivering. To maximise the Soyuz's endurance Musa had ordered that only essential systems should be run, at minimum power. So the ship had become progressively cold and damp. Black mildew was growing over the walls. The air, increasingly foul, was thick with dust, flaked-off skin, shaved-off bristle, and food debris, none of which, of course, settled out in the absence of gravity. Their eyes were gritty, and they all sneezed, all the time; yesterday Kolya had timed himself, and found he suffered twenty sneezes in a single hour.

The tenth day, he thought. Today they would complete another sixteen pointless orbits of the Earth, bringing their grand total, since the Station had winked out of existence, to perhaps a hundred and sixty.

He fixed his braslets to the tops of his legs. These elastic straps, a guard against fluid imbalances caused by microgravity, were adjusted to be tight enough to restrict the flow of fluids out of his legs, without being so tight that they stopped the flow in. Kolya pulled on his jumpsuit – actually another discard he had found in the trash piles in the living compartment.

Then he clambered down through the open hatch and into the descent compartment. Neither Musa nor Sable met his eyes; they were sick of the sight of each other. He swivelled in the air and slid into his left-side couch with a practised ease. As soon as he was out of the way Sable pushed herself up through the hatch, and Kolya heard her banging around.

'Breakfast.' Musa pushed a tray through the air towards Kolya. On it were taped tubes and cans of food, already opened, half-eaten. They had long since finished up the small stash of food aboard the Soyuz, and had broken into the emergency rations meant to sustain them after they landed: tins of meat and fish, squeeze tubes of creamed vegetables and cheese, even a few boiled sweets. But it was hardly filling. Kolya ran his finger over every empty tin, and sucked stray crumbs out of the air.

None of them was very hungry anyhow. The strange conditions of weightlessness ensured that. He did miss hot food, though, which he had not enjoyed since leaving the Station.

Musa had already begun his steady, determined working of the comms system. 'Stereo One, Stereo One . . .' Of course there was no reply, no matter how many hours he spent at the task. But what choice was there but to keep trying?

Sable meanwhile was bustling around 'upstairs' in the living compartment. She had discovered the components of an old ham radio rig, which the Station astronauts had once used to contact amateurs across the planet, especially school-children. Public interest in the Station had long waned, and the Station's ageing gear had been disassembled, boxed up and packed into the Soyuz for destruction. Now Sable was trying to make it work. Perhaps they would pick up signals, or even be able to send broadcasts, on wavelengths the con-ventional gear couldn't handle. Musa, almost routinely, had grumbled when she wanted to hook the gear up to the space-craft's power supply. Another blazing argument had ensued, but on this occasion Kolya had intervened. 'It's a long shot, but it might work. What harm can it do? . . .'

Kolya leaned forward and pressed the valve of the water tank. A globule a few centimetres across emerged and headed towards his face. Aware of Musa watching greedily – there would be a row if he wasted a single drop – Kolya opened his mouth wide. The water broke on his tongue, and he held it in his mouth, savouring its freshness, before swallowing it. Of all the rationing regimes Musa had imposed, the water was the hardest to bear. The Soyuz had none of the Station's recycling facilities; designed for short-duration hops from Earth to orbit and back, it was equipped only with a small water tank. But Sable had characteristically argued: 'Even when you're in a desert you don't ration your water. You drink it down when you need it. There's no other way . . .' Right or wrong, the water was running out anyhow.

He dug out a tooth cleaner from a compartment on the wall. This was a bit of muslin impregnated with highly flavoured toothpaste that you slipped over your finger and worked around your mouth. Kolya used this carefully, sucking every last bit of minty flavour out of the scrap of cloth; some-how the taste seemed to assuage his thirst a little.

And that was his day begun. He couldn't wash, for they had long since run out of the soft flannels that you usually used to wash your body and your hair. No doubt they all smelled as bad as the Cossack jockstraps upstairs. But at least they were all the same.

As Musa continued to call plaintively into the dark, Kolya turned to his own self-appointed programme of work, which was a study of the Earth.

In his long hours in space, Kolya had always derived great pleasure from watching Earth. The Station, like Soyuz now, orbited only a few hundred kilometres above the surface, so to him the planet had none of the sense of isolation and fragility that the travellers to Mars reported, when they looked back at the blue island where they had been born. To Kolya Earth was huge – and all but empty.

Half of every orbit took him over the great wastes of the Pacific, a sky-blue expanse broken only by the wakes of occa-sional ships, a dusting of islands. Even land masses were mostly empty of people: across Asia and north Africa the deserts stretched, unmarked save by the smoke of an occa-sional camp fire. Human habitation was confined largely to the coasts, or the river valleys. But even cities were difficult to make out from orbit; when he searched for Moscow or London, Paris or New York, he might make out only a bubb-ling greyness, fading into the green-brown of the countryside beyond.

It was not the fragility of the Earth that impressed him, then, but its immensity; and it was not the grandeur of man's conquest of the planet that was so obvious, but the smallness of human tenure, even in the mid-twenty-first century.

But all that was before the metamorphosis.

He clung to what was familiar. The geometry of Earth seen from low orbit was unchanged: every ninety minutes he could watch the sun rise with startling swiftness through the layers of atmosphere, the light brightening from crimson, orange, to yellow, in smoothly curving bands. And the shapes and positions of the continents, the deserts, the distribution of the mountains in their ranges – all those were much as they had been.

But beneath those sunrises, within the frames of the continents, there were many peculiarities.

There had been shifts in the patterns of the ice sheets. Over the Himalayas, he could clearly make out glaciers pouring off the sides of the mountains, clawing their way towards the lower ground. The Sahara, meanwhile, had not remained a desert, not entirely. Here and there new oases had sprung up, patches of green that could be fifty kilometres on a side, bordered by straight-line segments. Similarly he observed bits of desert somehow stuck into the green expanses of the South American rain forests. The world was suddenly a clumsy patchwork. But those odd patches of green in the desert were already fading, he observed as the days wore on, the greenery browning, visibly dying.

If the effect of the changes on the physical world were relatively subtle, the impact on humanity was dramatic.

By day the cities and farms had always been hard to make out from orbit. But now even the great roadways that had once spanned the red centre of Australia had vanished. Britain, its shape easily recognisable, seemed to be covered from the Scottish borders to the Channel coast by a thick blanket of forest: Kolya recognised the Thames, but it was much broader than he remembered – and there was no sign of London. Once Kolya made out a bright orange-yellow glow in the middle of the North Sea. It appeared to be a burning oil rig. A great black plume of smoke rose from it and feathered out over Western Europe. As their radio footprint crossed over, Musa tried desperately to make contact. But there was no reply, and no sign of ships or planes coming to the aid of the stricken rig.

And so on. If the day side of the world was transformed, the night side was heartbreaking. The city lights, once glowing necklaces around the necks of the continents, were gone, all extinguished.

Everywhere he looked it was the same, save for a few, a very few exceptions. In the middle of a desert, he would make out the spark of a camp fire, though he had learned he could be fooled by lightning-struck blazes. There was a denser scattering of fires in Central Asia, near the Mongolian border. There even seemed to be a city in what had been Iraq, but it was small and isolated, and at night its glow was flickering, as if from fires and lanterns, not electricity. Sable claimed she saw some signs of habitation at the site of Chicago. Once the Soyuz crew was excited by the glimpse of an extensive glow along the western seaboard of the continental United States. But that turned out to be a tectonic fault, rivers of lava pouring from a ruptured ground, soon obscured by great billows of ash and dust.

To a first approximation, humanity was gone: that was all you could say about it. And as for Kolya's own family, Nadia and the boys, Moscow had vanished; Russia was empty.

The crew cautiously discussed what could have caused this tremendous metamorphosis. Perhaps some great war could have left the world depopulated; that seemed the most likely hypothesis. But if so surely they would have heard the military commands, seen the sparks of ICBMs rising, heard desolate cries for help – seen cities burn, God help them. And what possible force could pick up blocks of ice or tracts of green, dozens of kilometres on a side, and plant them so out of place?

These discussions never went very far. Perhaps they all lacked the imagination to deal with what they saw. Or perhaps they feared that by talking about it they would somehow make it real.

Kolya tried to be analytical. The Soyuz's external sensor pod was functioning well. Designed to photograph the Station's exterior, the pod had a virtually unlimited electronic capacity for storing images. It had been easy for Kolya to reconfigure the pod so that it pointed downwards at the Earth. The Soyuz's orbit, a shadow of the vanished Station's, did not cover the whole planet, but it did loop far from the equator, and as the Earth turned beneath them so new segments of the planet were brought into the cameras' view. Kolya would be able to create a photographic record from orbit of the state of Earth, covering a great swathe to north and south.

Patiently, as the lonely Soyuz circled, Kolya tried to put aside preconceptions, to control his emotions and his fears, and simply to record what he saw, what was there. But it was strange to think that somewhere in the pod's vast electronic memory were stored the images of the Station they had taken just after separation – images of a Station now somehow vanished, its loss a grace note in the unfolding symphony of strangeness around them.

Sable demanded to know what was the point of this patient recording. Her ham radio project, by comparison, was aimed at establishing communications that could enable them to survive; what use were all these images? Kolya didn't feel the need to justify himself. There was surely nobody else in a position to do it, and Earth, he felt, deserved a witness to its metamorphosis.

And besides, as far as he knew, his wife and boys were gone. If that were true, then what was the point of *anything* they did?

The climate seemed restless: great low pressure systems prowled the oceans, and pushed their way towards the land, spinning off huge electrical storms. Seen from space the storms were wonders, with lightning flickering and branching between the clouds, releasing chain reactions that could span a continent. And at the equator clouds stacked up in vast heaps that seemed to be straining towards him, and sometimes he imagined the Soyuz might plunge into those thunderheads. Perhaps the sea and the air had been as churned up as the land. As the days wore by the visibility slowly worsened. But, oddly, the increasing obscurity made him feel better about his situation – as if he was a child, able to believe that the badness had gone away if he couldn't see it.

When it got too hard to bear Kolya would turn to his lemon tree. This tree, bonsai small, had been the subject of one of his experiments on Station. After the first day in the

Soyuz he had dug it out of its packaging and now kept it in the little space under his seat. One day, aboard liners sailing between the worlds, people would have grown fruit in space, and Kolya might have been remembered as a pioneer in a new way of cultivating life beyond the Earth itself. Those possibilities were all gone now, it seemed, but the little tree remained. He would hold it up to the sunlight that streamed in through the windows, and sprinkle precious water from his mouth on to its small leaves. If he rubbed the leaves between his fingers, he could smell their tang, and he was reminded of home.

The strangeness of the transformed world beneath its pond of air contrasted with the cosy kitchen-like familiarity of the Soyuz, so that it was as if what they saw beyond the windows was all a light show, not real at all.

About midday on that tenth day Sable stuck her head, upside down, out of the hatch to the living compartment. 'Unless you two have another appointment,' she said, 'I think we need to talk.'

The others huddled in their couches, under thin silvered survival blankets, avoiding each other's eyes. Sable twisted into her place.

'We're running out,' Sable said bluntly. 'We're running out of food, and water, and air, and wet wipes, and I'm out of tampons.'

Musa said, 'But the situation on the ground has not normalised—'

'Oh, come on, Musa,' Sable snapped. 'Isn't it obvious that the situation never is going to "normalise"? Whatever has happened to the Earth – well, it looks as if it's stuck that way. And we are stuck with it.'

'We can't land,' Kolya said quietly. 'We have no ground support.'

'Technically,' Musa said, 'we could handle the re-entry ourselves. The Soyuz's automated systems—'

'Yeah,' Sable said, 'this is the Little Spaceship That Could, right?'

'There will be no retrieval,' Kolya insisted. 'No helicopters, no medics. We have been in space for three months, plus ten unexpected days. We will be as weak as kittens. We may not even be able to get out of the descent compartment.'

'Then,' Musa growled, 'we must ensure we land somewhere close to people – any people – and throw ourselves on their mercy.'

'It's not a good prospect,' Sable said, 'but what choice do we have? To stay on orbit? Is that what you want, Kolya? To sit up here taking pictures until your tongue is stuck to the roof of your mouth?'

Kolya said, 'It might be a better end than whatever awaits us down there.' At least he was in a familiar environment, here in this failing Soyuz. He had literally no idea what might await them on the ground, and he wasn't sure if he had the courage to face it.

Musa reached over with his bear-like hand and pressed Kolya's knee. 'Nothing in our past – our training, our tradition – has prepared us for an experience like this. But we are Russians. And if we are the last Russians of all, as we may be, then we must live, or die, with suitable honour.'

Sable had the good sense to keep her mouth shut.

Kolya, reluctantly, nodded. 'So we land.'

'Thank God for that,' Sable said. 'Now, the question is – where?'

The Soyuz was designed to come down on land – happily, Kolya realised, for surely an ocean landing, as the Americans had once used, would have been the death of them without support.

'We can decide where to begin the re-entry,' Musa said. 'But after that we are in the hands of the automatic sequence; once we are dangling from our parachute, we will have little control over our fate. We don't even have a weather forecast. The wind could drag us hundreds of kilometres. We need the room for a messy landing. That means we have to land in Central Asia, just as our designers intended.'

He seemed to have expected an argument from Sable over that, but she shrugged. 'That's not necessarily a bad idea.

There are signs of people in Central Asia – nothing modern, but human habitation, quite a concentration – all those camp fires we saw. We need to find people, and that's as good a place as any to look.' This seemed logical, but Kolya saw a puzzling hardness in the set of her mouth, as if she was calculating, already thinking ahead to the situation beyond the landing.

Musa clapped his hands. 'Good. That's settled. There is no reason to hesitate. Now we must prepare the ship—'

A buzzer sounded from the living compartment.

'Shit,' said Sable. 'That's my ham radio rig.' With a single movement she launched herself up through the hatchway.

The simple detector Sable had rigged up had actually detected two signals. One was a steady pulse, strong but apparently automated, coming out of a site somewhere in the Middle East. The other, though, was a human voice, scratchy and faint.

'. . . Othic. This is Chief Warrant Officer Casey Othic, USASF and UN, at Jamrud Fort in Pakistan, broadcasting to any station. Please respond. I am Chief Warrant Officer Casey Othic . . .'

Sable grinned, showing gleaming teeth. 'An American,' she whooped. 'I knew it!' She began to adjust the tangled equipment, eager to reply before the radio footprint of the Soyuz drifted too far.

CHAPTER 12
ICE

On the day Bisesa's scouting party was to set off, the reveille was sounded by a trumpeter at five a.m. Bisesa woke blearily, her body still not quite accustomed to this new time zone, and went to look for her companions.

After a quick breakfast the party formed up, loaded with gear. A unit of twenty troopers, mostly sepoys, under the command of newly minted Corporal Batson, had been assigned to escort Bisesa, and here were Josh and Ruddy, both of whom insisted they couldn't possibly miss this jaunt. They were all on foot; Captain Grove, reasonably enough, didn't want to risk any of his dwindling population of mules. Grove was also uneasy about allowing the journalists to go. But there had been no sightings of Pashtuns to the north and west, not a single sniper's bullet. Even their villages seemed to have disappeared, as if apart from Jamrud humanity had been scraped off the planet. Grove relented about Ruddy and Josh, but he insisted that the party was to keep to tight military discipline at all times.

Off they marched. Soon Jamrud had disappeared over the horizon, and the world seemed empty, save for themselves. It was the tenth day since Bisesa's stranding.

The going was tough. They were clambering over country that was little more than a mountainous desert. At noon the heat climbed ferociously, though it was March – if this actually was still a slice of March 1885, of course – and at night, Bisesa was given to understand, the temperature would drop below freezing. Still, Bisesa expected to be comfortable enough in her flight suit, which was made of all-weather fabric manufactured in 2037. The British soldiers were much more poorly equipped, with their serge jackets and pith helmets, and laden down with heavy-duty kit, arms, ammunition, bedding, rations and water. But the men didn't complain. They were evidently used to their gear, and knowledgeable about ways around its shortcomings, such as using urine to soften boot leather.

As they advanced, following military drill, Batson sent picketing troops out ahead. In a country crowded by hillocks and ridges, three or four of them would clamber up the next commanding feature, covered by the rifles of their comrades, to be sure there were no Pashtuns hiding there. As they made their way further north, some of the hills rose as high as three hundred metres or so above the track, and it could be forty minutes or more before the pickets had reached the high point, but even so the rest of the column would not be moved forward until they were in position and had confirmed the way ahead was clear. It was frustrating, but the routine enforced plenty of rest halts, and they still made respectable progress.

As they marched they found more Eyes. There would be one every few kilometres or so, hovering silently, all apparently identical to the one at Jamrud. Batson marked their positions on a map. But soon these became as familiar as the first Eye, and nobody seemed to notice them – nobody save Bisesa. She found it hard to turn her back on an Eye, as if they really were eyes, watching her pass.

'What a place,' Ruddy announced to Bisesa as they plodded across one particularly barren stretch. He gestured at the file of sepoys ahead. 'Scraps of raw humanity, crushed between the empty sky and the used-up earth underfoot. All of India is like this, one way or another, you know. It's just that the Frontier is even more so than the rest – a sort of gritty quintessence. One finds it hard to retain one's dogmatism here.'

'You're a strange mix of young and old, Ruddy,' she said.

'Why, thank you. I suppose all this footslogging seems primitive to you, with your flying machines and thinking boxes, the marvellous war-making devilry of futurity!'

'Not at all,' she said. 'I'm a soldier myself, remember, and I've done my share of footslogging. Armies are all about discipline and focus, regardless of the technology. And anyhow British forces were – sorry, *are* – technologically advanced for their time. The telegraph can get a message from India to London in a few hours, you have the most advanced ships in the world, and your railways make inland journeys fast. You have what we'd call a rapid-reaction capability.'

He nodded. 'A capability that has enabled the inhabitants of a small island to build and hold a global empire, madam.'

As a walking companion Ruddy was always interesting, if not always exactly likeable. He was certainly no soldier. Something of a hypochondriac, he complained continually about his feet, his eyes, his headaches, his back, and other ways in which he felt 'seedy'. But he got on with it. During breaks he would sit in the shade of a boulder or a tree, and jot down notes or scraps of poetry in a battered notebook. When he was composing poetry he would sing a little melody, over and over, to serve as the basis of his meter. He was an untidy writer, and with his impulsive, jerky movements he blunted his pencils and tore his paper.

Bisesa still couldn't believe it was *him*. And for his part, he kept trying to get her to tell him his future.

'We've been through this,' she said steadily. 'I don't know that I have the right. And I don't think you see how strange this experience is for me.'

'How so?'

'To me you are Ruddy, here and now, alive, vivid. And yet there is a shadow from the future over you, a shadow cast by the Kipling you will become.'

'Good Lord,' Josh muttered. 'I hadn't thought of that.'

'And besides –' She waved a hand at the empty land. 'Things have changed, to say the least. Who knows if all the stuff in your biographies is still your true destiny?'

'Ah,' Ruddy said quickly. 'But if not – if my lost future has become a phantasm, a teasing dream of a blue devil – then what harm can there be in my hearing about it?'

Bisesa shook her head. 'Ruddy, isn't it enough that I've heard your name, a hundred and fifty years from now?'

Ruddy nodded, sagely enough. 'You're right. That bit of news is more than most men could ever know, and I should be grateful to whichever many-limbed deity is responsible for delivering it to me.'

Josh teased him. 'Ruddy, how can you be so equanimous about this? I think you're the most vain man I ever met. You know, Bisesa, he was convinced he was destined for greatness long before you appeared in our lives. Now he wants you to tell him in person – a correspondent from the future. I think he imagines all this dislocation has been arranged just for him!'

Ruddy's composure wasn't disturbed by this at all.

They faced one more bit of strangeness on that first day's walk.

They came to a disjunction in the ground. It was like a step, cut into the rubble-strewn ground, no more than half a metre high. The exposed wall of the cut was vertical and polished smooth, and the cut marched in a dead straight line from one horizon to another. It would be easy enough to jump up and over it, but the soldiers milled before it, uncertainly.

Josh stood with Bisesa. 'Well,' he said, 'what do you make of that? It looks to me like a place where somebody has stitched two bits of the world together.'

'I think that's exactly what it is, Josh,' she murmured. She squatted down and touched the sheer rock surface. 'This is a tectonically active region – India crashing into Asia – if you took two chunks of land, separated in time by a few hundred thousand years or more, this is the kind of shift in level you'd expect . . .'

'I scarcely understand you,' Josh admitted.

She stood up, brushing the dirt from her trousers. She reached forward, tentatively, until she had pushed her fingers over the line of disjunction, then she snatched her hand back. She muttered, 'What were you expecting, Bisesa – a force field?' Without further hesitation she leapt up to the upper layer, and walked a few paces ahead – into the future, or the past.

Josh and the others scrambled to follow, and they walked on.

At the next rest stop, she took a look at the weal on Ruddy's cheek, what he called his 'Lahore sore'. He thought it had been caused by an ant bite, and it had not responded to his doctor's prescription of cocaine. Bisesa knew only a little field medicine, but she thought this looked like Leishmania, an affliction caused by a parasite transmitted by sandflies. She treated it with the contents of her med kit. It soon began to clear up. Ruddy would say later that this small incident had convinced him more than anything else, even Bisesa's spectacular arrival in a crashing helicopter, that she really was from the future.

About four o'clock, Batson called a halt.

In the lee of a hill the troops began assembling the evening's camp site. They piled up their weapons, took off their equipment and boots, and pulled on the *chaplies* – sandals – they had been carrying in their packs. They passed out small shovels, and everybody, including Josh, Bisesa and Ruddy, set to building a low perimeter wall from loose rubble, and digging out sleeping pits. All of this was for protection against opportunistic attacks by Pashtuns, though they had still seen no Pashtuns that day. It was hard work after a day's march, but after about an hour it was done. Bisesa volunteered for 'stag', which, Josh worked out, meant sentry duty. Batson was polite enough, but refused.

They settled down for some food: just boiled meat and rice, but appetising to them all after the long day. Josh made sure he was close to Bisesa. She added little tablets to her food and 'Puritabs' to her water, which she said should protect her from infections from the water and the like; her supply of these twenty-first-century miracles wouldn't last for ever, but perhaps long enough to let her system acclimatise – or so she hoped.

She curled up in her pit under her own lightweight poncho, with her belt kit wrapped up as a pillow. She took out a little sky-blue device she called her 'phone', and set it up on the ground before her. Somehow it didn't seem surprising when the little toy *spoke* to her. 'Music, Bisesa?'

'Something distracting.'

Music poured out of the little machine, loud and vibrant. The troops stared, and Batson snapped, 'For God's sake turn it down!' Bisesa complied, but let the music play on quietly.

Ruddy had theatrically clamped his hands over his ears. 'By all the gods! What barbarity is that?'

Bisesa laughed. 'Come on, Ruddy. It's an orchestral reworking of a few classic gangsta rap anthems. It's decades old – grandmother music!'

Ruddy harrumphed like a fifty-year-old. 'I find it impossible to believe that Europeans will ever be seduced by such rhythms.' And, pointedly, he picked up his blanket and made for the furthest corner of the little compound.

Josh was left alone with Bisesa. 'Of course he likes you, you know.'

'Ruddy?'

'It's happened before – he is drawn to strong older women – there's a pattern to it. Perhaps he will select you as one of his muses, as he calls them. And perhaps, even if his destiny is now in flux, this startling experience will provide such an imaginative man with new creative directions.'

'I think he did write some futuristic fiction, in his old history.'

'More might be gained than is lost, then . . .'

She toyed with her phone, listening to her strange music, with an expression softened by what he took to be a kind of reverse nostalgia, a nostalgia for the future. He essayed, 'Does your daughter like this music?'

'When she was small,' Bisesa said. 'We'd dance to it together. But she's too grown up for it now – all of eight years old. She likes the new synth stars – entirely generated by computer, ah, by machines. Little girls like their idols to be safe, you see, and what's safer than a simulation?'

He understood little of this, but he was charmed by another glimpse of a culture he could barely understand. He said cautiously, 'There must be somebody else you miss – back on the other side.'

She looked at him directly, her eyes shadowed, and he realised to his chagrin that she knew exactly what he was fishing for. 'I've been single for a while, Josh. Myra's father died, and there's been nobody else.' She rested her head on her arm. 'You know, apart from Myra it's not people I'm missing so much as the texture. This little phone should connect me to the world, the whole planet. On every surface there is animation – ads, news, music, colour – twenty-four hours a day. It's a constant rush of information.'

'It sounds clamorous.'

'Perhaps it is. But I'm used to it.'

'There are pleasures to be had here. Breathe . . . Can you smell it? The touch of frost already in the air . . . The burning of the fire – you'll soon learn to tell one wood from another purely by the scent of its smoke, you know . . .'

'Something else, too,' she murmured. 'A musk. Like a zoo. There are animals out here. Animals that shouldn't *be* here, even in your time.'

He reached out impulsively and took her hand. 'We're safe here,' he said. She neither responded nor drew back, and after a while, unsure, he pulled his hand away. 'I'm a city boy,' he said. 'Boston-born. So all this – the openness – is new to me too.'

'What brought you here?'

'Nothing planned. I was always curious, you know, always wanted to see what was around the corner, in the next block. I kept volunteering for one crazy assignment after another, until I landed up here, at the ends of the earth.'

'Oh, you've gone rather further than that, Josh. But I think you're just the type to cope with our strange adventure.' She was watching him, a hint of humour in her eyes. Toying with him, perhaps.

He continued doggedly, 'You don't seem much like the soldiers I know.'

She yawned. 'My parents were farmers. They owned a big eco-friendly spread in Cheshire. I was an only child. The farm was going to be mine to work and develop. I loved that place. But when I was sixteen my father sold it out from under me. I suppose he thought I was never serious about running it.'

'But you were.'

'Yes. I'd even applied for a place at agricultural college. It caused a rift, or maybe showed one up. I wanted to get away. I moved to London. Then, as soon as I was old enough, I joined up. Of course I had no idea what the army would be like – the PT, the drill, the weapons, the field craft – but I took to it.'

'I don't see you as a killer,' he said. 'But that's what soldiers do.'

'Not in my day,' she said. 'Not in the British army anyhow. Peacekeeping: that's what we go out in the world for. Of course sometimes you have to kill, or even wage war to keep the peace – and that's a whole other set of issues.'

He lay back, staring at the stars. 'It's strange to hear you speak of your troubles with your family, failed communication, lost ambitions. I tend to imagine, when I think of it, that the people of a hundred and fifty years hence will be too wise for that – too *evolved*, as Professor Darwin would say!'

'Oh, I don't think we're very evolved, Josh. But we're getting smarter about some things. Religion, for instance. Take Abdikadir and Casey. Devout Muslim and jock Christian, you'd think they are as far apart as can be. But they are both Oikumens.'

'That word is from the Greek – like ecumenical?'

'Yes. Over the last few decades we've been close to an all-out conflict between Christianity and Islam. If you take a long view, it's absurd; both religions have deep common roots, and both are basically creeds of peace. But all the high-level attempts at reconciliation, conferences of bishops and mullahs, came to nothing. The Oikumens are a grass-roots movement trying to achieve what all the top-level contact has failed to do. They are so low-profile they are almost underground, but they're there, burrowing away.'

This talk made him realise how remote in time her age was, and how little he could understand of it. He said cautiously,

'And has God been banished in your day, as some thinkers would predict?'

She hesitated. 'Not banished, Josh. But we understand ourselves better than we used to. We understand why we *need* gods. There are some in my time who see all religion as a psychopathology. They point to those who are prepared to torture and kill their co-religionists, for the sake of a few per cent difference in obscure ideology. But there are others who say that for all their flaws the religions are attempts to address the most basic questions about existence. Even if they tell us nothing about God, they're surely telling us a great deal about what it means to be human. The Oikumens hope that by unifying religions, the result won't be a dilution but an enrichment – like the ability to study a precious gem from many angles. And maybe these tentative steps are our best hope of a true enlightenment in the future.'

'It sounds Utopian. And is it working?'

'Slowly, like the peacekeeping. If we're building a Utopia we're doing it in the dark. But we're trying, I guess.'

'It's a beautiful vision,' he breathed. 'The future must be a marvellous place.' He turned to her. 'How strange all this is. How exhilarating – to be here with you – to be castaways in time, together! . . .'

She reached out and touched his lips with one fingertip. 'Goodnight, Josh.' She rolled away, pulled her poncho over her body, and curled up.

He lay down, his pulse thumping.

The next day the ground rose steadily, becoming broken and lifeless. The clear air thinned and grew colder, bitterly cold when the wind from the north blew, despite the brightness of the sun. By now it was obvious there was no threat from Pashtuns or anybody else, and Batson allowed the troops to abandon the slow routine of picketing and march more briskly.

Though Bisesa's all-weather flight suit kept her reasonably protected, the others suffered. As they struggled into the wind the soldiers wrapped themselves up in their blankets and groused about how they should have brought their winter greatcoats. Both Ruddy and Josh became subdued, locked in themselves, as if the wind was leaching the energy out of them. But nobody had expected these conditions; even old Frontier hands said they had never known such a chill in March.

Still they marched doggedly along. Most of the time even Kipling didn't complain; he was too cold to bother, he said.

Fourteen of the twenty troopers were Indian. It seemed to Bisesa that the Europeans kept away from the sepoys, and that the Indians had poorer equipment and weapons.

Ruddy said, 'Once the proportion of British troops to Indian was about one in ten. But the Mutiny shattered all that. Now there's one European for every three Indians. The best weaponry, and all the artillery pieces, are in the hands of British troops, though the Indians may be used as muleteers. You don't want to train up and arm potential insurgents – common sense, that. Remember that the Indian Civil Service employs only about a thousand people – brave men of the plains, all! – to administer a country of four hundred *million*. It is only the backing of force that enables such a bluff to be played effectively.'

'But that's why,' she said gently, 'you have to train up an Indian elite. This isn't America, or Australia. There's no way British colonists or their descendants will ever outnumber the Indians.'

Ruddy shook his head. 'You're talking of our growing crowd of babus – with all respect to yourself! That notion might wash in London, but not here. You must know of Lucknow, where the whites were summarily slaughtered! *That's* the tinder-box we're sitting on. We may be withholding the best guns, but by filling a babu's head with visions of liberty and self-determination you are handing him the most potent weapons of all – weapons he isn't yet mature enough to use.'

Such casual patronising set Bisesa's teeth on edge. But she knew that Ruddy was actually representative of his class, if more articulate than most. It was some consolation to her to know that Ruddy was quite wrong about the future – even what would unravel in his own lifetime. The confrontation between Cossacks and sowars in Central Asia, so long feared in London, would never come to pass. In fact Russia and Britain came to be allies in the face of a new enemy common to both, in the person of the Kaiser. The Empire had always been about acquisition and profit, but Britain's legacy in this region wasn't all bad. It did leave India with a functioning civil service, and right up to Bisesa's time India remained the second-largest democracy in the world, second only to Europe. But the well-intended partition imposed when the Raj withdrew caused tensions from the beginning, tensions that resulted in the terrible destruction of Lahore.

That was the old history, though, she reminded herself. Just in the few days they had been here, she thought she detected a change in the sepoys' attitude. They were not quite so respectful to the whites, as if they now knew something of the future – that babus like Gandhi, and Bisesa herself, would eventually win. Even if time somehow stitched itself back together again, she couldn't believe that this bit of history, polluted by her own present, could ever be quite the way it had been before.

Soon they found themselves clambering through high-shouldered hills, and as the northern wind was funnelled into steep-walled valleys and gorges the going got tougher still. But these were just foothills.

At last they broke through a final cluttered valley, and emerged to face a view of the mountains themselves. The peaks were clad in bright grey-white glaciers that descended from their summits and tumbled down their flanks. Even from here, still kilometres away, Bisesa could hear the groan and crack of the ice rivers as they forced their way down the gouged flanks of the mountains.

They all stopped in their tracks, quite stunned.

'Good God,' said Ruddy. 'The sepoys are saying, it wasn't like *this* before.'

Bisesa dug out her night-vision goggles, and set them to a binocular setting. She scanned the base of the mountains.

Beyond the peaks the ice stretched away, she saw; this was the edge of an icecap. 'I think this is a piece of the Ice Age.'

Ruddy, shivering, had wrapped his arms around his bulk. *'Ice Age* . . . Yes . . . I have heard of the phrase. A Professor Agassiz, I think . . . controversial idea . . . Controversial no more, then!'

'Another time-slip?' Josh asked.

'Look.' Bisesa pointed at the base of the mountains. The glaciers there came to an abrupt halt, making a cliff. But the glaciers continued to pour off the mountains in their slow, inexorable way, and Bisesa could see how the cliff was splintering, calving off chunks like great landlocked icebergs, revealing clefts of a piercing blue. At the base of the cliff the ice was already melting, and slow floods were seeping out towards the lower ground. 'I think that's another interface. Like the step on the plain. Could be a jump anything from ten thousand years to two million years deep.'

'Yes,' said Josh, his breath steaming. 'I see it. Another boundary between worlds – eh, Ruddy?'

But poor short-sighted Kipling could see little through his frosted spectacles.

'We should head back,' Batson said, his teeth chattering. 'We've seen what we came to see, and can go no further.' The men concurred.

Bisesa's radio bleeped. She pulled her headset out of her pocket and wrapped it around her head. It was a short-wave message from Casey. One of Grove's scouting expeditions had spotted what appeared to be an army, a massive one, in the valley of the Indus. And Casey had received a signal on his lashed-up receiving station, he said. A signal from space. Her heart beat faster.

Time to go, then.

Before she turned away Bisesa ran her field of view along that crumbling base of ice one last time. No wonder the weather was screwed up, she thought. This big chunk of ice wasn't meant to be here. The cold winds pouring off it would mess up the climate for kilometres around, and when it melted there would be swollen rivers, floods. That was, of course, if things remained stable, and there wasn't more unravelling of time to come . . .

She glimpsed movement. She scanned back, upping the magnification. Two, three, four figures walked through the chill blue shadow of the glaciers. They were upright, and wore something dark and heavy, skins perhaps. They carried sticks, or spears. But they were squat, broad, their shoulders massive and rounded, their muscles immense. They were like pumped-up American footballers, she thought; Casey, eat your heart out. Tiny sparks of light, well-spaced, hovered over them: a string of Eyes.

One of the figures stopped and turned in her direction. Had he glimpsed a reflection off her goggles? She tapped the controls, and the magnification zoomed to its limit. The image grew blurred and shaky, but she could make out a face. It was broad, almost chinless, with powerful cheek-bones, a forehead that sloped back from a thick brow into a mass of black hair, and a great protruding nose from which steam snorted, white and regular, as if from some hidden engine. Not human – not quite – but still, something atavistic in her felt a shock of recognition. Then the image broke down into a blur of colour, white and blue.

CHAPTER 13

LIGHTS IN THE SKY

Things didn't get any easier. It was a rare day now when the sky didn't bubble with cloud. Jamrud began to be plagued by rain storms, and sometimes hail, that would boil up out of nowhere. The sepoys said they had never known such weather.

The British officers, though, had more on their minds than the weather. They were increasingly distracted by the sketchy reports their scouts brought back of an army of some kind to the south-west, and they were scrambling for ways to bring back more complete information.

But for all their difficulties the castaways of Jamrud were learning a great deal more about their new world, for as the crew of the Soyuz followed their lonely cycles around the planet, they downloaded images and other data to Casey's improvised receiving station. Casey used what was left of the Little Bird's avionics to store, process and display the data.

The Soyuz's storm-streaked images of a transformed world were bewildering, but they captivated all who studied them, in different ways. Bisesa thought that for Casey and Abdikadir, even though the images in themselves were disturbing, they were a reassuring reminder of home, where they had been used to having the ability to call up images like this whenever they chose. But soon the Soyuz must fall to earth, and their sole eye in the sky would close.

As for the men of 1885, Ruddy, Josh, Captain Grove and the rest were at first simply gosh-wowed by the display soft-screens and other gadgets: while Casey and Abdi were comforted by familiarity, Ruddy and the others were distracted by novelty. Then, once they got used to the technology, the British were struck by the marvel of looking at images of a world from space. Even though the Soyuz was only a few hundred kilometres up, a glimpse of a curved horizon, of cloud banks sailing on layers of air, or of familiar, recognisable features, like India's teardrop shape or Britain's fractal coastlines, would send them into paroxysms of wonder.

'I had never imagined such a godlike perspective was possible,' Ruddy said. 'Oh, you know how big the world is, in round, fat numbers.' He thumped his belly. 'But I had never *felt* it, not in here. How small and scattered are the works of man – how petty his pretensions and passions – how like ants we are!'

But the nineteenth-century crowd soon got past that and learned to interpret what they were seeing; even the stiffer military types like Grove surprised Bisesa with their flexibility. It took only a couple of days after the first download before the chattering, awestruck crowds around Casey's softscreen began to grow more sombre. For, no matter how marvellous the images and the technology that had produced them, the world they revealed was sobering indeed.

Bisesa took copies of all this to store in their only significant portable electronics, her phone. The data was precious, she saw. For a long time these images would be all they would have to tell them what was on the other side of the horizon. And besides, she agreed with cosmonaut Kolya that there should be a record of where they had come from. Otherwise people would eventually forget, and believe that *this* was all there ever had been.

But the phone had its own agenda. 'Show me the stars,' it said, in its small whisper.

So, each evening, she would set it up on a convenient rock, where it sat like a patient metallic insect, its small camera peering into the sky. Bisesa put up little screens of waterproofed canvas to protect it. These observation sessions could last hours as the phone waited for a glimpse of some key part of the sky through the scudding clouds.

One evening, as Bisesa sat with her phone, Abdikadir, Josh and Ruddy walked out of the fort to join her. Abdikadir brought a tray of drinks, fresh lemonade and sugar water.

Ruddy grasped the nature of the phone's project readily enough. By mapping the sky, and comparing the stars' positions to the astronomical maps stored in its database, the phone could determine the date. 'Just like astronomers at the Babylonian court,' he said.

Josh sat close to Bisesa, and his eyes were huge in the gathering dark of the evening. He could not be called handsome. He had a small face, with protruding ears, and cheeks pushed up by smiling; his chin was weak, but his lips were full, and oddly sensual. He was an endearing package, she admitted to herself – and, though she felt obscurely guilty about it, as if she was somehow betraying Myra, his obvious affection for her was coming to matter to her.

He said, 'Do you think that even the stars have been washed around the sky?'

'I don't know, Josh,' she said. 'Perhaps that's my sky up there; perhaps it's yours; perhaps it's nobody's. I want to find out.'

Ruddy said, 'Surely by the twenty-first century you have a much deeper understanding of the nature of the cosmos, even of time and space themselves, than we poor souls.'

'Yes,' said Josh eagerly. 'We may not know *why* all this has happened to us – but surely, Bisesa, armed with your advanced science, you can speculate on *how* the world has been turned upside down . . .'

Abdikadir put in, 'Maybe. But it's going to be a little difficult to talk about spacetime, as you wouldn't have even heard of special relativity for another couple of decades.'

Ruddy looked blank. 'Of special what?'

The phone whispered dryly, 'Start with chasing a light beam. If it was good enough for Einstein—'

'All right,' Bisesa said. 'Josh, think about this. When I look at you, I don't see you as you are *now*. I see you as you were a little way in the past, a few fractions of a second ago, the time it took starlight reflecting from your face to reach my eye.'

Josh nodded. 'So far so clear.'

Bisesa said, 'Suppose I chased the light from your face, going faster and faster. What would I see?'

98

Josh frowned. 'It would be like two fast trains, one over-taking the other. Both fast, but from the point of view of the one, the other seems to move slowly.' He smiled. 'You would see my cheeks and mouth moving like a glacier when I smiled to greet you.'

'Yes,' she said. 'Good, you've got the idea. Now, Einstein – ah, he was a physicist of the early twentieth century, an important one – Einstein taught us this isn't just an optical effect. It's not just that I *see* your face move more slowly, Josh. Light is the most fundamental way we have of measur-ing time – and so, the faster I travel, *the slower I see time pass for you.*'

Ruddy pulled at his moustache. 'Why?'

Abdikadir laughed. 'Five generations of schoolteachers since Einstein have failed to come up with a good answer to that, Ruddy. It's just the way the universe is built.'

Josh grinned. 'How wonderful – that light should be for-ever young, forever ageless – perhaps it's true that God's angels are creatures of light itself!'

Ruddy shook his head. 'Angels or no angels, this is damned fishy. And what does it have to do with our present situ-ation?'

'Because,' Bisesa said, 'in a universe where time itself ad-justs around you depending on how fast you travel, the con-cept of simultaneity is a little tricky. What is simultaneous for Josh and Ruddy, say, may not be simultaneous for me. It depends on how we move, how the light passes between us.'

Josh nodded, but he was evidently uncertain. 'And this isn't simply an effect of timing –'

'Not timing, but physics,' Bisesa said.

'I think I see,' Josh said. 'And if that can happen, it may be possible to take two events which were *not* simultaneous – let's say, a moment in my life in 1885, and a moment in Bisesa's in 2037 – and bring them together so that they touch, so closely we can even . . .'

'Kiss?' said Ruddy, mock-solemnly.

Poor Josh actually blushed.

Ruddy said, 'But all this is described from the point of view of one person or another. From what mighty point of view, then, is our new world to be seen? That of God – or of the Eye of Time itself?'

'I don't know,' Bisesa said.

'We need to learn more,' Josh said decisively. 'If we're ever to have a chance of fixing things—'

'Oh, yes.' Ruddy laughed hollowly. 'There is that. Fixing things!'

Abdikadir said, 'In our age we've grown used to our seas and rivers and air being fouled. Now time is no longer a steady, remorseless stream, but churned up, full of turbulence and eddies.' He shrugged. 'Perhaps it's just something we will have to get used to.'

'Perhaps the truth is simpler,' Ruddy said brutally. 'Perhaps your noisy flapping machines have shattered the cathedral calm of eternity. The whizzes and bangs of the terrible wars of your age have shocked the walls of that cathedral beyond their capacity to heal.'

Josh looked from one to the other. 'You're saying all this might not be natural – it might not even be the actions of some superior beings – it might be *our fault*?'

'Maybe,' said Bisesa. 'But maybe not. We only know a little more science than you, Josh – we really don't know.'

Ruddy was still brooding on relativity. 'Who was this fellow – did you say Einstein? Sounds German to me.'

Abdikadir said, 'He was a German Jew. In your time he was, umm, a six-year-old schoolboy in Munich.'

Ruddy was muttering, 'Space and time themselves can be warped – there is no certainty, even in physics – how Einstein's opinions must have helped the world towards flux and disintegration – and now you say he was Hebrew, *and* a German – it's so inevitable it makes one laugh!'

The phone said quietly, 'Bisesa, there's one more thing.'

'What?'

'Tau Ceti.'

Josh said, 'What is that? Oh. A star.'

'A star like the sun, about twelve light years away. I saw it nova. It was faint, and by the time I noticed it the light was

100

already fading, already past its peak. It lasted only a few nights, but—'

Abdikadir pulled his beard. 'What's so remarkable about that?'

'Just that it's impossible,' said the phone.

'How so?'

'Only binary systems nova. A companion has to add inert material to the star, which is eventually blown off in an explosion.'

'And Tau Ceti is solitary,' Bisesa said. 'So how can it have gone nova?'

'You can check my records,' the phone said tetchily.

Bisesa looked at the sky uncertainly.

Ruddy grumbled, 'In the circumstances that seems a rather remote and abstract puzzle to *me*. Perhaps we should concern ourselves with more immediate matters. Yon phone has been working on its Babylonian date-calculating for days already. How long will it take to deliver its marvellous news?'

'That's up to the phone. It's always had a mind of its own.'

He laughed. 'Sir Gadget! Tell me what you have surmised, as best you can, incomplete as it may be. I order it!'

The phone said, 'Bisesa?'

She had set up nanny safeguards to ensure the phone didn't say too much to the British. But now she shrugged. 'It's okay, phone.'

'The thirteenth century,' the phone whispered.

Ruddy leaned closer. '*When?*'

'It's hard to be more exact. The changes in the stars' positions are slight. My cameras are designed for daylight and I have to take long-exposure images, and the clouds are a pain in the ass . . . There are a number of lunar eclipses in the period; if I observe one of those I may be able to pin it down to the exact day.'

'The thirteenth century, though,' Ruddy breathed, and he peered up at a cloud-littered sky. 'Six centuries from home!'

'For us, eight,' Bisesa said grimly. 'But what does that mean? It might be a thirteenth-century sky, but for sure the world we are standing on isn't thirteenth-century Earth. Jamrud doesn't belong there, for instance.'

Josh said, 'Perhaps the thirteenth century is a – a foundation. Like the underlying fabric on to which the other fragments of time, making up this great chronological counterpane of a world, have been stitched.'

'Sorry to be the bearer of bad news,' the phone said.

Bisesa shrugged. 'I think it's more complex than bad.'

Ruddy lay back against the rock, hands clasped behind his broad head, the clouds reflected in his thick glasses. 'The thirteenth century,' he said wistfully. 'What a marvellous journey this is turning out to be. I thought I was coming to the Northwest Frontier, and that was adventure enough, but to be whisked to the Middle Ages! . . . But I admit it isn't wonder I feel at the moment. Nor even fear, over the fact that we are lost.'

Josh sipped his lemonade. 'What, then?'

Ruddy said, 'When I was five years old I was sent to stay with foster parents in Southsea. It's a common practice, of course, for if you're an émigré parent you want your children to be grounded in Blighty. But at five I knew nothing of that. I hated that place as soon as I set foot in it. Lorne Lodge, the House of Desolation! I was punished regularly, in truth, for the dreadful crime simply of being me. My sister and I would comfort ourselves by playing at Robinson Crusoe, never dreaming I would one day become a Robinson Crusoe in time! I wonder where poor Trix is now . . . But what hurt most about my situation, was that I had been abandoned – as I saw it then – betrayed by my parents and left in that desolate place of misery and pain.'

'And so it is here,' Josh mused.

'Once I was abandoned by my parents,' Ruddy said bitterly. 'Now we are abandoned by God Himself.'

That silenced them for a while. The night seemed huge, under a sky populated even by alien stars. Bisesa hadn't felt quite so stranded since the moment of the Discontinuity, and she ached for Myra.

Abdikadir said gently, 'Ruddy, your parents meant the best,

didn't they? It's just that they didn't understand how you felt.'

Josh said, 'Are you suggesting that whoever is responsible for what has happened to the world – God or not – actually means well?'

Abdikadir shrugged. 'We are human, and the world has been transformed by forces that are clearly superhuman. Why should we expect to understand the motives behind such forces?'

Ruddy said, 'All right. But do any of us actually *believe* there can be benevolence behind this meddling?'

Nobody replied.

CHAPTER 14

LAST ORBIT

Suddenly it was their last orbit: perhaps the last orbit of Earth ever to be travelled by humans, Kolya thought wistfully. But the necessary preparation was unchanged, and once their training kicked in the three of them began to work together as effectively as they had since the start of this strange adventure. In fact Kolya suspected they were all comforted by the familiar routine.

The first task was to pack the living compartment with their garbage, including most of the contents of their post-landing survival kit, already consumed. Sable stowed her scavenged ham radio gear in the descent compartment, however, for it could still be useful after landing.

Now it was time to suit up. They took turns in the living compartment. First Kolya pulled on his elasticated trousers, tight enough to squeeze body fluids up towards his head, which ought to help him avoid fainting after the landing – invaluable but grossly uncomfortable. Next he pulled himself into the suit itself. He had to climb in legs first through a hole in the stomach area. The inner layer, of a tough rubbery material, was airtight, and the outer layer, of a hardy man-made fabric, was equipped with pockets, zippers and flaps. Under gravity this assembly would have been all but impossible to don without the support of the ground crew. But here he thrashed around until he had got his legs in place, his arms in the sleeves, the back snugly fitting. He was used to his suit; it even smelled like him, and in case of disaster it would save his life. But after the freedom of weightlessness he felt as if he had been locked up inside a tractor tyre.

Suited, he scrambled back down into the descent compartment. The three of them strapped in. Musa had them don their helmets and gloves, and ran a pressure check on the suits.

For the last time the Soyuz passed over India, and their radio footprint reached Jamrud. The little speaker Sable had rigged to her ham radio gear crackled to life.

'. . . Othic calling Soyuz, come in. Soyuz, Othic, come in . . .'

Musa called, 'Soyuz here, Casey. How is our trusty capcom today?'

'The rain is pissing on me. More important, how are you?'

Musa glanced at his crew. 'We are strapped in, tight as three bugs in a rug. Our systems check out, despite the additional time we have spent in orbit. We are ready for the descent.'

'That Soyuz is a tough old bird.'

'That she is. I will be sorry to say goodbye to her.'

'Musa, you understand we have no way of tracking you. We won't know where you come down.'

'We know where you are,' Musa said. 'We will find you, my friend.'

'God and Karl Marx willing.'

Kolya, suddenly, urgently, didn't want this contact to be lost. They were all aware that Casey and his people were just another handful of castaways, as lost and helpless as they were. But at least Casey's was a twenty-first-century voice, reaching them from the ground; it was almost as if they had touched home again.

'I must say something.' Musa put his hand to his wraparound headset. 'Casey, Bisesa, Abdikadir – and Sable and Kolya, all of you. We are far from home. We have come on a journey whose nature we can't even grasp. And I think it's clear that this new world, made of patches snipped from space and time, is *not ours*: it is made from pieces of Earth, but it is not Earth. So I think we should not call this new world, our world, "Earth". We need a new name.'

Casey said, 'Like what?'

'I have thought about this,' Musa said. '*Mir*. We should call this new planet Mir.'

Sable guffawed. 'You want to call a planet after an antique Russian space station?'

But Kolya said, 'I understand. In our language the word "Mir" can mean both "world" and "peace".'

'We like the idea down here,' Casey said.

'Then Mir it is,' said Musa.

Sable shrugged. 'Whatever,' she said cruelly. 'So you got to name a world, Musa. But what does a name matter?'

Kolya murmured, 'You know, I wonder where we would all be if we hadn't happened to be in just that bit of the sky, just at that moment.'

Casey said, 'Too much double-dome horseshit for a jock like me. I can't even keep . . . rain out . . . neck.'

Musa glanced at Kolya. 'Your signal is breaking up.'

'Yeah . . . likewise . . . losing you . . .'

'Yes. Goodbye for now, Casey.'

'. . . won't be a welcome back. Welcome to your new home – welcome to Mir! . . .'

The signal faded out.

CHAPTER 15

NEW WORLD

Not long after dawn, Bisesa and Abdikadir made for the wreck of the chopper. The overnight rain continued un-relenting, stippling the muddy parade ground with tiny craters. Abdikadir briefly pulled back the hood of his poncho and lifted up his face to the rain, tasting it. 'Salty,' he said. '*Big* storms out there.'

A lean-to had been set up against the side of the downed chopper. Huddled under the canvas, Casey and the British were all so splashed with mud they looked as if they had been moulded out of the earth themselves. But Cecil de Morgan wore his customary suit, and was almost dapper despite a few splashes. Bisesa would never like the man, but she admired his defiance of nature.

Captain Grove had requested a briefing from Casey on what had been discovered so far. So Casey, propping himself up on a crutch, had used a bit of chalk to sketch an outline Mercator-projection world map on to the chopper's hull, and he had set up a softscreen on a trestle chair before it. 'Okay,' Casey said briskly. 'First the big picture.' The dozen officers and civilians, standing in the uncertain shelter of the lean-to, clustered to see as images of a changed world flickered by.

The shapes of the continents were familiar enough. But within their coastlines the land was a jigsaw of irregular slices, of browning green or melting white, showing how the peculiar fragmentation of time had occurred all across the planet. Few people seemed to have made it through the Discontinuity. The night side of the world was almost com-plete darkness, broken only by a scattered handful of brave, defiant manmade lights. And then there was the weather. Great storm systems boiled out of the oceans, or the poles, or the hearts of the continents, and thunderstorms spanned continents with branching purple-grey pyrotechnics.

Casey tapped the world map. 'We think we're looking at landmasses that have been replaced, in patches, by bits of themselves from earlier eras. But so far as we can tell – given the Soyuz wasn't properly equipped, and all – there's only a slight shift in the overall position of the landmasses. That limits us in time, even though we think the small shifts that do exist might be enough to trigger volcanism, later on.'

Already Ruddy had his hand up. 'Of course the landmasses haven't shifted, as you put it. Why should they?'

Casey growled, 'For you, Alfred Wegener is a five-year-old boy. Tectonic plates. Drifting continents. Long story. Take my word.'

Bisesa asked, 'How deep in time, Casey?'

'We don't think there can be any scrap that's more than two million years old.'

Ruddy laughed, a little wildly. '*Only* two million years! That's a comfort, is it?'

Casey said, 'The time slices presumably extend up from the surface of the Earth, and down at least some distance to its centre – maybe all the way. Maybe each slice is a great spiky wedge of core, mantle, crust and sky.'

Grove said, 'And each patch brought its own vegetation, inhabitants, a column of air above it?'

'Looks like it. It's the mixing of the patches that we think is stirring up the weather.' He tapped the softscreen. It displayed images of massive tropical storms, creamy-white swirls pouring up from the southern Atlantic to batter the eastern American seaboard, and fronts of bubbling black cloud laced across Asia. Casey said, 'Some of the slices must be from summer, some from winter. And the Earth's climate fluctuates on longer cycles. Ice Ages come and go, and that's all mixed in too.' He showed images of a slab of icebound land, a neat near-rectangle set square over the site of Paris in France. 'Hot air rises above cold, and that causes the winds; hot air holds more water vapour than cold air, and over cool land it dumps it out, and that's your rain. And so on. As all that works itself out, we get this screwed-up weather.'

Abdikadir said, 'How far do these slices extend upwards?'

'We don't know,' Casey said.

'Not as far as the Moon, surely,' piped up Corporal Batson. 'Or that body would have vanished, or be scattered about its orbit.'

Casey raised his eyebrows. 'Good point. Hadn't thought of that. But we do know it reaches out at least as far as low Earth orbit.'

'The Soyuz,' Bisesa said.

'Yeah. Bis, their clocks agree with ours, to the second. They must have been flying overhead – pure chance – when the Discontinuity hit, and they were brought along with us.' He rubbed his fleshy nose. 'We've tried to map the time slices, and in some places we can. Here's the Sahara . . .' He showed patches of greenery in the desert, mostly irregularly shaped, but some were bounded by geometrically pure arcs and straight lines. 'One patch of desert looks much the same as another, even if they're half a million years apart in time. Still, it's possible to date some of the patches, roughly, from geological changes.'

He turned and drew a big chalk asterisk on central Africa. 'This seems to be the oldest area of all. You can tell by the width of the Rift Valley . . . And look: the Sahara doesn't extend nearly so far south, and there are lakes, patches of green. That's just an average, though; on the ground it's all mixed up.' More images blurred by. 'We think much of Asia is from the last couple of thousand years or so. You see scattered human habitations out on those steppes, but nothing advanced – streaks of smoke from camp fires, no electric lights. The biggest concentration of people looks to be *here*.' He tapped an area north of China, in eastern Asia. 'We don't know who they are.'

He continued his show-and-tell, guiding his reluctant audience around a transformed world. Australia looked exotic. Though much of its centre was burned red raw, just as in Bisesa's time, around the coasts and in the river valleys the greenery was thick and luxurious. A few high-magnification shots were detailed enough to show animals. Bisesa made out a thing like a hippo, browsing at greenery at the edge of a forest scrap – and, in a short animated sequence, a herd of some huge upright creatures came leaping out of cover, perhaps fleeing some predator. They were giant kangaroos, Bisesa thought; Australia seemed to have reverted to its virgin state before the arrival of humans. South America meanwhile was a bank of solid green: the rain forest, decimated and dying in Bisesa's time, restored to its antique glory here.

In North America a great slab of ice lay sprawled across the north and east, extending up to the pole and down to the latitude of the Great Lakes. Casey said, 'The ice in this area comes from different ages. You can see that by the gaps, and the ragged edges.' He showed close-ups of the southern edge of the cap, which looked like a piece of paper, ripped across roughly. Bisesa could see glaciers pouring off that ragged edge, great ice-dammed lakes of floodwater building up and ferocious storm systems pooling, presumably where cold Ice Age air spilled off the cap and ran over warmer land. To the south of the ice the land was a bare green-brown: tundra, locked in by permafrost, scoured by the winds off the icecap. At first glance she could see no sign of people; but then, she recalled, people were a recent addition to America's fauna.

Abdikadir said, 'What about Alaska? The shape looks odd to me.'

Casey said, 'It's extending towards Beringia – you know, the land bridge that once stretched from Asia to America across the Bering Straits, the way the first humans walked into North America. But it's been cut off; the sea has broken through . . .'

The tour continued, relentlessly; they watched the flickering images uneasily.

'And Europe?' Ruddy asked, his voice tight. '*England?*'

Casey showed them Europe. Much of the continent was covered by dense green forest. On the more open southern regions in France, Spain, Italy there were settlements, but they were just scattered villages – perhaps not even constructed by humans, Bisesa mused, recalling that southern Europe had been in the range of the Neandertals. There was certainly nothing human to be seen in England, which, south of the line of what would have been Hadrian's Wall, was a slab of dense, unbroken forest. Further north the pine forest was marred by a great white scar that straddled the Scottish Highlands, a rogue section of icecap escaped from a glaciation age.

'It is gone,' said Ruddy. Bisesa was surprised to see his eyes, behind his thick spectacles, were misting. 'Perhaps it is because I was born abroad that this affects me so. But *Home is gone*, all of it, all that history down to the Romans and even deeper, vanished like dew.'

Captain Grove put a scarred hand on his shoulder. 'Chin up, man. We'll clear that bloody forest and build our own history if we have to, you'll see.'

Ruddy nodded, seeming unable to speak.

Casey watched this little melodrama wide-eyed, his gum-chewing briefly suspended. Then he said, 'I'll cut to the chase. The Soyuz found only three sites, on the whole damn planet, where there's signs of any advanced technical culture – and one of them is right here. The second –' He tapped his graffiti map, at the southern tip of the unmistakable shape of Lake Michigan.

'Chicago,' Josh breathed.

'Yeah,' Casey said. 'But don't get your hopes up. We can see dense urban settlement: a lot of smoke, as if from factories – even what look like steamboats on the lake. But they didn't respond to the Soyuz's radio signals.'

'They could be from any era before the development of radio,' Abdikadir said. '1850, say. Even then the population was sizeable.'

'Yeah,' Casey growled, pulling up images on his softscreen. 'But they have problems of their own right now. They are surrounded by ice. The hinterland has gone – no farmland and no trade, because there's nobody to trade with.'

'And where,' Bisesa said slowly, 'is the third advanced site?'

Casey pulled up an image of the Middle East. 'Here. There's a city – small, we think ancient, not like Chicago. But what's interesting about it is that Soyuz picked up a radio signal from there, the only one on the planet, save for ours. But it wasn't like ours. It's powerful, but regular, just an upwards chirp through the frequencies.'

'A beacon, perhaps,' Abdikadir said.

'Maybe. It's not one of our designs.'

Bisesa peered at the softscreen. The city was set in a broad expanse of green, apparently cultivated land, laced with suspiciously straight waterways, like shining threads. 'I think this is Iraq.'

'That,' said Cecil de Morgan firmly, 'is Babylon.'

Ruddy gasped. 'Babylon lives again! . . .'

'And that's all,' Casey said. 'Just us, and this beacon in Babylon.'

They fell silent. *Babylon*: the very name was exotic to Bisesa, and her head buzzed with speculation about how that strange beacon had got there.

Captain Grove seized the moment. The little man stepped forward, mighty moustache bristling, and he clapped his hands briskly. 'Well, thank you, Mr Othic. Here's the way I see it. We have to concentrate on our own position, since it's clear that nobody is about to come to our rescue, so to speak. Not only that, I think we have to find something to *do*, to give ourselves a goal – it's time we stop reacting to whatever the gods throw at us, and start taking command.'

'Hear, hear,' Ruddy murmured.

'I'm open to suggestions.'

'We must go to Chicago,' Josh said. 'With so many people, so much industry, so much potential—'

'They don't know we're here,' Casey said bluntly. 'Oh, perhaps they saw Soyuz pass overhead, but even if they did they won't have understood.'

'And we have no way to reach them,' Captain Grove said. 'We're scarcely in a position to mount a transatlantic crossing . . . Perhaps in the future. But for now we must put Chicago out of our minds.'

'Babylon,' said Abdikadir. 'It's the obvious goal. And there's that beacon: perhaps we will learn more of what has become of us.'

Grove nodded. 'Besides, I like the look of all that green. Wasn't Babylon an early centre of agriculture? The Fertile Crescent and all that? Perhaps we should consider a relocation there. A march wouldn't be impossible.'

Abdikadir smiled. 'You're thinking of farming, Captain?'

'It's hardly been my lifelong ambition, but needs must, Mr Omar.'

Bisesa pointed out, 'But somebody lives there already.'

Grove's face hardened. 'We'll deal with that when we get there.' In that moment, Bisesa glimpsed something of the steel that had enabled these British to build an empire that spanned a planet.

There was no serious alternative suggestion. Babylon it would be.

The party began to break up into smaller groups, talking, planning. Bisesa was struck by a new sense of purpose, of direction.

Josh, Ruddy and Abdikadir walked back across the mud with Bisesa. Abdikadir said, 'Grove is a smart cookie.'

'What do you mean?'

'His eagerness to go to Babylon. It's not just so we can plough fields. *There will be women there.*'

'Before his men start mutinying, you mean?'

Josh grinned uneasily. 'Think of it: five hundred Adams and five hundred Eves . . .'

Ruddy said, 'You're right that Grove is a good officer. He's very aware of the mood in the barrack rooms and the Mess.' Many of the men who had happened to be at Jamrud during the Discontinuity were 'three-year-olds', Ruddy said, short-service troops. 'Few of 'em have pipeclay in the marrow . . .' Pipeclay was the whitener the troops used on their belts. 'They're actually keeping their spirits up remarkably well. But that mood won't last long, once they realise how little chance there is that any of us is going home any time soon. Babylon might be just the thing.'

Abdikadir said, 'You know, we are fortunate in having the Soyuz, and so much data. But we've lots of unanswered questions. That two-million-year frame is interesting, for instance.'

'How so?' Bisea asked.

'Because two million years is about the date of the emergence of *Homo erectus*, the first hominid. Some predecessor species, like the pithecines the British captured, overlapped for a time, but—'

'You think the time frame has something to do with *us*?'

'It may be just a coincidence – but why not one million years, why not twenty, or two hundred million? And the oldest parts of this world-quilt seem to be where *we* are oldest, and the youngest, like the Americas, where we reached last . . . Perhaps this new world is somehow a representative sampling of human, and hominid, history.'

Bisea shuddered. 'But so much of the world is empty.'

'The history of *Homo sapiens* is just the last chapter of the long, slow story of hominid evolution. We are mere dust, floating on the surface of history, Bisea. Perhaps that's what the state of this world shows us. It's a fair sample across time.'

Josh tugged at Bisea's sleeve. 'Something has occurred to me. It may not have struck you or the others, but then my perspective, as a man of the nineteenth century, is different –'

'Spit it out, Josh.'

'You look out at this new world, and you see scraps of your past. But I see a little of my future, too, in *you*. Why should you be the last – why, Bisea, is there nothing of your *own* future?'

The thought struck her all at once, fully formed; she felt shocked it hadn't occurred to her. She had no reply.

'Captain Grove! Over here!' Corporal Batson, on the edge of the parade ground, was waving. Grove hurried over; Bisea and the others followed.

Batson was with a small group of soldiers, a British corporal

114

and a number of sepoys, who were holding two men. These strangers had their hands tied behind their back. They were shorter, stockier than the sepoys, and more muscular. They both wore knee-length smocks of faded purple, tied at the waist with bits of rope, and strapped-up leather sandals. Their faces were broad and swarthy and roughly shaved, their black hair curly and cropped short. They were crusted with dried blood, and they were evidently terrified of the sepoys' guns; when a soldier playfully lifted his rifle, one of the pair cried out and tumbled to his knees.

Grove stood before this pair, fists on his hips. 'Leave them alone, man, for God's sake. Can't you see they're terrified?'

The sepoy backed off sheepishly. Ruddy stared at the new-comers gleefully.

Grove snapped, 'Well, Mitchell, what have you brought home? What kind of Pashtuns are these?'

'Dunno, sir,' said the corporal. His accent was broad West Country English. 'Not Pashtuns, I don't think. Was patrolling down south-west . . .' Mitchell's party had been sent by Grove to scout out the 'army' they had spied down there; it seemed that the strangers were scouts sent the other way with the same idea in mind. 'Actually there was three of 'em, on podgy little horses like pit ponies. They had spears that they chucked and then they came at us with knives – three against half a dozen! We had to shoot the horses out from under them, and then one of the three dead, before these two would give up. Even when their horses went down they just rolled off and started tugging at 'em to get them up again, like they couldn't understand they had been shot.'

Ruddy said dryly to Grove, 'If you'd never seen a gun, Captain, you'd be dumbfounded if your horse just went down from under you like that.'

Captain Grove said, 'What's your point, sir?'

'That these men may come from a different time, a time more remote than any Pashtun.'

The two strangers listened to this conversation, mouths open. Then they jabbered excitedly, wide-eyed with fear, unable to drag their gaze from the sepoys' guns.

'That sounds like Greek,' Ruddy muttered.

Josh said, 'Greeks? In India?'

Bisesa held her phone up to the strangers. 'Phone, can you—?'

'I'm smart technology, but not that smart,' the phone said. 'I think it's some archaic dialect.'

Cecil de Morgan stepped out of the crowd, adjusting his mud-spattered morning jacket with an easy self-awareness. 'A rather fine education was once wasted on me. I still recall a little of my Euripides . . .' He spoke rapidly to the strangers. They jabbered back. De Morgan held his hands up, obviously telling them to slow down, and spoke again.

After a minute of this de Morgan turned to Grove. 'I think we're getting through, Captain, if imperfectly.'

Grove said, 'Ask them where they're from. And *when*.'

Ruddy said, 'They wouldn't understand the question, Captain. And we probably wouldn't understand the answer.'

Grove nodded; Bisesa admired his imperturbability. 'Then ask them who commands them.'

It took de Morgan a couple of tries to get that across. But Bisesa could understand the answer without interpretation.

'*Al-e-han-dreh! Al-e-han-dreh!* . . .'

Abdikadir stepped forward, his eyes alive with a wild surmise. 'He *did* come this way. Is it possible? Is it *possible*?'

CHAPTER 16

RE-ENTRY

The retro-rocket burn was brief, a push in the back. But it was enough to knock them out of orbit.

So it was done, the decision made, and whatever remained of Kolya's life – minutes or years – was irrevocably shaped as a consequence.

After launch, re-entry was the most dangerous part of a space mission, for the great energies expended to inject them into orbit now had to be dissipated in friction against the air. The only in-flight casualties of Kolya's country's space programme had occurred at re-entry, and he remembered those poor cosmonauts in his heart now – as he remembered the crew of the lost space shuttle *Columbia*. But there was nothing to do but wait. The Soyuz was designed to bring itself home without support from the ground, or instructions from its crew. Kolya, who had been trained as a pilot, longed to be less a passenger, to be more in control of events – to have a joystick in front of him, to do something to bring the ship home.

He glanced out of his window. The tangled jungles of South America, laced by cloud, passed for the last time beneath the prow of the spaceship. He wondered if anybody would ever see such a sight again, and how soon it would be before even the existence of such a place as this remote continent was forgotten. But as the Soyuz passed over the Americas towards the Atlantic he saw a storm, a creamy-white spiral that sat like an immense spider across the Gulf of Mexico. Minor storms spun off across the Caribbean islands, Florida, Texas and Mexico. These children of the monster in the Gulf were themselves devastatingly powerful, and had scratched deep gouges into the forest that covered central America. Worse, the central mother storm system was itself edging north, and surely little would be spared from Houston to New Orleans. This was the second superstorm system they had seen in the last few days; the remnants of the first were still coursing across the eastern United States and the western Atlantic. But there was nothing the cosmonauts could do for anybody on the ground, not even warn them.

Right on time there was a series of bangs from above and below. The craft shuddered, feeling subtly lighter. Explosive bolts had detonated, jettisoning the descent compartment from the other two sections of the Soyuz: the rocket engines and their garbage would now burn up like meteors, to baffle whoever was down there on the ground.

They endured the next few minutes in a silence broken only by the ticking of their instruments, the humming of the air supply. But the small noises of the various gadgets were almost cosy, like being in a home workshop, Kolya thought. He knew he was going to miss this environment.

As they fell across the sky, the resistance of the thickening air began to bite. Kolya watched the deceleration build up on the meter before him: 0.1 g, 0.2 g. Soon he began to feel it. Pushed back into his couch, his straps felt loose, and he tightened them. But the rise in pressure wasn't steady; the upper atmosphere was lumpy, and the compartment shuddered as it fell, like an airliner passing through turbulence. Kolya was aware, as he had been during no previous descent, of the smallness and fragility of the capsule within which he was falling to the ground.

Through his window now he could see only the blackness of space. But a deep colour seeped into that blackness: first brown, like old, dried blood, but quickly lighter, climbing the spectrum through red, orange, yellow. As the air thickened the deceleration became savage, rising rapidly through a single gravity and climbing to two, three, four g. The light outside, of atoms of air smashed to bits by their passage, climbed to white now, and a pearly glow shone through the windows, casting a pale, beautiful illumination over their suited laps. It was like being inside a fluorescent lightbulb, he thought. But the windows blackened as the outside of the capsule was scorched by the ionised air, and the angelic light was obscured.

And still the buffeting continued. The capsule shuddered, throwing them from side to side and against each other, despite the straps. It was a much more severe ride even than the launch had been, and after three months in space Kolya wasn't well equipped to cope with it. He found it hard even to breathe, and he knew that he could not have lifted a finger, no matter how urgent the task.

At last the ride smoothed out. There was another sharp bang from outside the wall, startling him. A window shield had blown off, taking the soot with it, to reveal a slab of startlingly clear blue sky. Not the sky of Earth: the sky of a new world, the sky of Mir.

The first parachute deployed, a drogue that snatched at the air. The descent compartment swung violently, through two, three, four swings, and then the main chute yanked at the capsule, making it rock again. Kolya could just make out the wide orange canopy of the main chute above him. It was hard to believe it was only ten minutes or so since they had jettisoned the other parts of the Soyuz, perhaps five since first entering the atmosphere. He could feel gravity's invisible fingers pulling at his internal organs: even his head was heavy, as if made of concrete, too heavy for his neck. But he felt only a huge relief; the most dangerous part of the descent was already over.

As touchdown approached compressed gas hissed. Kolya found his seat rising up as its base was pressurised to serve as a shock absorber, pushing him up against the instrument console and increasing his discomfort further.

'Christ,' Sable growled, similarly squashed up, 'I will be so damn glad to get out of this tractor cabin.'

'It has served you well,' was Musa's level reply. 'Only a few minutes more.'

But Kolya relished those minutes, uncomfortable as he was: the last minutes in which the ship's automated systems cushioned him, perhaps the last minutes of his old life.

'Proximity light,' called Musa.

Kolya braced. There was a brief roar as rockets fired, just a couple of metres from the ground. And then there was a slam as they hit the ground – and bounced up again. After a breathless second the cabin came down again, scraped loudly, and leapt into the air once more with a shudder. Kolya knew what that meant: the Soyuz was being dragged over the ground by its parachute.

'Shit!' Sable shouted. 'There must be a wind—'

'If we tip over,' Musa said, his voice made uneven by the jarring, 'we could have trouble extricating ourselves.'

'Maybe you should have thought of that before!' Sable yelled.

Another slam, a scraping ride, a bounce. Though the padding of his suit protected his body, Kolya found his head rattling inside his helmet, his forehead slamming against the faceplate. There was nothing they could do but endure the ride, and pray that the capsule didn't tip.

But then, with a final bounce and scrape, the capsule was still – and it was upright. They sat there, scarcely breathing. Musa quickly punched a button to release the parachute.

Kolya was unbearably hot; he could feel sweat puddled under his back inside the suit. He reached out – his arm felt enormously heavy – and searched for Musa's gloved hand. For a moment they held each other, reassuring themselves of their continued existence.

'We are all right,' panted Musa. 'We are *down*.'

'Yes,' said Sable, her voice a gasp. 'But down *where*?'

Even now there was some routine, as they worked to close down the spacecraft's remaining systems. Kolya turned off the ventilator, and took off his helmet and gloves. A valve to allow in air from outside had opened some minutes before the landing, and Kolya tasted air that was noticeably free of the dust that had plagued the Soyuz.

Musa grinned at him. 'I can smell polin.'

'Yes.' It was a sweet, smoky aroma. Polin, a kind of worm-wood, grew all over the steppe. The familiar scent seemed to invigorate Kolya. 'Perhaps this Mir of yours won't be so strange after all!'

Musa grunted. 'There's only one way to find out.' He punched another button. Latches clicked. The hatch above their heads sprung open, and Kolya saw a circle of cloud-choked grey sky. More fresh air pushed into the cabin.

Musa released his straps and pushed at his couch. 'This is the part I have been dreading.' He had to be the first to move because of his central position. Slowly, moving like a very old man, he struggled to his feet. Normally a team of rescuers and medics would be on hand to help him out of the cabin, like lifting a china doll from its packaging; but today there was nobody to help. Kolya and Sable both leaned over, pushing at his rump and legs, but Kolya felt weak as a kitten himself. Musa said, 'This damn suit is so stiff, it fights against me.'

At last he was upright, and he pushed his head outside the capsule. Kolya saw him squint in the light, and his thick thatch of hair was blown by the wind. Then his eyes widened. He got his hands on the hull – it was still hot from the re-entry, and he had to be cautious – then, with what seemed a superhuman effort to Kolya, he lifted himself up until he was sitting on the lip of the hatch.

'Me next,' Sable said. She was visibly weakened, but compared to Musa she seemed agile and eager. She swarmed up out of her couch, and allowed Musa to help pull her up until she was sitting beside him. 'My, my,' she said.

Kolya, left alone in the capsule, could see nothing but their dangling legs. 'What's happening? What's out there?'

Musa said to Sable, 'Help me.' He lifted his legs out of the hatch, turned ponderously on his belly, and held up his hands to her. Then he slid down the curving side of the Soyuz and out of Kolya's sight.

Sable peered down at Kolya, grinning. 'Come see the show.'

When Kolya forced himself to his feet, he felt as if all the blood was draining from his brain. He stood still until the feeling of fainting had dissipated a little. Then he reached up to the hatch, and let Sable help him haul himself up until he was sitting at the top of the hull.

Kolya was maybe two metres up from the ground. The descent compartment was a dome of metal sitting on the grass. From this elevation he saw the eternal steppe, flat and semi-infinite, stretching away under a great lid of cloud. It had been marked by their landing: a series of crude gouges and craters led up to the final position of the craft, and further away the discarded main chute lay on the ground, billowing forlornly, a startling orange against the yellow-green ground.

Directly ahead of him there was a kind of village. It was just a huddle of grubby, dome-shaped tents. People stood, men, women and children, all bundled up in furs. They were staring at him, open-mouthed. Beyond, horses grazed, loosely tethered, unperturbed.

A man walked out of the tent village. He had a broad face, deep-set black eyes that seemed very close together, and he wore a heavy full-length coat and a conical cap, both made of fur. He was holding a heavy sword of beaten iron.

'A Mongol warrior,' Sable whispered.

Kolya glanced at her. 'You expected this, didn't you?'

'I thought there was a good chance, based on what we saw from orbit . . .'

The breeze shifted, and a stench of cooked meat, unwashed flesh, and horse sweat hit Kolya. It was as if a veil had been torn away from his face, and suddenly he was confronted with the reality: this really was the past, or a fragment of it, and he was stranded in it.

Musa was managing to stand, with one hand on the hull of the spacecraft for support. 'We have fallen from space,' he said to the man, smiling. 'Isn't that a marvellous thing? Please . . .' He held out his empty hands. 'Can you help us?'

The warrior reacted so quickly Kolya could barely follow the move. That sword flashed through the air, blurring like a helicopter blade. Musa's head flipped into the air, cut off as easily as the head of a steppe daisy, and it rolled like a football in the dirt. Musa's body still stood, the arms still outstretched. But blood gushed in a sudden fountain from the stump of his neck, running down the scuffed orange of his spacesuit. Then the body fell, rigid.

Kolya stared down at Musa's severed head, scarcely able to believe what had happened.

The warrior raised his sword again. But with his free hand he beckoned the others to climb down to the ground.

'Welcome to Mir,' Sable muttered. Kolya, horrified, thought he heard a note of triumph in her voice.

CHAPTER 17

A HARD RAIN

Grasper wasn't troubled by her confinement. She was so young, perhaps she had forgotten that any other way of life had ever existed. She would roam around the cage floor or climb up the netting; she would swing from the shining object that held it all up; she explored her own ears and nostrils with ruthless efficiency.

As the days wore on the men beyond the netting seemed to be growing more agitated, but they never failed to bring the man-apes their food and water. Grasper would come clambering up the net walls and try to reach out to them, and the men would reward her with extra bits of food. Seeker, though, grew withdrawn. She hated this prison, and the strange creatures who had trapped her. Nobody praised *her*, or gave her extra bits of fruit; there was nothing cute about Seeker's sullen hostility.

It got worse when the rains started.

The rains were sometimes so hard that the heavy drops pounded against your skin like a hundred tiny fists. The man-apes were always cold and sodden, and even Grasper's bright curiosity was subdued. Sometimes the rain stung when it hit your bare flesh, your hands or feet or lips, and if it got in your eyes it could be very painful indeed.

The rain was full of acid because of events half a world away.

The new world had been stitched together from fragments of the old – but those fragments had been plucked from many different eras, across two million years. The mixing of air masses had caused the unstable weather that plagued those first days after the Discontinuity. In the oceans, too, the invisible Amazons of the great currents sought a new equilibrium.

And the land had been rent apart. In the Atlantic a belt of volcanic mountains, stretching south from Iceland, marked the position of a mid-ocean ridge, a place where sea bed was born, molten material welling up from the planet's interior. This birthing zone had been ripped open by the Discontinuity. The Gulf Stream, which for millennia had delivered warm southern water to Europe, now faced a fresh obstacle, a new volcanic island that would eventually dwarf even Iceland, thrusting its way out of the ridge.

Meanwhile the 'Ring of Fire' around the Pacific, where great tectonic plates jostled each other, lived up to its name. There was turmoil all down the western seaboard of North America, from Alaska to Washington State: most of the twenty-seven volcanoes in the Cascades were triggered.

Mount Rainier's explosion was the worst. Its noise was a great shout that spread right around the planet. In India it sounded like distant artillery, and the survivors of the nineteenth and twenty-first centuries stirred uneasily in their sleep. A vast mushroom cloud of ash and debris lifted high into the air's upper layers, spreading at hurricane-force speeds. Most of the debris washed out quickly, but the thin stuff lingered, blotting out the sun. Temperatures dropped. As the air cooled, it could hold less water.

All over the world it rained. And rained, and rained.

In a sense, all of this was beneficial. A Frankenstein's monster of a world was trying to knit itself together, and a new equilibrium, in the air, the sea and the rocks, would eventually emerge. But the painful thrashing of that healing process was devastating for anything, plant or animal, struggling to survive.

Seeker had no long-term perspective. For her there was only the present, and her present was drenched in misery, confined in the humans' cruel cage, and by the acid rain that lanced down at her from the sky. When the rain was at its worst Grasper huddled under her mother, and Seeker curled over her baby, taking the scalding downpour on her own back.

Time's Eye

PART THREE

ENCOUNTERS AND ALLIANCES

CHAPTER 18

EMISSARIES OF HEAVEN

Still wielding his sword, the Mongol yelled over his shoulder. More armed men came running out of the tents – no, Kolya thought, the *yurts*. Women and children followed. The children were little bundles in felt coats, wide-eyed with curiosity.

The men had classic Asiatic features, Kolya thought, with broad faces and small dark eyes, and jet-black hair which they wore tied back. Some had bands of cloth around their heads. They wore baggy dun-coloured trousers, and went barefoot, or wore boots into which the trousers were tucked. If they weren't bare-chested they wore simple light tunics, heavily mended.

They looked mean, and strong. And they gathered threateningly around the gravity-laden cosmonauts. Kolya tried to hold his ground. He was shaking; Musa's headless corpse still lay against the side of the Soyuz, the last blood trickling from its neck.

Musa's killer walked up to Sable, who glared back at him. Uncompromisingly he grabbed her breast and compressed it.

Sable did not flinch. 'Holy crap, but this guy *stinks*.' Kolya could hear the brittleness in her voice, sense the fear under her resolve. But the warrior backed away.

The men talked rapidly, eyeing the cosmonauts and their spacecraft, and the parachute silk which lay sprawled across the dusty steppe.

'You know what I think they're saying?' Sable whispered. 'That they're going to kill you. Me they'll rape, *then* kill.'

'Try not to react,' Kolya said.

The tension was broken by a squeal. A little girl of about five, with a face round as a button, had touched the wall of the Soyuz and had come away with a burned hand.

129

The men growled as one. Musa's killer pressed his sword against Kolya's neck. His mouth was open, his eyes small, and Kolya could smell meat and milk on his breath. Suddenly the world was very vivid: the animal stink of the man before him, the rusty scent of the steppe, even the surge of blood in his ears. Was this to be his last memory, before he followed Musa into the dark? . . .

'*Darughachi*,' he said. '*Tengri. Darughachi.*'

The man's eyes widened. He backed away, but he kept the sword raised, and the rapid conversation resumed, but now the men stared even harder.

Sable hissed, 'What did you say?'

'Schoolboy memories.' Kolya tried to keep his voice level. 'I was guessing. It mightn't have been their language at all; we could have landed anywhere in time—'

'What language, Kolya?'

'Mongolian.'

Sable snorted. 'I knew it.'

'I said we were emissaries. Emissaries of Eternal Heaven. If they believe it, they will have to treat us with respect. Hand us over to local officials, maybe. I'm bluffing – just bluffing.'

'Good thinking, Batman,' Sable said. 'After all these guys saw us fall from the sky. *Take me to your leader*. Always works in the movies.' She actually laughed, a forced, ugly sound.

At last the circle around the cosmonauts began to break up, and nobody came to kill them. One man pulled on a jacket and felt hat, ran to a hobbled horse tied up beside a yurt, mounted it and rode briskly away.

The cosmonauts' hands were tied behind their backs and they were prodded in the direction of one of the yurts. It would have been difficult to walk even without tied hands; Kolya felt as if he was encased in lead, and his head sang. Staring children, picking their noses, formed a sort of honour guard as they passed. One nasty-looking brat threw a rock that bounced off Kolya's shoulder. It was hardly a dignified return to Earth, he thought. But at least they were alive; at least he had won them some time.

The door-flap of the yurt was pulled open, and they were shoved inside.

Sable and Kolya were thrust down on to felt mats. In their stiff pressure suits the cosmonauts were huge in the yurt, and their legs stuck out comically in front of them. But it was a relief just to sit down.

The yurt's single doorway faced south; Kolya could see the sun beyond a layer of haze. That was a Mongol tradition, Kolya knew; in their rudimentary theology there was a strand of sun-worship, and here on the plains of northern Asia the sun wheeled through its daily circles predominantly in the south.

Mongols came and went, apparently to inspect the newcomers, squat men and muscular-looking women. They stared at the cosmonauts, especially Sable, with greedy calculation.

Some of the cosmonauts' gear was brought in from the Soyuz capsule. Much of this – emergency medical kits, an inflatable life-raft – was incomprehensible to the Mongols. But Sable and Kolya were allowed to change out of their bulky spacesuits into the lighter orange jumpsuits they had worn on orbit. The Mongol children stared at their underwear, and the rubberised trousers they stripped off. The spacesuits were stacked up in a corner of the grubby yurt like abandoned cocoons.

The cosmonauts both managed to conceal the existence of their sidearms, tucked behind their backs, from the Mongols.

After that, to Kolya's huge relief, they were left alone for a while. He lay against the yurt's grimy wall, his limbs trembling, trying to still the beating of his heart and clear the fog in his head by sheer willpower. He should have been in hospital right now, surrounded by state-of-the-art twenty-first-century technology, beginning a programme of physiotherapy and recuperation, not stuck in the corner of this stinking tent. He was weak as an old man, and before these stocky, powerful Mongols he was utterly helpless; he was resentful as well as frightened.

131

He tried to think, to take stock of his surroundings.

The yurt was sturdy and well-worn. Perhaps it belonged to the chief of this little community. Its main support was a stout pole, and lighter wooden stakes and slats shaped a dome of felt. Grubby mats covered the floor, and metal pots and goatskins hung from hooks. Stacked around the walls were chests of wood and leather, the furniture of a travelling people. The yurt had no windows, but a hole in the roof had been cut over a fireplace of hearthstones, where lumps of dried dung burned continually.

At first Kolya puzzled about how the yurt could be taken down and re-erected, as it must be at least twice a year as the nomads travelled between their summer and winter pastures. But he had noticed a broad cart, parked a short distance away. Its bed was easily wide enough to take the intact yurt, contents and all.

'But they didn't always do that,' he whispered to Sable. 'The Mongols. Only in the early thirteenth century. Otherwise they just dismantled the yurts like tents and carried them folded up. So that fixes us in time . . . We have landed in the middle of the Mongol Empire, at its peak!'

'Lucky for us you know so much about them.'

Kolya grunted. 'Lucky? Sable, the Mongols came to Russia – *twice*. You don't forget an experience like that, not even after eight centuries.'

After a time a meal was prepared. A woman hauled in a big iron pot. Half a sheep carcass was chopped up and thrown into the pot – not just flesh and bones, but lungs, stomach, brains, intestines, hooves, eyeballs; evidently nothing was wasted. The woman had a face like leather and arms like a shot-putter's. As she worked steadily at the meat she paid absolutely no attention to Sable and Kolya, as if two humans from the future stacked in the corner of her yurt were an everyday occurrence.

The stranded cosmonauts did what they could to speed their adaptation to Earth's ferocious pull, surreptitiously flexing their joints, shifting their posture to favour one muscle group over another. Aside from that they had nothing to do but wait, Kolya supposed, for that rider to return from his mission to the local official, at which point the decision about their fate would be made – a decision which could still, he knew, mean their deaths. But despite that grim prospect, as the afternoon wore by, Kolya, astonishingly, grew bored.

The mass of meat and offal in the pot was boiled for a couple of hours. Then more adults and children crowded into the yurt. Some of them brought in more meat for the pot, bits of what looked like foxes, mice, rabbits. These were roughly skinned but not cleaned; Kolya could see bits of grit and dried blood sticking to them.

When it was time to eat the Mongols just dived in. They scooped out chunks of meat with wooden bowls and ate with their fingers. They washed it down with cups of what looked like milk, poured from a sweating goatskin. Sometimes, if they didn't like the flavour of a piece of meat after a few bites, they would throw it back, and they would spit bits of gristle back into the pot.

Sable watched this in horror. 'And nobody washed their hands before lunch.'

'To the Mongols water has divine purity,' Kolya said. 'You don't sully it by using it to wash.'

'So how do they keep clean?'

'Welcome to the thirteenth century, Sable.'

The Mongols kept their distance from the cosmonauts, but otherwise their social life seemed unimpeded.

After a time one of the younger men approached the cosmonauts, carrying a bowl of meat. Kolya saw how the mutton fat that shone on the boy's lips was only the topmost layer in a smear of fat and dirt that covered his face; there was even wind-dried snot under his broad nostrils, and his stink, like over-ripe cheese, was just overwhelming. The boy reached behind Kolya and released one of his hands. Then he picked out a piece of meat from his bowl and held it out to Kolya. His fingernails were black with dirt.

'You know,' Kolya murmured, 'the Mongols would soften their meat by riding with it under their saddle. This bit of mutton might have spent days being pumped full of methane from some fat herdsman's ass.'

'Eat it,' murmured Sable. 'We need the peptides.'

Kolya took the meat, closed his eyes, and bit into it. It was leathery, and tasted of fat and butter. Later, the boy brought him a cup of milk. It actually had a kick, and he vaguely remembered that the Mongols would ferment mares' milk. He drank as little as he could.

After the meal the cosmonauts were allowed out, separately, to relieve themselves, heavily watched all the time.

Kolya took the chance to look around. The plain stretched on all sides, huge and empty, an elemental sheet of yellow dust broken by splashes of green. Under an ashen sky fat clouds sailed, casting shadows like lakes. But the land, vast and flat and featureless, seemed to dwarf the sky itself. This was the Mongolian plateau – he knew that much from their navigation during the descent. Nowhere much less than a thousand metres above sea level, it was shut off from the rest of Asia by great natural barriers: mountain ranges to the west, the Gobi desert to the south, the Siberian forests to the north. From orbit, he remembered, it had been a vast blank, a faintly crumpled plain stitched here and there with the threads of rivers – barely there at all, like the preliminary sketch of a landscape. And now here he was, stuck in the middle of it all.

And in this vast emptiness the village huddled. The yurts, mud-coloured, weather-beaten and rounded, looked more like eroded boulders than anything made by humans. The battered Soyuz descent compartment did not, somehow, look particularly out of place here. But children ran and laughed, and neighbours called from one yurt to the next. Kolya could see animals, sheep, goats and horses, moving in unfenced herds, their lows and bleating carrying in the still air. Though he might be as much as eight centuries out of time, and though there could hardly have been a greater contrast in his origins with these people's – spaceman and nomad, the most technologically advanced humans put together with some of the most primitive – the basic grammar of human discourse was unchanged, he saw, and he had come to a little island of human warmth in the midst of the huge silent emptiness of the plain. Somehow that was reassuring, even if he was a Russian fallen into the hands of Mongols.

That night, Kolya and Sable huddled together under a foul-smelling blanket of what smelled like horse hair. The snores of the Mongols were all around them. But whenever Kolya looked up one of them always seemed to be awake, his eyes gleaming in the dim firelight. Kolya didn't believe he slept at all. Sable, on the other hand, just rested her head against Kolya's shoulder and slept for hours at a time; he was astonished at her courage.

In the night the wind rose up, and the yurt creaked and rocked, like a boat adrift on the sea of the steppe. Kolya, relentlessly awake, wondered what had become of Casey.

CHAPTER 19

THE DELTA

His breakfast over, Secretary Eumenes dismissed his pages. He pulled his purple cloak over his shoulders, and, pushing the heavy leather door flap out of his way, walked out of his tent.

The clouds had cleared away, revealing a washed-out blue sky, pale like faded paint, and the morning sun was hot. At least the rain had stopped for once. But when he looked west, to the sea, Eumenes could see more black clouds bubbling and boiling, and he knew that another storm was on its way. Even the natives who clustered around the army camp selling charms, and gewgaws, and the bodies of their children, claimed never to have known such weather.

Eumenes set off towards Hephaistion's tent. It was difficult going. The ground had been turned to soft, yellow mud, churned up by the feet of men and animals, that clung to Eumenes's cavalry boots.

Around him the smoke of a thousand fires rose to the pale sky. The men were emerging from their tents, hefting clothing and gear heavy with mud. Some of them shaved off their stubble: an order to be clean-shaven had been one of the King's earliest initiatives when he had taken over the army from his assassinated father, ostensibly so that enemies would not be given an easy handhold in close quarters. The Macedonians moaned, as usual, about this fancy Greek practice, and about the wretched, barbarous state of this place the King had brought them to.

Soldiers always liked to grumble. But when the fleet had first arrived here in the delta, having sailed down the Indus from the King's camp, Eumenes himself had been appalled by the heat, the stink, the clouds of insects that had hovered over the marshy ground. But Eumenes prided himself on his

136

disciplined mind; a wise man got on with his business whatever the weather. It even rains on god-Kings, he thought.

Hephaistion's tent was a grand affair, far grander than Eumenes's, a sign of the favour with which the King regarded his closest companion. The living quarters were surrounded by a series of vestibules and antechambers, and were guarded by a detachment of Shield Bearers, the army's elite infantry, reputed to be the finest foot soldiers in the world.

As Eumenes neared the tent he was challenged. The guard was a Macedonian, of course. He certainly knew Eumenes, yet he stood before the Secretary now, holding up his stabbing sword. Eumenes held his ground, his gaze unflinching, and eventually the soldier backed down.

The hostility of a Macedonian warrior for a Greek administrator was as inevitable as the weather – even if it was founded on ignorance, for how did these half-barbarians imagine that the great machinery of the army kept them all alive and provisioned, organised and directed, if not for the meticulous work of Eumenes's Secretariat? Eumenes pushed his way into the tent without glancing back.

The vestibule was a mess. Chamberlains and pages righted tables, gathered up fragments of smashed crockery and bits of ripped clothing, and mopped up wine and what looked like blood-stained vomit. Last night Hephaistion had evidently once more been entertaining his commanders and other 'guests'.

Hephaistion's usher was a small, fat, fussy man with peculiar strawberry-blond hair. When he had kept Eumenes waiting in the vestibule for just the precise time required to reinforce his own position, he bowed and waved Eumenes forward into Hephaistion's private chambers.

Hephaistion was on his couch, loosely covered by a sheet, and still in his nightshirt. He was the centre of industry: chamberlains laid out clothes and brought in food, and a file of pages brought in jugs of water. Hephaistion himself, propped up on one elbow, picked languidly at a tray of meat.

There was a stirring under the sheet. A boy, eyes heavy with sleep, emerged and sat up, looking bewildered. Hephaistion smiled at him. He touched his fingers to his own lips, and then the boy's, and patted his shoulder. 'Go now.' The boy clambered off the couch, naked. A chamberlain pulled a cloak around him and led him from the chamber.

Eumenes, waiting by the entrance, tried not to show his disdain for all this. He had lived and worked with these Macedonians long enough to understand them. Under their Kings they had been welded into a force capable of conquering the world, but they were highland tribesmen only a couple of generations removed from their ancestral traditions. Eumenes would even strive to join in with their revels when it was politic to do so. But still, some of these pages were the sons of Macedonian nobility, sent to serve the King's officers in order to complete their education. Eumenes could only imagine what impression it must make on such young men when they spent their mornings mopping up the stinking detritus of some barbarian-warrior in his cups – or spent their nights serving his needs in other ways.

At length Hephaistion acknowledged Eumenes. 'You're early today, Secretary.'

'I don't think so – not unless the sun has begun to jump around the sky again.'

'Then I must be late. Hah!' He waved a meat-laden skewer at Eumenes. 'Try some of this. You'd never think a dead camel could taste so good.'

'The reason the Indians spice their food so heavily,' Eumenes said, 'is because they eat rotten meat. I'll stick to fruit and mutton.'

'You really are a bore, Eumenes,' Hephaistion said tensely.

Eumenes bit back his irritation. Despite his endless rivalry with Hephaistion, he thought he understood the Macedonian's mood. 'And you miss the King. I take it there has been no word.'

'Half our scouts don't even return.'

'Does it comfort you to lose yourself between the thighs of a page?'

'You know me too well, Secretary.' Hephaistion dropped the skewer back on the plate. 'Perhaps you're right about these spices. Still, they cut a passage through the gut like the Companion Cavalry through Persian lines . . .' He clambered off his couch, stripped off his nightshirt and pulled on a clean tunic.

This Macedonian was a contradiction, Eumenes had always thought. He was taller than most, with regular features, though a rather long nose, startling blue eyes and close-cropped black hair. He held himself well. But there was no doubt he was a warrior, as the many scars on his body attested.

Everybody knew that Hephaistion had been the King's closest companion since they were boys, and his lover since adolescence. Though the King had since taken wives, mistresses and other lovers, the latest being the worm-like Persian eunuch Bagoas, he had once, drunk, confided in Eumenes that he always regarded Hephaistion as the only true companion, the only true love of his life. The King, no fool even when it came to his friends, had put Hephaistion in command of this army group, and before that made him his Chiliarch – that is, his Vizier, in the Persian style. And as for Hephaistion there were no others, none but the King; his pages and other concubines were no more than ciphers to warm him when the King was away.

Hephaistion said now as he dressed, 'Does it give you satisfaction to see me suffer over the King?'

'No,' Eumenes said. 'I fear for him too, Hephaistion. And not just because he is my King – not because of the devastation his loss would cause in all our lives – but for *him*. You can believe that or not, but it's nevertheless true.'

Hephaistion eyed him. He went to his bath, took a flannel and dabbed at his face. 'I don't doubt you, Eumenes. After all, we have been through a great deal together, following the King on his great adventure.'

'To the ends of the Earth,' Eumenes said softly.

'The ends of the Earth – yes. And now, who knows, perhaps even beyond . . . Give me a moment more. Please, sit, have some water, wine, fruit.'

Eumenes sat and took some dried figs. It had indeed been a

long journey, he thought. And how strange, how – disappointing – if it was all to end here, in this desolate place, so far from home.

With Iron Age soldiers pointing spears at their back, Bisesa, Cecil de Morgan, Corporal Batson and their three sepoy companions climbed over a final ridge. The delta of the Indus opened up before them, a plain striped by the glimmering surface of the broad, sluggish river. On the western horizon Bisesa could make out the profiles of ships on the sea, made indistinct by the dense, misty air.

The ships looked like triremes, she thought, wondering.

Before her an army camp was laid out. Tents had been set up along the riverbanks, and the smoke of countless fires coiled up into the morning air. Some of the tents were huge, and had open fronts like shops. Everywhere there was movement, a steady churning. There weren't just soldiers: women walked slowly, many heavily laden, children ran over the muddy ground, and dogs, chickens and even pigs scampered through the churned-up lanes. Further out, big enclosures held horses, camels and mules, and flocks of sheep and goats fanned out over the marshy land. Everybody and everything was muddy, from the loftiest camel to the smallest child.

De Morgan, despite mud and weariness, seemed exhilarated. Thanks to his 'wasted education', he knew a lot more than she did about what was going on here. He pointed to the open tents. 'See that? The soldiers were expected to buy their provisions, and so you have these traders – many of them Phoenicians, if I remember correctly – following after the marching troops. There are all sorts of emporia, travelling theatres, even courts to administer justice . . . And remember this army has been in the field for years. Many of the men have acquired mistresses, wives, even children on the way. This is truly a travelling city.'

Bisesa was prodded in the back by a Macedonian's long iron-tipped spear: his 'sarissa', as de Morgan had called it. Time to move on. They began to plod down the ridge towards the camp.

She tried to hide her fatigue. At Captain Grove's request she had set off with a scouting party to try to make contact with this Macedonian army. After several days' hike down the valley of the Indus, at dawn that morning they given themselves up to a Macedonian patrol, hoping to be taken to the commanders. Since then they had been marched maybe ten klicks.

Soon they were in among the tents, and Bisesa found herself picking her way over mud and dung; the animal stink was overwhelming. It was more like a farmyard than a military camp.

They were soon surrounded by people, who stared at Bisesa's flight suit, de Morgan's morning suit, and the glaring red serge jackets of the British troops. Most of the people were short, shorter even than the nineteenth-century sepoys, but the men were broad, stocky, obviously powerfully strong. The soldiers' tunics had been recut and patched, and even the leather tents showed signs of wear and repair – but the soldiers' shields shone, gilded, and even the horses had silver bits in their mouths. It was a peculiar mixture of shabbiness and wealth. Bisesa could see that this army had been a long time away from home – but it had been successful, acquiring wealth beyond its soldiers' dreams.

De Morgan seemed more interested in Bisesa's reaction than in the Macedonians themselves. 'What are you thinking?'

'I'm telling myself that I'm really here,' she said slowly. 'I am really seeing this – that twenty-three centuries have some-how been peeled back. And I'm thinking of all the people back home who would have loved to be here, to see this.'

'Yes. But at least *we* are here, and that's something.'

Bisesa stumbled, and was rewarded with another prod from the sarissa. She said softly, 'You know, I have a pistol in my belt.' The Macedonians, as they had anticipated, had not recognised the party's firearms and had let them keep them, while confiscating knives and bayonets. 'And I am very tempted to take off the safety and make my escort here shove that pointy tip up his own Iron Age arse.'

'I wouldn't advise it,' de Morgan said equably.

When Hephaistion was ready to face the day, Eumenes had his chamberlain bring forward the muster rolls and conduct sheets. This paperwork was spread out over a low table. As they spent most mornings, Eumenes and Hephaistion began to work through the endless details of administering an army of tens of thousands of men – the strengths of the army's various units, the distribution of pay, reinforcements, arms, armour, clothing, baggage animals – work which went on even when an army had been static for so many weeks, like this one. In fact the task was made more complicated than usual by the demands of the fleet that stood idle in the mouth of the delta.

As always the report of the Secretary of Cavalry was especially troublesome. Horses died in huge numbers, and it was the duty of provincial governors across the empire to procure replacements and dispatch them to the various remount centres from where they would be sent to the field. But with the continuing lack of communication, there had been no resupply for some time, and the Cavalry Secretary, growing worried, recommended a sequestration from the local population – 'If any fit horses can be found outside the cooking pot,' Hephaistion joked grimly.

Hephaistion was commander of this army group. But Eumenes, as Royal Secretary, had his own hierarchy that ran in parallel to the army's command structure. He had subsidiary Secretaries attached to each of the main army units – the infantry, the cavalry, the mercenaries and others – each assisted by Inspectors who did much of the detailed information-gathering. Eumenes prided himself on the accuracy and currency of his information: quite an achievement in the service of Macedonians, most of whom, even the nobility, were illiterate and innumerate.

But Eumenes was well equipped for the task. Older than most of the King's close companions, he had served the King's father Philip, as well as the son.

Philip had seized Macedon three years before the birth of his heir. In those days the kingdom had been a loose coalition of feuding principalities, under threat from the barbarian tribes to the north and the devious Greek city-states to the south. Under Philip the northern tribes had soon been subdued. A confrontation with the Greeks had been inevitable – and when it had come Philip's crucial military innovation, a highly trained, highly mobile cavalry division called the Companions, had sliced through the Greeks' slow-moving hoplite infantry.

Eumenes, himself a city-state Greek from Cardia, knew that resentment against the Greeks' barbarian conquerors was unlikely ever to fade. But in a time when civilisation was limited to a few pockets surrounded by great seas of barbarism and the unknown, the more politically aware of the Greeks knew that a strong Macedon shielded them from worse dangers. They lauded Philip's wider ambition to invade the immense empire of Persia, ostensibly in order to revenge earlier Persian atrocities against Greek cities. And the education of the King's son at the hands of Greek tutors, including the famous Aristotle, pupil of Plato, had served to reinforce an impression of Philip's Hellenism.

It had been just as Philip was preparing for his great Persian adventure that he had been assassinated.

The new King was just twenty, but he had shown no hesitation in continuing where his father had left off. A series of rapid campaigns had consolidated his position in Macedonia and Greece. Then he had turned his attention to the prize which had been almost in Philip's grasp. The Persian empire sprawled from Turkey to Egypt and Pakistan, and its Great King could field forces that could number a *million*. But after six years of a short, brutal and brilliant campaign, a King of Macedon had mounted the throne of Persepolis itself.

This King had not wanted simply to conquer, but to rule. He had sought to spread Greek culture through Asia: he had planted or rebuilt cities to the Greek model throughout his empire. And, more controversially, he had tried to weld together the disparate people who now came under his rule. He had adopted Persian dress and mannerisms, and shocked his men by kissing Bagoas the eunuch on the lips in their sight.

Meanwhile Eumenes' own career had advanced with the King's. His efficiency, intelligence and political subtlety had earned him the King's undying confidence, and his responsibilities had swollen with the growing empire until Eumenes felt as if he was carrying the burden of a world on his shoulders.

But a mere empire was not enough for this King. With Persia won he had launched his battle-hardened army, all fifty thousand of them, to the south and west, towards the rich, mysterious prize of India. They headed ever east into unexplored and unmapped country, heading for a coast which would, the King believed, be the shore of the Ocean that ran around the world. The country was strange: there were crocodiles in the rivers, and forests full of gigantic snakes, and there were rumours of empires nobody had ever heard of before. But the King would not stop.

Why did he go on? Some said he was a god in mortal flesh, and the ambitions of gods transcended those of men. Some said that he sought to ape the achievements of the great hero Achilles. There was curiosity too; a man who had been tutored by Aristotle could not help but grow up with a deep desire to know the world. But Eumenes suspected the truth was simpler. This King was his illustrious father's creation, and it was no wonder that the new King had wanted to eclipse his father's very ambitions, and so to prove himself the greater man.

At last, at the river Beas, the troops, exhausted from years of campaigning, had rebelled, and even the god-King could go no further. Eumenes believed that the men's gut wisdom was sound. Enough was enough; they would do well to hold what had already been taken.

Besides, on a deep level of his sophisticated mind, Eumenes was subtly calculating his own advantage. He had always faced rivalries in the court: the Macedonian contempt for the Greek, the fighting man's derision of mere 'scribes', and Eumenes's very competence were enough to make him many enemies. Hephaistion particularly was notoriously jealous of anybody who had his lover's confidence. Often the tensions among the King's companions could be lethal. But Eumenes had survived – and he was not without his own ambitions. As the emphasis of the King's reign turned from conquest to political and economic consolidation, Eumenes's more subtle skills might find greater purchase, and he intended to be well placed to advance his own position beyond that of mere Secretary.

After that reverse at the Beas, the King still had one grand ambition, though. Still deep in India, he built an immense fleet to be sailed down the Indus and then along the coast of the Persian Gulf, intending to establish a new trade route which might further unify his empire. He had split his forces: Hephaistion was to take the fleet to the mouth of the delta, followed by the baggage train and the King's prized elephants; Eumenes and his staff had travelled with the fleet. The King himself stayed behind to campaign against rebellious tribesmen in his new Indian province.

All had gone well, until the King had taken on a people called the Malloi and their fortress city of Multan. The King, with typical daring, had led the attack himself – but he had taken an arrow in the chest. The last dispatch Hephaistion had received had reported that the wounded King was to be placed on a ship and floated down the river to join the rest of the fleet, while his army followed later.

But that had been days ago. It was as if the world-conquering army upriver had utterly disappeared. And the sky had been full of unimaginably strange portents: some of the men muttered that they had seen the sun itself lurch across the sky. Such strange signs could only signify a huge and terrible event – and what could that be but the death of the god-King? Eumenes believed more in hard fact than any number of omens, but it was hard for him to decipher this information, or rather the lack of it, and unease grew steadily.

Still, the unrelenting routine of running the army was a distraction from the greater uncertainty of the situation.

Eumenes and Hephaistion had to deal with contentious issues that could not be resolved at lower levels of the bureaucracy. Today they turned to the case of a commander of a division of Foot Companions who, on discovering his favourite prostitute in the bed of a fellow officer, had lopped off the man's nose with his dagger.

'It's a nasty little case,' said Eumenes, 'which sets a bad example.'

'But it's more complicated than that. This is a shameful act.' So it was; such disfiguring had been meted out, on the King's orders, for example to an assassin of the defeated Darius, Great King of Persia. 'And I know these men,' Hephaistion went on. 'Rumour has it they were lovers too! Somehow this girl has come between them, perhaps hoping to profit by turning one against another.' He rubbed his long nose. 'Who is the girl, by the by?'

It was a good question. It wasn't impossible for members of resentful, defeated peoples to work their way into the command structure of the King's army, to do as much damage as they could. Eumenes riffled through his scrolls.

But before he could find the answer Hephaistion's usher came bustling in. 'Sir! You must come . . . The strangest thing, the strangest people—'

Hephaistion snapped, 'Is it news of the King?'

'I don't know, sir. Oh, come, come!'

Hephaistion and Eumenes glanced at each other. Then they stood, carelessly toppling the table with its scrolls, and hurried out. Hephaistion snatched up his sword on the way.

Bisesa and de Morgan were brought to a grander collection of tents, though no less mud-spattered than the rest. Severe-looking guards armed with spears and stabbing swords stood at the entrance, glaring at them. Bisesa's escort stepped forward and began to jabber in his fast Greek. One of the guards nodded curtly, stepped into the first tent, and spoke to somebody within.

De Morgan was tense, edgy, excited – a state he got into,

146

Bisesa had learned, when he sensed opportunity. She tried to keep herself calm.

More guards, in subtly different uniforms, came pouring out of the tent. They surrounded Bisesa and the others, their swords pointed at the travellers' bellies. Then out came two figures, obviously more senior; they wore military-looking tunics and cloaks, but their clothes were clean. One of these commanders, the younger, came pushing through the guards. He had a broad face, a long nose, short dark hair. He looked them up and down and peered into their faces; like his troops he was shorter than any of the moderns. He seemed tense, gaunt, unhappy to Bisesa, but his body language was so alien it was hard to be sure.

He stood before de Morgan and yelled in his face. De Morgan quailed, flinching from the rain of spittle, and stammered a reply.

Bisesa hissed, 'What does he want?'

De Morgan frowned, concentrating. 'To know who we are . . . I think. His accent is thick. His name is Hephaistion. I asked him to slow down. I said my Greek was poor – and so it is; the stuff I was taught to parrot at Winchester wasn't much like *this*.'

Now the other commander stepped forward. He was evidently older, bald save for a frosting of silver hair, and his face was softer, narrow – shrewd, Bisesa thought. He put his hand on Hephaistion's shoulder, and spoke to de Morgan in more measured tones.

De Morgan's face lit up. 'Oh, thank God – a genuine Greek! His tongue is archaic but at least he can speak it properly, unlike these Macedonians . . .'

So, with a double translation through de Morgan and the older man, who was called Eumenes, Bisesa was able to make herself understood. She gave their names and pointed back up the valley of the Indus. 'We are with an army detachment,' she said. 'Far up the valley.'

'If that is true we should have encountered you before,' snapped Eumenes.

She didn't know what to say. Nothing in her life had

147

prepared her for an incident like this. *Everything was strange*, everything about these people from the depths of time. They were short, grimy, vigorous, powerfully muscled, and they seemed closer to the animal than the human. She wondered how they saw *her*.

Eumenes stepped forward. He walked around Bisesa, fingering the fabric of her clothes. His fingers lingered over the butt of Bisesa's pistol, and she tensed; but happily he left it alone. 'Nothing about you is familiar.'

'But everything is different now.' She pointed to the sky. 'You must have seen it. The sun, the weather. Nothing is as it was before. We have been brought on a journey against our will, without our understanding. As have you. And yet we have been brought together. Perhaps we can – help each other.'

Eumenes smiled. 'With the army of a god-King I have journeyed through strangeness these past six years, and everything we have encountered we have conquered. Whatever strange power has stirred up the world, I doubt it holds any fear for *us*—'

But now a cry went up, rustling through the camp. People started running to the river, thousands of them moving at once, as if a wind had run over a field of grass. A messenger ran up and spoke rapidly to Eumenes and Hephaistion.

Bisesa asked de Morgan, 'What is it?'

'He's coming,' the factor said. 'He's coming at last.'

'Who?'

'The King . . .'

A small flotilla of ships sailed down the river. Most were broad flat-bottomed barges, or magnificent triremes with billowing purple sails. But the craft at the head of the flotilla was smaller and, without a sail, was pulled along by fifteen pairs of oarsmen. At its stern was an awning, stitched with purple and silver. As the boat neared the camp the awning was pulled back to reveal a man, surrounded by attendants, lying on what looked like a gilded couch.

A muttering ran through the watching crowd. Bisesa and

de Morgan, forgotten by all but their guards, pressed with the rest towards the shallow bank. Bisesa said, 'What are they saying now?'

'That it's a trick,' de Morgan said. 'That the King is dead, that this is merely his corpse being returned for burial.'

The boat put in to the shore. Under Hephaistion's command a team of soldiers ran forward with a kind of stretcher. But, to general astonishment, the figure on the couch stirred. He waved the stretcher-bearers away, and then, slowly, painfully, with the help of his white-robed attendants, he got to his feet. The crowds on the banks, all but silent, watched his painful struggle. He was wearing a long-sleeved tunic and a cloak of purple, and a heavy cuirass. The cloak was inlaid and edged with gold, and the tunic ornately worked with patterns of sunbursts and figures.

He was short, stocky, like most of the Macedonians. He was clean-shaven, and he wore his brown hair brushed back from a centre parting and long enough to touch his shoulders. His face, if weather-beaten red, was strong, broad and handsome, and his gaze steady and piercing. And as he faced the gathering on the bank he held his head oddly, tilted a little to the left, so that his eyes were uplifted, and his mouth was open.

'He looks like a rock star,' Bisesa whispered. 'And he holds his head like Princess Diana. No wonder they love him . . .'

A new muttering began to spread through the crowd.

'*It's him*,' de Morgan whispered. 'That's what they are saying.' Bisesa glanced at him and was startled to see tears in his eyes. '*It is him!* It is Alexander himself! By God, by God.'

The cheering started, spreading like fire through dry grass, and the men waved their fists and their spears and swords. Flowers were thrown, and a gentle rain of petals settled over the boat.

149

CHAPTER 20
THE CITY OF TENTS

At dawn, two days after his departure, the Mongol envoy returned. The cosmonauts' fate, it seemed, had been decided.

Sable had to be prodded awake. Kolya was already alert, his eyes gritty with sleeplessness. In the musty dark of the yurt, where children snored gently in their cots, the cosmonauts were given breakfast of a little unleavened bread, and a bowl of a kind of hot tea. This was aromatic, presumably made from steppe herbs and grasses, and was surprisingly refreshing.

The cosmonauts moved stiffly. They were both recovering quickly from their orbital sojourn, but Kolya longed for a hot shower, or even to be able to rinse his face.

They were led out of the yurt, and allowed a toilet break. The sky was brightening, and the customary lid of cloud and ash seemed comparatively light today. Some of the nomads were paying their respects to the dawn, with genuflections to the south and east. This was one of their few public displays of religious feeling; the Mongols were shamanists, eschewing public rituals for oracles, exorcisms and magic displays in the privacy of their yurts.

The cosmonauts were led to a small group of men. They had saddled up half a dozen horses, and had harnessed two more to a small wooden-wheeled cart. The horses were stocky and undisciplined-looking, like their owners; they looked around impatiently, as if eager to get this chore over with.

'At last we're out of here,' Sable grunted earnestly. 'Civilisation here we come.'

'There is a Russian saying,' Kolya warned. 'Out of the frying pan—'

'Russian my ass.'

The cosmonauts were prodded towards the cart. They had to climb aboard, hands still bound. As they sat down on the bare floor a Mongol man, strong-looking even by the standards of these people, approached them and began to harangue them loudly. His leathery face was creased like a relief map.

Sable said, 'What's he saying?'

'No idea. But we've seen him before, remember. I think this is the chief. And his name is Scacatai.' The chief had come to inspect them during their first hours of captivity.

'This little asshole is going to try to make capital out of us. What were those words you used?'

'*Darughachi. Tengri.*'

Sable glared at Scacatai. 'Did you get that? *Tengri, Tengri.* We're ambassadors from God. And I'm not about to ride off to the Pleasure Dome with my arms tied behind my back. Let us loose, or I'll fry your sorry butt with a thunderbolt.'

Scacatai, of course, understood nothing but the fragments of Mongolian, but Sable's tone carried the day. After more mutually incomprehensible argument, he nodded to one of his sons, who cut Sable's and Kolya's bonds.

'Good work,' Kolya said, rubbing his wrists.

'Piece of cake,' Sable said. 'Next.' She started pointing, at the Soyuz, and at the parachute silk stacked up against one of the yurts. 'I want what's mine. Bring that silk to the cart. And the stuff you stole out of the Soyuz . . .' It took much gesturing to get this point across, but at length, with much bad grace, Scacatai ordered his people to load up the parachute, and bits of kit were brought out of the yurt. Soon the cart was incongruously piled high with parachute, spacesuits and other gear. Kolya checked that the emergency medical supplies and flare guns were there – and the components of the ham radio gear, their only possible line to the outside world, and to Casey and the others in India.

Sable rummaged through the gear and dug out a life-raft. She handed it ceremonially to Scacatai. 'Here you go,' she said. 'A gift from Heaven. When we've gone, pull this toggle like *so*. You dig?' She mimed the action repeatedly until it was clear that the Mongol understood. Then she bowed, and Kolya followed suit, and they clambered on to the cart.

The horsemen set off, one of them leading the carthorses by a rope, and the cart lumbered into motion. 'Thanks for the mutton, buster,' Sable called back.

Kolya studied her. Bit by bit, starting from a position of utter weakness and vulnerability, she was assuming control of the situation. In the days since the landing she seemed to have burned her fear out of herself by an effort of will, but her intensity of purpose made Kolya uneasy. 'You have nerve, Sable.'

Sable grinned. 'A woman doesn't get to the top of the Astronaut Office without learning to be tough. Anyhow, it's nice to leave with a little more style than when we arrived—'

There was a loud bang, a chorus of confused cries. Scacatai had pulled the ripcord on the raft. The Mongols stared in open-mouthed astonishment at this bright orange artefact that had exploded into existence out of nowhere. Before the village had receded into the distance, the children were starting to bounce on the raft's inflated rim.

The party made remarkably rapid progress. For hours on end the riders kept their horses moving at a trot, a pace which Kolya was sure would quickly exhaust the animals, but the horses were obviously bred for such treatment. The Mongols ate in the saddle, and expected the cosmonauts to do the same. They didn't even stop for toilet breaks, and Sable and Kolya learned to keep out of the way when a rider's volley of urine was caught by the wind.

As they travelled on, Kolya would sometimes glimpse sparks in the distance, floating silently above the ground. He wondered if these were examples of the 'Eyes' Casey had described in India. If so, were the Eyes a worldwide phenomenon? He would have welcomed the chance to study one, but their track never brought them close, and the Mongols showed no curiosity.

Before the sun had climbed to its highest, they arrived at a waystation. It was just a huddle of yurts, lost in the middle of the emptiness of the steppe, but several horses were tied up outside, and Kolya glimpsed a herd of others, moving with the silence of distance across the steppe. As they approached, the riders rang a bell and the keepers of the station came running out. The riders quickly negotiated with the keepers, exchanged their horses, and were on their way.

Sable grumbled, 'I could have done with a break. The suspension on this thing is a little stiff.'

Kolya gazed back at the station. 'I think this must be the *yam*.'

'The what?'

'At one time the Mongols held all of Eurasia from Hungary to the South China Sea. They kept it all unified with fast communications – a system of routes and waystations where you could change your horses. The Romans had a similar system. A courier could cross two or three hundred kilometres in a day.'

'This isn't exactly a road. We're just riding over empty steppe. So how did these guys know how to find this place?'

'Mongols learn to ride before they can walk,' Kolya said. 'Crossing this vast plain, they have to be expert navigators. They probably don't even have to think about it.'

Even when night came the Mongols rode on. They slept in the saddle, with one or two of them leading the others. Sable found the jolting of the cart kept her awake. But Kolya, exhausted by two sleepless nights, over-stressed, overwhelmed by the oxygen-rich air of the steppe, slept from sunset to dawn.

At times, though, the riders did hesitate. They had to cross peculiar straight-line boundaries between bare, baked-dry steppe and areas of bright green grass, and other places where flowers lay scattered, wilting – and other areas, stranger yet, where banks of snow lay half-melted in pools of shadow.

It was obvious to Kolya that these suspiciously straight borders were transitions between one time-slice and another,

153

and that this steppe was stitched together from a myriad fragments drawn from different times of the year – even different eras. But just as the snow was melting in the warmth, the spring flowers were quickly wilting, and the summer grass screeds were mottled and curled. Perhaps there would be some recovery, some knitting together, Kolya thought, after a full cycle of seasons. But he suspected that it would take more than a single year to assemble a new ecology from these time-shifted bits of the old.

The Mongol nomads could understand none of this, of course. Even the horses bucked and whinnied as they crossed these disturbing transitions.

Once the riders, evidently baffled, stopped at a site that seemed as empty and undistinguished as the rest of the steppe. Perhaps, Kolya speculated, a waystation had been sited here, and the riders couldn't imagine why they hadn't found it. The station was lost, not in space, but in time. The nomads, evidently a practical people, took this in their stride. After a brief discussion marked with much shoulder-shrugging, they moved on, but at a slower pace; evidently they had decided that if they couldn't rely on the way-stations they should spare the horses.

In the afternoon of the second day, the character of the country began to change, becoming more broken and hilly. Now they rode through shallow valleys, sometimes fording streams, and passed copses of larch and pine. It was a much more human landscape, and Kolya felt relieved to be away from the oppressive, unchanging immensity of the steppe. Even the Mongols seemed to be happier. As they pushed through one small stand of trees, one brute-faced young man leaned down to pluck handfuls of wild geraniums that he attached to his saddle.

The area was relatively densely populated. They passed many yurt villages, some of them large and sprawling, with smoke rising everywhere, the fine threads leaning in the prevailing wind. There were even roads, after a fashion, or at least heavily worn and rutted trails. This part of the Mongol empire seemed to have come through the Discontinuity almost intact, even though it was studded with time-slice incongruities.

They came to a broad, sluggish river. A ferry had been set up here, a platform guided by ropes slung across the river. The platform was big enough for the riders, cosmonauts, horses and even the cart to be loaded on and transferred in one go.

On the far bank they turned south, following the river. Kolya saw that a second great river snaked across the countryside, glistening; they were heading for a mighty confluence. Clearly the nomads knew where they were going.

But at the foot of a hill, close to a big oxbow loop of one of the rivers, they came to a slab of stone, closely inscribed. The nomads slowed and stared.

Kolya said grimly, 'They haven't seen this before, that's clear. But *I* have.'

'You've been here?'

'No. But I've seen pictures. If I'm right this is the confluence of the Onon and Balj rivers. And that monument was set up in the 1960s, I think.'

'So this is a little teeny time-slice. No wonder these guys are staring.'

'The script is supposed to be old Mongolian. But nobody knows for sure if they got it right.'

'You think our escorts can read it?'

'Probably not. Most of the Mongols were illiterate.'

'So this is a memorial? A memorial to what?'

'To an eight hundredth birthday . . .'

They rode on and climbed over a last ridge. There, set out before them on a lush green plain, was another yurt village – no, not a village, Kolya realised, a *city*.

There must have been thousands of tents, set out in a regular grid pattern, spanning hectares of ground. Some of the yurts seemed no more impressive than those in Scacatai's village out on the steppe, but at the centre was a much grander structure, a vast complex of interconnected pavilions. All this was enclosed by a wall, but there were outer 'suburbs', a kind of shanty town of cruder-looking yurts that huddled outside the wall. Dirt roads cut across the plain from all directions, leading to the gates in the wall. A lot of traffic moved on the roads, and inside the city itself smoke rose from the yurts, merging into a pale brown smog that hung over the city.

'Christ,' said Sable. 'It's a tent Manhattan.'

Perhaps. But on the green land beyond Kolya saw vast herds of sheep, goats and horses, grazing contentedly. 'Just as the legends described,' he murmured. 'They were never anything more than nomads. They ruled a world, yet cared only about having somewhere to graze their flocks. And when the time comes to move to the winter pastures, this whole city will be uprooted and moved south . . .'

Once more the horses jolted into motion, and the party rode down the shallow ridge towards the yurt city.

At the gate, a guard in a blue, star-spangled tunic and felt cap held them up.

Sable said, 'You think our guys are trying to sell us?'

'Negotiating a bribe, perhaps. But in this empire everything is owned by the ruling aristocracy, the Golden Family. Scacatai's people *can't* sell us – the Emperor already owns us.'

At last the party was allowed to go ahead. The guard commander attached a detail of soldiers, and Sable, Kolya, and just one of their Mongol companions, along with the cart laden with their gear, were escorted into the city.

They made their way down a broad lane, heading directly for the big tent complex at the centre. The ground was just churned-up mud. The yurts were grand, and some were decorated in rich fabrics. But the stench was Kolya's overwhelming first impression – like Scacatai's village, but multiplied a thousandfold; it was all he could do to keep from gagging.

Smell or not, the streets were crowded, and not just by Asiatics. There were Chinese and perhaps even Japanese, Middle Eastern types, maybe Persians or Armenians, Arabs – even round-eyed west Europeans. The people wore finely made tunics, boots and hats, and many had heavy jewellery around their necks, wrists and fingers. The cosmonauts' gaudy jumpsuits attracted some eyes, as did the spacesuits and other gear piled on their cart, but nobody seemed much interested.

'They are used to strangers,' Kolya said. 'If we're right about our location in time, this is the capital of a continental empire. We must be sure not to underestimate these people.'

'Oh, I won't,' said Sable grimly.

As they neared the central complex of pavilions, the presence of soldiers became more obvious. Kolya saw archers and swordsmen, armed and ready. Even those off duty glared at the party as it passed, breaking off from their eating, and gambling over dice. There must have been a thousand troops guarding this one big tent.

They reached an entrance pavilion, itself big enough to have swallowed Scacatai's yurt whole. A standard of white yak tails hung over the entrance. There were more negotiations, and a messenger was sent deeper into the complex.

He returned with a taller man, obviously Asiatic but with startling blue eyes, and expensively dressed in an elaborately embroidered waistcoat and pantaloons. This figure brought a team of advisors with him. He studied the cosmonauts and their equipment, running his hands briefly over the fabric of Sable's jumpsuit, and his eyes narrowed with curiosity. He conversed briefly and unintelligibly with his advisors. Then he snapped his fingers, turned, and made to leave. Servants began to take the cosmonauts' goods away.

'No,' Sable said loudly. Kolya cringed inwardly, but she was standing her ground. The tall man turned slowly and stared at her, wide-eyed with surprise.

She walked up to the cart, took a handful of parachute fabric, and spread it out before the tall man. 'All this is our property. *Darughachi Tengri.* Comprende? It stays with us. And *this* material is our gift for the Emperor, a gift from the sky.'

Kolya said nervously, 'Sable—'

'We really don't have a lot to lose, Kolya. Anyhow you started this charade.'

The tall man hesitated. Then his face split briefly into a

grin. He snapped orders, and one of his advisors ran off deeper into the complex.

'He knows we're bluffing,' Sable said. 'But he doesn't know what to make of us. He's a smart guy.'

'If he's that smart we should be careful.'

The advisor returned with a European. He was a small, runty man who might have been about thirty, but, under the customary layer of grime, and with his hair and beard raggedly uncut, it was hard to tell. He studied the two of them with fast, calculating eyes. Then he spoke rapidly to Kolya.

'That sounds like French,' Sable said.

And so it turned out to be. His name was Basil, and he had been born in Paris.

In a kind of anteroom they were served with food and drink – bits of spiced meat, and a kind of lemonade – by a serving girl. She was plump, no older than fourteen or fifteen, and wore little but a few veils. She looked vaguely European too to Kolya, and her eyes were empty; he wondered how far she had been brought from home.

The tall grandee's purpose soon became clear. Basil was proficient in the Mongol tongue, and was to serve as an interpreter. 'They assume all Europeans speak the same language,' Basil said, 'from the Urals to the Atlantic. But this far from Paris it's an understandable error.'

Kolya's French was quite good – better than his English, in fact. Like many Russian schoolchildren he had been taught it as his second language. But Basil's version of French, dating only a few centuries after the birth of that nation itself, was difficult to grasp. 'It's like meeting Chaucer,' Kolya explained to Sable. 'Think how much English has changed since then . . . save that Basil must have been born a century or more *before* Chaucer.' Sable had never heard of Chaucer.

Basil was bright, his mind flexible – Kolya supposed he wouldn't have made it so far if not – and it took them only a couple of hours to build up a reasonable understanding.

Basil said he was a trader, come to the capital of the world to make his fortune. 'The traders love the Mongols,' he said. 'They've opened up the east! China, Korea—' It took a while to identify the place names he used. 'Of course most of the traders here are Muslims and Arabs – most people in France don't know the Mongols even exist . . . !' Basil had his eye on the main chance, and he began to ask questions – where the cosmonauts had come from, what they wanted, what they had brought with them.

Sable intervened. 'Listen, pal, we don't need an agent. Your job is to speak our words to – uh, the tall man.'

'Yeh-lu,' said Basil. 'His name is Yeh-lu Ch'u-ts'ai. He is a Khitan.'

'Take us to him,' Sable said simply.

Though Basil argued, her tone of command was unmistakable, even without translation. Basil clapped his hands, and a chamberlain arrived to escort them into the presence of Yeh-lu himself.

They walked through corridors of felt, ducking their heads; the roofs were not built for people their height.

In a small chamber in a corner of this palace of tents, Yeh-lu was reclining on a low couch. Servants hovered at his elbow. Before him on the floor he had spread out faded diagrams that looked like maps, a kind of compass, blocks carved into figures that looked vaguely Buddhist, and a pile of small artefacts – bits of jewellery, small coins. It was the stock in trade of an astrologer, Kolya guessed. With an elegant gesture Yeh-lu bade them sit down, on more low couches.

Yeh-lu was patient; forced to speak to them through an uncertain chain of translation via Basil and Kolya, he asked them their names, and where they had come from. At the answer that had become their stock reply – from *Tengri*, from Heaven – he rolled his eyes. Astrologer he might be, but he was no fool.

'We need a better story,' Kolya said.

'What do these people know of geography? Do they even know what shape the world is?'

'Damned if I know.'

Briskly Sable got to her knees and pulled aside a felt mat, exposing dusty earth. With a fingertip she began to sketch a rough map: Asia, Europe, India, Africa. She stabbed her finger into the heart of it. 'We are here . . .'

Kolya remembered that the Mongols always oriented themselves to the south, while Sable's map had north at the top; with that simple inversion things became much clearer.

'Now,' said Sable. 'Here's the World Ocean.' She dragged her fingers through the dust beyond the continents, making a ridged circle. 'We come from far away – far beyond the World Ocean. We flew over it like birds, on our orange wings . . .' It wasn't quite true, but was close to the truth, and Yeh-lu seemed to accept it for now.

Basil said, 'Yeh-lu is asking about the *yam*. He has ordered riders out along all the main routes. But some are broken. He says he knows the world has undergone a great disturbance. He wants to know what you understand about this strangeness, and what it means for the empire.'

'We don't know,' said Sable. 'That's the truth. We are just as much victims of this as you are.'

Yeh-lu seemed to accept this. He stood languidly, and spoke again.

Basil gasped with excitement. 'The Emperor himself is impressed by your gift, the orange cloth, and wants to see you.'

Sable's eyes hardened. 'Now we're getting somewhere.'

They stood, and a party quickly formed up, headed by Yeh-lu, with Sable, Kolya and Basil at the centre, surrounded by a phalanx of tough-looking guards.

Kolya was rigid with fear. 'Sable, we have to be careful. We're the Emperor's property, remember. He will speak only to members of his family, perhaps a few key aides like Yeh-lu. Everybody else just doesn't count.'

'Yeah, yeah. Even so. We've done well, Kolya. Just a few days here and we've got this far already . . . Now we just have to figure the angles.'

They were taken into a much grander chamber. The walls were hung with rich embroidery and tapestry, the floors covered with layers of rugs and carpets so thick they were soft to walk on. The place was crowded. Courtiers milled and beefy-looking soldiers stood around the walls, laden with weapons, glaring at the cosmonauts and everybody else – even each other. In one corner of the yurt an orchestra played softly, a harmony of lutes. All the instrumentalists were beautiful, all very young girls.

And yet for all its opulence this was still just a yurt, Kolya thought, and the prevailing stink, of greasy flesh and stale milk, was just as bad as in Scacatai's humble home.

'Barbarians,' he muttered. 'They didn't know what towns and farms were *for* save as sources of booty. They plundered a world, but they still live like goat-herders, their tents piled with treasures. And in our time their descendants will be the last nomads of all, still trapped by their barbaric roots—'

'Shut *up*,' Sable hissed.

Following Yeh-lu, they walked slowly to the centre of the yurt. Around the throne that was the focus of this wide space stood a number of smooth-faced young men. They looked similar: perhaps the Emperor's sons, Kolya thought. There were many women here, sitting before the throne. All were handsome, though some looked as old as sixty; the younger ones were quite stunningly beautiful. Wives, or concubines?

Yeh-lu stepped aside, and they stood before the Emperor.

He looked about sixty. Sitting on his ornately carved throne, he was not tall. But he was slim, upright; he looked very fit. His face was full, his features small – very Asiatic – with only a trace of grey in his hair and neatly groomed beard. He held a swatch of parachute cloth in his hand, and he regarded them steadily. Then he turned aside and muttered something to one of his advisors.

'He has eyes like a cat's,' said Sable.

'Sable – you know who this is, don't you?'

'Of course.' To his astonishment she grinned, more excited than fearful.

Genghis Khan watched them, his black eyes unreadable.

CHAPTER 21

RETURN TO JAMRUD

At dawn Bisesa was woken by the peals of trumpets. When she emerged from the tent, stretching, the world was suffused with blue-grey. All across the river delta the trumpet notes rose up with the smoke of the night's fires.

She really was in the camp of Alexander the Great; this was no dream – or nightmare. But mornings were the times she missed Myra the most, and she ached for her daughter, even in this astonishing place.

While the King and his advisors decided what to do, Bisesa, de Morgan and the others had spent the night at the Indus delta camp. The moderns were kept under guard, but they were given a tent of their own to sleep in. The tent itself was made of leather. Battered, scuffed, it *stank*, of horses, food, smoke, and the sweat of soldiers. But it was an officer's tent, and only Alexander and his generals had more luxurious accommodation. Besides, they were soldiers, and used to roughing it, all save Cecil de Morgan, and he had learned better than to complain.

De Morgan had been quiet all night, in fact, but his eyes were alive. Bisesa suspected he was calculating how much leverage he could apply in his new role as an irreplaceable interpreter. But he grumbled about the Macedonians' 'barbaric' Greek accent. 'They turn *ch* into *g* and *th* into *d*. When they say "Philip" it sounds like "Bilip" . . .'

As the day gathered, Eumenes, the Royal Secretary, sent a chamberlain to Bisesa's tent to communicate the King's decision. The bulk of the army would stay here for now, but a detachment of troops – a mere thousand! – would make their way up the Indus valley to Jamrud. Most of them would be Shield Bearers, the shock troops who were used on such ventures as night raids and forced marches, and who were entrusted with Alexander's own safety. The King himself was to make the journey, along with Eumenes and his favourite and lover, Hephaistion. Alexander was evidently intrigued by the prospect of seeing these soldiers from the future in their bastion.

Alexander's army, tempered by years of campaigning, was remarkably well disciplined, and it took only a couple of hours for the preparations to be completed, and the orders for the march to be sounded.

Infantrymen formed up with weapons and light packs on their backs. Each unit, called a *dekas* although it typically contained sixteen men, had a servant and a pack animal to carry its gear. The animals were mostly mules, but there were a few foul-smelling camels. A couple of hundred of Alexander's Macedonian cavalry would ride along with the infantry. Their horses were odd-looking little beasts; Bisesa's phone said they were probably of European or central Asian stock, and they looked clumsy to eyes used to Arabian breeds. The horses had only soft leather shoes and would surely have quickly been ruined by being over-ridden on rocky or broken ground. And they had no stirrups; these short, powerful-looking men gripped their horses' flanks hard with their legs and controlled their mounts with vicious-looking bits.

Bisesa and the British would travel with the Macedonian officers, who walked like their troops – as did even the King's companions and the generals. Only the King was forced by his injuries to ride, on a cart drawn by a team of horses. His personal physician, a Greek called Philip, rode with him.

But after they had set off Bisesa realised that the thousand troops, with their military gear, their servants, pack animals and officers, were only the core of the column. Trailing after them was a rabble of women and children, traders with laden carts, and even a couple of shepherds driving a flock of scrawny-looking sheep. After a couple of hours' marching, this ragged, uncoordinated train stretched back half a kilometre.

Hauling this army and its gear across the countryside

involved an enormous amount of labour, unquestioned by everybody concerned. Still, once they had entered the rhythm of the march, the troopers, some of whom had already marched thousands of kilometres with Alexander, simply endured, setting one hardened foot before the other, as foot-slogging soldiers had always done. Marching was nothing new to Bisesa and the British troops either, and even de Morgan endured it in silence with a fortitude and determination Bisesa grudgingly admired. Sometimes the Macedonians sang odd, wistful songs, in strange keys that sounded out of tune to Bisesa's modern ears. These people of the deep past still seemed so odd to her: short, squat, vivid, as if they belonged to a different species altogether.

When she got the chance, Bisesa studied the King.

Seated on a gloriously heavy-looking golden throne, being hauled across India by animal-power, Alexander was dressed in a girdle and striped tunic, with a golden diadem around the purple Macedonian hat on his head, and holding a golden sceptre. There wasn't much of the Greek to be seen about Alexander. Perhaps his adoption of Persian ways was more than just diplomatic; perhaps he had been seduced by the grandeur and wealth of that empire.

As he travelled his tame prophet Aristander sat at his side, a bearded old man in a grimy white tunic and with sharp, calculating eyes. Bisesa speculated that this hand-waver might be concerned about the impact of people from the future on his position as the King's official seer. Meanwhile the Persian eunuch called Bagoas leaned nonchalantly against the back of the throne. He was a pretty, heavily made up young man in a kind of diaphanous toga, who from time to time stroked the back of the King's head. Bisesa was amused by the weary glares Hephaistion shot at this creature.

Alexander, though, slumped on his throne. It hadn't been hard for Bisesa to figure out, with the help of the phone, just *when* in his career she had encountered him. So she knew he was thirty-two, and though his body was powerful, he looked exhausted. After years of campaigning, in which he led his men into the thick of it with a self-sacrificing bravery that must have sometimes bordered on folly, Alexander bore the results of several major injuries. He even seemed to have difficulty breathing, and when he stood it was only through extraordinary willpower.

It was strange to think that this still-young man had already come to rule more than two million square kilometres, and that history was a matter of his whim – and stranger yet to remember that in the time-line of Earth his campaign had already passed its high water mark. His death would have been only months away, and the proud, loyal officers who followed him now would have begun the process of tearing apart Alexander's domains. Bisesa wondered what new destiny awaited him now.

In the middle of the afternoon the march broke, and the travelling army quickly organised itself into a suburb of the sprawling tent city of the Indus delta.

Cooking, it seemed, was a slow and complicated process, and it took some time before the fires were lit, the cauldrons and pots bubbling. But in the meantime there was plenty of drinking, music, dancing, even impromptu theatrical performances. Traders set up their stalls, and a few prostitutes shimmered through the camp before disappearing into the soldiers' tents. Most of the women here, though, were the wives or mistresses of the soldiers. As well as Indians, there were Macedonians, Greeks, Persians, Egyptians – even a few exotic souls whose origin Bisesa barely knew, like Scythians and Bactrians. Many of them had children, some as old as five or six, their complexions and hair colours betraying their complicated origins, and the camp was filled with the incongruous noise of wailing babies.

In the night Bisesa lay in her tent trying to sleep, listening to the crying of babies, the laughing of lovers, and the mournful, drunken wailing of homesick Macedonians. Bisesa had been trained for missions where you were flown in over a few hours, and that usually didn't last more than a day away from base. But Alexander's soldiers had walked out of Macedonia and across Eurasia, travelling as far as the Northwest Frontier.

She tried to imagine how it must have been to have followed Alexander for *years*, to have walked to places so remote and unexplored that this city-army might as well have been campaigning on the Moon.

After a few days of the march, there were complaints of peculiar sicknesses among the Macedonians and their followers. These infections hit hard, and there were some deaths, but the crude field medicine of Bisesa and the British was able to diagnose them and to some extent treat them. It was obvious to Bisesa that the British, and she, had brought bugs from the future to which the Macedonians had no immunity: the Macedonians had been subject to many novel plagues during their odyssey, but the far future was a place even they hadn't breached. It was probably lucky for all concerned that these infections quickly died out. There was no sign of reverse infections, of the British by bugs carried by the Macedonians; Bisesa imagined an epidemiologist could work up an academic paper about that chronological asymmetry.

Day by day the march went on. Guided by Alexander's own scouts, and the careful surveys he had had made of the Indus valley, they followed a different route back to Jamrud than that taken by Bisesa on the way down.

One day, no more than a couple of days out of Jamrud, they came to a city that none of them recognised. The march halted, and Alexander sent a party of scouts to investigate, accompanied by Bisesa and some of the British.

The city was well laid out. About the size of a large shopping mall, it was based on two earth mounds, each walled by massive ramparts of hard-baked mud brick. It was a well planned place, with wide, straight avenues set out according to a grid system, and it looked to have been recently inhabited. But when the scouts passed cautiously through its gates, they found nobody within, no people at all.

It wasn't old enough to be a ruin; it was too well preserved for that. Such features as wooden roofs were still intact. But the abandonment was not recent. The few remaining bits of furniture and pottery were broken, if any food had been left behind the birds and dogs had long taken it away, and everything was covered by rust-brown, drifting dust.

De Morgan pointed out a complicated system of sewers and wells. 'We'll have to tell Kipling,' he said with dry humour. 'A big fan of sewers, is Ruddy. The mark of civilisation, he says.'

The ground was heavily trampled and rutted. When Bisesa dug her hand into the dust she found it was full of flotsam: bits of broken pottery, terracotta bangles, clay marbles, figurine fragments, bits of metal that looked like a trader's weights, tablets inscribed in a script unknown to her. Every square centimetre of the ground seemed to have been heavily trodden, and she walked on layers of detritus, the detritus of centuries. This place must be old, a relic of a time deeper than the British, deeper even than Alexander's foray, old enough to have been covered by the drifting dirt by her own day. It was a reminder that this bit of the world had been inhabited, indeed civilised, for a long, long time – and that the depths of time, dredged by the Discontinuity, contained many unknowns.

But the town had been emptied out, as if the population had just packed up and marched away across the stony plain. Eumenes wondered if the rivers had changed their courses because of the Discontinuity, and the people had gone in search of water. But the abandonment looked too far in the past for that.

No answers were forthcoming. The soldiers, Macedonian and British alike, were spooked by the empty, echoing place, this Marie Celeste of a town. They didn't even stay the night before moving on.

After several days' march, Alexander's train arrived at Jamrud, to astonishment and consternation on all sides.

Still on crutches, Casey hobbled out to meet Bisesa and embraced her. 'I wouldn't have believed it. And Jeez, the stink.'

She grinned. 'That's what a fortnight eating curry under a

leather tent does for you. Strange – Jamrud seems almost like home to me now, Rudyard Kipling and all.'

Casey grunted. 'Well, something tells me it's all the home you and I are going to have for a while, for I don't see any sign of a way back yet. Come on up to the fort. Guess what Abdikadir managed to set up? *A shower.* Goes to show heathens have their uses – the smart ones anyhow . . .'

At the fort Abdikadir, Ruddy and Josh crowded around her, eager for her impressions. Josh was predictably glad to see her, his small face creased by smiles. She was pleased to get back to his bright, awkward company.

He asked, 'What do you think of our new friend Alexander?'

Bisesa said heavily, 'We have to live with him. His forces outnumber ours – I mean, Captain Grove's – by maybe a hundred to one. I think for now that Alexander is the only show in town.'

'And,' said Ruddy silkily, 'Bisesa undoubtedly thinks that Alexander is a fine fellow for his limpid eyes and his shining hair that spills over his shoulders—'

Josh blushed furiously.

Ruddy said, 'What about you, Abdi? It's not everybody who gets to confront such a deep family legend.'

Abdikadir smiled, and ran his hand over his blond hair. 'Maybe I'll get to shoot my great-to-the-nth grandfather and prove all those paradoxes wrong after all.' But he wanted to get down to business. He was keen to show Bisesa something – and not just his patent shower. 'I took a trip back to the bit of the twenty-first century that brought us here, Bisesa. There was a cave I wanted to check out . . .'

He led her to a storeroom in the fort. He held up a gun, a big rifle. It had been wrapped in dirty rags, but its metal gleamed with oil. 'There was an intelligence report that this stuff was here,' he said. 'It was one of the objectives for our mission in the Bird that day.' There were flash-bang grenades, a few old Soviet-era grenades. He bent and picked one up; it was like a soup can mounted on a stick. 'Not much of a stash, but here it is.'

Josh touched the barrel of the gun cautiously. 'I've never seen such a weapon.'

'It's a Kalashnikov. An antique in my day, a weapon left over from the Soviet invasion, which is to say maybe fifty years before our time. Still works fine, I should imagine. The hill fighters always loved their Kalashnikovs. Nothing so reliable. You don't even have to clean it, which many of those boys never bothered to do.'

'Twenty-first-century killing machines,' Ruddy said uneasily. 'Remarkable.'

'The question is,' Bisesa said, 'what to do with this stuff. Could we justify using twenty-first-century guns against, say, an Iron Age army, no matter what the odds?'

Ruddy peered at the gun. 'Bisesa, we have no idea what waits out there for us. We did not choose this situation, and whatever manner of creature or accident has stranded us here did not take much notice of our welfare. I would say nice moral questions are beside the point, and that pragmatism is the order of the day. Wouldn't it be foolish not to preserve these muscles of steel and gunpowder?'

Josh sighed. 'You're as pompous as ever, Ruddy, my friend. But I have to agree with you.'

Alexander's army unit set up its camp half a kilometre from Jamrud. Soon the fires were lit, and the usual extraordinary mixture of military base and travelling circus established itself. That first evening there was a great deal of suspicion between the two camps, and British and Macedonian troops patrolled up and down an implicitly agreed border.

But the ice began to break on the second day. It was Casey who started it, in fact. After spending some time in the border zone, facing down a short, squat Macedonian veteran who looked about fifty, Casey, with gestures, challenged him to a milling. Bisesa knew what this was about: a tradition among some military units where you joined in a one-minute, no-rules, no-holds-barred boxing match and simply tried to beat the living shit out of your opponent.

Despite his aggression, it was obvious to everybody that

one-legged Casey was in no shape for such a contest, and Corporal Batson stepped into the breach. Stripped to trousers and braces, the Geordie might have been a twin of the squat Macedonian. A crowd quickly gathered, and as the contest was joined the baying of each side for its champion rose up. 'Get stuck in, Joe!' '*Alalalalai!*' Casey timed the contest, breaking it up after its regulation minute, by which time Batson had taken a lot of blows to his body, while the Macedonian's nose looked broken. There was no clear winner, but Bisesa could see a grudging respect had been established, the crude regard of one fighting soldier for another, just as Casey had intended.

There was no shortage of volunteers for the next match. When one sepoy came away with a broken arm, the officers stepped in. But a new sporting contest began at the Macedonians' suggestion, this time a game of *sphaira*. This Macedonian tradition turned out to be a game played with a leather ball, a pick-up-and-run affair a bit like British rugby or American football, but a *lot* more violent. Again Casey got involved, marking out the pitch, agreeing rules, and acting as referee.

Later, some of the Tommies tried to teach the Macedonians the rules of cricket. Bowlers hurled a hard cork ball, battered by overuse, down a strip of dirt marked by sets of improvised stumps, and batsmen swung homemade bats with abandon. Bisesa and Ruddy paused to watch. The game went well, even if the rule of leg before wicket was a challenge to the Tommies' miming skills.

All this went on right beneath a floating Eye. Ruddy snorted. 'The human mind has a remarkable capacity to swallow strangeness.'

One wild drive sent the ball flying into the air, where it collided with the hovering Eye. It sounded as if the ball had hit a wall of solid rock. The ball bounced back into the hands of a fielder, who raised his hands in triumph at his dismissal of the batsman. Bisesa saw that the Eye was quite unperturbed by this clout.

The cricketers gathered into an arguing knot. Ruddy pulled

his nose. 'As far as I can tell, they are arguing about whether a bounce off the Eye constitutes a valid catch.'

Bisesa shook her head. 'I never understood cricket.'

Thanks to all these initiatives, by the end of that second day much of the tension and mute hostility had bled away, and Bisesa wasn't surprised to see Tommies and sepoys slipping into the Macedonian camp. The Macedonians were happy enough to exchange food, wine and even souvenirs like boots, helmets and Iron Age weapons for glass beads, mouth organs, photographs and other trinkets. And, it seemed, some of the camp prostitutes were prepared to offer their services to these wide-eyed men from the future for no payment at all.

On the third day Eumenes sent a chamberlain to the fort, who summoned Captain Grove and his advisors into the presence of the King.

CHAPTER 22

THE MAP

It was the dirt that Kolya hated most. After a couple of days in the tent city he felt as filthy as a Mongol himself, and as lice-ridden – in fact he believed the parasites were homing in on him, a source of untapped, fresh meat. If the food poisoning didn't kill him, he'd probably be bled to death.

But Sable said they had to fit in. 'Look at Yeh-lu,' she said. 'He's a civilised man. You think he grew up covered in shit? Of course not. And if he can stand it, you can.'

She was right, of course. But it didn't make life with the Mongols any easier.

Genghis Khan, it seemed, was a patient man.

Something incomprehensible had happened to the world. And whatever it was had fractured the Mongol empire, as was shown by the severing of the *yam*, the great empire-wide arteries of waystations and couriers. Well, Genghis Khan had built an empire once, and whatever the state of the world, he would do it again – he, or his able sons. Yeh-lu, however, was advising Genghis Khan to wait. It was always the Mongol way to allow information to be gathered before determining which way to strike, and Genghis Khan listened to his advisors.

During this period of deliberation, though, Genghis Khan was aware of the need to keep his troops fit and occupied. He set up a rigorous programme of training, including long forced marches and rides. And he ordered a *battue* to be organised. This would be a mighty hunt spanning kilometres, and it would take a week to organise. It would be an exercise in manoeuvring troops, using weapons, maintaining discipline, communications, and hardship. It was a significant event; the hunt was at the core of the Mongols' self-image as well as their military methods.

Sable, meanwhile, explored the yurt city. She particularly targeted the troops, hoping to learn how they fought.

The Mongol warriors saw Sable as an irritation. Kolya learned that, given that the usual pattern of courtship here was to kidnap your wife from the yurt of your neighbour, women had surprising influence in Mongol society – as long as they were members of the Golden Family anyhow. Genghis Khan's first wife Borte, about the same age as the emperor, was a key voice in the decision-making of the court. But women didn't fight. The warriors were wary of this strange Heaven-woman in her orange clothes, and they weren't about to submit to her inspections.

The turning point came when one cavalryman, drunk on rice wine, forgot about the power of Heaven and tried to rip open Sable's jumpsuit. He was a stocky, powerful man, a veteran of the Mongols' first Russian campaign, and so probably personally responsible for hundreds of deaths – but he was no match for twenty-first-century martial arts disciplines. With one pale breast exposed, Sable floored him in seconds and left him screaming on the ground, with a leg broken in two places.

After that, Sable rapidly grew in stature and in aura. She was allowed to come and go where she pleased – and she took care to ensure that the tale of her victory, suitably embellished, found its way back to the court. But the Mongols were growing nervous of her, Kolya saw, and that surely wasn't a good thing.

Come to that, *he* was nervous of her. Her fear had long burned away, and as the days wore by, and she pushed against one barrier or another with impunity, she grew in confidence and determination. It was as if her stranding in this bit of the thirteenth century had liberated something primeval inside her.

Kolya, meanwhile, spent his time with Yeh-lu, the empire's chief administrator.

Born in one of the neighbouring nations, Yeh-lu had been

brought into the Mongol camp as a prisoner; an astrologer by training, he had quickly risen in this empire of illiterates. Yeh-lu and other educated men in the court had been appointed by a farsighted Genghis Khan to administer the growing empire.

Yeh-lu had used China as his model for the new state. He selected the most able of the prisoners the Mongols brought back from their raids into northern China to help him in this project, and extracted books and medicines from their booty. Once, he said modestly, he had been able to save many lives during an epidemic in Mongolia by using Chinese medicines and methods.

Yeh-lu sought to moderate the Mongols' cruelty by appealing to higher ambitions. Genghis Khan had actually considered depopulating China to provide more pasture for his horses, but Yeh-lu had deflected him. 'The dead don't pay taxes,' he had said. Kolya suspected his long-term ambition was to civilise the Mongols by allowing the sedentary cultures they conquered to assimilate them, just as China had absorbed and acculturated previous waves of invaders from the northern wastes.

Kolya had no idea how his personal adventure would turn out. But if he was stuck here on Mir, in people like Yeh-lu he saw the best hope for the future. And so he was happy to consult with Yeh-lu about the nature of the new world, and to draw up plans for what to do about it.

Yeh-lu had been taken by Sable's first attempt to sketch a world map on the dirt floor. He and Kolya now assembled a detailed map of the entire world, based on Kolya's memories and charts from the Soyuz. Yeh-lu was an intelligent man who had no difficulty accepting that the world was a sphere – like the Greeks, Chinese scholars had long ago pointed out the curving profile of the Earth's shadow cast on the Moon during a lunar eclipse – and it was easy for him to grasp the mapping of a globe's surface to a flat sheet.

After some preliminary sketching Yeh-lu assembled a team of Chinese scribes. They began work on an immense silk version of the world map. When finished it would cover the floor of one of the yurts in the Emperor's great pavilion.

Yeh-lu was fascinated by the emerging image. He was intrigued how little remained of Eurasia for the Mongols to conquer; from the Mongols' continent-spanning point of view, it seemed a short step from Russia through the countries of western Europe to the Atlantic coast. But Yeh-lu worried about how he would present the map to Genghis Khan, with so many territories in the New World, the Far East and Australasia, southern Africa and Antarctica, of which Genghis Khan had had no knowledge.

The scribes' work was truly beautiful, Kolya thought, with the icecaps picked out in delicate white threads, spun gold following principal rivers, precious stones marking major cities, and the whole covered with careful Mongol lettering – although Kolya learned to his surprise that the Mongols had had no written script at all before Genghis Khan, who had adopted the script of his neighbours the Uighurs as his standard.

The labouring clerks clearly took pride in their work, and Yeh-lu treated them well, congratulating them on their prowess. But the clerks were slaves, Kolya learned, captured during the Mongols' raids on the Chinese nations. Kolya had never met slaves before, and he couldn't help but be fascinated by them. Their posture was always submissive, their eyes dropped, and the women especially cringed from any contact with the Mongols. Perhaps they were favoured in the presence of Yeh-lu, but they were defeated, owned.

Kolya missed his home: his wife, his children, lost in the time streams. But each of these wretched slaves had been ripped from her home, her life trashed, and not by a god-like manipulation of time and space but simply through the cruelty of other human beings. The slaves' plight didn't make his own loss any easier to bear, but it warned him against self-pity.

If he found the presence of the slave clerks difficult to accept, Kolya took comfort in the civilised intelligence of Yeh-lu. After a time it seemed to him that he was finding it easier to trust Yeh-lu, a man from the thirteenth century, than Sable, a woman of his own time.

Sable grew impatient with the careful mapping sessions. And she was not impressed with the plans Yeh-lu was tentatively assembling to present to Genghis Khan.

The first priority ought to be consolidation, in Yeh-lu's view. The Mongols had come to rely on the import of grain, cloth and many other essentials, and so trade had become important to them. As there were few working links left with China, the first and richest part of Genghis Khan's Asiatic empire ought to be explored first. At the same time, Kolya urged, a party should be sent to the valley of the Indus, to seek out Casey and the other refugees from his own time.

But this wasn't bold enough for Sable. After a week she walked into Yeh-lu's chamber and stabbed a knife into the world map. The slave clerks fluttered away like frightened birds. Yeh-lu regarded her with cold interest.

Kolya said, 'Sable, we are still strangers here—'

'Babylon,' she said. She pointed to her knife, which quivered at the heart of Iraq. 'That's where the Khan should be directing his energies. Grain stores, trade routes, the cowing of Chinese peasants – all these are dirt compared to that. Babylon is where the true power behind this new world lies – as you know as well as I do, Kolya – a manifestation of a power which has torn up space and time themselves. If the Khan gets hold of *that*, then his divine mission to rule the planet might come about after all, even in his lifetime.'

In English, incomprehensible to any of their interpreters, Kolya said, 'Power like that, in the hands of *Genghis Khan*? Sable – you're crazy.'

She looked at him, eyes blazing. 'We're eight centuries ahead, remember. We can harness these Mongols.' She waved her hand over the world map, as if laying claim to it. 'It would take generations for anything like a modern civilisation to be built on the fragments of history we have inherited. With the Mongols behind us we could shortcut

176

that to less than a lifetime. Kolya, we can do this. In fact it's more than an opportunity. It's a *duty*.'

Before this fierce woman, Kolya felt weak. 'But this is a raging horse you're trying to ride . . .'

Yeh-lu leaned forward. Through Basil he said, 'You will speak in the common tongues.'

They both apologised, and Kolya repeated a sanitised version of the cosmonauts' discussion.

Delicately Yeh-lu plucked the knife out of the gleaming map, and picked at the damaged threads. To Sable he said, 'Your case is not made. Perhaps we could close our hand on the beating heart of the new world. But we cannot maintain that grip if we starve.'

She shook her head. 'I will take this to the Khan. He would not be so timid as to pass by an opportunity like this.'

Yeh-lu's face closed up, the nearest Kolya ever saw to him growing angry. 'Emissary of Heaven, you do not yet have the ear of Genghis Khan.'

'Just wait,' Sable said in English, and she grinned defiantly, apparently without fear.

CHAPTER 23

CONFERENCE

Answering Alexander's summons, they headed for the King's tent: Captain Grove and his officers, Bisesa, Abdikadir, Cecil de Morgan in his role as interpreter, and Ruddy and Josh, who would record this astonishing conference in their notebooks. On the Macedonian side there would be Alexander himself, Eumenes, Hephaistion, Philip the King's doctor, and an inordinate number of courtiers, advisors, chamberlains and pages.

The setting was magnificent. Alexander's official tent, hauled all the way from the delta, was immense, supported by golden columns and roofed with spangled cloth. Silver-legged sofas had been set up before the King's golden throne for the visitors. But the atmosphere was tense: there must have been a hundred troops standing alert throughout the tent, the infantrymen known as Shield Bearers dressed in scarlet and royal blue, and Immortals from Persia in beautifully embroidered if impractical tunics.

Eumenes, seeking to minimise unnecessary friction, had quietly briefed Bisesa on the protocol expected in the King's presence. So, on entering, the visitors from the future paid the King *proskynesis*, a Greek name for a Persian form of obeisance which involved blowing a kiss at the King and bowing. Abdikadir was predictably uncomfortable with this, but Captain Grove and his officers were unfazed. Evidently these British, stuck out on the edge of their own empire and surrounded by petty princes, rajahs and amirs, were accustomed to respecting eccentric local customs.

Aside from that, Bisesa could see that Abdikadir was enjoying himself hugely. She had met few people as hard-headed as Abdikadir, but he was obviously indulging himself in a pleasant fantasy that these magnificent Macedonians were indeed his ancestors.

The party settled on the couches, pages and ushers circulated with food and drink, and the conference began. The translation, channelled by Greek scholars and de Morgan, was slow and sometimes frustrating. But they got there steadily, sometimes with the aid of maps, drawings or even lettering scrawled on Macedonian wax tablets, or on bits of paper Ruddy or Josh ripped out of their notebooks.

They started with a sharing of information. Alexander's people were not surprised by Jamrud's Evil Eye, which continued to hover over the parade ground. Since 'the day on which the sun had lurched across the sky', as the Macedonians put it, their scouts had seen such things all over the Indus valley. Like the British, the Macedonians had quickly become used to these silent, floating observers, and treated them just as disrespectfully.

Hard-headed Secretary Eumenes was less interested in such silent mysteries than in the politics of the future, which had brought these strangers to the Frontier. It took some time to make Eumenes and the others understand that the British and Bisesa's party were actually from two different eras – though the gap between them, a mere hundred and fifty years or so, was dwarfed by the twenty-four centuries between Alexander's time and Bisesa's. Still, as Captain Grove sketched in the background to the nineteenth-century Great Game, Eumenes showed his quick understanding.

Bisesa had expected her twenty-first-century conflict to be less comprehensible to the Macedonians, but when Abdikadir talked about central Asia's oil reserves Eumenes spoke. He remembered that on the banks of a river in what Bisesa gathered was modern-day Iran, two springs of a strange fluid had welled out of the ground near where the royal tent had been pitched. 'It was no different in taste or brightness from olive oil,' said Eumenes, 'though the ground was unsuited to olive trees.' Even then, he said, Alexander had mused on the profit to be made out of such finds if they were extensive, though his tame prophet Aristander had declared the oil an omen of hard labour ahead. 'We come here in our different times for our different ambitions,' said Eumenes. 'But still we come, even across millennia. Perhaps this is the cockpit of the world for eternity.'

Alexander himself spoke little. He sat on his throne with his head propped on one fist, eyes half-lidded, occasionally looking up with that odd, head-turned, beguiling shyness. He left the conduct of the meeting largely to Eumenes, who struck Bisesa as a very smart cookie, and to Hephaistion, who would interrupt Eumenes, seeking clarification or even contradicting his colleague. It was obvious that there was a lot of tension between Eumenes and Hephaistion, but perhaps Alexander was content for these potential rivals to be divided, Bisesa speculated.

Now the discussion turned to the meaning of what had happened to them all, how history could have been chopped up into pieces, and why.

The Macedonians did not seem as awestruck as Bisesa had naïvely imagined. They had absolutely no doubt that the time-slips were the work of the gods, following their own inscrutable purposes: their world view, which had nothing to do with science, was alien to Bisesa's, but it was easily flexible enough to accommodate such mysteries as this. They were tough-minded warriors who had marched thousands of kilometres into strangeness, and they, and their Greek advisors, were intellectually tough too.

Alexander himself seemed entranced by the philosophical aspects. 'Can the dead live again?' he murmured in his throaty baritone. 'For *I* am long dead to *you* . . . And can the past be restored – old wrongs undone, regrets wiped away?'

Abdikadir murmured to Bisesa, 'A man with as much blood on his hands as this King must find the notion of correcting the past appealing . . .'

Hephaistion was saying, 'Most philosophers view time as a cycle. Like the beating of a heart, the passing of the seasons, the waxing and waning of the Moon. In Babylon the astronomers assembled a cosmic calendar based on the motions of the planets, with a Great Year that lasts, I believe, more than four hundred thousand years. When the planets congregate in one particular constellation, there is a huge fire, and the "winter", marked by a planetary gathering elsewhere, marked by a flood . . . Some even argue that past events repeat *exactly* from one cycle to the next.'

'But that notion troubled Aristotle,' said Alexander, who, Bisesa recalled, had actually studied under that philosopher. 'If I live as much before the fall of Troy as after it, then what *caused* that war?'

'But still,' Hephaistion said, 'if there is something in the notion of cycles, then many strange things can be justified. For instance, oracles and prophets: if time cycles, perhaps prophecy is as much a question of a memory of the deep past as it is a vision of the future. And the strange mixing of times we endure now seems much less inexplicable. Do you agree, Aristander?'

The old seer bowed his head.

So the conversation continued, rattling between Alexander, Hephaistion and Aristander, often too rapidly for the creaky chain of translators to keep up.

Ruddy was entranced. 'How marvellous these men are,' he whispered.

'Enough philosophy,' said Eumenes, practical as ever. He challenged the meeting about what they should do next.

Captain Grove replied that he had a proposal. The British officer had brought along an atlas – a rather antiquated thing, even by his standards, from a Victorian schoolroom – and he now displayed it.

The Macedonians were familiar with maps and mapmaking. Indeed, throughout his campaigns Alexander had brought along Greek surveyors and draughtsmen to map the lands he explored and conquered, many of them barely known to the ancient Greek world he came from. So the Macedonians were fascinated by the atlas, and crowded around the little book excitedly. They were intrigued by the quality of the printing, the regularity of the type and the pages' bright colouring. The Macedonians seemed to have little trouble accepting that the Mediterranean-centred world they knew was only a section of the planet, and that the planet was a sphere, as predicted by Pythagoras centuries before Alexander's time. In fact Aristotle, Alexander's tutor, had written a whole book about the notion. For her part Bisesa was amused by the great swathes inked in pink, to show the territories of the British Empire at its zenith.

At last Alexander, in some exasperation, demanded that the atlas be brought up to his throne. But he was dismayed when he saw the outline of his empire sketched on a whole-Earth map. 'I thought I had made a mighty footprint on the world, but there is so much I never even saw,' he said.

Using the atlas, Captain Grove said that his proposal was that the forces, combined, should make for Babylon.

Abdikadir tried to explain about the radio signals picked up by the Soyuz. This was predictably baffling, until Ruddy and Josh hit on happy metaphors. 'Like the sound of inaudible trumpets,' Ruddy said. 'Or the flash of invisible mirrors . . .'

Abdikadir said, 'And the only signal we have found came from *here*.' He pointed to Babylon. 'There is surely our best chance of determining what has happened to us, and to the world.' All this was transmitted to Alexander.

Babylon struck chords with the Macedonians too. There had been no news from Macedon or anywhere else beyond the Indus valley for many days now, and nor had the British received any messages from their own time. There was the question of where they should settle, if no news was forthcoming. Alexander had always planned to make Babylon a capital of an empire which might have stretched from the Mediterranean to India, united by sea and river routes. Perhaps even now that dream might be achievable, even with the resources the King had to hand, even if the rest of the world he had known had vanished.

For all these reasons the best path seemed clear. As the consensus emerged Ruddy was thrilled. 'Babylon! By God – where will this adventure not take us?'

The meeting quickly got down to detailed questions of timetables and logistics. The light beyond the tent grew dimmer, circulating servants brought more wine, and the assembly slowly grew more raucous.

When they could get away from the Macedonians, Josh, Abdikadir, Ruddy and Bisesa gathered.

Bisesa said, 'We'll have to leave something for Sable, Musa and Kolya, in case they ever make it here.' They discussed markers such as big stone arrows on the ground, cairns with messages, even leaving radios for the stranded cosmonauts.

'And are you happy,' said Abdikadir, 'that we are throwing in our lot with Alexander and his crew?'

'Yes,' said Ruddy immediately. 'Aristotle taught these fellows openness of mind and heart, and a curiosity about the world. Alexander's journey was as much an exploration as an expedition of conquest.'

'Captain Cook with a fifty-thousand-man army,' Abdikadir mused.

'And surely,' Ruddy said, 'it was this very openness that enabled them to accept the customs of unfamiliar peoples – and so to weld an empire that, if not for the untimely death of Alexander, might have endured for centuries, and advanced civilisation by a thousand years.'

'But *here*,' Josh said, 'Alexander isn't dead . . .'

Bisesa was aware that Alexander was watching them. He leaned back and murmured something to the eunuch, and she wondered if he heard what they said.

Ruddy finished, 'I can think of no finer legacy than to have established a "British Empire" in Asia and Europe two thousand years or more before its time!'

'But Alexander's empire,' Josh said, 'had nothing to do with democracy or Greek values. He committed atrocities – he burned Persepolis, for instance. He paid for each section of his endless campaign with the loot from the last. And he spent lives like matches – perhaps three quarters of a million, by some estimates.'

'He was a man of his time,' said Ruddy, stern and cynical as if he were twice his age. 'What can you expect? In his world, order derived only from empire. Within the empire's borders you had culture, order, a chance at civilisation. Outside there were only barbarians and chaos. There was no other way to run things! *And* his achievement endured, even if his empire did not. He spread the Greek language from Alexandria to Syria like jam over toast. When the Romans pushed east they found, not barbarians, but Greek-speakers. If not for that Greek legacy, Christianity would have had a hard time spreading out of Judea.'

'Perhaps,' Abdikadir said, grinning. 'But, Kipling – I'm not a Christian!'

Captain Grove joined them. 'I suspect our business is done,' he said quietly. 'I'm jolly pleased we came to such a quick agreement, and it's remarkable how much we hold in common. I suppose nothing fundamental has changed in two thousand years when it comes to carting an army around the place . . . But look here: I think the gathering is starting to degenerate a bit. I've heard about Alexander and his debaucheries,' he said with a rueful grin, 'and much as I'd rather give it a miss I fear it would be politic of me to stick around, and do a little getting-to-know-you with these chaps. Don't worry, I can handle my wine! My lads will stay on too, but if you want to slip away . . .'

Bisesa accepted the excuse. Ruddy and Josh agreed to leave too, though Ruddy looked back with envy at the shimmering interior of the royal tent, where a curvaceous young woman dressed only in a floor-length veil was starting to dance.

Outside the tent Bisesa found Philip, Alexander's Greek doctor, waiting for her. Bisesa hastily summoned de Morgan. The factor was half-drunk already, but able to translate.

Philip said, 'The King knows you spoke of his death.'

'Ah. I'm sorry.'

'And he wants you to tell him how he will die.'

Bisesa hesitated. 'We have a legend. A tale of what happened to him . . .'

'He will die soon,' Philip breathed.

'Yes. He would have.'

'Where?'

She hesitated again. 'Babylon.'

'Then he will die young, like Achilles, his hero. That's just like Alexander!' Philip glanced back at the King's tent, where, judging from the noise, the debauch was gathering steam. He looked troubled, but resigned. 'Well, it's no surprise. He drinks as he fights, enough for ten men. And he was nearly killed by an arrow in his lung. I fear he will not allow himself time to recover, but—'

'He won't listen to his doctor.'

Philip smiled. 'Some things never change.'

Bisesa made a quick decision. She dug into her survival pack, under her jumpsuit, and pulled out a plastic sheet of malaria tablets. She showed Philip how to pop the pills out of their bubbles. 'Have your King take these,' she said. 'Nobody knows for sure how it happened. The truth was obscured, by rumour, conflict and false history. But some believe it will be of the sickness these tablets will prevent.'

Philip frowned. 'Why do you give me these?'

'Because I think your King is going to be important for all our futures. If he dies, at least it won't be *this* way.'

Philip closed his hand over the sheet of tablets, and smiled. 'Thank you, lady. But tell me . . .'

'Yes?'

'Will they remember him, in the future?'

Again, the strange dilemma of too much knowledge, compounded for Bisesa by long sessions with her phone as she had researched Alexander's story. 'Yes. They even remember his horse!' Bucephalus had died in a battle on the river Jhelum. 'More than a thousand years from now, in the land beyond the Oxus, the rulers will claim that their horses once all had horns on their heads, and were descended from Bucephalus when Alexander passed there.'

Philip was enchanted. 'Alexander had a headdress with golden horns made for Bucephalus in battle. Lady, if the King is ever close to death –'

'Tell him then.'

When he had gone, she turned on de Morgan. 'And *you* keep that to yourself.'

He spread his hands. 'Of course. We must keep Alexander alive. If we are stuck here, he may indeed be our best hope of salvaging something of our future. But by all the gods, Bisesa! Why not *sell* those pills to him? Alexander is a thousand times richer than any other man of his time! What a waste!'

Laughing, she walked away.

CHAPTER 24

THE HUNT

At last the *battue* was ready.

An enormous area of the steppe had been designated for the hunt, which was run as a military exercise. Army units were deployed in a great cordon, each with a full general in command. The beaters closed in towards the centre, moving as if on manoeuvres, with scouts in advance of the main body of troops, and flanking sections to either side. Trumpets and flags were used to communicate around this mass of troops, and once it was closed the circle was maintained with great precision.

When the beating began, Genghis Khan himself led the imperial procession to a low ridge, which would serve as a good viewpoint. All the Golden Family were required to be present, along with Genghis's wives and concubines, chamberlains and servants. Yeh-lu travelled with the royal party, and brought Kolya, Sable and their interpreters with him.

The scale of the exercise was startling. When he took his place at the summit of the ridge Kolya could see only a couple of military units, drawn up in formation, standards flying, horses restless, on the plain below; the rest were somewhere over the horizon. And he was stunned by the opulence of the food, drink and other hospitality laid on for the royal party.

While they waited for the beating to be completed, the Golden Family were kept amused by falconry displays. One man brought forward a mighty eagle, perched on a massive hawking glove. When the bird stretched its wings, their span was wider than the keeper was tall. A lamb was released, and the bird lunged with a ferocity that dragged the keeper off his feet, to the hilarity of the royal party.

The falconry was followed by horse races. Mongol races were conducted over kilometres, and only the finishing stages were visible from Kolya's position. The child jockeys, surely no older than seven or eight, rode their full-sized mounts bareback and barefoot. The riding was ferocious, and the finishes, masked by a billowing cloud of dust, were close. The Golden Family threw gold and jewels at the victors.

As far as Kolya was concerned, all this was another example of the Mongols' mixture of barbarity and vulgar ostentation – or, as Sable put it, 'These people really don't have any taste.' But Kolya could not deny the calm aura of Genghis Khan himself.

Militarily disciplined, politically astute, single-minded and incorruptible, Genghis Khan had been born the son of a clan chief. He was called Temuchin, which meant 'smith'; his adopted name meant 'universal ruler'. It took a decade of fratricidal conflict for Temuchin to unite the Mongols into a single nation for the first time in generations, and he became 'the ruler of all tribes who live in felt tents'.

Mongol armies consisted almost entirely of cavalry, highly mobile, disciplined and fast-moving. Their fighting style had been honed over generations in hunting and warring across the plains. For the sedentary nations of farms and cities around the fringe of the steppe, the Mongols were difficult neighbours, but they weren't exceptional. For centuries the great land-ocean of Asia had spawned armies of marauding horsemen; the Mongols were just the latest in that long and bloody tradition. But under Genghis Khan they became a fury.

Genghis Khan began his campaigns against the three nations of China. Rapidly growing rich on plunder, the Mongols next turned west, assailing Khwarazm, a rich and ancient Islamic state that stretched from Iran to the Caspian Sea. After that the Mongols pushed on through the Caucasus into the Ukraine and Crimea, and struck north in an out-rageous raid on Russia. By the time of Genghis Khan's death, his empire, built in a single generation, was already four times as extensive as Alexander's, and twice as large as Rome's ever became.

But Genghis Khan remained a barbarian, his only purpose the empowerment and enrichment of his Golden Family. And the Mongols were killers. Their ruthlessness derived from their own traditions: illiterate nomads, they saw no purpose in agriculture, no value in cities save as mines of plunder – and they placed no value on human life. This was the creed applied to each conquest.

Now Kolya had been magically transported to the heart of the Mongol empire itself. Here, the benefits of the empire were more apparent than in history books written by descendants of the vanquished. For the first time in history Asia had been united, from the boundaries of Europe to the South China Sea: the tapestries that adorned Genghis's tents combined Chinese dragon designs with Iranian phoenixes. Though contact would be lost after the Mongols' empire decayed, myths of eastern nations were replaced by memory – a memory that would one day inspire Christopher Columbus to strike out across the Atlantic Ocean, seeking a new route to Cathay.

But in the overrun lands the suffering was vast. Ancient cities were erased, whole populations slaughtered. Compared to the human misery Kolya was able to perceive, even in the pavilion of Genghis Khan himself, the benefits of the empire seemed of little worth indeed.

But Sable, he saw clearly, was drawn to the Mongols' rapacious glamour.

At last the beating troops appeared over the horizon, yelling and crying, and converged on the hunting ground. Runners stretched ropes between the army groups, making a cordon. Cornered animals lumbered or raced to and fro, dimly visible in the great cloud of dust they raised.

Kolya peered into the dust clouds. 'I wonder what they've caught. I see horses – asses maybe – wolves, hyenas, foxes, camels, hares – they are all terrified.'

Sable pointed. 'Look over there.'

A larger shape loomed through the dust. It was like a great

boulder, Kolya thought at first, a thing of the earth, much taller than a human being. But it moved massively, immense shoulders working, and curtains of rust-brown hair shimmered. When it raised its head, he saw a curling trunk, spiral tusks, and he heard a peal like a Bach trumpet.

'*A mammoth*,' he breathed. 'Genghis's hunters, crossing the time-slips, have trapped more than they bargained for – it is the dream of ages to witness this. If only we had a camera!'

But Sable was indifferent.

A little stiffly, Genghis Khan mounted his horse. He rode forward, with a couple of guards to either side. It was his privilege to make the first kill. He took position not twenty metres below Kolya, and waited for the prey to be shepherded to him.

Suddenly there were screams. Some of Genghis's guards broke ranks and fled, despite the howls of their commanders. Through the billowing dust before Genghis, Kolya saw a red rag flung through the air – no, not a rag, it was a *human being*, a Mongol warrior, his chest ripped open, entrails dangling.

Genghis Khan held his ground, holding his horse steady, his lance and scimitar raised.

Kolya saw the beast coming, emerging from the dust. It was like a lion in its stealthy advance, but it was massively muscled, its shoulders more like a bear's. And when it opened its mouth it revealed teeth that curved like Genghis Khan's scimitar. In a moment of deadly stillness, Emperor and sabre-tooth cat faced each other.

Then a single shot rang out, as unexpected as a clap of thunder from a clear sky. It was so close to Kolya his ears rang, and he heard the hiss of the bullet as it flew. Around Kolya the royal party and their attendants screamed and quailed. Suddenly the cat lay in the dirt, its hind legs twitching, its head exploded to a bloody mass. Genghis's horse was shying, but the Emperor had not flinched.

It had been Sable, of course. But she had already hidden the pistol.

Sable spread her arms. '*Tengri!* I am the Emissary of Heaven, sent to save you, great one, for you are intended to

190

live for ever, and to rule all the world!' She turned to a whimpering Basil. In broken French she hissed, 'Translate, you dog, or it will be your head I take off next.'

Genghis Khan stared up at her.

The slaughter of the animals inside the cordon took days. It was customary for some of the animals to be let loose, but on this occasion, as Genghis's life had been threatened, none was allowed to live.

Kolya inspected the remains curiously. The heads and tusks of several mammoths were presented to Genghis, along with a pride of lions of a size nobody had seen before, and foxes with coats of a beautiful snowy whiteness.

And there were a strange kind of people, too, caught up in the Mongols' net. Naked, fast-running but unable to escape, they were a small family, a man, woman and boy. The man was dispatched immediately, and the woman and child brought in chains to the royal household. The creatures were naked and filthy, and seemed to have no speech. The woman was given to the soldiers for their sport, and the child was kept in a cage for a few days. Without his parents, the child would not eat, and rapidly weakened.

Kolya saw him close to just once. Sitting squat on the ground inside his cage, the boy was tall – taller than all the Mongols, even taller than Kolya – but his face and body had the unformed look of a child. His skin was weather-beaten and his feet were callused. There wasn't an ounce of fat on his body, but his muscles were hard. He looked as if he could run all day without a break. Over his eyes was a heavy ridge of bone. When he looked at Kolya his eyes were startling blue, clear as the sky. There was intelligence there, Kolya thought, but it wasn't a human intelligence; it was a blank knowingness, without a centre in self, like the eyes of a lion.

Kolya tried to talk about this with Sable. Perhaps this was some pre-human, a *Homo erectus* perhaps, haplessly caught up in the Discontinuity. But Sable was nowhere to be found.

When Kolya went back, the cage had gone. He learned the

boy had died, his body removed and burned with the rest of the waste from the hunt.

Sable reappeared about noon the day after that. Yeh-lu and Kolya were in the middle of another of their strategy sessions.

Sable was wearing a Mongol tunic, of the expensive, embroidered sort the Golden Family sported, but she had bits of bright orange parachute silk in her hair and around her neck, a badge of her different origins. She looked wild, a creature neither of one world nor the other, out of control.

Yeh-lu sat back and watched her steadily, wary, calculating.

'What happened to you?' Kolya said in English. 'I haven't seen you since you pulled that gun.'

'Spectacular, wasn't it?' she breathed. 'And it worked.'

'What do you mean, "it worked"? Genghis could have had you killed, for violating his priority in the hunt.'

'But he didn't. He called me to his yurt. He sent out everybody, even the interpreters – there were just the two of us. I think he really believes now that I am from his *Tengri*. You know, when I went to him Genghis had been drinking for hours, so I cured his hangover. I kissed his cup of wine. I slipped in a few aspirins I'd put in my mouth. It was so easy. I tell you, Kolya—'

'What did you offer him, Sable?'

'What he wants. Long ago he was given a divine mission, via a shaman. Genghis is *Tengri*'s representative on Earth, sent to rule over all of us. He knows his mission isn't complete yet – and since the Discontinuity he's actually gone backward – but he also knows he's getting older. That Communist monument recording the date of his death spooked the bejasus out of him. He wants time to complete his mission – *he wants immortality*. And that's what I offered him. I told him that in Babylon he will find the philosopher's stone.'

Kolya gasped, 'You're crazy.'

'How do you know, Kolya? We've no idea what waits for us in Babylon. Who knows what's possible? And who is to stop us?' She sneered. 'Casey? Those dumb-ass Brits in India?'

192

Kolya hesitated. 'Did Genghis take you to his bed?'

She smiled. 'I knew he would be put off by clean flesh. So I took a little dung from his favourite horse, and rubbed it in my scalp. I even rolled around in the dirt a bit. It worked. And you know, he liked my skin. The smoothness – the absence of disease scars. He may not like hygiene, but he likes its results.' Her face darkened. 'He took me from behind. The Mongols make love about as subtly as they wage war. Some day that hard-faced bastard will pay for that.'

'*Sable*—'

'But not today. He got what he wanted, and so did I.' She beckoned Basil. 'You, Frenchie. Tell Yeh-lu that Genghis has decided. The Mongols would have reached Iraq anyhow, in a generation or so; the campaign won't be a challenge for them. The *quriltai*, the council of war, has already been called.' She took a dagger from her boot, and thrust it into the map, where she had placed it before, into Babylon. This time nobody dared remove it.

Time's Eye

PART FOUR

THE CONFLUENCE
OF HISTORY

CHAPTER 25

THE FLEET

Bisesa thought that Alexander's fleet, gathered offshore, looked magnificent despite the rain. There were triremes with their banks of oars, horses whinnied nervously on flat-bottomed barges, and most impressive of all were the *zohruks*, shallow-draught grain-lighters, an Indian design that would persist to the twenty-first century. The rain fell in sheets, obscuring everything, washing out colours and softening lines and perspectives, but it was hot, and the oarsmen went naked, their brown, wiry bodies glistening, the water plastering their hair flat and running down their faces.

Bisesa couldn't resist taking snaps of the spectacle. But the phone was complaining. 'What do you think this is, a theme park? You're going to fill my memory long before we get to Babylon, and then what will you do? *And* I'm getting wet.'

Alexander meanwhile was seeking the gods' approval of the coming journey. Standing at the bow of his ship, he poured libations from a golden bowl into the water, and called on Poseidon, the sea-nymphs, and the spirits of the World Ocean to preserve and protect his fleet. Then he went on to make offerings to Heracles, who he supposed was his ancestor, and Ammon, the Egyptian god he had come to identify with Zeus, and indeed had 'discovered' to be his own father at a shrine in the desert.

The few hundred nineteenth-century British troops, drawn up in rough order by their officers, watched with amazement, and some ribald comments, as the King did his divine duty. But Tommies and sepoys alike had been happy enough to accept the hospitality of the Macedonian camp; Alexander's gestures today were the finale of days of sacrifices and celebration, of musical festivals and athletic contests. Last night the King had given a 'sacrificial' animal, a sheep, cow or goat, to each platoon. It had been, Bisesa thought, like the mightiest barbecue in history.

Ruddy Kipling, standing with his broad face sheltered by a peaked cap, pulled irritably at his moustache. 'What nonsense fills the minds of men! You know, as a child my ayah was a Roman Catholic, who would take us children to church – the one by the Botanical Gardens in Parel, if you know it. I liked the solemnity and dignity of it all. But then we had a bearer called Meeta who would teach us local songs and take us to Hindu temples. I rather liked their dimly seen but friendly gods.'

Abdikadir said dryly, 'An interestingly ecumenical childhood.'

'Perhaps,' Ruddy said. 'But stories told to children are one thing, and the ludicrous Hindu pantheon is little more than that: monstrous and inane, and littered with obscene phallic images! And what is it but a remote echo of this nonsensical crew on whom Alexander wastes good wine – indeed, of whom he believes himself to be a part?'

'Ruddy, when in Rome, do as the Romans do,' Josh said.

Ruddy clapped him on the back. 'But, chum, hereabouts Rome probably hasn't been built! So *what* am I to do? Eh, eh?'

The ceremonies finished at last. Bisesa and the others made for the boats that would transfer them to the ships. They and most of the British troops were to sail with the fleet, with about half of Alexander's army, while the rump would follow the shore.

The army camp broke up, and the baggage train began to form. It was a chaotic scene, with thousands of men, women, children, ponies, mules, bullocks, goats and sheep, all milling around. There were carts laden with goods and tools for the cooks, carpenters, cobblers, armourers and other craftsmen and traders who followed the army. More enigmatic shapes of wood and iron were catapults and siege engines, broken down into kit form. Prostitutes and water-carriers worked the crowd, and Bisesa saw the proud heads of camels lifting above the crush. The noise was extraordinary, a clamour of voices, bells and trumpets, and the complaints of draught animals. The presence of the bewildered man-apes, confined in a lashed-up cage on their own cart, only added to the circus-like atmosphere of the whole venture.

The moderns marvelled. 'What a gagglefuck,' Casey said. 'I have never seen anything like it in my life.'

But it was all somehow coming together. The coxes began to shout, and oars splashed in the water. And on land and on the sea, Alexander's followers began to join in rhythmic songs.

Abdikadir said, 'The songs of Sinde. A magnificent sound – tens of thousands of voices united.'

'Come on,' Casey said, 'let's get aboard before those sepoys grab the best deckchairs.'

The plan was that the fleet would sail west across the Arabian Sea and then into the Persian Gulf, while the army and baggage train would track its movements following the southern coasts of Pakistan and Iran. They would meet again at the head of the Gulf, and after that they would strike overland to Babylon. These parallel journeys were necessary; Alexander's boats could not last more than a few days at sea without provisioning from the land.

But on land the going was difficult. The peculiar volcanic rain continued with barely a break, and the sky was a lid of ash-grey cloud. The ground turned to mud, bogging down the carts, animals and humans alike, and the heat remained intense, the humidity extraordinary. The baggage train was soon strung out over kilometres, a chain of suffering, and in its wake it left behind the corpses of broken animals, irreparable bits of equipment – and, after only a few days, people.

Casey couldn't bear the sight of Indian women who had to walk behind the carts or the camels with great heaps of goods piled up on their heads. As Ruddy remarked, 'Have you noticed how these Iron Age chaps lack so much – not just the obvious like gaslights and typewriters and trousers – but blindingly simple things like carthorse collars? I suppose it's just that nobody's thought of it yet, and once it's invented it *stays* invented . . .'

That observation struck Casey. After a few days he sketched a crude wheelbarrow, and went to Alexander's advisors with it. Hephaistion would not consider his proposal, and even Eumenes was sceptical, until Casey put together a hasty, toy-sized prototype to demonstrate the idea.

After that, at the next overnight stop, Eumenes ordered the construction of as many wheelbarrows as could be managed. There was little fresh wood to be had, but the timber from one foundered barge was scavenged and reused. In that first night, under Casey's direction, the carpenters put together more than fifty serviceable barrows, and the next night, having learned from the mistakes of the first batch, nearly a hundred. But then, this was an army that had managed to build a whole fleet for itself on the banks of the Indus; compared to that, knocking together a few wheelbarrows wasn't such a trick.

For the first couple of days after that the train happened to pass over hard, stony ground, and the barrows worked well. It was quite a sight to see the women of Alexander's baggage train happily pushing along barrows that might have come from a garden centre in Middle England, laden with goods, and with children balancing precariously on top. But after that the mud returned, and the barrows bogged down. The Macedonians soon abandoned them, amid much derision of the moderns' new-fangled technology.

Every three days or so the ships had to put in to shore for provisioning. The shore-based troops were expected to live off the land, providing for themselves *and* for the crews and passengers of the ships. That became increasingly difficult away from the Indus delta, as the land grew more barren.

So the sailors would vary their rations with the contents of tidal pools: oysters and sometimes mussels. Once, as Bisesa took part in one of these enjoyable scavenging expeditions, a whale broke the surface of the water, its breath-hole plume erupting perilously close to some of the anchored ships. At first the Macedonians were terrified, though the Indians laughed. A troop of foot soldiers ran into the sea, yelling and hammering at the water with their shields and spears and the flats of their swords. The next time the whale surfaced it was a hundred metres further away from shore, and it was not seen again.

Where the army passed, its scouts surveyed the land and made maps, as Alexander's army had always done. Map-making had also been a crucial tool for the British in establishing and holding their own empire, and now the Greek and Macedonian scouts were joined by British cartographers armed with theodolites. Everywhere they went they drew new maps and compared them with the old, from before the Discontinuity.

They encountered few people, however.

Once the army scouts found a crowd of around a hundred, men, women and children, they said, dressed in strange, bright clothes that were nevertheless falling to rags. They were dying of thirst, and they spoke in a tongue none of the Macedonians could recognise. None of the British or Bisesa's party got a first-hand glimpse of this crowd. Abdikadir speculated that they could have come from a hotel from the twentieth or even twenty-first century. Cut off when their home vanished into the corridors of time, left to wander, such refugees were like negative-image ruins, Bisesa thought. In a normally flowing history the people would vanish and leave their city slowly to decay into the sand; here it was the other way round. Alexander's troops, ordered to protect the baggage train, had killed a couple of refugees as an example, and driven the rest off.

If people were rare, the Eyes were a continual presence. As they worked along the coast, they found Eyes hovering like lamps along the shoreline, one every few kilometres, and in a loose array covering the interior.

Most people ignored them, but Bisesa remained queasily fascinated by the Eyes. If an Eye had popped into existence in the old world – if it had come to hover over that old favourite of UFO dreamers, the White House lawn – it would have been an extraordinary event, the sensation of the century.

But most people didn't even want to talk about it. Eumenes was a notable exception; he would stare at the Eyes, hands on hips, as if challenging them to respond.

Despite the attrition of the march, Ruddy's spirits seemed to rise as the days passed. He wrote when he could, in a tiny, crabbed, paper-preserving hand. And he speculated on the state of the world, expounding to whoever would listen.

'We should not stop at Babylon,' he said. He, Bisesa, Abdikadir, Josh, Casey and Cecil de Morgan were sitting under the awning of an officers' ship; the rain rattled on the awning, and hissed on the surface of the sea. 'We should go on – explore Judea, for example. Think about it, Bisesa! The ethereal eye of your space boat could make out only scattered settlements there, a few threads of smoke. What if, in one of those mean huts, even now the Nazarene is taking His first lusty breath? Why, we would be like ten thousand magi, following a strange star.'

'And then there is Mecca,' Abdikadir said dryly.

Ruddy spread his hands expansively. 'Let's be ecumenical about it!'

Bisesa asked, 'So, after your complicated origins, you've ended up a Christian, Ruddy?'

He stroked his moustache. 'Put it this way. Believe in God. Not sure about the Trinity. Can't accept eternal damnation, but there must be some retribution.' He smiled. 'I sound like a Methodist! My father would be pleased. Anyhow I'd be delighted to meet the chap who started it all.'

But Josh said, 'Be careful what you wish for, Ruddy. This is not some vast museum through which we travel. Perhaps you would find Christ in Judea. But what if not? It's unlikely, after all – in fact it's far more likely that all of the Judea we find here has been ripped out of a time *before* Christ's birth.'

'*I* was born after the Incarnation,' Ruddy said firmly. 'There is no doubt about that. And if I could summon up one grandfather after another in a great chain of predecessors I could have them attest to that fact.'

'Yes,' said Josh. 'But you are not in the history of your

grandfathers any more, Ruddy. *What if there has been no Incarnation here?* Then you are a saved man in a pagan world. Are you Virgil, or Dante?'

'I – ah.' Ruddy fell silent, his broad brow furrowed. 'It would take a better theologian than I to puzzle that out. Let's add it to the itinerary: we must seek Augustine, or Aquinas, and ask them what *they* think. And what about you, Abdikadir? What if there is no Mecca – what if Muhammad has yet to be born?'

Abdikadir said, 'Islam is not time-bound, as Christianity is. *Tawhid*, unicity, remains true: on Mir as on Earth, in the past as in the future, there is no god but God, and every particle of the universe, every leaf on every tree, is an expression of His immanence. And the Quran is the unmediated word of God, in this world as in any other, whether His prophet exists here to speak it or not.'

Josh nodded. 'It's a comforting point of view.'

'*As salaam alaikum*,' said Abdikadir.

'Anyhow it may be even more complicated than that,' Bisesa said. 'Mir didn't come from one time-frame, remember. It is a patchwork, and that surely applies in Mecca and Judea. Perhaps there are bits of Judea dating from before Christ's birth, but bits later, where He once walked. So does the Incarnation apply to this universe, or not?'

Ruddy said, 'How strange it is! We are each granted twenty-five thousand days of our lives, say. Is it possible that *we too* are fragmented – that each day has been cut out of our lives like a square from a quilt?' He waved a hand at the ash-grey sky. 'Is it possible there are twenty-five thousand other Ruddys out there somewhere, each picking up his life where he can?'

'One of you mouthy assholes is enough for me,' Casey growled, his first contribution to the debate, and he took a pull from his skin of watered-down wine.

Cecil de Morgan listened to such talk, mostly silently. Bisesa knew he had formed a loose alliance with Alexander's Greek Secretary, Eumenes, and de Morgan reported back such speculations to his new partner. They were both in it for themselves, of course: Eumenes's priority was his own jostling with Alexander's other courtiers, notably Hephaistion; and Cecil was, as always, playing both ends against the middle. But everybody knew that. And Bisesa saw no harm in information flowing through Cecil to Eumenes. They were all in this together, after all.

The fleet sailed on.

CHAPTER 26

THE TEMPLE

When Mongols broke camp, the first task was to round up horses.

Mongol horses lived semi-wild, in herds that were allowed to roam around the plains until needed. There had been some concern that the time-slips might have magicked away many of the herds Genghis Khan's plans relied on, but riders were sent out into the field to bring them in, and after a day great clouds of horses came thundering across the plain towards the metropolis of yurts. The men closed around the horses brandishing long poles with lassos on the end. As if they knew that a march of thousands of kilometres lay ahead of them, the horses bucked and darted defiantly. But once bound, they allowed themselves to be led away stoically.

Kolya thought it was typical of the Mongols' whole uncivilised enterprise that even the greatest campaign should have to start with a rodeo.

After the spectacle of the round-up, the preparations for the march were rapid. Most of the yurts were collapsed and loaded on to carts or baggage animals, but some of the larger tents, including those that had made up Genghis's pavilion, were loaded on to broad-based carts drawn by teams of oxen. Even the Soyuz capsule was to be dragged along. It had been brought here at Genghis's orders from the village of Scacatai; Kolya understood that a siege engine had been adapted to lift it. Sitting on a heavy-duty cart, strapped on by horsehair ropes, it looked like a metal yurt itself.

For his march on Babylon Kolya estimated that Genghis Khan would be accompanied by around twenty thousand warriors, most of them cavalrymen, and each of these accompanied by at least one attendant and two or three spare horses. Genghis organised his travelling force into three divisions: armies of the left wing, and of the right, and of the centre. The centre, commanded by Genghis Khan himself, included the elite imperial guard, including Genghis's own thousand-strong bodyguard. Sable and Kolya would travel with the centre, in the retinue of Yeh-lu.

Some forces were left behind to garrison Mongolia itself, and to continue the task of piecing together what had become of the empire. The garrison would be left under the command of one of Genghis Khan's sons, Tolui. Genghis Khan was not significantly weakened by leaving Tolui behind. As well as his chancellor Yeh-lu he had with him another son, Ogodei, and his general Subedei. Considering that Ogodei was the man who would have succeeded Genghis Khan in the old time-line, and that Subedei was perhaps Genghis's most able general – the man who would have masterminded the invasion of Europe after Genghis's death – it was a formidable team indeed.

Kolya witnessed the moment when Genghis Khan took leave of his son. Genghis drew Tolui's face to his own with his two hands and touched his lips to one of Tolui's cheeks, inhaling deeply. Sable dismissed it as an 'Iron Age air-kiss'. But Kolya was oddly moved.

At last Genghis's standard was raised, and with a clamour of shouts, trumpets and drums, the force set off, followed by long baggage trains. The three columns, under the command of Genghis, Ogodei and Subedei, were to travel independently, perhaps diverging hundreds of kilometres from each other, but they would keep in touch daily, through fast riders, trumpet blasts and smoke signals. Soon the great clouds of kicked-up dust were separating across the plains of Mongolia, and by the second day the forces were out of each other's sight.

Travelling west from the region of Genghis Khan's birthplace, they followed a tributary of the Onon river through a country of rich meadows. Kolya rode in a cart with Sable, Basil and other subdued-looking foreign traders, and some of

Yeh-lu's staff. After the first couple of days, they entered a country of gloomy, somewhat sinister forests, broken by boggy valleys that were frequently difficult to ford. The skies remained leaden, and the rain beat down. Kolya felt oppressed in this dismal, gloomy place. He warned Yeh-lu about acid rain, and the administrator passed on orders that the soldiers should ride with their caps on and collars raised on their coats.

Genghis's troops were no more hygienic than the common Mongols. But they took pride in their appearance. They rode on saddles high at the back and front, with solid stirrups. They wore conical felt caps, lined with fur from fox, wolf or even lynx, and long robe-like coats that opened from top to bottom. The Mongols had worn such garments since time immemorial, but these were a wealthy people now, and some of the officers wore coats embroidered with silk or gold thread, and silken underwear from China. But even Genghis's generals would wipe their mouths on their sleeves, and their hands on their trousers.

The Mongols' field craft was slick and practised – but then it was the product of centuries of tradition. The march was broken each night, and rations distributed: dried milk curd, millet meal, *kumis*, an alcoholic drink made from fermented milk curd, and cured meat. In the morning a rider would put a bit of dried curd and water into a leather bag, and the shaking as he rode along would soon turn it into a kind of yoghurt, consumed with great relish and much belching. Kolya envied the Mongols' skills: how they made rawhide from cow skin, even how they used a distillate of human urine as a purgative when one man had a fever.

Genghis's army moved efficiently, and orders and changes of plan were transmitted rapidly and without confusion. The army was rigidly governed by a hierarchy based on rules of ten. That way, the chain of command was simplified, with each officer having no more than ten subordinates. The Mongols empowered their local commanders as much as possible, which enhanced the army's flexibility and responsiveness. And Genghis made sure that all units of his army, down to the poorest platoon, were made up of a mix of nationalities, clans and tribes. He wanted nobody to have any loyalty, save to the Khan himself. It was, Kolya thought, a remarkably modern way of structuring an army: no wonder these Mongols had overwhelmed the ragbag forces of medieval Europe. But the system relied heavily on efficient and loyal staff. The officer corps was ruthlessly weeded out in training, through such tests as the *battue* – and, of course, in battle.

After a few days, still deep in the heart of Mongolia, the army crossed a grassy plain towards Qaraqorum. This city had once been the power centre of the Uighurs, and Genghis Khan had established it as his own permanent seat of power. But even from a distance Kolya could see the city's walls were ruined. Inside the walls a few abandoned temples huddled in one corner, but the rest of the city had been conquered by the eternal grass.

Genghis Khan himself, accompanied by burly guards, stalked with Ogodei around this place. To Genghis it was only a few years since he had established the city, and now here it was, eroded to rubble. Kolya saw him return to his travelling yurt, his face like thunder, as if he was angry with the very gods who would make such a mockery of his ambitions.

In the days that followed the army passed through the valley of the Orkhon river, an immense walled plain bounded to the east by blue mountains. It was almost like a Martian *vallis*, Kolya thought idly. The earth here was grey and flaking, the river languid. Sometimes they had to ford tributaries and river channels. At night they camped on islands of bare mud, and made huge aromatic fires of dead willow wood.

They crossed one last river, and the country began to rise. Sable said they were leaving the modern Mongolian province of Arhangay, and crossing the Hangayn massif. Behind Kolya, the country folded up into a complex patchwork of forests and valleys, but beyond the massif he could see a more elemental landscape of yellow grassland stretching away.

At the massif's broad summit there were many small ridges and folds, littered by shattered pebbles, as if many time-slips had criss-crossed. But a cairn stood here, a heap of stones that had somehow survived the time shocks. As the army passed each man added a pebble or rock to the cairn. Kolya saw that by the time they had all gone by it would be a mighty mound.

They descended at last to the steppe. The massif receded over the horizon, leaving nothing but flatness, and they walked across a treeless plain where the long grass rippled around the horses like parting water. As the world opened up around him, the immense scale of central Asia at last diminishing even Genghis Khan and his ambitions, Kolya felt a huge relief.

But they encountered no people. In this huge place there could sometimes be seen the circular shadows of yurts, the scars of fires, the ghosts of small villages packed up and moved on to another pasture. The steppe was timeless, people had always lived here much the same way, and these scars could have been made by Huns, Mongols or even Soviet-era Communists – and those who left these shadows might have walked across the plain and into another time entirely. Maybe, Kolya thought, when the last shreds of civilisation wore away, when the Earth was forgotten and nothing was left but Mir, they would all become nomads, drawn into this great pit of human destiny.

But no people. Sometimes Genghis would send out search parties, but nobody was found.

Then, lost in the middle of the steppe, the scouts unexpectedly came upon a temple.

A party was sent ahead to investigate. Yeh-lu included Kolya and Sable, hoping that their perspective might be of use.

The temple was a small, box-like building with tall doors, ornately carved and decorated with lion-head knockers. Out front was a porch framed by lacquered pillars, and the beams at the top were decorated by gold skulls. Kolya, Sable and some of the Mongols stepped cautiously inside. On low tables manuscript rolls had been set out amid the debris of a meal. The walls were wooden, the air full of strong incense, and the feeling of enclosure was powerful.

Kolya found himself whispering. 'Buddhists, you think?'

Sable had no qualms about raising her voice. 'Yes. And at least some of them are still around. No telling *when* this place is from. Buddhists are as timeless as nomads.'

'Not quite,' Kolya said grimly. 'The Soviets tried to purge Mongolia of the temples. This place must predate the twentieth century . . .'

Two figures came shuffling forward from the shadows at the back of the temple. The Mongol soldiers drew their daggers, to be stopped by a sharp word from Yeh-lu's advisor.

At first Kolya thought they were two children, they seemed so similar in size and build. But as they came into the light he saw that one of them was indeed a child, but the other an old man. The old one, evidently a lama, wore a red satin robe and slippers, and he carried a string of amber prayer beads. He was astonishingly thin, his wrists protruding from his sleeves like the bones of a bird. The child was a boy, no older than ten, as tall as the old one, and nearly as skinny. He wore some kind of red robe too, but on his feet were training shoes, Kolya noted with a start. The lama had one skinny arm wrapped around the boy, but the lama was so frail his weight could have been no burden even to a child.

The lama grinned, showing an almost toothless mouth, and began to speak in a rustling voice. The Mongols tried to reply, but it was soon obvious there was no point of contact.

Kolya whispered to Sable, 'Look at the boy's shoes. Maybe this place is more recent than we think.'

Sable grunted. 'The *shoes* are recent. Proves nothing. If these two have been left alone here, the kid must have been out foraging . . .'

'The lama's so old,' Kolya whispered. So he was: his skin looked paper-thin and, stained by age, hung in gentle folds from his bones, and his eyes were a blue so pale they almost seemed transparent. It was as if he had sublimated with age, his substance just evaporated away.

'Yeah,' said Sable. 'Ninety if he's a day. But *look at the two of them*, Kol. Put aside the age gap. Look at their eyes, the bone structure, the chin . . .'

Kolya stared, wishing the light were brighter. The shape of the boy's skull was hidden by a mop of black hair, but his face, his pale blue eyes – 'They look alike.'

'So they do,' Sable said dryly. 'Kolya, when you come to a place like this, it's for life. You arrive as a cadet at eight or nine, you stay here and chant and pray, and you're still at it when you're ninety, if you live that long.'

'Sable—'

'*These two are one*: the same man, the youthful cadet, the aged lama, brought together by faults in time. And the boy knows that when he grows old, he will one day see his own younger self come walking across the steppe.' She grinned. 'They don't seem fazed, do they? Maybe Buddhist philosophy doesn't have to be stretched too far to accommodate what's happened. It's just a circle closing, after all.'

The Mongol soldiers searched desultorily for plunder, but there was nothing to be had save for a few scraps of food, and the petty treasures of worship: prayer-wheels, sacred texts. The Mongols made to kill the monks. They prepared for this without emotion, just a matter of routine; killing was what they did. Kolya plucked up his courage and interceded with Yeh-lu's advisor to stop this.

They left the temple to its paradoxical slumber, and the army moved on.

CHAPTER 27

THE FISH-EATERS

After three weeks of the journey along the coast of the Gulf, Eumenes let the moderns know that the scouts had found an inhabited village.

Driven by curiosity and a need for a break from the sea, Bisesa, Abdikadir, Josh, Ruddy, and a small squad of British soldiers under Corporal Batson joined an advance party at the head of the sprawling train that Alexander's army had become. All the moderns were discreetly equipped with firearms. As they disembarked, Casey, his leg still weak, watched from the boat with envy.

It was a day's walk to the village, and it was a tough slog. Though Ruddy was the first to grumble, they were all soon suffering. If they walked too close to the shore there was nothing but salt and stony ground where nothing grew, but if they went inland, they hit sand dunes over which the going would have been tough even without the rain. There was always a danger of flash floods, as water came pouring down overloaded courses. And even when the rain stopped falling, the horseflies would rise up like clouds.

Snakes were a constant hazard. None of the moderns was able to recognise the varieties they encountered here – but as they might have been drawn from a line of descent that spanned two million years or more, perhaps that wasn't surprising.

Bisesa glared at the unmoving Eyes, effortlessly placed over the most difficult country, which watched her petty struggles as she passed.

At the end of the day the party came to the village. With the Macedonian soldiers, Bisesa and the others crept up the crest of a bluff to see. Close to the shore, it was a poor-looking place. Round-shouldered huts sat squat on the stony ground. A few scrawny sheep grazed the scrubby grass behind the village.

The natives weren't prepossessing. Adults and children alike had long, matted, filthy-looking hair, and the men trailed beards. Their main source of nourishment was fish, which they caught by wading into the water and casting nets made of palm bark. They went about their business dressed crudely in what looked like the treated skin of fish, or maybe even whale.

Ruddy said, 'They are clearly human. But they are Stone Age.'

De Morgan said, 'But they may have come from a time not much before now – I mean, Alexander's era. One of the Macedonians has seen people like this before; he calls them "Fish-Eaters".'

Abdikadir nodded. 'We tend to forget how empty Alexander's world was. A couple of thousand kilometres away you have the Greece of Aristotle – but *here* you have Neolithics, living as they have since the Ice Age, perhaps.'

Bisesa said, 'Then perhaps this new world won't seem so strange to the Macedonians as it does to us.'

The Macedonians treated the Fish-Eaters briskly, driving them off with a volley of arrows. Then the advance party marched into the deserted village.

Bisesa looked around curiously. The stink of fish permeated everything. She found a kind of knife on the ground made of bone, perhaps the scapula of a small whale or dolphin. It had been finely carved, and dolphins danced over its surface.

Josh inspected the huts. 'Look at this. The huts are just skins thrown over frames of whale bones, or – look here – banks of heaped-up oyster shells. Almost everything they have they get from the sea – even their clothes, tools and homes – remarkable!'

As an example of living archaeology, Bisesa thought, this was an unimaginably rich place, and she recorded as much as she could, despite the phone's bleating. But she felt depressed at how much of the past was lost and forever unknowable; this shard of a vanished way of life, torn out of its context, was just another page ripped out of an untitled book, salvaged from a vanished library.

The soldiers were here for provision, not archaeology. But there was little here for them. A store of powdered fish-meal was dug up and taken away. The few wretched sheep were captured and quickly slaughtered, but even their meat turned out to taste dreadfully of fish and salt. Bisesa was dismayed at this casual destruction of the village, but there was nothing she could do about it.

A single Eye hovered over the village of the Fish-Eaters. It watched the Macedonians leave as it had watched them come, with no reaction.

They spent the night not far from the village, close to a stream. The Macedonians set up camp with their customary efficiency, stretching some of their leather tents out on poles as a rough awning to keep off the rain. The British soldiers helped with the work.

Bisesa decided it was time for some proper admin; the toilet facilities on Alexander's ships weren't exactly advanced. The relief at getting her boots off was huge. Briskly she treated her feet. Her socks crackled with sweat and dust, and the gaps between her toes were caked with dirt and what looked like the beginnings of athlete's foot. She was sparing with what was left of her medical kit, which was after all just a small emergency pack, though out in the field like this she continued to use her Puritabs.

She stripped off and dunked herself in the cold water of the stream. She wasn't too concerned by the attentions of her male companions. Lusts were slaked easily enough in the Macedonian camp. Josh watched her, of course, as he always did – but boyishly, and if she caught him he would duck his head and blush. She rinsed out her clothes and left them to dry.

By the time she was done, the Macedonians had built a fire. She lay down on the ground close to the fire, slipped under her poncho, and set her pack as a pillow beneath her head. Josh, as always, manoeuvred himself closest to her, and settled into a position where he could just stare at her when he thought nobody was looking. But behind his back Ruddy and Abdikadir mimed blowing kisses.

Ruddy started holding forth, as he always did. 'We are so few. We've seen a great swathe of the new world now, from Jamrud to the coast of Arabia. Humans are spread thin, and thinking humans thinner! But we keep seeing the emptiness of the land as an absence. We should regard it rather as an opportunity.'

Josh murmured, 'What are you on about, Giggers?'

Ruddy Kipling took off his spectacles and rubbed eyes that looked small and deep. 'Our English Empire has gone now, wiped away like a bridge suit in a card shuffle. Instead we have *this* – Mir, a new world, a blank canvas. And *we*, we few, might be the only source of rationality and science and civilisation left in the world.'

Abdikadir smiled. 'Fair enough, Ruddy, but there aren't too many Englishmen here on Mir to translate that dream into reality.'

'But an Englishman always was a mongrel. And that's not a bad thing. He is the sum of his influences, from the solemn might of the Romans to the fierce intelligence of democracy. Well, then, we must start to build a new England – and forge new Englishmen! – right here in the sands of Arabia. And we can found our new state from the beginning on solid English principles. Every man absolutely independent, so long as he doesn't infringe his neighbour's rights. Prompt and equal justice before God. Toleration of religions and creeds of any shape or form. Every man's home his castle. That sort of thing. It's an opportunity to clear out a lot of clutter.'

'That all sounds marvellous,' said Abdikadir. 'And who's to run the new world empire? Shall we leave it to Alexander?'

Ruddy laughed. 'Alexander achieved marvellous things for his time, but he is a military despot – worse, an Iron Age savage! You saw that display of idol-bothering by the sea. Perhaps he had the right instincts, buried under his armour –

he did cart along the Greeks – but he's not the chap. For the time being we civilised folk must guide. We are few, but *we* have the weapons.' Ruddy lay back, arm behind his head, and closed his eyes. 'I can see it now. The forges will ring out! The Sword will being peace – and peace will bring wealth – and wealth will bring the Law. It's as natural as the growth of a sturdy oak. And *we*, who have seen it all before, will be there to water the sapling.'

He meant to inspire them, but his words seemed hollow to Bisesa, and their camp seemed a small and isolated place, a speck of light in a land empty even of ghosts.

The next day, during the walk back, Ruddy took ill with a severe dose of gut infection. Bisesa and Abdikadir dug into their dwindling twenty-first-century medical packs to give him antibiotics, and made up drinks of sugar and water. Ruddy asked for his opium, insisting it was one of the oldest analgesics in the Indian pharmacopoeia. Still the diarrhoea weakened him, and his broad head looked too heavy on his neck. But he talked and talked.

'We need a new set of myths to bind us,' Ruddy wheezed. 'Myths and rituals; *that's* what makes a nation. That's what America lacks, you know: a young nation, no time yet to grow tradition. Well, America is gone now, and Britain too, and the old stories won't do – not any more.'

Josh said wryly, 'You're just the man to write new ones, Ruddy.'

'We are living in a new age of heroes,' he said. '*This* is the age when the world is built. *That's* our opportunity. And we must tell the future what we did, how we did it and *why* . . .' On Ruddy talked, filling the air with his dreams and plans, until dehydration and breathlessness forced him to stop, and they walked slowly on through the huge, empty desert.

CHAPTER 28

BISHKEK

The army of Genghis Khan skirted the northern edge of the Gobi desert.

The land was vast, a mirror of the dust-clogged sky. Sometimes they would see eroded, tired-looking hills, and once a herd of camels trotted by in the distance, stiff-backed and pompous. When the wind blew, a storm of yellow sand blocked out the light: sand that tasted of iron, sand that might have been formed a million years ago, Kolya thought, or a month. The Mongols, their heads wrapped in cloth, looked like Bedouins.

As the desert crossing wore on, Kolya sank within himself. His mind numbed, his senses dulled, he would sit in the back of the cart, never speaking, a cloth drawn across his face to keep out the dust. The land was so huge and still that sometimes it was as if they weren't moving at all. He grudgingly admired the strength of spirit, the sheer bloody-minded resilience that enabled the Mongols to conquer the immense distances of their Asiatic stage. And yet he had flown in space; and once he would have spanned the distance he had travelled, so vast on the human scale, in fifteen minutes or less.

They came to a great mound of stone and earth, a barrow. It looked like some trapped chthonic beast struggling to escape the clutches of the bone-dry ground. Kolya thought this was a Scythian tomb, a relic of a people who had lived before the birth of Christ, but who had ridden horses and built yurts just like the Mongols. The mound looked fresh, the stones unworn, but the tomb had been broken open, robbed of whatever gold or other wealth it had contained.

And then they came to an almost modern relic. Kolya

glimpsed it only from the distance: tin-roofed cement barns, silos, what looked like a convoy of rusted tractors. Perhaps it was a government agricultural project, abandoned apparently long before the Discontinuity. Perhaps as they moved away from central Mongolia, Kolya mused, they were leaving behind the centre of gravity of this vast continent's history, the terrible reign of Genghis Khan; perhaps here the shards of shattered time had been more free to settle as they willed, bearing refugees from wider expanses. The Mongol scouts inspected the site, pulled around a few sheets of rusted corrugated iron, abandoned it as worthless.

Slowly the country changed. They passed a lake – dry, a sheet of salt. At its edge lizards hopped between the rocks, and flies rose up, troubling the horses. Kolya was startled to hear the desolate cries of seabirds, for there could scarcely be a place in the world further from the sea than this desiccated heartland. Perhaps the birds had followed Asia's complicated network of rivers and become lost here. The parallel with his own situation was obvious, the irony banal.

And still the journey wore on.

To leave modern Mongolia, they would have to pass southeast through a range called the Altay Mountains. Day by day the ground rose, becoming more fertile and better watered. In places there were even flowers: once Kolya found primulas, anemones, orchids, stranded in a dying fragment of steppe spring. They crossed a wide, marshy plain, where plovers wheeled over sodden grass, and the horses plodded carefully through murk that rose to their ankles.

The ground became mountainous. The army squeezed through valleys, each more narrow and higher than the one before. The Mongols called to each other, and their voices echoed from the walls. Sometimes Kolya would see eagles high above, their unmistakable silhouettes painted against the lead-grey sky. Genghis's generals muttered darkly about their vulnerability to ambush here.

At last the land opened up into a vast canyon bounded by walls of shattered rock that reared up towards the sky. Kolya found himself on the ridge at the head of the canyon. An enormous flat-topped mountain loomed over him, streaked by snow and ice like the droppings of immense birds. He looked back, and saw the army of Genghis Khan strung out along the canyon's length, people and animals the colour of mud, with here and there the sparkle of polished armour. But this thin line of people was dwarfed by the towering pinnacles of purple-red rock around them.

They moved on, tracking the north-western border of modern China, heading south-west towards Kyrgyzstan. After that it was only a few more days' ride until they came to the town.

The Mongols, great believers in intelligence, sent scouts and spies creeping around the town, and eventually envoys who walked boldly up its main streets. Citizens in flat caps and buttoned-up jackets marched out, hands extended in friendship to these rank-smelling strangers.

The place was obviously modern, or nearly so. The news of it seemed to jolt Kolya out of the trance into which the journey had plunged him. It was a shock when he heard that the army, and he, had been travelling for nearly three months.

And it was here, as it turned out, that the final stage of his own journey would begin.

Sable was taken forward to help spy out the town. It was Bishkek, she thought, in the twenty-first century the capital of Kyrgyzstan. The place as they had found it was obviously from some pre-electric age, but there were water-mills and factories. 'It could be late nineteenth century,' she said. Metalled roads led into the town, but they were truncated by time-slides a kilometre or so outside town.

More scouts were sent in, and Kolya was taken to translate. The town was a pretty place, its streets lined with trees, wilting a little under the persistent acid rain. Reflecting a deeper history, its main thoroughfare was called Silk Road Street. The townsfolk, cut off and with no idea what had happened, were disturbed by the lack of visits by their tax inspectors, and wanted to know if there were any directives from Moscow, any news of the Tsar. Kolya longed to speak directly to them, but the Mongols wouldn't allow it.

Kolya was excited by the town, the most modern place they had yet encountered. Surely there was a base of equipment and expertise here that could be built on. He pressed Yeh-lu to make friendly contact. But his pleas went unheard, and he began to grow disturbed: the Mongols did not like towns, and knew only one way to deal with them. Sable wouldn't back him up; she merely watched and waited, playing her own complicated game.

Kolya witnessed some of what followed.

The Mongols came in the night, riding in silence. When they charged they roared, and the sound of their voices and the horses' hooves overwhelmed the little town. The killing began in the main street, and swept through the town, a wave of butchery with a bloody froth of slaughter at its leading edge. The townsfolk could put up no resistance save for a few futile pot-shots with antiquated firearms.

Genghis had ordered that the town's ruler be brought out alive. The mayor tried to hide himself and his family in the town's small library, and the building was taken apart brick by brick. His wife was killed before him, his daughters raped, and the man himself trampled to death.

The Mongols found little of value in the town. They broke up the newspaper office's small printing press, bringing out the iron to melt down and reuse. It was the Mongols' habit when taking a town to pick out artisans and other skilled folk who might serve their purposes later, but in Bishkek they were capable of recognising little of what they found: the skills of a clockmaker or accountant or lawyer meant nothing to them. Few men were allowed to live. Most of the children and some of the younger women were taken prisoner, though many of the women were raped. All this was done mechanically, joylessly, even the rapes; it was just what the Mongols did.

When they were done, the Mongols torched the town systematically.

The surviving prisoners were driven out into the countryside towards Genghis's encampment, where they huddled in desolate misery. To Kolya they looked like classic peasant stock, and their waistcoats and trousers, thick skirts and headscarves were the subject of stares from the Mongols. One beauty was picked out for Genghis himself, the fifteen-year-old daughter of an innkeeper, called Natasha. He always took the most beautiful women, and impregnated many of them. Genghis had intended to drive the prisoners on with him, for there were always uses for such wretched souls; they could be driven into battle, for instance. But when he found that one of the Golden Family had been injured by the bullet of a wild-eyed solicitor, he ordered the prisoners to be slain. Yeh-lu's weary pleas for leniency counted for nothing. The women and children submitted meekly.

By the time the army moved on the town was reduced to a smoking ruin, little left of the buildings above foundation level. The Mongols left a heap of severed heads, some of them heartbreakingly tiny. A few days later, Genghis ordered his rearguard to return to the town. A handful of citizens had escaped the slaughter, hiding in cellars and other hideaways. The Mongols rounded these up and put them to death, after enjoying a little more sport.

Sable showed no reaction to this, no emotion at all. But as for Kolya, after Bishkek, his mind seemed clear about what he must do.

CHAPTER 29

BABYLON

It took two months of sailing to reach the head of the Gulf. From there, Alexander was anxious to move inland quickly. He formed up an advance party of a thousand troops, accompanied by Eumenes, Hephaistion and others. Bisesa and her companions made sure they were attached to the expedition.

Within a day of disembarking the party set off for the short march inland to Susa, in Alexander's time the administrative centre of his conquered Persian empire. Alexander was still too weak to ride or walk far, so he rode on a cart covered with purple awnings, a hundred Shield Bearers marching in step around him. They reached Susa without incident, but it was not the Susa Alexander remembered.

Alexander's surveyors had no doubt about the site, at the heart of a sparsely greened plain. But there was no sign of the city, none at all. They might have been the first humans ever to set foot here – as perhaps they were, Bisesa thought.

Eumenes joined the moderns, his face grim. 'I was here only a few years ago. This was a rich place. Every province of the empire contributed to its magnificence, from craftsmen and silversmiths from the Greek cities of the coast, to wooden pillars from India. The treasure here was remarkable. And now . . .' He seemed overcome, and Bisesa glimpsed again the rage she had sensed building in him, as if this intelligent Greek took the Discontinuity personally.

Alexander himself got out of his cart and walked around, peering at the earth, and kicking at clods of dirt. Then he retreated to his awning, and refused to emerge again, as if in disgust.

They camped that night near the vacant site of Susa. The

next morning, guided by Alexander's cartographers, they set off due west, making for Babylon, crossing a vast and echoing land. After Susa, everybody seemed subdued, as if the vast weight of time bore down on them all. Sometimes Bisesa would catch the Macedonians looking at her, and sensed what they were thinking: that here was a woman, living and breathing, who would not be born until everybody they knew, everything they had touched, had eroded to dust, as if she was a living symbol of the Discontinuity.

To everyone's relief they had not gone many kilometres before they reached a junction in time where the surface of the ground dropped a few centimetres, and a road was revealed. It was crudely laid to Bisesa's eyes, topped with coarsely cut stone blocks, but it was undoubtedly a road. In fact, Eumenes told them, it was a section of the Royal Road which had once united Persia – and which Alexander had found extraordinarily useful in his conquest of the empire.

Even on the road, the march took several more days. The land around the road was dust dry, colonised only by scrub vegetation. But it was marked here and there by anonymous mounds of rubble and scarred by great straight-line ditches, evidently artificial but long abandoned, their purpose forgotten.

Each night, when the march broke to make camp, Casey would set up his radio gear and listen for any signals coming from the Soyuz crew, lost somewhere in the unknowable expanses of Asia. It was a time they'd agreed with the crew, but he'd heard nothing since the day of their attempted re-entry. Casey also monitored the radio signal that continued to emanate from the unknown beacon that was presumed to lie in Babylon. Its content remained the same: just a 'chirp', a sweep up through the frequencies like an engineering test signal. But it continued to repeat, over and over. Casey kept a log of his observations, with position, time, signal strength and bearings, and his rough triangulations continued to predict a source inside Babylon.

And then there were the Eyes – or rather, the lack of them. As they walked west, the Eyes were fewer, more spaced out, until at last Bisesa realised she had marched through a whole day without seeing a single one. Nobody had any idea what to make of this.

At last they approached another transition. The advance party came to a line of green that stretched, dead straight, from the northern horizon to the south. The party hesitated on the desiccated side of the border.

To the west, beyond the line, the land was split up into polygonal fields, and striped by glistening canals. Here and there crude-looking wattle-and-daub shacks sat amid the fields, squat and ugly, like lumps of shaped mud. The shacks were clearly occupied, for Bisesa could see traces of smoke rising from some of them. A few goats and bullocks, tethered to posts, patiently chewed on grass or stubble. But there were no people.

Abdikadir stood with Bisesa. 'Babylon's famous irrigation canals.'

'I suppose they must be.' Some of the canals were extensions of the dry, worn-out ditches she had noticed before: the same bits of ancient engineering, severed by centuries. But this crude coupling of the eras obviously caused practical problems; the sections from later eras, ditches silted up by erosion, blocked off the canals from their riverside sources, and some of the farmers' channels were drying up.

Abdikadir said, 'Let's show the way.' He took a deliberate step forward and crossed the invisible, intangible line between the two world slices.

The party crossed the disjunction and moved on.

The richness of the land was obvious. Most of the fields seemed to be stocked with wheat, of a tall, fat-headed variety farmer's daughter Bisesa didn't recognise. But there was also millet and barley, and, here and there, rich stands of date palms. Once, Cecil de Morgan said, the Babylonians would sing songs about these palms, listing their three hundred and sixty uses, one for every day of their year.

Whether the farmers were hiding or not, this obviously wasn't an empty landscape – and it was on the produce of these fields that Alexander's army was going to depend.

There would have to be some gentle diplomacy here, Bisesa realised. The King had the manpower to take whatever he wanted, but the natives knew the land, and this vast and hungry army couldn't afford a single failed crop. Perhaps the first priority ought to be to get Alexander's soldiers and engineers to rebuild the irrigation system . . .

Abdikadir said, 'You know, it's impossible to believe this is Iraq – that we're only a hundred kilometres or so south-west of Baghdad. The agricultural wealth of this place fuelled empires for millennia.'

'But where is everybody?'

Abdi said, 'Can you blame these farmers for hiding? Their rich farmland is sliced in half and replaced by semi-desert. Their canals fail. A stinging rain withers their crops. And then, what looms over the horizon? Only the greatest army the ancient world ever saw – Ah,' he said. '*There*.' He stopped and pointed.

On the western horizon she saw buildings, a complicated wall, a thing like a stepped pyramid, all made grey and misty by distance.

'Babylon,' Abdikadir whispered.

Josh said, 'And *that* is the Tower of Babel.'

'Holy crap,' said Casey.

The army and its baggage train caught up with its head, and spread out into a camp over the mud flats near the banks of the Euphrates.

Alexander chose to wait a day before entering the city itself. He wanted to see if the dignitaries of the city would come out to greet him. Nobody came. He sent out scouts to survey the city walls and its surroundings. They returned safe but, Bisesa thought, they looked shocked.

Time-slips or not, Alexander was going to enter the ancient city in the grand style. So, early in the morning, wearing his gold-embroidered cloak and his royal diadem on his head, he rode ahead towards the city walls, with Hephaistion walking at his side, and a phalanx of a hundred Shield Bearers around him, a rectangle of ferocious muscle and iron. The King showed no sign of the pain the effort to ride must be causing him; once again Bisesa was astounded by his strength of will.

Eumenes and other close companions walked in a loose formation behind the King. Among this party were Captain Grove and his senior officers, a number of British troops and Bisesa and the Bird crew. Bisesa felt oddly self-conscious in the middle of this grand procession, for she and the other moderns towered over the Macedonians, despite the finery of their dress uniforms.

The city's walls were impressive enough in themselves, a triple circuit of baked brick and rubble that must have stretched twenty kilometres around, all surrounded by a moat. But there were no signs of life – no smoke from fires, no soldiers watching vigilantly from the towers – and the great gates hung open.

Eumenes muttered, 'It was different last time, on Alexander's first entry to the city. The satrap rode out to meet us. The road was strewn with flowers, and soldiers came out with tame lions and leopards in cages, and priests and prophets danced to the sound of harps. It was magnificent! It was fitting! But *this* . . .'

This, conceded Bisesa, was scary.

Alexander, as was his reputation, led by example. Without hesitating he walked his horse over the wooden bridge that spanned the moat, and approached the grandest of the gates. This was a high-arched passage set between two heavy square towers.

The procession followed. Even to reach the gate they had to walk up a ramp to a platform perhaps fifteen metres above ground level. As Bisesa walked through it, the gate itself towered twenty metres or more above her head. Every square centimetre of its walls was covered in glazed brick-work, a haunting royal blue surface across which dragons and bulls danced.

Ruddy walked with his head tilted back, his mouth gaping open. Still a little 'seedy' from his illness, he walked uncertainly, and Josh kindly took his arm to lead him. 'Can this be the Ishtar Gate? Who would have thought, who would have thought? . . .'

The city was laid out in a rough rectangle, its plan spanning the Euphrates. Alexander's party had entered from the north, on the east side of the river. Inside the gate, the procession moved down a broad avenue that ran south, passing magnificent, baffling buildings, perhaps temples and palaces. Bisesa glimpsed statues, fountains, and every wall surface was decorated with dazzling glazed bricks and moulded with lions and rosettes. There was so much opulence and detail she couldn't take it all in.

The phone, peeking out of her pocket, tried to help. 'The complex to your right is probably the Palace of Nebuchadnezzar. Babylon's greatest ruler, who—'

'Shut up, phone.'

Casey was hobbling along. 'If this is Babylon, where are the Hanging Gardens?'

'In Nineveh,' said the phone dryly.

'No people,' said Josh uncertainly. 'I see some damage – signs of fires, looting, perhaps even earthquake destruction – but still *no people*. It's getting eerie.'

'Yeah,' growled Casey. 'All the lights on but nobody at home.'

'Have you noticed,' said Abdikadir quietly, 'that the Macedonians seem overwhelmed too? And yet they were here so recently . . .'

It was true. Even wily Eumenes peered around at the city's immense buildings with awe.

'It's possible this isn't their Babylon either,' said Bisesa.

The party began to break up. Alexander and Hephaistion, with most of the guard, made for the royal palace, back towards the gate. Other parties of troops were instructed to spread out through the city and search for inhabitants. The officers' cries rang out peremptorily, echoing from the glazed walls of the temples; de Morgan said they were warning their men of the consequences of looting. 'But I can't imagine anybody will dare touch a thing in this haunted place!'

Bisesa and the others continued on down the processional

way, accompanied by Eumenes and a handful of his advisors and guards. The way led them through a series of walled plazas, and brought them at last to the pyramid-like structure that Bisesa had glimpsed from outside the city. It was actually a ziggurat, a stepped tower of seven terraces rising from a base that must have been a hundred metres on a side. To Bisesa's eyes, conditioned by images of Egyptian pyramids, it looked like something she might have expected to find looming above a lost Mayan city. South of the ziggurat was a temple which the phone said must be the 'Esagila' – the Temple of Marduk, the national god of Babylonia.

The phone said, 'The Babylonians called this ziggurat the "Etemenanki", which meant "the house that is the foundation of Heaven and Earth". It was Nebuchadnezzar who brought the Jews here as slave labour; by bad-mouthing Babylon in the Bible the Jews took a long revenge . . .'

Josh grabbed Bisesa's hand. 'Come on. I want to climb that blooming heap.'

'Why?'

'Because it's the Tower of Babel! Look, there's a staircase on the south side.' He was right; it must have been ten paces wide. 'Race you!' And, dragging her hand, he was off.

She was intrinsically fitter than he was; she had trained as a soldier, and had come from a century far better provided for with food and health care. But he was younger and had been hardened by the relentless marching. It was a fair race, and they kept holding hands until, after a hundred steps or so, they took a break and collapsed on the steps.

From up here the Euphrates was a broad silver ribbon, bright even in the ashen light, that cut through the heart of the city. She couldn't make out clearly the western side of the city, but on this eastern side grand buildings clustered closely – temples, palaces, presumably government departments. The city plan was very orderly. The main roads were all straight, all met at right angles, and all began and ended in one of the many gates in the walls. The palaces were riots of colour, every surface covered with polychrome tiles on which dragons and other fantastic creatures gambolled.

She asked, 'Where are we in time?'

Her phone said, 'If this is the age of Nebuchadnezzar, then perhaps the sixth century BC. The Persians took Babylonia two centuries before Alexander's time, and they bled the area dry. When Alexander arrived it was still a vibrant city, but its best days were already far in the past. We, however, are seeing it at something close to its best.'

Josh studied her. 'You look wistful, Bisesa.'

'I was just thinking.'

'About Myra—'

'I'd love her to be here, to be able to show her this.'

'Maybe someday you'll be able to tell her about it.'

'Yeah, right.'

Ruddy, Abdikadir, Eumenes and de Morgan had followed more slowly up the ziggurat. Ruddy was wheezing, but he made it, and as he sat down Josh clapped him on the back. Eumenes stayed standing, apparently not winded at all, and gazed out at Babylon.

Abdikadir borrowed Bisesa's night goggles and looked around. 'Take a look at the western side of the river . . .'

The line of the walls crossed the river, to complete the city's bisected rectangle. But on the far side of the river, though Bisesa thought she could make out the lines of the streets, there was no colour but the orange-brown of mud-stone, and the walls were reduced to ridges of broken rubble, the gates and watchtowers just mounds of core.

Josh said, 'It looks as if half the city has been melted.'

'Or nuked,' said Abdikadir grimly.

Eumenes spoke. 'It was not like this,' de Morgan translated. 'Not like this . . .' While the eastern half of the city had been ceremonial and administrative, the western half had been residential, crowded with houses, tenement blocks, plazas and markets. Eumenes had seen it that way only a few years before, a vibrant, crowded human city. Now it was all reduced to nothing.

'Another interface,' Abdikadir said grimly. 'The heart of a young Babylon, transplanted into the corpse of the old.'

Eumenes said, 'I believed I was coming to terms with the

strangeness of the faults in time which afflict us. But to see *this* – the face of a city rubbed away into sand, the weight of a thousand years descended in a heartbeat.'

'Yes,' Ruddy said. 'The terrible cruelty of time.'

'More than cruelty,' Eumenes said. 'Arrogance.' Bisesa was insulated from the Secretary's emotions by translation and two millennia of different body language. But again she thought she detected a growing, cold anger in him.

A voice floated up from the ground, a Macedonian officer calling for Eumenes. A search party had found somebody, a Babylonian, hiding in the Temple of Marduk.

CHAPTER 30

THE GATE OF THE GODS

The Macedonians' captive was brought to Eumenes. He was clearly terrified, his eyes wide in a grimy face, and two burly troopers had to drag him. The man was dressed in fine robes, rich blue cloth inlaid with threads of gold. But the robes, ragged and dirty, hung off his frame, as if he hadn't eaten for days. He might once have been clean-shaven and his scalp scoured bare, but now a stubble of black hair was growing back, and his skin was filthy. As he was brought close, Bisesa shrank from a stink of stale urine.

Prodded with a Macedonian stabbing sword, he gabbled freely, but in an antique tongue that none of the moderns recognised. The officer who had found him had had the presence of mind to find a Persian soldier who could understand this language, and so the Babylonian's words were translated into archaic Greek for Eumenes, and then English for the moderns.

De Morgan, frowning, translated uncertainly. 'He says he was a priest of a goddess – I can't make out the name. He was abandoned when the others finally left the temple complex. He has been too frightened to leave the temple. He has been here for six days and nights – he has had no food – no water but that which he drank from the sacred font of the goddess—'

Eumenes snapped his fingers impatiently. 'Give him food and water. And make him tell us what happened here.'

Bit by bit, between ravenous mouthfuls, the priest told his story. It had begun, of course, with the Discontinuity.

One night the priests and other temple staff had been woken by a dreadful wailing. Some of them ran outside. It was dark – *but the stars were in the wrong place*. The wailing

231

came from a temple astronomer, who had been making observations of the 'planets', the wandering stars, as he had every night since he was a small boy. But suddenly his planet had disappeared, and the very constellations had swum around the sky. It had been the astronomer's shock and despair that had begun to rouse the temple, and the rest of the city.

'Of course,' Abdikadir muttered. 'The Babylonians kept careful records of the sky for millennia. They based their philosophy and religion on the great cycles in the sky. It's a strange thought that a less advanced people mightn't have been so terrified . . .'

But that first astronomical trauma, really perceptible only to a religious elite, was just the precursor. For at the end of that night the sun was late rising, by six hours or more. And by the time it did rise, a strange hot wind was washing over the city, and rain fell, hot salty rain of a type nobody had known before.

The people, many still dressed in their nightclothes, fled to the religious district. Some ran to the temples and demanded to be shown that their gods had not abandoned them on this, the strangest dawn of Babylon's history. Others climbed the ziggurat, to see what other changes the night had brought. The King was away – it wasn't clear to Bisesa whether the priest meant Nebuchadnezzar himself, or perhaps a successor – and there was nobody to impose order.

And then the first panicked reports came of the erasure of the western districts. Most of the city's population had actually lived there; for the priests, ministers, court favourites and other dignitaries left on the eastern side, the shock was overwhelming.

The last vestiges of order quickly broke down. A mob had stormed the Temple of Marduk itself. As many as could force their way in had rushed to the innermost chamber, and when they saw what had become of Marduk himself, King of the ancient Babylonian gods—

The priest could not complete his sentence.

After that final shock, a rumour had swept through the city

that the eastern half would be rubbed into dust as had the western. People flung open the gates and ran, screaming, out of the city and into the land beyond. Even government ministers, army commanders and the priests had gone, leaving only this poor wretch, who had huddled in his defiled temple.

Around mouthfuls of food the priest described the nights since, as he had heard looting, burning, drunken laughter, even screaming. But whenever he had dared to poke his head out of doors in the daylight he had seen nobody. It was clear that most of the population had vanished into the parched land beyond the cultivated fragment, there to die of thirst or starvation.

Eumenes ordered his men to clean up the priest and present him to the King. Then he said, 'This priest says the old name of the city is "the gate of the Gods". How appropriate, for now that gate has opened . . . Come.' Eumenes strode forward.

The others hurried after him. Ruddy gasped, 'Where are we going now?'

Bisesa said, 'Why, to the Temple of Marduk, of course.'

The temple, another great pyramidal pile, was like a cross between a cathedral and an office building. Hurrying down corridors and climbing from level to level, Bisesa passed through a bewildering variety of rooms, each elaborately decorated, containing altars, statues, friezes, and obscure-looking equipment like crosiers, ornate knives, headdresses, musical instruments like lutes and sackbuts, even small carts and chariots. In some of the deeper rooms there were no windows, and the light came from oil lamps burning smokily in little alcoves in the walls. There was a powerful smell of incense, which de Morgan told her was frankincense. There was some evidence of minor damage: a door smashed off its heavy wooden hinges, broken pottery, a tapestry ripped off one wall.

Ruddy said, 'More than one god is worshipped here, that's for sure. This is a library of worship. More gaudy polytheism!'

De Morgan muttered, 'I can barely make out the gods for the gold. *Look* at it – it's everywhere.'

Bisesa said, 'Once I visited Vatican City. It was like this – wealth plastered to every surface, so dense you could barely pick out details.'

'Yes,' Ruddy said. 'And the same causes: the peculiar hold religion has on the mind of man – and the accumulation of wealth by an ancient empire.'

There was some evidence of looting, though: the smashed doors, a few sockets where gems might have been lodged. But it seemed to have been half-hearted.

Marduk's own chamber was at the very apex of the complex. But it was ruined, and they stood at the doorway in shock.

Bisesa learned later that the great statue of Marduk that had stood here had consumed twenty tonnes of gold. The last time Eumenes had been in this temple the statue had gone: centuries before Alexander's visit, the conqueror Xerxes had looted these buildings and had taken away the great golden statue. Well, the statue had been *here* – but it had been destroyed, melted to a puddle of gleaming slag on the floor. The walls had been reduced to bare brick, scorched by some intense heat; Bisesa saw ashen fragments, the remains of tapestry or carpet. Only the statue's base remained, softened and rounded, with perhaps the faintest trace of two mighty feet.

And, hanging in the air at the centre of the burned-out temple, mysterious, unsupported, perfect, was an Eye – immense, much bigger than any others they had seen, perhaps three metres across.

Josh whistled. 'Abdi, you're going to need a big bucket to dunk that.'

Bisesa walked towards the Eye. In the uncertain light from the oil lamps, she could see her own distorted reflection looming larger, as if the other Bisesa, contained in the Eye like a fish in a bowl, was swimming to the glass to see her. She felt no heat, no sign of the great energies that had gutted this chamber. She lifted her hand and held it close to the Eye. She felt as if she was pushing against some invisible but resilient barrier. The harder she pushed, the more she was repelled, and she felt a subtle sideways pull.

Josh and Abdikadir were both watching her with some concern. Josh came up to her. 'Are you all right, Bis?'

'Can't you feel it?'

'What?'

She looked into the sphere. 'A – presence.'

Abdikadir said, 'If this is the source of the electromagnetic signals we have been monitoring—'

'I can hear them now,' her phone whispered from her pocket.

'More than that,' she said. There was something here, she thought. An awareness – yes. Or at least a watchfulness, a huge cathedral-like watchfulness, which drew her up helplessly. But she didn't even know how she knew this. She shook her head, and something of that mysterious sense of presence dissipated.

Eumenes's face was like thunder. 'So now we know how Babylon was destroyed.' To Bisesa's astonishment he picked up a golden staff from the floor. He wielded it over his head like a club, bringing it down on the unresponsive hide of the Eye. The club was left bent over, the Eye unmarked. 'Well, this arrogant god of the Eye may find Alexander, son of Zeus-Ammon, a tougher opponent than Marduk.' He turned to the moderns. 'There is much to do. I will need your help and insight.'

Abdikadir said, 'We should use the city as a base—'

'That much is obvious.'

'Move the army in. We have to think about the water supply, food. And we need to set up routines like fire watches, guard patrols, repair crews.'

Josh said, 'If the residential half of the city has gone we've a lot of building to do.'

'I think we will all be under tents for a while yet,' Abdikadir said ruefully.

'We will send out scouts to map the countryside,' Eumenes said. 'And we will coax the farmers from their mud huts – or we will take their farms and run them for them. I don't know any more if it is summer or winter, but here in Babylonia we can grow crops all year round.' He gazed up at the impassive Eye. 'Alexander was to make this his imperial capital. Well, so it will become – the capital of a new world, perhaps . . .'

Casey came bustling into the chamber. His expression was grim. 'We've had a message.'

Bisesa remembered what time of day it was; he had been due to try to pick up the cosmonauts' radio signals. 'From Kolya and Sable?'

'Yeah.'

'That's wonderful!'

'No, it isn't. We've got a problem.'

CHAPTER 31

HAM RADIO

In the luggage he had been allowed to bring on the Mongols' transcontinental trek, Kolya had made sure he packed up the ham radio gear from the Soyuz. Some instinct had always made him keep this secret even from Sable, who had long lost interest in what had once been her project, and he was glad of that now. Once Genghis Khan established his base camp a few tens of kilometres from Babylon, he retrieved the gear and set it up.

Oddly this wasn't difficult. In the retinue of Yeh-lu, the Mongol guards were watchful, but they had no idea what he was doing with his anonymous boxes and cables and spidery antennae. It was more difficult, in fact – but crucial – to keep what he was doing secret from Sable, at least for a few more hours.

He knew he would get only one chance at this. He prayed for a decent transmission path, and for Casey to be listening. Well, the path was poor – the post-Discontinuity ionosphere seemed to be suffering, and the signal was obscured by static, pops and whoops – but Casey was indeed listening, at the daily times they had agreed when Kolya was still orbiting the world in Soyuz, in the impossible and lost past. Kolya wasn't surprised to know that Casey and the others had travelled to Babylon; it was a logical destination, and they'd discussed the possibility before he had left orbit. But he was stunned to learn who Casey had travelled with – stunned, yet hopeful; for perhaps there was after all a force in the world that could resist Genghis Khan.

Kolya longed to prolong the contact, to listen to this man from the twenty-first century, his own time. He felt that

237

Casey, who he had never even met in person, had become his closest friend in the world.

But there was no time for that. There were no choices left, no more luxuries for Kolya. He talked, and talked, describing everything he knew about Genghis Khan, his army, his tactics; and he spoke of Sable, and what she had done – and what he suspected she was capable of.

He talked for as long as he could. It turned out to be about half an hour. Then Sable showed up with two burly Mongol guards, who hauled him back from the radio, and briskly smashed up the gear with the butts of their lances.

CHAPTER 32

COUNCIL OF WAR

Alexander's scouts brought the news that the vanguard of the Mongol army was only a few days' ride away. To his advisors' surprise, the King ordered that a parley should be attempted.

Alexander was horrified by what the moderns had to tell him of the destruction that had been wrought by the Mongol expansion. Alexander might be a blood-stained conqueror himself, but he had 'ambitions beyond simple conquest: his intent was certainly more sophisticated than Genghis Khan's, fifteen centuries after his own time. He was determined to oppose the Mongols. But Alexander was of a mind to build something new in this empty world, not to destroy. He said to his advisors, 'We, and our red-coated comrades from beyond the ocean, and these horsemen from the wastes of Asia, are all survivors of dislocations in time and space, wonders beyond the anticipation of any man. Do we have no other response to all this than to slaughter each other? Is there nothing for us to learn from each other but weapons and tactics . . . ?'

So he ordered a party of envoys to be sent out, with gifts and tributes, to open a dialogue with the Mongol leaders. It would travel with an impressive force of a thousand men, and was to be under the command of Ptolemy.

Ptolemy was one of the King's closest companions, a Macedonian and a friend of Alexander from childhood. A hard-faced warrior, he was a dark, silent man, and evidently shrewd. Perhaps he was a good choice for such a delicate mission: Bisesa's phone told her that in another reality Ptolemy would, in the carve-up of Alexander's conquests after his death, have become Pharaoh of the ancient kingdom of Egypt. But as he prepared for the mission, Ptolemy stamped around the royal palace looking thunderous. Bisesa wondered if his appointment to this perilous, and highly likely fatal, mission had anything to do with the end-less manoeuvrings and intrigues among Alexander's inner circle.

At Abdikadir's suggestion, Captain Grove attached the competent Geordie Corporal Batson and a few British troops to the party. It had been proposed that one of Bisesa's group should go along, since Sable was believed to be at the heart of the assault they anticipated. But Alexander decreed that his three refugees from the twenty-first century were too few to be risked on such a venture, and that was that. Still, at Eumenes's suggestion, Bisesa drafted a note for Batson to give to Kolya, in case he encountered the cosmonaut.

The party marched out of the gates of Babylon. They set off to the east, with the Macedonian officers in their dress uni-forms with bright purple cloaks, and Corporal Batson and the other British in their kilts and their serge, all to the din of trumpets and drums.

Alexander was a hardened warrior, and while he hoped for peace, he prepared for war. In Babylon, Bisesa, Abdikadir and Casey, along with Captain Grove and a number of his officers, were summoned to a war council.

Like the Ishtar Gate, the royal palace of Babylon sat on a platform raised some fifteen metres above the riverside plain, so it loomed over the city and its surroundings.

The palace was staggering – if, to Bisesa's modern perspect-ive, it was an obscene demonstration of wealth, power and oppression. Walking towards the centre of the complex, they passed terraced gardens built on the *roofs* of the buildings. The trees looked healthy enough, but the grass was a little yellow, the flowers sickly; the gardens had been neglected since the Discontinuity. But the palace was a symbol of the city and Alexander's new reign, and there was a great flurry of activity as servants ran back and forth with jars of fresh water and nutrients. These were not slaves, Bisesa learned, but some of Babylon's former dignitaries, who had come creeping back from the countryside where they had fled. In the aftermath of the Discontinuity, they had proved themselves cowardly; now, at Alexander's orders, they were reduced to menial chores.

At the heart of the palace complex was the King's throne room. This room alone was about fifty paces long, and every surface from floor to ceiling was coated with multi-coloured glazed bricks showing lions, dragons and stylised trees of life. The moderns walked in, their feet echoing on the glazed floor, trying not to be overwhelmed by the scale of it all.

A table had been set up in the middle of the room, bearing a giant plaster model of the city, its walls and the surrounding countryside. Perhaps five metres across, the model was brightly painted and full of detail, right down to the human figures in the streets and the goats in the fields. Toy canals glimmered, full of real water.

Bisesa and the others settled to their couches before the table, and servants brought them drinks. Bisesa said, 'This was my idea. I thought a model might be easier for everyone to grasp than a map. I had no idea they would put together something on this scale, and so quickly.'

Captain Grove said levelly, 'Shows what you can do when you can draw on an unlimited resource of human mind and muscle.'

Eumenes and his advisors entered and took their places. To his huge credit in Bisesa's eyes, Eumenes showed little taste for elaborate protocols; he was far too intelligent for that. But as a member of Alexander's court he couldn't avoid some flummery, and his advisors fluttered around him as he grandly settled to his couch. These advisors now included de Morgan, who had taken to wearing elaborate Persian dress, like others in Alexander's court. Today his face was bloated and red, his eyes marked by deep shadows.

Casey said bluntly, 'Cecil, my man, you look like shit, despite that cocktail dress you're wearing.'

De Morgan grunted. 'When Alexander and his Mace-donians get started on one of their debauches, they make

British Tommies in the brothels of Lahore look like school-boys. The King is sleeping it off. Sometimes he misses whole days, though he's always awake for the evenings when it all starts again . . .' De Morgan accepted a goblet of wine from a servant. 'And this Macedonian wine is like goat's urine. But still – hair of the dog.' He took a deep draught, shuddering.

Eumenes called the meeting to order.

Captain Grove began to set out ideas on how to strengthen Babylon's already formidable defences. He said to Eumenes, 'I know you already have crews out reinforcing the walls and digging out the moat.' That was especially important on the western side where the walls had been all but rubbed out by time; in fact the Macedonians had decided to abandon the western side of the city and use the Euphrates itself as a natural barrier, and were building up defences on its bank. 'But,' said Grove, 'I would recommend setting up deeper defences further out, especially to the east, where the Mongols will be coming from. I'm thinking of pillboxes and trenches – fortifications we can set up quickly.' Many of these concepts took a little translating, through Eumenes's assistants and a hung-over de Morgan.

Eumenes listened patiently for a while. 'I will have Diades look into this.' Diades was Alexander's chief engineer. 'But you must know that the King is not mindful simply to defend. Of all the fields on which he has fought, Alexander is most proud of his victorious sieges – at Miletus and Tyre and a dozen other examples – these are epic triumphs which will surely echo down the ages.'

Captain Grove nodded. 'Indeed they do. What I think you're telling us is that Alexander won't be content to be the victim of a siege himself. He is going to want to ride out on the field and meet the Mongols in open battle.'

'Yes,' murmured Abdikadir, 'but the Mongols, by comparison, were poor at siege warfare, and much preferred to meet their enemies on open ground. If we ride out we meet our enemies on the field of their choice.'

Eumenes growled, 'The King has spoken.'

Grove said quietly, 'Then we must listen.'

'But,' said Abdikadir, 'Alexander and Genghis are separated by more than fifteen centuries, far longer than separates Genghis from *us*. We should exploit every advantage we have.'

Eumenes said smoothly, 'Advantages. You mean your *guns* and *grenades*.' Again he used the English words.

Since meeting Alexander's army, the British and the moderns had tried to keep back some secrets from the Macedonians. Now Casey jumped off his couch and reached across the table towards de Morgan. 'Cecil, you bastard. What else have you given away?'

De Morgan cowered back out of his reach, and two of Eumenes's guards hurried forward, their hands on their stabbing swords. Abdikadir and Grove grabbed Casey and pulled him back down.

Bisesa sighed. 'Come on, Casey, what did you expect? You know what Cecil's like by now. He'd offer Eumenes your testicles on a plate if he thought it would be to his advantage.'

Abdikadir said, 'And Eumenes probably knew about it all anyhow. These Macedonians aren't fools.'

Eumenes followed these exchanges with interest. He said, 'You forget that Cecil may not have had a choice in what he told me.' De Morgan translated this hesitantly, his eyes averted, and Bisesa saw the dark side of the choice he had made. 'And besides,' Eumenes went on, 'my foreknowledge will save us time now we need it, won't it?'

Captain Grove leaned forward. 'But you must understand, Secretary, that our weapons, though formidable, are limited. We have only a small stock of grenades, and ammunition for the guns . . .' The most significant armament was nineteenth-century vintage, a few hundred Martini rifles brought from Jamrud. Such a number of weapons wouldn't count for much against a fast-moving horde numbered in the tens of thousands.

Eumenes quickly grasped these ideas. 'So we have to be selective about how we use these weapons.'

'Exactly,' Casey growled. 'Okay, if we commit to this

we should use the modern weapons to blunt their first attack.'

'Yes,' said Abdikadir. 'Flash-bang grenades will spook the horses – and the men, if they're unused to firearms.'

Bisesa said, '*But they have Sable*. We don't know what weapons came down in that Soyuz with her – surely at least a couple of pistols.'

'That won't help her much,' said Casey.

'No. But if she's thrown in her lot with the Mongols, she may have used them to familiarise the Mongols with firearms. And she has modern training. We have to plan for the possibility that they'll come in anticipating what we might do.'

'Shit,' said Casey. 'Hadn't thought of that.'

'All right,' Captain Grove said. 'Casey, what else do you suggest?'

'Prepare for firefights in the city,' Casey said. Quickly the moderns sketched out the discipline for Eumenes: how you could anticipate the enemy's likely approaches, and set up interlocking firing positions, and so forth. 'We'll have to train up some of your men in using the Kalashnikovs,' said Casey to Grove. 'The key will be not to waste ammo – not to fire until you have a clear target. If we draw the Mongols into the city it's possible we could soak up a large proportion of their forces.'

Again Eumenes grasped the ideas quickly. 'But Babylon would be destroyed in the process,' he said.

Casey shrugged. 'Winning this war is going to be costly – and if we lose, Babylon dies anyhow.'

Eumenes said, 'Perhaps this tactic should be a last resort. Anything else?'

Bisesa said, 'Of course it's not just guns we've brought with us from the future, but knowledge. We may be able to suggest weapons that could be built with the resources available here.'

Casey said, 'What are you thinking, Bis?'

'I've seen those kit-form catapults and siege engines the Macedonians have. Maybe we could come up with some improvements. And then, how about Greek fire? Wasn't that a primitive form of napalm? Just naphtha and quicklime, I think . . .'

They discussed such possibilities for a while, but Eumenes cut them short. 'I only dimly grasp what you describe, but I fear there will not be enough time to implement such schemes.'

'I've got something that could be delivered quickly,' Abdikadir murmured.

'What?' Bisesa asked.

'Stirrups.' Sketching quickly, he described what he meant. 'A kind of foot-rest for horsemen, attached by leather straps.'

When Eumenes understood that these devices, quickly and simply manufactured, could multiply a cavalry's manoeuvrability, he became extremely interested. 'But our Companions are men of tradition. They will resist any innovation.'

'But,' Abdikadir pointed out, 'the Mongols have stirrups.'

There was a great deal to be put in place, and little time to do it; the meeting broke up.

Bisesa drew Abdikadir and Casey to one side. 'You really think this battle is inevitable?'

'Yeah,' Casey growled. 'Alternatives to war – non-violent means of resolving disputes – depend on the willingness of everybody concerned to back down. Back in the Iron Age, these guys haven't had the benefit of our experience of two thousand years of bloodshed, give or take a few Hiroshimas and Lahores, to learn that it is sometimes *necessary* to back down. For them, war is the only way.'

Bisesa studied him. 'That's surprisingly thoughtful for you, Casey.'

'Shucks,' he said. But he quickly relapsed into his jock act; he cackled and rubbed his hands. 'But it's fun too. You know, we've got ourselves in a crock of shit here. But, think about it – Alexander the Great versus Genghis Khan! I wonder what they'd charge on pay-per-view for *that*.'

Bisesa knew what he meant. She had trained as a soldier

too; mixed in with her dread, and her wish that none of this was happening – that she could just go home – was anticipation.

They walked out of the throne room, talking, speculating and planning.

CHAPTER 33

A PRINCE OF HEAVEN

After a day and night alone in the dark, Kolya was taken to Yeh-lu. His arms pinned behind his back by horsehair rope, he was thrown to the ground.

He had no desire to face torture, and he talked fast, telling Yeh-lu what he had done, as much as he could remember. At the end of it Yeh-lu walked out of the yurt.

Sable's face loomed over him. 'You shouldn't have done it, Kol. The Mongols know the power of information. You saw that for yourself at Bishkek. You could hardly have committed a worse crime if you'd taken a swipe at Genghis himself.'

He whispered, 'Can I have some water?' He'd had nothing since being discovered.

She ignored his request. 'You know there's only going to be one verdict. I tried to plead your case. I said you were a prince, a prince of Heaven. They'll be lenient. They don't spill royal blood—'

He found the phlegm to spit in her face. The last time he saw her, she was laughing down at him.

They took him outside, hands still behind his back. Four burly soldiers held him down at his shoulders, his legs. Then an officer emerged from a yurt, his hands heavily gloved, carrying a ceramic cup. The cup turned out to contain molten silver. They poured it into one eye, then the other, and then one ear, and the other.

After that he could feel them pick him up, carry him, throw him into a hole lined with soft, fresh-dug earth. He could not hear the hammering as they nailed down the floorboards over his head, nor could he hear his own screams.

CHAPTER 34

DWELLERS ALL IN TIME AND SPACE

Alexander threw his army into a strict regime of training. Most of this followed traditional Macedonian methods, involving a lot of forced marching, running under weights, and hand-to-hand combat.

But there were attempts to integrate the British troops into the Macedonian force. After a few trials it was clear that no British rider or sowar was good enough to ride with Alexander's cavalry, but the Tommies and sepoys were accepted into the heart of the Macedonian infantry, the Foot Companions. Given the language and culture clashes a unified chain of command was hardly possible, but the Tommies were trained to understand the Macedonian trumpeters' key signals.

Abdikadir's work with the cavalry made fast strides, even though, as Eumenes had predicted, the first attempts to have the Macedonians ride with Abdikadir's prototype stirrups were farcical. The Companion cavalry, the army's senior regiment, was recruited from the youth of Macedonian nobles; Alexander sported a version of their uniform himself. And when they were first offered stirrups the proud Companions just sliced off the dangling leather attachments with their scimitars.

It took a brave sowar to climb on to one of the Macedonians' stocky horses and, inexpertly but effectively, show how tightly he was able to control even an unfamiliar horse. After that, and with some heavy pressure relayed from the King, the training began in earnest.

Even without stirrups, though, the Macedonians' horsemanship was astonishing. The rider steadied himself by holding on to the horse's mane, and steered his horse purely by the pressure of his knees. Even so, the Companions were able to skirmish and wheel sharply, a flexibility and agility that had made them the hardened cutting edge of Alexander's forces. Now, with stirrups, their manoeuvrability was vastly improved, and a Companion could brace his legs against impact and support a heavy lance.

'They're just remarkable,' Abdikadir said as he watched wedges of a hundred men wheel and dart as one across the fields of Babylon. 'I almost regret giving them stirrups; a couple of generations and this kind of horsemanship will be forgotten.'

'But we'll still need horses,' Casey growled. 'Makes you think. Horses would be the main engine of war for another twenty-three centuries – until World War One, for God's sake.'

'Maybe it will be different here,' Bisesa mused.

'Right. We're *not* the same half-insane bunch of squabbling, over-promoted primates we were before the Discontinuity. The fact that we're immersed in a battle with the Mongols five minutes after arriving here is just an aberration.' Casey laughed, and walked away.

Grove arranged for the Macedonians to be given some exposure to gunfire. In squads of a thousand or more, the Macedonians watched as Grove or Casey sacrificed a little of their stock of modern weaponry: a grenade, or a few shots squeezed off a Martini or a Kalashnikov at a tethered goat. Bisesa had argued that this kind of conditioning was essential: let them piss their pants now but hold the line against the Mongols, in case Sable had similar surprises up her spacesuit sleeve. The Macedonians had no trouble in grasping the principles of firearms; killing at a distance with bows was familiar to them. But the first time the Macedonians saw a relatively harmless flash-bang grenade go off they yelled and ran, regardless of the harangues of their officers. It would have been comical if not so alarming.

With Grove's support, Abdikadir insisted that Bisesa shouldn't take part in the fighting directly. A woman would be particularly vulnerable; Grove, quaintly, actually used the phrase 'a fate worse than death'.

So Bisesa threw herself into another project: establishing a hospital.

She requisitioned a small Babylonian townhouse. Philip, Alexander's personal physician, and the British Surgeon-Captain both assigned her assistants. She was grievously short of any kind of supplies, but what she lacked in resources she tried to compensate for in modern know-how. She experimented with wine as an antiseptic. She established casualty collection points across the likely battlefield, and trained pairs of Alexander's powerful, long-legged Agrarian scouts to work as stretcher-bearers. She tried to set up trauma chests, simple packs of equipment to serve the basis of the most likely injuries they would encounter – even gunshot wounds. This was an innovation of the British army in the Falklands: you made a quick assessment of the injury, then just grabbed the most appropriate kit.

The hardest thing to impart was the need for hygiene. Neither Macedonians nor nineteenth-century Brits grasped the need even to wipe off the blood between treating one patient and another. The Macedonians were baffled by her vague talk of invisible creatures, like tiny gods or demons, attacking broken flesh or exposed organs, and the British were scarcely any the wiser about bacteria and viruses. In the end, she had to appeal to their respective command structures to enforce her will.

She gave her assistants what practice she could. She sacrificed more goats, hacking at the animals with a Macedonian scimitar, or shooting them in the gut or pelvis. There was no substitute for getting your hands in real gore. The Macedonians were not squeamish – to have survived with Alexander, most of them had seen enough terrible injuries in their time – but the notion of doing something about it was new to them. The effectiveness of even simple techniques like tourniquets startled them, and inspired them to work harder, learning all the time.

Once again she was changing the trajectory of history, Bisesa thought. If they survived – a big if – she wondered what new medical synthesis, two thousand years early, might develop from the rough-and-ready education she was struggling to impart: perhaps a whole new body of knowledge, functionally equivalent to the mechanical Newtonian models of the twenty-first century, but couched in the language of Macedonian gods.

Ruddy Kipling insisted on 'joining up', as he called it. 'Here I stand at the confluence of history, as mankind's two greatest generals join in combat, with the prize the destiny of a new world. My blood is up, Bisesa!' He had, he claimed, trained with the First Punjab Volunteer Rifles, part of an Anglo-Indian initiative to fend off the threats emanating from the rebellious Northwest Frontier. 'Granted I didn't last very long,' he admitted, 'after mocking my fellow recruits' shooting skills in a little poem about having my carcass peppered with bullets while walking down a neighbouring street . . .'

The British took one look at this broad-faced, podgy, somewhat pompous young man, still pale from his lingering illness, and laughed at him. The Macedonians were simply baffled by Ruddy, but wouldn't have him either.

After these rebuffs, and somewhat against Bisesa's better judgement, Ruddy insisted on joining her makeshift medical corps. 'I once had some ambition to be a doctor, you know . . .' If that was true he turned out to be astoundingly squeamish, fainting dead away the first time he glimpsed a goat's fresh blood.

But, determined to play his part in the great struggle, he stuck with it. Gradually he became inured to the atmosphere of a hospital, the stink of blood, and the bleating of wounded and frightened animals. Eventually he was able to apply a bandage to a goat's hacked-open leg, all but finishing the job before fainting.

Then came his greatest triumph, when a Tommy came in with a gashed-open hand from a training accident. Ruddy was able to clean it and bind it up without referring to Bisesa, although he threw up later, as he cheerfully admitted.

After that, Bisesa took his shoulders, ignoring the faint stink of vomit. 'Ruddy, courage on the battlefield is one thing, but no less is the courage to face one's inner demons, as you have done.'

'I will persuade myself to believe you,' he said, but he blushed through his pallor.

Though Ruddy became able to stand the sight of blood, suffering and death, he was still greatly moved by the spectacle – even by the death of a goat. Over dinner he said, 'What is life that it is so precious, and yet so easily destroyed? Perhaps that wretched kid we shot to bits today thought himself the centre of the universe. And now he is snuffed out, evanescent as a dewdrop. Why would God give us something so precious as life, only to hack it short with the brutality of death?'

'But,' de Morgan said, 'it isn't just God that we can ask now. We can no longer regard ourselves as the pinnacle of Creation, below God Himself, for now we have in our world these creatures whom Bisesa senses inside the Eyes, perhaps below God but higher than us, as we are higher than the kid goats we slaughter. Why should God listen to *our* prayers when *they* stand over us to call to Him?'

Ruddy looked at him with disgust. 'That's typical of you, de Morgan, to belittle your fellow man.'

De Morgan just laughed.

Josh said, 'Or maybe there is no god of the Discontinuity.' He sounded unusually troubled. 'You know, this whole experience, everything since the Discontinuity, is so like a terrible dream, a fever dream. Bisesa, you have taught me about the great extinctions of the past. You say this was understood in my time, but barely accepted. And you say that in all the fossil record there is no trace of mind – nothing until man and his immediate precursors. Perhaps, then, if we are to die ourselves, it will be the first time an intelligent species has succumbed to extinction.' He flexed his hand, studying his fingers. 'Abdikadir says that according to the scientists of the twenty-first century, mind is bound up with the structure of the universe – that mind somehow makes things *real*.'

'The collapse of quantum functions – yes. Perhaps.'

'If that is so, and if *our* kind of minds are about to be snuffed out, then perhaps *this* is the consequence. They say that when you face death your past life flickers before your eyes. Perhaps we as a race are undergoing a final psychic shock as we succumb to darkness – shards of our bloody history have come bubbling to the surface in the last instants – and perhaps, in falling, we are smashing apart the structure of space and time itself . . .' He was talking rapidly now, disturbed.

Ruddy just laughed. 'Not like you to brood so, Josh!'

Bisesa reached out and took Josh's hand. 'Shut up, Ruddy. Listen to me, Josh. This is no death dream. I think the Eyes are artefacts, the Discontinuity a purposeful act. I think there *are* minds involved – minds greater than ours, but like ours.'

'But,' de Morgan said grimly, 'your creatures of the Eye can shuffle space and time themselves. What is that but the preserve of a god?'

'Oh, I don't think they are gods,' Bisesa said. 'Powerful, yes, far beyond us – but not gods.'

Josh said, 'Why do you say that?'

'Because they have no compassion.'

They had four days' grace. Then Alexander's envoys returned.

Of the thousand men who rode out, only a dozen came back. Corporal Batson lived, but his ears and nose had been sliced off. And, in a bag on his saddle, he carried the severed head of Ptolemy.

When she heard the news, Bisesa shuddered, both at the imminent prospect of war, and the loss of another thread from history's unravelling fabric. The news about Batson, the competent Geordie soldier, broke her heart. She heard that Alexander simply mourned the loss of his friend.

The next day, the Macedonian scouts reported much activity in the Mongol camp. The assault, it seemed, was close.

That afternoon, Josh found Bisesa in the Temple of

253

Marduk. She was sitting against one scorched and blackened wall, a British blanket over her legs to keep out the gathering cold. She stared up at the Eye, which they had labelled the Eye of Marduk – although some of the Tommies called it 'God's Bollock'. Bisesa had taken to spending much of her spare time in here.

Josh sat down beside her, arms wrapped around his thin torso. 'You're supposed to be resting.'

'I am resting. Resting and watching.'

'Watching the watchers?'

She smiled. 'Somebody has to. I don't want them to think –'

'What?'

'That we don't *know*. About them, and what they've done to us, our history. And besides, I think there is power here. There must be, to have created this Eye and its siblings across the planet, to have melted twenty tonnes of gold to a puddle . . . I don't want Sable, or Genghis Khan come to that, to get their hands on it. If it all goes pear-shaped when the Mongols come I'll be standing in that doorway with my pistol.'

'Oh, Bisesa, you are so strong! I wish I was like you.'

'No, you don't.' He was holding her hand, very tightly, but she didn't try to pull away. 'Here.' She fumbled under the blanket and produced a metallic flask. 'Have some tea.'

He opened the flask and sipped. 'It's good. The milk is a little, umm – not authentic.'

'From my survival pack. Condensed and irradiated. In the American army they give you suicide pills; in the British, tea. I've been saving it for a special occasion. What more special than this?'

He sipped the tea. He seemed turned in on himself.

Bisesa wondered if the shock of the Discontinuity was at last working its way through Josh. It had hit them all, she suspected, in different ways. She asked, 'Are you okay?'

'Just thinking of home.'

She nodded. 'None of us talks much about home, do we?'

'Perhaps it's too painful.'

'Tell me anyhow, Josh. Tell me about your family.'

'As a journalist I'm following my father. He covered the War between the States.' Which was, Bisesa reflected, only twenty years in the past for Josh. 'He took a bullet in the hip. Eventually got infected – took him a couple of years to die. I was only seven,' Josh whispered. 'I asked him why he had become a journalist, rather than go fight. He said that somebody has to watch, to tell others. Otherwise it's as if it never really happened at all. Well, I believed him, and followed in his footsteps. Sometimes I resented the fact that the pattern of my life was somewhat fixed before I was born. But I suppose that's not uncommon.'

'Ask Alexander.'

'Yeah . . . My mother is still alive. Or was. I wish I could tell her I'm safe.'

'Maybe she knows, somehow.'

'Bis, I know who you would be with, if—'

'My little girl,' Bisesa said.

'You never told me about her father.'

She shrugged. 'A good-looking bum from my regiment – think of Casey without the charm and sense of personal hygiene – we had a fling, and I got careless. Drunkenness, against which there is no prophylactic. When Myra was born, Mike was – confused. He wasn't a bad guy, but I didn't care by then. I wanted her, not him. And then he got himself killed anyhow.' She felt her eyes prickle; she pressed the heel of her palm into their sockets. 'I was away from home for months at a time. I knew I wasn't spending enough time with Myra. I always promised myself I'd do better, but could never get my life together. Now I'm stuck here, and I have to deal with Genghis fucking Khan, when all I want is to go home.'

Josh cupped her face with his hand. 'None of us wants this,' he said. 'But at least we have each other. And if I die tomorrow – Bis, do you believe that we will come back? That if there is some new chopping-up of time, we will live again?'

'No. Oh, there may be another Bisesa Dutt. But it won't be *me*.'

'Then this moment is all we have,' he whispered.

After that it seemed inevitable. Their lips met, their teeth touched, and she pulled him under her blanket, ripping at his clothes. He was gentle – and fumbling, a near-virgin – but he came to her with a desperate, needy passion, which found an echo in herself.

She immersed herself in the ancient liquid warmth of the moment.

But when it was over she thought of Myra and probed at her guilt, like a broken tooth. She found only emptiness inside, like a space where Myra had once been, and was now vanished for good.

And she was always aware of the Eye, hovering above them both balefully, and the reflections of herself and Josh like insects pinned to its glistening hide.

At the end of the day Alexander, having completed his sacrifices in advance of the battle, gave orders that his army should be assembled. The tens of thousands of them drew up in their squads before the walls of Babylon, their tunics bright and shields polished, their horses whinnying and bucking. The few hundred British, too, were drawn up by Grove in parade order, their khaki and red serge proud, their arms presented.

Alexander mounted his horse and rode before his army, haranguing them with a strong, clear voice that echoed from Babylon's walls. Bisesa would never have guessed at the wounds he carried. She couldn't follow his words, but there was no mistaking the response: the rattle of tens of thousands of swords against shields, and the Macedonians' ferocious battle cry: 'Alalalalai! Al-e-han-dreh! Al-e-han-dreh! . . .'

Then Alexander rode to the small section of British. Holding his horse steady with his hand wrapped in its mane, he spoke again – but in English. His voice was heavily accented, but his words were easily comprehensible. He talked of Ahmed Khel and Maiwand, battles of the British Empire's Second Afghan War that loomed large in the barrack-room mythology of these troops, and the memory of some of them. And Alexander said: ' "From this day to the ending of the world, but we in it shall be remembered; we few, we happy few, we band of brothers; for he today that sheds his blood with me shall be my brother." '

The Europeans and sepoys alike cheered as loud as any Macedonian. Casey Othic bellowed, 'Heard! Acknowledged! Understood!'

When the parade broke up Bisesa sought out Ruddy. He was standing on the platform of the Ishtar Gate, looking out over the plain, where the fires of the soldiers' camp were already alight under a darkling slate-grey sky. He was smoking, one of his last Turkish cigarettes – saved for the occasion, he said.

'Shakespeare, Ruddy?'

'*Henry the Fifth*, to be exact.' He was puffed up, visibly proud of himself. 'Alexander heard I was something of a wordsmith. So he called me to the palace to concoct a short address for him to deliver to our Tommies. Rather than something of my own, I turned to the Bard – and what could be more fitting? And besides,' he said, 'as the old boy probably never even existed in this new universe he can hardly sue for plagiarism!'

'You're quite a package, Ruddy.'

As the light faded, the soldiers had begun singing. The Macedonian songs were the usual mournful dirges about home and lost loved ones. But tonight Bisesa heard English words, an oddly familiar refrain.

Ruddy smiled. 'Do you recognise it? It's a hymn, "Praise, My Soul, the King of Heaven". Given our situation, I think one of those Tommies has a sense of humour! Listen to the last verse . . .'

'Angels, help us to adore Him,/Ye behold Him face to face;/ Sun and Moon, bow down before Him/Dwellers all in Time and Space./Praise Him! Praise Him! Praise Him! Praise Him!/ Praise with us the God of grace . . .' As they sang, the accents of London, Newcastle, Glasgow, Liverpool and the Punjab merged into one.

But a soft wind blew from the east, wafting the smoke of

the fires over the walls of the city. When Bisesa looked that way she saw that the Eyes had returned, dozens of them, hovering expectantly over the fields of Babylonia.

CHAPTER 35

CONFLUENCE

The dust: that was what Josh saw first, a great cloud of it kicked up by racing hooves.

It was about midday. For once it was a clear, bright day, and the rolling bank of dust, perhaps half a kilometre wide, was filled with smoky light, elusive shapes. Then, in Josh's clear view, they emerged from the dusty glow, shadows at first, coalescing into figures of stocky menace. They were Mongol warriors, identifiable at a glance.

Despite all that had happened to him Josh had found it hard to believe that a Mongol horde, under the control of Genghis Khan himself, was really and truly approaching, intent on killing *him*. And yet it was so; he could see it with his own eyes. He felt his heart beat faster.

He was sitting in a cramped guard position on the Ishtar Gate, looking out over the plain to the east, towards the Mongol advance. With him were Macedonians and a couple of British. The British had decent pairs of binoculars, Swiss-made. Grove had impressed on them the importance of keeping the lenses shielded: they had no idea how much information Genghis Khan had about their situation here in Babylon, but Sable Jones would surely understand the significance of a glinting reflection. The best-equipped of all was Josh, though, for Abdikadir – who had gone off to fight – had bequeathed him his precious NODs, the farsighted night-vision glasses that one wore like goggles.

At the first glimpse of the Mongols, among Macedonians and British observers alike there was an air of tension, and yet of excitement, a palpable thrill. On the next gate, Josh thought he saw the brightly coloured chestplate of Alexander himself, come to view this first clash.

The Mongols came in a long line, and seemed to be grouped into units of ten or so. Josh counted the units quickly: the Mongol line was perhaps twenty men deep but two hundred wide – a force of four or five thousand men, just in this first approach.

But Alexander had drawn up ten thousand of his own men on the plain before Babylon. Their long scarlet cloaks billowed in the breeze, and their bronze helmets were painted sky blue, the spines of their crests marked with the insignia of rank.

It started.

The first assault was with arrows. The front ranks of the advancing Mongols lifted complicated-looking compound bows, and fired into the air. The bows were of laminated horn, and could strike accurately over hundreds of yards, as fast as a warrior could pull arrows from his quiver.

The Macedonians had been drawn up into two long files, with the Foot Companions at the centre and the elite Shield Bearers guarding either flank. Now, as the arrows flew, to brisk drumbeats and trumpet peals, they quickly regrouped into a close order, a box-like formation eight men deep. They raised their leather shields over their heads and locked them together, like the formation the Romans had called the turtle.

The arrows fell on the shields with audible thumps. The shell formation held, but it wasn't perfect. Here and there men dropped, to sharp cries, and there would be a brief hole in the cover, a fast flurry as the wounded man was dragged from the formation, and the shell would close up again.

So men had already started to die, Josh thought.

Perhaps a quarter-mile from the city walls, the Mongols suddenly broke into a charge. The warriors roared, their war drums banged like a pulse, and even the clatter of the horses' hooves was like a storm. The wave of noise was startling.

Josh didn't believe he was a coward, but he couldn't help but quail. And he was astonished how calmly Alexander's seasoned warriors held their places. To more trumpet peals and yelled commands – *'Synaspismos!'* – they broke up their turtle formation and formed their open lines once more, though some kept their shields raised to ward off arrows. They were in a line four deep now, with some troops held in reserve at the back. They were infantrymen facing the Mongols' cavalry charge: a thin line of flesh and blood was all that stood between Babylon and the oncoming Mongols. But they locked their button shields together and rammed the butts of their long spears in the ground, and foot-long iron blades bristled at the oncoming Mongols.

In the last moments Josh saw the Mongols very clearly, even the eyes of their armoured horses. The animals seemed crazed; he wondered what goads, or drugs, the Mongols used to induce their horses to attack packed infantry.

The Mongols fell on the Macedonian lines. It was a brutal collision.

The armoured horses battered a way through the Macedonian front line, and the whole formation buckled at the centre. But the Macedonians' rear lines cut at the animals, killing or hamstringing them. Mongols and their horses began to fall, and their rear lines slammed into the stalled advance.

All along the Macedonian line now there was a stationary front of fighting. A stink of dust and metal, and the coppery smell of blood, rose up to Josh. There were cries of rage and pain, and the clash of iron on iron. There were no gunshots, no cannon roars, none of the dark explosive noises of the warfare of later centuries. But human lives were erased with industrial efficiency, all the same.

Josh was suddenly aware of a silvered sphere hovering before him, high over the ground, but almost at his own eye level. It was an Eye. Perhaps, he thought grimly, there were other than human observers here today.

The first assault lasted only minutes. And then, to a trumpet-call, the Mongols suddenly broke away. Those still mounted galloped back from the fray. They left behind a line of broken and writhing bodies, severed limbs, maimed horses.

The Mongols paused in loose order, a few hundred yards from the Macedonian position. They called insults in their incomprehensible language, shot off a few arrows, even spat at the Macedonians. One of them had dragged a wretched Macedonian foot soldier with him, and now, with mocking elaboration, began to carve a hole in the living man's chest. The Macedonians responded with insults of their own, but when a unit ran forward, weapons raised, their officers roared commands for them to hold their positions.

The Mongols continued to withdraw, still taunting the Macedonians, but Alexander's soldiers would not follow. As the lull continued, stretcher-bearers ran out from the Ishtar Gate.

The first Macedonian warrior to be brought into Bisesa's surgery had suffered a leg wound. Ruddy helped her haul the unconscious figure on to a table.

The arrow had been broken and pulled out, but it had passed right through the calf muscle and out the other side of the leg. It didn't look to have broken any bones, but flaps of muscle tissue spilled out of the raw wound. She stuffed the muscle tissue back into the hole, packed some wine-soaked cloth into it, and then, with Ruddy's brisk help, bound it up tight. The soldier was stirring. Bisesa had no anaesthetic, of course, but perhaps, if he woke, fear and adrenalin would keep the pain at bay for a while.

Ruddy, working with both hands, wiped sweat from his broad, pale brow on to the shoulder of his jacket.

'Ruddy, you're doing fine.'

'Yes. And this man will live, will he not? And walk out, scimitar and shield in hand, to die on some other battlefield.'

'All we can do is patch them up.'

'Yes . . .'

But there was no time, no time. The leg wound was just the first of a flood of stretcher-bound invalids which suddenly flowed in through the Ishtar Gate. Philip, Alexander's physician, ran to meet the flow and, as Bisesa had taught him, began to operate a brisk triage, separating those who could be helped from those who could not, and sending the invalids to where they could best be treated.

She had Macedonian porters take the leg wound away to a casualty tent, and grabbed the next stretcher in line. It turned out to be a fallen Mongol warrior. He had taken a sword blow to his upper thigh, and blood pumped from an artery. She tried to press the edges of the wound together, but it was surely too late, and already the flow was stilling of its own accord.

Ruddy said, 'This man shouldn't have been let in here in the first place.'

Her hands soaked in blood, panting hard, Bisesa stepped back. 'There's nothing we can do for him anyhow. Get him out of here. Next! . . .'

It continued through the early afternoon, a flow of maimed and writhing bodies, and they all worked on until they felt they could work no more, and continued anyhow.

Abdikadir was with the forces outside the walls of Babylon. He had already come close to the fighting, when the Macedonian line had nearly buckled. But he and the British – and Casey, somewhere else in the line – had been kept in the reserves, their firearms concealed under Macedonian cloaks. Their moment would come, Alexander had promised them, but not yet, not yet.

Alexander and his modern advisors had the perspective of a different history to aid them. They knew the Mongols' classic tactics. The first Mongol assault had been only a feint, intended to draw the Macedonians into a pursuit. They would have been prepared to withdraw for days if necessary, exhausting and dividing Alexander's forces, until at last they were ready to snap closed their trap. The moderns had told Alexander how the Mongols had once broken an army of Christian knights in Poland by luring them in this way – and in fact Alexander himself had faced Scythian horsemen who used similar tactics. He would have none of it.

Besides, Alexander was playing his own game of concealment, with half his infantry and all his cavalry still hidden inside the walls of Babylon, and with the weapons of the nineteenth and twenty-first centuries still unused. It might work. Though Mongol scouts had been spotted in the countryside around Babylon, it was scarcely possible for spies of Genghis Khan to penetrate the city undercover.

Despite the defenders' tense anticipation, the Mongols did not come again that day.

As the evening gathered, a great line of camp fires could be seen on the horizon, stretching from north to south, as if encircling the world. Abdikadir was aware of muttering among the men at the apparent awesome size of the Mongol force. They might have been more scared, he mused, if they had been told that among the long lines of the Mongols' yurts had been spotted the unmistakable dome shape of a spacecraft.

But Alexander himself came walking through the camp, with Hephaistion and Eumenes at his side. The King was limping slightly, but his helmet and breastplate of iron gleamed like silver. Everywhere he walked he joked with his men. The Mongols were faking, he claimed. They had probably lit two or three fires for every man they had out in the field – why, they had been known to go into battle with stuffed dummies riding their spare horses, to addle the wits of their enemies. But Macedonians were too sharp to fall for such ruses! And meanwhile Alexander himself had allowed so few fires to be lit that the Mongols would seriously under-estimate the strength of those opposing them, as well as never guessing at the Macedonians' indomitable valour and will!

Even Abdikadir felt his spirit rise as the King passed. Alexander was a remarkable man, he thought – if, like Genghis Khan, a terrible one.

With his Kalashnikov at his side, curled up under his poncho and a coarse British blanket, Abdikadir tried to sleep.

He felt oddly at peace. This confrontation with the Mongols seemed to have focused his own determination. It was one thing to know of the Mongols in abstract, as a page of long-dust history, and another to see their destructive ferocity in the flesh.

The Mongols had done huge damage to Islam. They had

come to the rich Islamic state of Khwarazm – a very ancient nation, stable and centralised since the mid-seventh century BC. In fact Alexander the Great, on his cross-Eurasian jaunt, had come into contact with it. The Mongols sacked its beautiful cities of Afghanistan and northern Persia, from Herat to Kandahar and Samarkand. Like Babylonia Khwarazm had been built on an elaborate underground irrigation system that had survived since antiquity. The Mongols destroyed this too, and with it Khwarazm; some Arab historians claimed the region's economy had never recovered. And so on. The soul of Islam had been forever darkened by these events.

Abdikadir had never been a zealot. But now he discovered in himself a passion to put history right. *This* time Islam would be saved from the Mongol catastrophe, and be reborn. But this wretched war had to be won first – at any cost.

It was comforting, he thought, in the confusion left by the Discontinuity, to have something to do: a goal of unambiguous value to aim at. Or maybe he was just rediscovering his own Macedonian blood.

He wondered what Casey would say to all this: Casey the jock Christian, born in Iowa in 2004, now caught between armies of Mongols and Macedonians, in a time that had no date. 'A good Christian soldier,' Abdikadir murmured, 'is only ever a klick away from Heaven.' He smiled to himself.

Kolya had lain in his hole in the ground under Genghis's yurt for three days – three days, blind and deaf and in agonising pain. And yet he lived. He could even sense the passage of time by the vibration of the feet on the floorboards above him, footsteps coming and going like a tide.

If the Mongols had searched him they would have found the plastic bag of water under his vest, the sips of which had kept him alive for so long – and the one other item which this great gamble had been all about. But they had not searched him. A gamble, yes, and it had paid off, at least so far.

He had known far more about the Mongols than Sable ever could, for he had grown up with their memory, eight centuries old yet still potent. And he had heard of Genghis's habit of sealing enemy princes under the floor of his yurt. So Kolya had leaked what information he could to Casey, knowing he would be caught; and, once caught, he had let the treacherous Sable manipulate the Mongols into granting him this 'merciful' release. All he had wanted was to be here in the dark, still alive, holding the device he had made, just a metre or so from Genghis Khan.

The Soyuz had not carried any grenades, which would have been ideal. But there were explosive bolts. The Mongols would not have recognised what he had brought out of the spacecraft, even had they been watching him carefully. Sable would have known, of course, but in her arrogance she had assumed Kolya was an irrelevance, not capable of hindering her own ambitions. Disregarded, it had been a simple matter for Kolya to rig up a simple trigger, and to conceal his improvised weapon.

He had to wait for the right time to strike. That was why he had to wait, in the dark and the agony. *Three days*. It was like surviving three days beyond his own death. But how odd that his body kept functioning, that he had to urinate and even defecate, as if the body thought his story had an epilogue. But these were like the twitches of a fresh corpse, he thought, of a manikin, meaningless in themselves.

Three days. But Russians were patient. They had a saying: that the first five hundred years are always the worst.

First light gathered. The Macedonians started to move around, coughing, rubbing their eyes, urinating. Abdikadir sat up. The pink-grey of the brightening sky was oddly beautiful, scattered sunlight against volcano ash clouds, like cherry blossom scattered on pumice.

But he had only moments of peace after waking.

First and last light are the most dangerous times for a soldier, when the eye struggles to adjust to fast-changing light. And, in that moment of maximum vulnerability, the Mongols struck.

They had approached the Macedonian positions in silence. Now the great *naccara* called out, their camel-borne war drums, and the Mongols surged forward, screaming wildly. The sudden eruption of noise was blood-curdling, as if some immense force of nature was approaching, a flood or a landslide.

But the Macedonians' trumpet peals followed only a heartbeat later. Soldiers rushed to their positions. There were brisk commands in the Macedonians' harsh dialect: *Form up, hold your position, hold the line!* The Macedonian infantry, eight deep, made a wall of hardened leather and iron.

Alexander had, of course, been prepared. Anticipating this assault, he had let his foe approach as close as he dared. Now was the time to spring his trap.

Abdikadir took his place, three ranks back from the front. To either side were nervous Tommies. Catching their glances, Abdikadir forced a smile and raised his Kalashnikov.

He got his first good look at a Mongol warrior through a gun sight.

The Mongols' heavy cavalry was at the centre of the charge, with the light cavalry following behind. They wore body armour made of strips of buffalo leather, and metal helmets with leather guards over their necks and ears. Each man was loaded with weapons: two bows, three quivers, a lance with a vicious-looking hook on the end, an axe, a curved sabre. Even the horses were armoured, with broad leather sheets that guarded their sides, and metal caps on their heads. The Mongols, carapaced, bristling with weapons, looked more insectile than human.

But they weren't having it all their own way. At a trumpet peal, archers popped up over the parapets of the walls of Babylon, and arrows hissed through the air, over Abdikadir's head, thudding into the advancing Mongols. When a rider fell there would be a tangle, briefly disrupting the charge.

Now more arrows fell, ablaze, their tips dipped in pitch. They were aimed at flame pits, bales of hay soaked in pitch in the ground. Soon great pockets of flame and smoke were bursting up beneath the Mongols. Men screamed, and their horses shied and refused. But, though the grit of casualties slowed the Mongol advance, it did not halt it.

And once again the Mongol heavy cavalry slammed into the Macedonians.

All along the line the Macedonians fell back. The momentum of the Mongols' charge, and the sheer ferocity with which the horsemen wielded their swords and maces, made that inevitable.

Abdikadir, now only a metre or so from the worst of the fighting, saw rearing horses, flat Mongol faces looming above the struggling crowd, men fighting and dying. He could smell blood, dust, the sweat of terrified horses – and, even now, a rank, buttery stink that could only be the Mongols themselves. The sheer density of men and animals, the roar of ten thousand voices, made it difficult to fight, even to raise a weapon. As blades hissed in the air, blood and body parts flew in scenes of almost absurd, impossible carnage, and gradually the screams of rage turned to howls of pain. More pressure came when the Mongol light cavalry followed up their heavy counterparts, pressing forward where the heavy cavalry had made room, jabbing with their swords and javelins.

But Alexander struck back. Brave infantrymen rushed from the back of the Macedonian line carrying long hooked lances; if the lance missed, the hook could dismount a warrior. Mongols fell, but the Macedonian infantrymen were cut down like flowers before a scythe.

Now, through the clamour, a Macedonian trumpet sounded a clear peal.

At the centre of the field, just before Abdikadir, the surviving Macedonian front ranks pulled back, melting through the ranks behind them, leaving their wounded and dead. Suddenly there was nothing left, nothing between Abdikadir and the most ferocious horseback warriors who had ever lived.

The Mongols, startled, their horses shying, hesitated for a

second. One immense man, short but wide like a bear, stared into Abdikadir's eyes and raised a stubby mace that was already dripping with blood.

Captain Grove was at Abdikadir's side. 'Fire at will!'

Abdikadir raised his Kalashnikov and pulled the trigger. The Mongol's head exploded into a mist of blood and bone, his metal cap hurled absurdly into the air. His horse bolted, the headless body sliding from the saddle into the pressing crowd.

All around Abdikadir the British fired into the mass of Mongols, antique British Martini-Henrys and Sniders making precise coughs against the clatter of the Kalashnikovs. Men and horses disintegrated before the withering hail of bullets. Grenades flew. Most of them were just flash-bangs, but that was enough to terrify the horses and at least some of the warriors. But one exploded under a horse. The animal seemed to burst, and its rider, screaming, was hurled away.

One grenade landed too close to Abdikadir. The blast was like a punch to the stomach. He fell backwards, his ears ringing, his nose and mouth filled with the sour, metal taste of blood, and the chemical tang of the ignition. He felt somehow dislocated, as if he had been knocked through another Discontinuity. But if he was down, a corner of his mind told him, there was a hole in the line before him. He raised his rifle, fired without looking, and struggled to his feet.

The order came to advance. The line of British strode forward, firing continually.

Abdikadir moved ahead with them, snapping a new magazine into his weapon as he did so. There was no open ground; he had to climb over earth littered by corpses and body parts, in places slippery with entrails. He even had to step on to the back of a wounded man, who screamed in agony, but there was no other way.

It was working, he thought at first. To left and right, as far as he could see, where they were not dying in their saddles, the Mongols were falling back, their weapons unable to match the firearms of six hundred years and more after their time.

But now Abdikadir heard a high-pitched voice – *a woman's voice* – and some of the Mongols clambered off their horses. They actually advanced *towards* the gunfire, using the bodies of their comrades and their horses as cover. Abdikadir recognised the tactics: scan for threats, move, take cover, scan again. They were using their bows, the only weapon they had that could match the guns' range, and took turns to cover each other as they made their way forward: a manoeuvre called pepperpotting. And as they fired, Macedonian screams and a torrent of fluent Geordie oaths told Abdikadir that some arrows were striking home.

These Mongols had been trained to withstand gunfire, he realised. *Sable* – it had to be, just as they had feared. His heart sank. He snapped in another magazine, and fired again.

But the Mongols were closing. Abdikadir and the other riflemen had been assigned a shield bearer each, but these were being brushed aside. One horseback rider almost got through to Abdi, and he had to swing the rifle, using the butt as a club. He got a lucky hit on the man's temple, and the Mongol reeled back. Before he could recover Abdikadir had shot him dead, and was looking for the next target.

From his elevated position on the Ishtar Gate Josh could see the great sweep of the battle. Its bloody core was still the slab of struggling men and animals, directly before the gate, where the Mongol heavy cavalry had collided with Alexander's Foot Companions. The Eyes were everywhere, like floating pearls above the heads of the struggling warriors.

The heavy cavalry was the Mongols' most powerful instrument, designed to smash the enemy's strongest forces in a single blow. It had been hoped that a sudden assault with gunfire would do enough damage to the heavy cavalry to blunt that blow. But for whatever reason the Mongols had not fallen back as had been hoped, and the armed troops were getting bogged down.

This was bad news. There had only been three hundred

British troops in Jamrud, after all. Their numbers were no match for the Mongols, and even if every single bullet took a Mongol life, Genghis's troops would surely overwhelm them at last, through sheer numbers.

And now the Mongols threw more cavalry around the wings of the battlefield to envelop the enemy. This was again expected – it was a classic Mongol manoeuvre called the *tulughma* – but its sheer ferocity, as the new units smashed into the Macedonians' flanks, was staggering.

But Alexander wasn't done yet. Trumpets pealed out again from the city walls. With a great clang, gates were thrown open, and the Macedonian cavalry at last rode out into the field. Even as they emerged they were in their tight wedge formation. At a glance Josh could see how much more skilful these horsemen of ancient times were than the Mongols. And, at the head of the Companions who rode out from the right-hand side, Josh recognised the bright purple cloak and white-plumed helmet of Alexander himself, a panther skin thrown over his saddle cloth, as ever leading his men to glory or death.

The Macedonians, fast, agile, and tightly disciplined, wheeled to cut into the Mongol flank like a scalpel. The Mongols tried to turn, but, compressed now between the stolid Macedonian infantry and the Companions, their movements were constricted, and the Macedonians began to jab at their unprotected faces with their long wooden spears. It was another classic tactic, Josh knew – a battle formation perfected by Alexander the Great, yet inherited from his father before him, with cavalry on the right delivering the killer blow, and the central infantry following up with its dogged pressure.

Josh was no advocate of war. But he saw a kind of elation in the eyes of warriors on both sides as they hurled themselves into the fray: a kind of release that the moment in which all inhibitions could be shed was here at last, and a sort of joy. Even Josh felt a deep visceral thrill as he watched this ancient, brilliant manoeuvre unfold before his eyes – even as men fought and died in the dirt below, each one a unique life snuffed out. This is why we fight wars, we humans, he thought; this is why we play this game with the highest of stakes: not for profit, or power, or territory, but for this intense pleasure. Kipling is right: war is *fun*. It is the dark secret of our kind.

Perhaps that was why the Eyes were here – to enjoy the unique spectacle of the universe's most vicious creatures dying in the dirt. Josh felt resentment, and a certain squalid pride.

Save for some reserves, nearly all the forces were in the field now. Apart from a few cavalry skirmishes on the fringe, the battle was concentrating into that tight, bloody mass of carnage at the centre of the field, where men lashed at each other relentlessly. Still the fire pits burned, throwing up smoke that obscured the action, and still arrows rained down from the walls of Babylon.

Josh could no longer tell which way the advantage of the battle went. It wasn't a time for tactics now, and the opposing generals, perhaps the greatest of all time, could do no more – save, like Alexander, to swing swords themselves. It was a time to fight, or die.

Bisesa's medical station was overwhelmed. There was no other word for it.

Working alone, she struggled to save a Macedonian, sprawled unconscious on the table before her, dumped like a carcass in a butcher's store. He was a boy, no more than seventeen or eighteen years old. But he had taken a javelin thrust to the stomach. She cleaned, padded and patched the wound as best she could, her hands trembling with fatigue. But she knew that what would finish the boy off was the infection caused by the garbage that spear point would have carried in with it.

And still, all around her, the bodies flowed in. Those selected by the triage teams were no longer carried to the townhouse she had designated as a morgue but were rudely dumped on the ground, where they were piling up, their dark blood staining the Babylonian dirt. Of those selected for treatment, a handful had been patched up and gone back out to fight, but more than half her patients had died on the treatment tables.

What did you expect, Bisesa? she asked herself. You're no doctor. Your only experienced assistant is an ancient Greek who once shook hands with Aristotle himself. You've no supplies, you're running out of everything from clean bandages to boiled water.

But she knew she had saved some lives today.

It might be futile – the great wave of Mongol aggression might break over the walls and destroy them all – but, for now, she found she really and truly didn't want this boy with the punctured stomach to die. She dug into the guiltily hoarded contents of her twenty-first-century medical kit. Trying to hide her actions from the others, she jabbed a shot of streptomycin into the boy's thigh.

Then she called for him to be taken away, like all the others. 'Next!'

Kolya believed that the Mongols' expansion was pathological. It was a ghastly spiral of positive feedback, born of Genghis Khan's unquestioned military genius and fuelled by easy conquests, a plague of insanity and destruction that had spread across most of the known world.

Russians especially had reasons to despise the memory of Genghis Khan. The Mongols had struck twice. Great cities grown fat on trade, Novgorod, Ryazan and Kiev, were reduced to bone yards. In those dread moments the heart had been torn out of the country, for ever.

'Not again,' Kolya whispered, unable to hear the words himself. 'Not again.' He knew Casey and the others would resist the Mongol menace as hard as they could. Maybe the Mongols had made too many enemies in the old time-line; maybe in some transcendent way they were now facing payback.

Of course his own gamble was still to be played out – was his weapon powerful enough, would it even work? But he had confidence in his own technical abilities.

Reaching the target, though, was another matter. He had observed Genghis. Unlike Alexander, Genghis was a commander who had watched battles from the safety of the rear, and retired to his yurt at the close of the day; aged nearly sixty, he was predictable to that degree.

Could Kolya be sure, though, any longer, after three days, quite what time it was? Could he be sure that the heavy tread he sensed now was indeed the man he sought to destroy? His only real regret was that he would never know.

Kolya smiled, thought of his wife, and closed the trigger. He had no eyes, no ears, but he felt the earth lurch.

Abdikadir was back to back with a handful of British and Macedonians, fighting off Mongols who swirled around them, most still on horseback, lashing and cutting. His ammunition long exhausted, he had dropped the useless Kalashnikov and fought with bayonet, scimitar, lance, javelin, whatever came to hand, the detritus of dead warriors from ages separated by more than a thousand years.

As the battle had closed around him, at first he had felt as if he had become more alive – as if his life had reduced to this instant, of blood, noise, intense effort and pain, and all that had gone before was a mere prologue. But as fatigue poisons built up, that sense of vividness had been replaced by a coppery unreality, as if he was on the point of fainting. He had trained for this: the 'drone zone', they called it, a place where the body ignored pain, grew impervious to hot or cold, and a new form of consciousness cut in, a kind of dogged autopilot. But that didn't make it any easier to bear.

This little group was surviving where others had already been cut down, an island of resistance in a sea of blood across which the Mongols surged at will. He himself had taken blow after blow. But he knew he couldn't take much more. The battle was being lost, and there was nothing he could do about it.

Over the carnage of the battlefield, he heard the cry of a trumpet, an uneven rhythm played on a war drum. He was briefly distracted.

A mace swung down from the sky, smashing the scimitar from his hand. Pain lanced; he had broken a finger. Unarmed, one-handed, he turned to face a Mongol cavalryman who reared above him, raising the mace again. Abdikadir lunged, his good hand stretched out stiff as a board, and stabbed at the Mongol's thigh, aiming for a nerve centre. The cavalryman stiffened and flopped backwards, and his horse stumbled back. Abdikadir got to his knees, found his scimitar in the bloody dirt, and straightened up, panting hard, looking for his next assailant.

But there was none.

The Mongol cavalrymen were wheeling their horses around, turning back towards their distant encampment. As they galloped away, occasionally one would stop to pick up a dismounted comrade. Abdikadir, standing there panting, clutching his scimitar, simply couldn't take it in. It was as surprising as if a tide had suddenly reversed.

He heard a snapping sound, close to his ear, almost insectile. He knew what that was, but his mind seemed to grind slowly, dredging up the memory. A sonic boomlet. *A bullet*. He turned to look.

Before the Ishtar Gate there was one exception to the general withdrawal. Perhaps fifty Mongols, packed tight on their horses, charged at the open gate. And somebody in there, somebody in the middle of the charge, was shooting at him.

He dropped the scimitar. The world wheeled, and he found the earth, sodden with blood, reaching up to him.

Bisesa heard the screams and roars, right outside her casualty point. She rushed out of the door to see what was happening. Ruddy Kipling, the whole front of his shirt sticky with blood, followed her.

A pack of Mongol warriors had smashed through the defenders' lines and pushed into the gate. Macedonians were closing around them like antibodies around an infection, and their officers screamed orders. Though the Mongols

275

slashed hard at those around them, already they were being pulled from their horses.

But a single figure burst from the struggling pack, and ran down Babylon's processional way. It was a woman. The Macedonians hadn't noticed her – or if they had, didn't take her seriously enough to stop her. She was dressed in leather armour, Bisesa saw, but her hair was tied back by a strip of material, bright orange.

'Day-Glo,' Bisesa muttered.

Ruddy said, 'What did you say?'

'That has to be Sable. Shit, she's heading for the temple—'

'The Eye of Marduk—'

'It's what this has been all about. Come on!'

They ran after Sable down the ceremonial way. Worried-looking Macedonian soldiers rushed past them towards the incursion at the gate, and baffled, terrified Babylonian citizens cowered. Over their heads, Eyes hovered, like strings of CCTV cameras, impassive; Bisesa was shocked by how many there were.

Ruddy was first to the chamber of Marduk. The great Eye still hovered over its puddle of congealed gold. Sable stood before the Eye, panting, her hair dishevelled over her Mongol armour, gazing up at a distorted reflection of herself. She raised a hand to touch the Eye.

Ruddy Kipling stepped forward. 'Madam, get away from there, or—'

With a single movement she turned, raised a pistol and shot him. In the ancient chamber the crack of the weapon was loud. Ruddy was hurled backwards, slammed against the wall, and slumped to the floor.

Bisesa screamed, '*Ruddy!*'

Sable had raised the gun to Bisesa. 'Don't try it.'

Ruddy looked up helplessly at Bisesa, his brow dotted with sweat, his thick glasses spattered with the blood of strangers. He clutched his hip. Blood gushed from between his fingers. He grinned foolishly. 'I'm shot.'

Bisesa longed to go to Ruddy. But she stood still and raised her hands. 'Sable Jones.'

'My fame spreads.'

'Where's Kolya?'

'Dead . . . Ah.' She smiled. 'A thought occurs. The Mongols sounded the retreat. There was me thinking it was a coincidence. But you know what must have happened? Genghis Khan is dead, and his sons and brothers and generals are hurrying back for a *quriltai* to decide who gets the big prize. The Mongols have the social structure of a pack of chimpanzees. But, just like the chimps, when the alpha male falls all bets are off. And Kolya used that against them.' She shook her head. 'You have to admire the scrawny little bastard. I wonder how he did it.' The gun in her hand never wavered.

Ruddy groaned.

Bisesa tried not to be distracted. 'What do you want, Sable?'

'What do you think?' Sable jerked her thumb over her shoulder. 'We could hear this thing's signal from orbit. Whatever's going on here, *this* is the key – to past, present and future.'

'To a new world.'

'Yeah.'

'I think you're right. I've been studying it.'

Sable's eyes narrowed. 'In that case you might be able to help me. What do you say? You're either with me or against me.'

Bisesa looked directly at the Eye. She let her eyes open wider, and forced a smile. 'Evidently it's been expecting you.'

Sable turned her head. It was a simple trick, but Sable's vanity had trapped her – and Bisesa had won a single half-second. It took one kick to shatter Sable's wrist and get the gun out of her hand, another to bring her down.

Panting hard, she stood over the fallen cosmonaut. Bisesa thought she could smell her, a stink of milk and fat, like the Mongols she had fallen in with. 'Sable, did you really think the Eye would care about you, and your petty ambitions? May you rot in hell.' She glared up at the Eye. 'And *you* – have

277

you seen enough? Is this what you wanted? *Have we suffered enough for you?* . . .'

'Bisesa.' It was a groan, barely formed as a word.

Bisesa ran to Ruddy.

CHAPTER 36
AFTERMATH

Hephaistion was dead.

Alexander had won a great battle in almost impossible circumstances, in a new world, against a foe more than a thousand years more advanced. But in doing so he had lost his companion, his lover, his only true friend.

Alexander knew what was expected of him, at this moment. He would retire to his tent, and drink himself to oblivion. Or else he would refuse to drink or eat at all for days on end, until his family and companions feared for his health. Or he would order the construction of an impossibly grandiose memorial: perhaps a carving of a majestic lion, he thought idly.

Alexander decided he would do none of those things. He would grieve for Hephaistion in private, true. Perhaps he would order that all the horses in camp should have their manes and tails clipped. Homer told of how Achilles had shorn his horses in honour of his dead, beloved Patroculus; yes, that was how Alexander might mourn Hephaistion.

But for now there was too much to do.

He walked over the blood-soaked ground of the battle-field, and through the tents and buildings that housed the wounded. His advisors and companions fluttered anxiously at his heels – and his doctor, for Alexander had taken more than a few more blows himself. Many of the men were glad to see him, of course. Some boasted of what they had done in the battle, and Alexander listened patiently and, straight-faced, commended them on their valour. But others were sunk in shock. He had seen this before. They would sit numbly, or they would tell their petty stories over and over. The men would recover, as they always did, as would this bloodied ground, when the spring came and the grass grew again. But nothing could erase the anger and guilt of those who had survived where companions had fallen, as their King would never forget Hephaistion.

Ruddy lay back against the wall, arms limp, palms up, fingers curled. His small hands, coated in blood, looked like two crabs, she thought. Blood was gushing from a puncture wound, just below his left hip. 'We're seeing a lot of blood today, Bisesa.' He was still smiling.

'Yeah.' She dragged Curlex from her pocket, and tried jamming it in the hole. But the blood was still pumping. Sable's shot seemed to have ruptured a femoral artery, one of the primary avenues by which blood reached the lower half of the body. There was no way she could move him – no transfusions she could give him, no casevac she could call in.

No time for sentiment: she had to treat Ruddy as a broken machine, a truck with the bonnet up, that she had to fix. She thought desperately. She began to rip open his trouser leg. 'Try not to talk,' she said. 'Everything will be fine.'

'As Casey would say, *bullshit.*'

'Casey is a bad influence.'

'Tell me,' he whispered.

'What?'

'What becomes of me . . . Or would have.'

'No time, Ruddy.' Exposed, the wound gaped, a bloody crater from which crimson liquid still flowed. 'Here, help me.' She got hold of his hands and pushed them against the wound, and she pressed herself, pushing her fingers into the hole up to the knuckle.

He squirmed, but he didn't cry out. He seemed terribly pale. His blood was forming a lake beneath him on the floor of the temple, a mirror to the melted gold of the god. 'There's time for nothing else, Bisesa. Please.'

'You become loved,' she said, still working frantically. 'The voice of a nation, of an age. You're internationally famous too. Wealthy. You refuse honours, but they're repeatedly offered to you. You help shape national life. You win a

280

Nobel prize for literature. They will say of you that your voice is heard around the world whenever it drops a remark . . .'

'Ah.' He smiled and closed his eyes. She shifted her fingers. Blood spurted out, as strongly as ever, and he grunted. 'All those books I will never write.'

'But they exist, Ruddy. They're in my phone. Every last damn word.'

'There's that, I suppose – even if it makes no logical sense if the author doesn't survive to write them . . . And my family?'

Trying to staunch the flow this way was like trying to stop up a broken pipe by pushing down on it through a pillow. The only thing she could do, she knew, was to find the femoral artery and tie it off directly. 'Ruddy, this will hurt like hell.' She dug her fingers into the wound and ripped it wider open.

His back arched, his eyes closed. 'My family. Please.' His voice was a flutter, dry as autumn leaves.

She dug into his leg, picking through layers of fat, muscle and blood vessel, but she couldn't find the artery. It might have retracted when it was severed. 'I could cut you open,' she said. 'Search for the damn artery. But the blood loss . . .' She couldn't believe how much blood had already poured from the young man; it was all over his legs, her arms, the floor.

'It hurts, you know. But it's cold.' His words were laboured. He was going into shock.

She pressed down on the wound. 'You have a long marriage,' she said quickly. 'Happy, I think. Children. A son.'

'Yes? . . . What is his name?'

'John. John Kipling. There is a great war, that consumes Europe.'

'The Germans, I suppose. Always the Germans.'

'Yes. John volunteers to fight in France. He dies.'

'Ah.' Ruddy's face was almost expressionless now, but his mouth twitched. 'At least he will be spared that pain, as will I – or perhaps not. That damn logic again! I wish I understood.' He opened his eyes, and she saw reflected in them the impassive sphere of the Eye of Marduk. 'The light,' he said. 'The light in the morning . . .'

She pressed a bloody hand to his chest. His heart fluttered, and stopped.

Refusing help, Alexander clambered stiffly to the top of the Ishtar Gate. He looked out to the east, over the plain, to where the fires of the Mongols still burned. The hovering spheres the men called Eyes, that had littered the air during the battle, had all evaporated now, all save the great monstrosity in the Temple of Marduk. Perhaps these new indifferent gods had seen all they wanted to see.

There were tribunals to arrange. It had turned out that the strange Englishman Cecil de Morgan had been feeding information to Mongol spies, information that included the route by which Sable Jones had reached the Eye of Marduk so quickly. The English commander Grove, and those others, Bisesa and Abdikadir, were demanding the right to try these renegades, de Morgan and Sable, according to their own customs. But Alexander was King, and he knew there was only one justice his men would accept. De Morgan and Sable would be tried before the whole army, drawn up on the plain outside the city; in his own mind their fate was assured.

This war was not done, he thought, even if this mighty figure Genghis was dead. He was confident he could destroy the Mongols eventually. But why should Macedonian and Mongol fight at the behest of the gods of the Eye, like dogs thrown into a pit? They were men, not beasts. Perhaps there was another way.

It amused him that Bisesa and the others called themselves 'modern', as if Alexander and his time were pale stories from long ago, told by a tired old man. But from Alexander's point of view these strange, spindly, gaudy creatures, from a far and uninteresting future, were a froth. There was only a handful of them, compared to the great crowds of his Macedonians, and of the Mongols. Oh, their gadgets had been briefly useful in the battle against the Khan, but they had soon been exhausted, and then it had been back to the most ancient weapons of all, iron and blood, discipline and raw courage. The moderns didn't matter. It was clear to him that the beating heart of the new world lay here – with him, and these Mongols.

He had always known that his moment of hesitation at the river Beas had been an aberration. Now it was behind him. He decided he would instruct Eumenes to approach the Mongols once again and seek common ground. If he defeated the Mongols he would be strong; but if he combined with them stronger still. There was surely not a power in this wounded world that could match them. And then, armed with the knowledge that Bisesa and the others had brought, there was no limit to the possibilities of the future.

Thinking, planning, Alexander tasted the wind which blew from the east, the heart of the world continent, rich and full of time.

Time's Eye

PART FIVE

MIR

CHAPTER 37
LABORATORY

You could hardly call it a cage.

Five years after the Discontinuity and their capture, the man-apes were still trapped under a bit of camouflage net, thrown loosely over a conveniently hovering Eye, and weighted down with boulders. Nobody had given any thought to putting together anything better – though some quirk of the military mind had ordered the boulders to be painted white; there was always somebody who needed his attitude adjusted with a bit of pointless work.

It was under this net that Seeker spent her days, alone save for the fast-growing Grasper. Grasper was nearly six years old now. Her young mind still forming, she had adjusted to the reality of their confinement. Seeker couldn't adjust. But she had to accept it.

The soldiers came in once a day to give her food and water and scrape out her dung. Sometimes they held her down and pushed their fat penises into her body. Seeker didn't care about that. She wasn't hurt, and she had learned to let her captors do what they want, while she kept an eye on Grasper. She had no idea why the soldiers did what they did. But whether she knew or not didn't matter, of course, for she had no power to stop them.

She could break out of here. On some level she still knew that. She was stronger than any of the soldiers. She could rip open that netting with her teeth and hands or even her feet. But she hadn't seen a single other of her kind, save Grasper, since the day of her capture. Through the holes in the net she could see no trees, no welcoming green shade. If she did break out there was nowhere for her to go, nothing waiting for her but clubs, fists and rifle butts. She had had to be taught that brutal lesson.

Suspended between animal and human, she had only a dim grasp of future and past. Her memory was like a gallery hung with vivid images – her mother's face, the warmth of her nest, the overwhelming scent of the male who first took her, the sweet agony of child-bearing, the dreadful limpness of her first child. And her sense of the future was dominated by an inchoate vision of her own death, a fear of the blackness that lurked behind the yellow eyes of cats. But there was no sense of narrative about her memories, no logic or order: like most animals she lived in the present, for if the present could not be survived the past and future meant nothing anyhow. And her present, this helpless captivity, had expanded to encompass her whole consciousness.

She was a captive. That was all she was. But at least she had Grasper.

Then, one morning, something changed.

It was Grasper who saw it first.

Seeker woke up slowly, as always clinging to her ragged dreams of the trees. She yawned hugely and stretched her long arms. The sun was already high, and she could see bright glimmers pushing through the gaps in the netting.

Grasper was staring up into the tent's apex. There was light on her face. Seeker looked up.

The Eye was shining. It was like a miniature sun, caught in the net.

Seeker stood up. Side by side, their gazes fixed on the Eye, mother and child walked forward, fully upright. Seeker raised a hand towards the Eye. It was out of reach, but it cast shadows of the two of them on their floor of trampled dirt. It gave off no heat, only light.

Seeker had only just woken up. She badly needed to urinate, to defecate, to groom to get rid of the night's ticks, to get some food and water. But she couldn't move. She just stood there, eyes wide, one arm raised. Her eyes began to prickle with dust and cold, but she couldn't so much as blink.

She heard a soft whimpering. Seeker couldn't even turn to look at Grasper. She had no idea how much time went by.

Her hand was before her face. She hadn't consciously raised it; it was like looking at somebody else's hand. The fingers clenched, opened; the thumb worked back and forth.

She was made to raise her arms and twist them at shoulders, elbows and wrists; she bent and flexed her legs. She walked up and down, as far as the netting would let her, first upright, then knuckle-walking. She probed with her fingers at every orifice in her body. She fingered her high rib cage, the shape of her skull, even her pelvis. It was as if somebody else was doing this to her, exploring her in a cruel grooming.

The man-apes were released, just for a heartbeat. Panting, hungry, thirsty, they reached for each other. But then the invisible grip closed around them again.

This time, as patterns of light pulsed over their heads, Grasper got down on her haunches and began to examine the floor, digging in the dirt. She found twigs, bits of reed. She rubbed the twigs against each other, split and folded the reed, banged pebbles together.

Meanwhile Seeker marched to the netting wall. She took hold of the net and began to climb. Her body proportions were like those of her ape-like ancestors, and she could climb better than any of her human captors. But as she clambered up the net, fear gathered, for she knew she wasn't supposed to do this.

Sure enough, one of the soldiers came running. *'Here, you! Get down from there!'*

A rifle butt smashed into her face. She couldn't even scream. Despite the grip of the Eye she fell back from the netting and clattered on her back to the ground. Her mouth full of coppery blood, she tried to raise her head.

She could see Grasper, sitting on the gritty ground. Grasper held up a reed, tied into a knot. Seeker had never seen such a thing.

Again she was forced to stand, despite the blood that dripped from her mouth, and stared up at the Eye.

There was something new again, she realised dimly. The

glow of the Eye was no longer uniform: a series of brighter horizontal bands straddled an underlying greyness, a pattern that might have reminded a human of lines of latitude on a globe of the Earth. These lines swept up past the Eye's 'equator', dwindling until they vanished at the north pole. Meanwhile another set, vertical this time, began the same pattern of emergence, sweeping from a pole on one side of the equator, disappearing on the other side. Now a third set of lines, sweeping to poles set at right angles to the first two pairs, came shining into existence. The shifting, silent display of grey rectangles was entrancing, beautiful.

And then a *fourth* set of lines appeared – Seeker tried to follow where they went, but suddenly something inside her head hurt badly. She cried out.

Again those unseen hands released her, and she collapsed to the ground. She rubbed the heels of her palms into her weeping eyes. For the first time she was aware of a warmth along her inner thighs. She had urinated where she stood, and never been aware of it.

Grasper was standing, trembling but upright, gazing up at the washing lights, which cast complex patterns of shadows across her small face. A fifth set of lines – a *sixth* set, disappearing in impossible directions—

Grasper went rigid, her head locked back, her fingers grabbing at nothing, and then she fell, rigid as a block of wood. Seeker grabbed her child and cradled her on her own piss-soaked lap. The stiffness went out of Grasper, and she became a bundle of limp fur. Seeker stroked her and let her suckle, though her flaccid breast had been dry for years.

Even now the Eye watched them, recording the bond between mother and child, draining the man-apes of every sensation. It was all part of the test.

The respite was only brief. Soon the Eye resumed its steady, pearly glow, and it was as if unseen hands poked and prodded at Seeker's limbs. She pushed aside her child and stood once more, her face lifted to the unearthly light.

CHAPTER 38

THE EYE OF MARDUK

Bisesa moved into the Temple of Marduk. She brought in a pallet and blankets and had her food delivered; she even set up a chemical toilet that had come from the Bird. She spent most of her time here now, alone save for the small company of the phone – and the brooding mass of the Eye.

She could *feel* there was something there, a presence behind that impenetrable hide. It was a feeling beyond the immediate senses, like the feeling she would get if she was blindfolded and thrust through a door, and still able to tell if the space she was in was open, or confined.

But it wasn't like being with a person. Sometimes all she felt was watchfulness, as if the Eye was no more than a huge camera. But sometimes she felt she glimpsed something *behind* the Eye. Was there a Watcher who stood, metaphorically, behind all the Eyes in the world? Sometimes she sensed there was a whole hierarchy of intelligences, in fact, escalating up from the simple constructs of Watchers and Eyes that she could imagine, up in some impossible direction, filtering and classifying the distillation of her actions, her reactions, her very self.

She spent more and more of her time exploring these sensations. She avoided everybody, her twenty-first-century companions – even poor Josh. She would turn to him for comfort, though, when she felt cold, and too desolately lonely. But afterwards, though she felt genuine affection for him, she would be guilty, as if she had used him.

She tried not to examine these feelings, tried not even to decide if she loved Josh or not. She had the Eye, and that was the centre of her world. It had to be. And she wouldn't share herself with anybody or anything else, not even Josh.

She tried to apply physics to the Eye.

She began with simple geometric measurements, like those Abdikadir had tried on the smaller Eye in the Northwest Frontier. She used laser instruments to prove that for this bauble too the famous ratio pi was not about three and one-seventh, as Euclid, schoolbook geometry and the rest of the world demanded, but simply three. Like all the Eyes, this was an intruder from somewhere else.

She went beyond geometry. With a party of Macedonians and British she went back to the Northwest Frontier and the crash site of the Little Bird. Months of acid rain hadn't helped to preserve what was left. Still, there were usable electro-magnetic sensors, working in visible light, infra-red and ultraviolet – twenty-first-century spy-in-the-sky electronic eyes – and various chemical sensors, 'noses' designed to sniff out explosives and the like. She dug out instrumentation, components, cabling, any usable gear – including that small chemical toilet.

She set up her equipment in the temple chamber. She improvised scaffolding around the Eye, and fixed the Bird's amputated sensors to gaze at the alien object from all angles, twenty-four hours a day. In the end she filled this ancient Babylonian temple chamber with a tangle of cables and infra-red comms beams, all leading to an interface box on which her phone patiently sat. She had little electrical power, though, only the batteries from the Bird and smaller cells in the gear itself. So her twenty-first-century sensors peered at this impossibly advanced alien artefact by the smoky light of animal-fat lamps.

She got some answers.

The Bird's radiation sensors, souped-up Geiger counters designed to sniff out illicit nukes, detected traces of high-frequency X-rays and very high-energy particles emanating from the Eye. These results were tantalising and elusive, and she guessed this was just leakage, that there was a whole spectrum of exotic high-energy radiation products flowing from the Eye, beyond the capacity of the Bird's crude Geigers to pick up. The radiation must be traces of some immense expenditure of energy – the great straining required to keep this Eye in existence in an inimical reality, perhaps.

And then there was the question of time.

She used the Bird's altimeter to bounce laser beams off the Eye's hide. The laser light was reflected with a hundred per cent efficiency; the surface of the Eye acted like a perfect mirror. But the beams came back with a measurable Doppler shift. It was as if the surface of the Eye was receding, fast, at more than a hundred kilometres per hour. Every point on the surface she tested gave the same result. According to these results the Eye was imploding.

To her naked eye, of course, the Eye sat fat and immovable, hovering complacently in the air as it always did. Nevertheless, in some direction she couldn't perceive, that slick surface was *moving*. She suspected that in some sense the Eye's existence escalated up in directions beyond her power to see, or her instruments to measure.

And if that was possible, she mused, perhaps there was only *one* Eye, projecting down from some higher dimension into the world, like fingers from a single hand pushing through the surface of a pond.

But sometimes she thought that all this experimentation was just to divert herself from the main issue, which was her intuition about the Eye.

'Maybe I'm just being anthropomorphic,' she said to the phone. 'Why should there be *mind*, anything like my mind, involved in this at all?'

'David Hume wondered about that,' the phone murmured. '*Dialogues Concerning Natural Religion* . . . Hume asked why we should look for "mind" as the organising principle of the universe. He was talking about traditional constructs of God, of course. Maybe the order we perceive just *emerges*. "For aught we know *a priori*, matter may contain the source, or spring, of order originating within itself, as well as the mind does." He wrote that down a full century before Darwin proved it was possible for organisation to emerge from mind-less matter.'

'So you do think I'm anthropomorphising?'

'No,' said the phone. 'We don't know any way for an object like this to be formed except by intelligent action. Assuming a mind is responsible is probably the simplest hypothesis. And anyhow, perhaps these feelings you have are based in some physical reality, even if they don't come through your senses. Your body, your brain, are complicated instruments in their own right. Perhaps the subtle electrochemistry that underpins your mind is being influenced, somehow, by *that*. It's not telepathy – but it may be real.'

'Do *you* sense there's something here?'

'No. But then I'm not human,' the phone sighed.

Sometimes she suspected the Eye was feeding her these insights, deliberately. 'It's as if it is downloading information into me, bit by bit. But my mind, my brain, is just incapable of taking it all. It's as if I tried to download modern virtual reality software on to a Babbage difference engine . . .'

'That's a simile I can sympathise with,' said the phone dryly.

'No offence.'

Sometimes she would simply sit in the ponderous company of the Eye, and let her mind roam where it would.

She kept thinking of Myra. As time passed, as the months turned into years, and the Discontinuity, that single extraordinary event, receded into the past, she felt herself embedding more deeply into this new world. Sometimes, in this drab antique place, her memories of twenty-first-century Earth seemed absurd, impossibly gaudy, like a false dream. But her feelings of loss about Myra didn't fade.

It wasn't even as if Myra had been taken from her somehow, to continue her life in some other part of the world. It was no comfort to her to imagine how old Myra would be now, how she must look, where she would be in her school career, what they might have been doing together if they had been reunited. None of those comprehensible human situations applied, because she couldn't know if she and Myra had a time-line in common. It was even possible that there were many copies of Myra on multiple fragmented worlds, some of them even with copies of *herself*, and how was she supposed to feel about that? The Discontinuity had been a superhuman event, and the loss she had suffered was superhuman too, and she had no human way of coping with it.

As she lay on her pallet, brooding through the night, she sensed the Eye watching her, drawing up her baffled grief. She sensed that mind, but there was no compassion there, no pity, nothing but a vast Olympian watchfulness.

She would get to her feet and beat on the Eye's impassive hide with her fist, or hurl bits of Babylonian rubble at it. 'Is this what you wanted? Is this why you came here, why you ripped apart our world and our lives? Did you come here to break my heart? *Why won't you just send me home*? . . .'

There was a certain receptivity, she felt. Mostly it felt like the reverberant receptivity of a vast cathedral dome, in which her tiny cries were lost and meaningless.

But sometimes she thought someone was listening to her.

And just occasionally, compassionless or not, she felt they might respond to her pleas.

One day the phone whispered to her, 'It's time.'

'Time for what?'

'I have to go to safe mode.'

She had been expecting this. The phone's memory contained a cache of invaluable and irreplaceable data – not just her observations of the Eye, and a record of the Discontinuity events, but the last of the treasures of the old vanished world, not least the works of poor Ruddy Kipling. But there was nowhere to download the data, not even a way to print it out. During her sleep times she had given up the phone to a team of British clerks, under the supervision of Abdikadir, who had copied out by hand various documents and diagrams and maps. It was better than nothing, but the phone's capacious memory had barely been scratched.

Anyhow Bisesa and the phone had agreed that when the phone's batteries dropped to a certain critical level it should make itself inert. It would only take a trickle of power to preserve its data almost indefinitely, until such time as Mir's new civilisation advanced enough to access the phone's invaluable memories. 'And bring you back to life,' she had promised the phone.

It was all quite logical. But now the moment was here, Bisesa was bereft. After all this phone had been her companion since she was twelve.

'You have to press the buttons to shut me down,' the phone said.

'I know.' She held the little instrument before her, and found the right key combination through eyes embarrassingly blurred with tears. She paused before hitting the final key.

'I'm sorry,' said the phone.

'It's not your fault.'

'Bisesa, I'm frightened.'

'You don't have to be. I'll wall you up if I have to and leave you to the archaeologists.'

'I don't mean that. I've never been switched off before. Do you think I will dream?'

'I don't know,' she whispered. She pressed the key, and the phone's surface, glowing green in the gloom of the chamber, turned dark.

CHAPTER 39

EXPLORATIONS

After a six-month exploratory jaunt into southern India, Abdikadir returned to Babylon.

Eumenes took him on a tour of the recovering city. It was a cold day. Though it was midsummer – according to the Babylonian astronomers, who patiently tracked the motion of stars and sun through a new sky – the wind was chill, and Abdikadir wrapped his arms around his body.

After months away, Abdikadir was impressed with the latest developments; the inhabitants of the city had been hard at work. Alexander had repopulated the depleted city with some of his own officers and veterans, and had installed one of his generals in a joint governorship of the city with one of Babylon's pre-Discontinuity officials. The experiment seemed to be working; the new population, a mixture of Macedonian warriors and Babylonian grandees, seemed to be getting along tolerably well.

There was much debate about what to do with the region on the western bank, reduced to rubble by time. To the Macedonians it was a wasteland; to the moderns it was an archaeological site which could perhaps one day offer up some clues about the great displacement in time that had split this city in two. To leave it alone for now was the obvious compromise.

But downstream of the city walls, Alexander's army had dug out a huge natural harbour, deep enough to take ocean-going ships, which were being constructed from local timber in hastily assembled dry docks. There was even a small lighthouse, illuminated by oil lamps with polished shields as mirrors behind them.

'This is magnificent,' Abdikadir said. They were standing

on the new harbour's wall, which towered over the small vessels that already ventured on to the water beneath it.

Eumenes said that Alexander knew that fast transport and effective communications were the key to holding together an empire. 'The King learned that lesson the hard way,' Eumenes said dryly. In five years he had learned some halting English, Abdikadir some uncertain Greek; with a little co-operation they could communicate without interpreters now. Eumenes went on, 'Alexander's progress through Persia owed much to the quality of the imperial roads. When we reached the end of the Persian roads, far to the east, his infantrymen knew they could go no further, no matter what his vaulting ambition desired. And so we had to stop. But the ocean is the road of the gods, and requires no labour to lay it.'

'Even so, I can't believe you've achieved so much so quickly.' Abdikadir, viewing all this industry, felt faintly guilty. Perhaps he had been away too long.

He had enjoyed his explorations. In India Abdikadir and his party had hacked a path through dense jungle, encountering all manner of exotic plants and animals – though few people. Similar expeditions were being sent out to east, west, north, south, across Europe, Asia, Africa. To map out this new and rich world seemed to fill a void in Abdikadir's heart left by the loss of his own world – and the trauma of the great killing during the Mongol assault. Perhaps he was exploring the outer world in order to distract himself from the turmoil of the inner – and perhaps he had been evading his true responsibilities too long.

He turned away from the city and gazed towards the south, where the glistening tracks of irrigation canals lanced across fields of green. Here was the real work of the world: growing food. This was the Fertile Crescent, after all, the birthplace of organised agriculture, and once its artificially irrigated fields had provided a third of the food supply for the Persian empire. There surely couldn't have been a better place to start farming again. But Abdikadir had already inspected the fields, and he knew that things weren't going well.

'It is this wretched cold,' Eumenes complained. 'The astronomers may call this midsummer, but I have known no summer like it . . . And then there are the locusts, and other plagues of insects.'

The recovery programme was indeed impressive, even if it had been slow starting. The quest to save Babylon from the Mongols was long over, and there seemed no real prospect of a revival of the Mongol threat in the near future. Alexander's ambassadors reported that the Mongols seem stunned by the sudden emptying of China, to their south: fifty million people, vanished into thin air. The war with the Mongols had been a great adventure – but it had been a diversion. With the battle won, there had been a deep sense of anticlimax among the British, Macedonians and Little Bird crew alike, and everyone in Babylon was suddenly left to face the unpleasant truth that this was one campaign from which none of them was ever going home.

It had taken some time for them to discover a new purpose: to build a new world. And Alexander, with his energy and indomitable will, had been central to establishing that sense of purpose.

'And what is the King working on himself?'

'That.' Eumenes pointed grandly to the ceremonial heart of the city.

Abdikadir saw that a broad area had been cleared, and the lower levels of what looked like a new ziggurat had been laid out. He whistled. 'That looks like it will rival Babel itself.'

'Perhaps it will. Nominally, it is a monument for Hephaistion; its deeper purpose will be to commemorate the world we have lost. These Macedonians always did treasure their funerary arts! And Alexander, I think, has an ambition to rival the massive tombs he once saw in Egypt. But with things as they are in the fields, it is hard for us to afford the manpower for such a venture, no matter how magnificent.'

Abdikadir studied the Greek's finely chiselled face. 'I have a feeling you're asking me for something.'

Eumenes smiled. 'And I have a feeling you have a little Greek in you too. Abdikadir, although the King's wife Roxana delivered a son – a boy who is now four years old – so that we have an heir, Alexander's continued well-being over the next few years is essential to us all.'

'Of course.'

'But *this*,' Eumenes said, meaning the dockyards and fields, 'is not enough for him. The King is a complex man, Abdikadir. *I* should know. He is a Macedonian, of course – and he drinks like one. But he is capable of cold calculation, like a Persian; and he can be a statesman of startling insight – he is like a Greek of the cities!

'But for all his wisdom, Alexander has the heart of a warrior, and there is a tension between his warmongering instincts and his will to build an empire. I don't think he always understands that himself. He was born to fight men, not locusts in a field, or silt in a canal. Let's face it, there are few men to be found out there to fight!' The Greek leaned towards Abdikadir. 'The truth is, the running of Babylonia has devolved to a handful of those close to him. There is myself, Perdiccas and Captain Grove.' Perdiccas was one of Alexander's long-serving officers, and among his closest associates; Perdiccas, a commander of the Foot Companion infantrymen, had been formally given the title Hephaistion had enjoyed before his death, which meant something like 'Vizier'. Eumenes winked. 'They need my Greek cleverness, you see, but *I* need Macedonians to work through. Of course we each have our own followers – especially Perdiccas! There are cliques and conspiracies, as there always have been. But as long as Alexander towers over us, we work together well enough. We all need Alexander; New Babylon needs its King. But—'

'It doesn't need him hanging around here with nothing to do, soaking up manpower on monuments while there are fields to be tilled.' Abdikadir grinned. 'You want me to distract him?'

Eumenes said smoothly, 'I wouldn't put it like that. But Alexander has expressed curiosity to know if the greater world you described to us is still there to be had. And I think he wants to visit his father.'

'His father?'

'His divine father, Ammon, who is also Zeus, at his shrine in the desert.'

Abdikadir whistled. 'That would be quite a tour.'

Eumenes smiled. 'All the better. There is the question of Bisesa, too.'

'I know. She's still locked away with that damn Eye.'

'I'm sure it's invaluable work. But we don't want to lose her to it: you *moderns* are too few to spare. Take her with you.' Eumenes smiled. 'I hear that Josh is back from Judea. Perhaps he might distract her . . .'

'You're a wily devil, Secretary Eumenes.'

'One does what one must,' said Eumenes. 'Come. I'll show you round the shipyards.'

The temple chamber was a rat's nest of cables and wires and bits of kit from the crashed chopper, some of them scarred where they had been crudely cut from the wreck, or even scorched by the fires that had followed the crash. This tangle enclosed the Eye, as if Bisesa had been seeking to trap it, not study it. But she knew that Abdikadir thought it was she who had become trapped.

'The Discontinuity was a physical event,' Bisesa said firmly. 'No matter how mighty the power behind it. Physical, not magical or supernatural. And so it's explicable in terms of physics.'

'But,' said Abdikadir, 'not necessarily *our* physics.'

She glanced vaguely about the temple chamber, wishing she still had the phone to help her explain.

Abdikadir, and a wide-eyed, scared-looking Josh, had settled down in a corner of the chamber. She knew Josh hated this place – not just for the awesome presence of the Eye, but because it had taken her away from him. Now Josh cracked a flask of hot tea with milk, English-style, as Bisesa tried to explain her current theories about the Eye, and the Discontinuity.

Bisesa said, 'Space and time were ruptured during the Discontinuity, ruptured and put back together again. We know

301

that much, and in a way we can understand it. Space and time are in some senses real. You can bend spacetime, for instance with a strong enough gravity field. It's as stiff as steel, but you can do it . . .

'But if spacetime is *stuff*, what's it made of? If you look really closely – or if you subject it to enough bending and folding – well, you can see the grain. Our best idea is that space and time are a kind of tapestry. The fundamental units of the tapestry are strings, minuscule strings. The strings vibrate – and the modes of the vibration, the tones of the strings, are the particles and energy fields we observe, and their properties, such as their masses. There are many ways the strings can vibrate – many notes they can play – but some of them, the highest energy modes, have not been seen since the birth of the universe.

'All right. Now, the strings need a space to vibrate in – not our own spacetime, which is the music of the strings, but a kind of abstraction, a stratum. In many dimensions.'

Josh frowned, visibly struggling to keep up. 'Go on.'

'The way the stratum is set up, its topology, governs the way the strings behave. It's like the sounding board of a violin. It's a beautiful image if you think about it. The topology is a property of the universe on the largest scale, but it determines the behaviour of matter on the very smallest scales.

'But imagine you cut a hole in the sounding board, make a change to the structure of the underlying stratum. Then you would get a transition in the way the strings vibrate.'

Abdikadir said, 'And the effect of such a transition in the world we observe—'

'The strings' vibrations govern the existence of the particles and fields that make up our world, and their properties. So if you go through a transition, those properties change.' She shrugged. 'The speed of light might change, for instance.' She described her measurements of Doppler shifts in the reflections from the Eye of Marduk; perhaps that was something to do with stratum-level transitions.

Josh leaned forward, his small face serious. 'But, Bisesa –

what about causality? You have the Buddhist monk, who Kolya described, living with his own younger self! Now, what if that old man were to strangle the boy – would the lama pop out of existence? And then there is poor Ruddy – dead, now, and so forever incapable of writing the novels and poems which you claimed, Bisesa, to have stored in your phone! What does your physics of strings and sounding-boards say about that?'

She sighed and rubbed her face. 'We're talking about a ripped-apart spacetime. The rules are different. Josh, do you know what a black hole is? Imagine a star collapsing, becoming so dense that its gravity field deepens hugely – in the end, not even the most powerful rocket could escape from its grasp. In the end, *even light itself* can't escape. Josh, a black hole is a tear in the orderly tapestry of spacetime. And it eats information. If I throw an object into a black hole – a rock, or the last copy of the complete works of Shakespeare, it doesn't matter – almost all the information about it is lost, beyond retrieval, nothing but its mass, charge and spin.

'Now, the interfaces between the chunks of Mir, drawn from different eras, were surely not like the event horizons of black holes. But they *were* spacetime rips. And perhaps information is lost in the same way. And *that's* why causality has broken down. I think our new reality, here on Mir, is – knitting up. New causal chains are forming. But the new chains are part of *this* world, this reality, and have nothing to do with the old . . .' She rubbed tired eyes. 'That's the best I can do. Depressing, isn't it? Our most advanced physics offers us nothing but metaphors.'

Abdikadir said gently, 'You must write this down. Have Eumenes assign you a secretary to record it all.'

'In Greek?' Bisesa laughed hollowly.

Josh said, 'We are talking of the *how* of the Discontinuity. I am no closer to understanding the *why*.'

'Oh, there was a purpose,' said Bisesa. She glared up at the Eye resentfully. 'We just haven't figured it out yet. But *they* are up there, somewhere – beyond the Eye, beyond all the Eyes – watching us. Playing with us, maybe.'

'Playing?'

She said, 'Have you seen the way the Eye in the cage has been experimenting with the man-apes? They run around that damn net like rats with wires in their heads.'

Josh said, 'Perhaps the Eye is trying to' – he spread his hands – 'stimulate the man-apes. Uplift them to greater intelligence.'

'Look in their eyes,' said Bisesa coldly. 'This has nothing to do with uplift. They are draining those wretched creatures. The Eyes aren't here to give. They are here to take.'

'We are no man-apes,' said Abdikadir.

'No. But maybe the tests they are running on us are just more subtle. Maybe the peculiar features of the Eye, like its non-Euclidean geometry, are there solely as a puzzle-box for us. And you think it was a *coincidence* that Alexander and Genghis Khan were both brought here? The two greatest warlords in Eurasian history, knocking their heads together, by *chance*? They are laughing at us. Maybe that's all there is to this whole damn thing.'

'Bisesa.' Josh took her hands in his. 'You believe the Eye is the key to everything that is happening. Well, so do I. But you are letting the work destroy you. And what good will that do?'

She looked at him and Abdikadir, alarmed. 'What are you two cooking up?'

Abdikadir told her about Alexander's planned European expedition. 'Come away with us, Bisesa. What an adventure!'

'But the Eye—'

'Will still be here when you get back,' Josh said. 'We can delegate somebody else to continue your monitoring.'

Abdikadir said, 'The man-apes can't leave their cage. You are a human. Show this thing it can't control you, Bisesa. Walk out.'

'Bullshit,' she said tiredly. Then she added, 'Casey.'

'What?'

'Casey's got to run this shop. Not some Macedonian. And not some British, who would be worse, because he'd think he understands.'

304

Abdikadir and Josh exchanged a glance. 'Bags I don't tell him he's got to do it,' said Josh quickly.

Bisesa stared at the Eye. 'I'll be back, you bastards. And be nice to Casey. Remember I know more about you than I've told them yet . . .'

Abdikadir frowned. 'Bisesa? What do you mean by that?'

That I might know a way home. But she couldn't tell them that, not yet. She stood up. 'When do we leave?'

CHAPTER 40

THE BOATING LAKE

The journey would begin at Alexandria. They were to sail anticlockwise around the complicated shore of the Mediterranean: starting from Egypt, they would travel north and then west along the southern coast of Europe, all the way to the Straits of Gibraltar, and back along the northern coast of Africa.

Nothing this King did was modest. He was, after all, Alexander the Great. And his jaunt around the Mediterranean, which his advisors had, wryly, taken to calling 'Alexander's Boating Lake', was no exception.

Alexander had been terribly disappointed to find that the city he had planted at the mouth of the Nile, his Alexandria-on-the-Nile, had been obliterated by the Discontinuity. But, undeterred, he ordered units of his army to begin the construction of a new city there, on the plan of the vanished old. And he set his engineers the task of building a new canal between the Gulf of Suez and the Nile. In the meantime he ordered the hasty construction of a temporary harbour at Alexandria, and had many of the ships he had constructed in India sailed up the Gulf of Suez, broken down into sections, and hauled overland.

To Bisesa's amazement it took only a couple of months before the fleet was reassembled at the site of Alexandria and ready to sail. After a two-day festival of sacrifices and merriment in the tent compound that housed the city's workers, the fleet set off.

At first Bisesa, separated from the Eye of Marduk for the first time in five years, found the voyage strangely relaxing. She spent a lot of time on deck, watching the land unravel past her, or listening to complicated cross-cultural discussions. Even the ocean was a curiosity. In her time the Mediterranean, recovering from decades of pollution, had become a mixture of game reserve and park, fenced off with great invisible barriers of electricity and sound. Now it was wild again, and she glimpsed dolphins and whales. Once she thought she saw the torpedo shape of an immense shark, bigger than anything from her day, she was sure.

It was never warm, though. Often in the mornings she would smell frost in the air. Every year it seemed a little colder, though it was hard to be sure; she wished they had thought to keep climate records from the beginning. But despite the chill she found she had to keep out of the sun. The British took to wearing knotted handkerchiefs on their heads, and even the nutmeg-brown Macedonians seemed to burn. On the royal boats thick awnings were erected, and Alexander's doctors experimented with ointments of asses' butter and palm sap to block the suddenly intense rays of the sun. The storms of the early days after the Discontinuity had long passed, but clearly the climate remained screwed.

At night there was more strangeness, too. Under the tented canopies Alexander and his companions drank the night away. But Bisesa would sit in the darkened quiet of the deck, watching land go by on which there was generally not a single light to be seen. She would peer up, if the sky was clear, at subtly altered constellations. But often she would see auroras, vast walls and sheets and curtains of light, visibly three-dimensional structures towering over the darkened world. She had never known of auroras visible at such low latitudes, and she had an uneasy feeling about what they might portend; the Discontinuity wasn't cosmetic, and might have cut deep indeed into the fabric of the world.

Sometimes Josh would sit with her. And sometimes, if the Macedonians were quiet, they would find a dark corner, and make love, or perhaps just huddle together.

But most of the time she kept to herself. She suspected her friends were right, that she had been in danger of losing herself in the Eye. She needed to ground herself in the world once more, and even Josh was a distraction. But she knew she was hurting him, once again.

The ostensible point of the trip was to survey the new world, and every few days Alexander sent parties inland. He had selected a small force of Iranians, colonial Greeks and Agrarians to carry out these missions: highly mobile, flexible troops, brimming with initiative and daring. Some British were attached to each party, and each foray was accompanied by surveyors and map-makers.

The first reports were desolating, though. From the beginning the explorers reported wonders: strange rock formations, islands of extraordinary vegetation, even more extraordinary animals. But these marvels were all aspects of the natural world; of the works of mankind barely a trace survived. The ancient civilisation of Egypt, for example, had vanished completely. The blocks of its monumental buildings were uncut from their sandstone beds, and in the Valley of the Kings there was no sign of anything like humanity save a few of the cautious chimp-like creatures the British called man-apes, clinging to patches of forest.

It was a relief to sail up the coast of Judea. Of Nazareth and Bethlehem there wasn't a trace – and no sign of Christ or His Passion. But close to the site of Jerusalem, under the command of British engineers, a small industrial revolution was being kick-started. Josh and Bisesa toured foundries and yards where cheerful British engineers and sweating Macedonian labourers, and a few bright Greek apprentices, constructed pressure vessels like giant kettles, and experimented with prototype steamship screws and lengths of railway track. The engineers were learning to communicate in an archaic Greek studded with English words like 'crank-shaft' and 'head of steam'.

As everywhere, there was a rush to build quickly, before the memories and capabilities of the first generation, transmitted across the Discontinuity, were lost. But Alexander himself, a lead-from-the-front warrior King, had turned out to be something of a sceptic when it came to technology. It had taken the construction of a prototype to impress him. This had been something like the famous *aeolipile* of Hero – in a lost time-line, a manufacturer of mechanical novelties in Alexandria – just a pressure vessel with two canted nozzles that would vent steam and spin around like a lawn sprinkler. But Eumenes had immediately seen the potential of this new form of power.

It was a difficult job, though. The British had only a handful of the necessary tools, and the industry's infrastructure would have to be built literally from the ground up, including establishing mines for coal and iron ore. Bisesa thought it might be twenty years before it was possible to manufacture engines as efficient and powerful as James Watt's, say.

'But it begins again,' Abdikadir said. 'Soon, all across Alexander's domain, there will be pumps labouring in mines dug deeper and deeper, and steamships cruising a shrinking Mediterranean, and rail networks spreading east across Asia towards the capital of the Mongols. This new Jerusalem will be the workshop of the world.'

'Ruddy would have loved it,' Josh said. 'He was always very impressed with machines. Like a new breed of being in the world, he said. And Ruddy said that transport *is* civilisation. If the continents can be united by steamships and railway trains, perhaps this new world need see no more war, no more nations, indeed, save the single marvellous nation of mankind!'

Abdikadir said, 'I thought he said sewage was the basis of civilisation.'

'That too!'

Bisesa fondly took Josh's hand. 'Your optimism is like a caffeine hit, Josh.'

He frowned. 'I'll take that as a compliment.'

Abdikadir said, 'But the new world is going to be nothing like ours. There are overwhelmingly more of *them*, the Macedonians, than *us*. If a new world-state does come into existence, it will be speaking Greek – if not Mongol. And it's likely to be Buddhist . . .'

In a world stripped of its messiahs, the strange time-twin Buddhists in their temple deep in Asia had been gathering interest from both Macedonians and Mongols. The lama's circular life seemed a perfect metaphor for both the Discontinuity and the strange condition of the world it had left behind, as well as for the religion the lama gently espoused.

'Oh,' said Josh wistfully, 'I wish I could spring forward through two or three centuries and see what grows from the seeds we are planting today! . . .'

But as the journey continued such dreams, of building empires and taming worlds, came to seem petty indeed.

Greece was empty. No matter how hard Alexander's explorers probed the dense tangle of forest that coated much of the mainland, there were no signs of the great cities, no Athens, no Sparta, no Thebes. There were barely signs of humans at all: a few rough-looking tribesmen, said the explorers, and what they described as 'sub-men'. More in hope than anticipation Alexander sent a party north to Macedon, to see what might have survived of his homeland. It took weeks for the scouts to return, with negative news.

'It seems,' Alexander said with a dry wistfulness, 'there are more lions in Greece now than philosophers.'

But even the lions weren't doing too well, Bisesa noted sadly.

Everywhere they travelled they saw signs of ecological damage and collapse. The Greek forests were wilted and fringed by scrubby grassland. In Turkey, the inland areas had been baked clean of life altogether, leaving the ground an exposed rust brown – 'Red as Mars,' Abdikadir said after taking part in one jaunt. And, as they explored the island that had once been called Crete Josh asked: 'Have you noticed how few birds there are?'

It was hard to be sure about the extent of what was being lost, as there was no way of knowing what had crossed through the Discontinuity in the first place. But Bisesa suspected there was a major die-back under way. They could only guess at the causes.

'Just mixing everything up must have done a great deal of damage,' Bisesa said.

Josh protested, 'But mammoths in Paris! Sabre-tooth cats in the Colosseum of Rome! Mir is a bringing-together of fragments, but so is a kaleidoscope, and its effect is beautiful.'

'Yeah, but whenever you get mixing of populations you get extinctions: when the land bridge between North and South America is joined, when humans carried rats and goats and such around the world to devastate native wildlife. So it must be here. You have creatures from the depth of the Ice Age side by side with rodents from modern cities, in a climate suited to neither. Whatever survived the Discontinuity is wiping out its neighbour, or being wiped out in turn.'

'Just like us,' Abdikadir said blackly. 'We couldn't stand being mixed up either, could we?'

Bisesa said, 'There must be booms and crashes: maybe that explains our plagues of insects, a symptom of an out-of-kilter ecology. Diseases must be transmitted across the old boundaries too. I'm a little surprised that we've had no real epidemics.'

Abdikadir said, 'We humans are too thinly scattered. Even so, perhaps we've been lucky . . .'

'But no birds trill from the trees!' Josh complained.

'Birds are bell-wethers, Josh,' Bisesa said. 'Birds are vulnerable. Their habitats, like wetlands and beaches, are easily damaged in climate shifts. The loss of the birds is a bad sign.'

'Then if things are so difficult for the animals' – Josh pounded his bunched fist on to a rail – 'we must do something about it.'

Abdikadir laughed, then stopped himself. 'What, exactly?'

'You mock me,' said Josh, red-faced. He waved his hands, grasping at ideas. 'We should gather the animals in zoos, or reserves. The same with the vegetation, the trees and plants. The birds and insects too – especially the birds! And then, when things settle down we can release the beasts into the wild.'

'And let a new Eden build itself?' Bisesa said. 'Dear Josh, we're not mocking you. And we should put your idea of

311

gathering zoo specimens to Alexander: if the mammoth and the cave bear have been brought back to life, let's keep a few. But it's just that we've learned it's more complicated than that – learned the hard way. Conserving ecospheres, let alone repairing them, isn't so easy, especially as we never understood how they worked anyhow. They aren't even static; they are dynamic, undergoing great cycles. Extinctions are inevitable; they happen at the best of times. No matter what we try, *we can't keep it all.*'

Josh said, 'Then what are we to do? Simply throw up our hands and accept whatever fate has decreed?'

'No,' said Bisesa. 'But we have to accept our limits. There are only a handful of us. We can't save the world, Josh. We don't even know how to. We will do well to save ourselves. We must be patient.'

Abdikadir said grimly, 'Patience, yes. But it took only a fraction of a second for the wounds of the Discontinuity to be inflicted. It will take millions of years for them to heal.'

'And it had nothing to do with fate,' Josh said. 'If the gods of the Eye were wise enough to rip apart space and time, could they not have foreseen what would become of our ecologies?'

They fell silent, and the jungles of Greece, dense, wilting, menacing, slid by.

CHAPTER 41

ZEUS-AMMON

Italy seemed as deserted as Greece. They found no sign of the city-states the Macedonians remembered, or the modern cities of Bisesa's time. Even at the mouth of the Tiber there was no trace of the extensive harbour workings which the imperial Romans had constructed, to service the great grain fleets which had kept their bloated city alive.

Alexander was intrigued by accounts of how Rome, just an ambitious city-state in his day, would one day have built an empire to rival his own. So he put together a handful of riverboats and, reclining under a brilliant purple canopy, led a party up the river.

The seven hills of Rome were immediately recognisable. But the site was uninhabited, save for a few ugly hill forts sitting squat on the Palatine, where the palaces of the Caesars would have been built. Alexander thought this was a great joke, and decided graciously to spare the lives of his historical rivals.

They spent a night camped close in the marshy lowland that should have become the Forum of Rome. There was another startling aurora, which brought gasps from the Macedonians.

Bisesa was no geologist, but she wondered what must have happened deep in the core of the world when the new planet had been assembled from its disparate fragments. Earth's core had been a spinning worldlet of iron as big as the Moon. If the stitching-together of Mir went to the very centre of the world, that great sub-planet, crudely reassembled, must be thrashing and roiling. The currents in the outer layers, the mantle, would be disturbed too, with plumes of molten rock, fountains hundreds of kilometres tall, breaking and crashing against each other. Maybe the effects of such deep storms were now being felt on the surface of the planet.

The planet's magnetic field, generated by the great iron dynamo of the spinning core, must have collapsed. Maybe that explained the auroras, and the continuing failure of their compasses. In normal times this magnetic shield protected fragile life forms from a hard rain from space: heavy particles from the sun, sleeting remnants from supernova explosions. Before the magnetic field restored itself there would be radiation damage: cancers, a flood of mutations, almost all of them harmful. And if the battered ozone layer had collapsed too, the flood of ultraviolet would explain the intensified sunlight, and would do even more damage to the living creatures exposed on Earth's surface.

But there were other domains of life. She thought of the deep hot biosphere, the ancient heat-loving creatures that had survived from Earth's earliest days, lingering around ocean vents and deep in the rocks. *They* wouldn't be troubled by a little surface ultraviolet, but if the world had been sliced to its core their ancient empire must have been partitioned, just as on the surface. Was there some slow extinction event unfolding deep in the rocks, as on the surface? And were there Eyes buried in the body of the world to watch that too?

The fleet sailed on, tracking the southern coast of France, and then along eastern and southern Spain, making towards Gibraltar.

There were few signs of humans, but in the rocky landscape of southern Spain the scouts found a stocky kind of people with beetling brows and great strength, who would flee at the first sight of the Macedonians. Bisesa knew this area had been one of the last hold-outs of the Neandertals as *Homo sapiens* had advanced west through Europe. If these were late Neandertals, they were well advised to be wary of modern humans.

Alexander was much more intrigued by the Straits themselves, which he called the Pillars of Heracles. The ocean beyond these gates was not quite unknown to Alexander's generation. Two centuries before Alexander the Carthaginian Hanno had sailed boldly south along the Atlantic coast of Africa. There were less well documented reports, too, of explorers who had turned to the north, and found strange, chill lands, where ice formed in the summer and the sun would not set even at midnight. Alexander now seized on his new understanding of the shape of the world: such strangeness was easy to explain if you believed you were sailing over the surface of a sphere.

Alexander longed to brave the wider ocean beyond the Straits. Josh was all for this, eager to get in touch with the community at Chicago which might not be far removed from his own time. But Alexander himself was more interested in reaching the new mid-Atlantic island the Soyuz had reported: he had been stirred by Bisesa's descriptions of voyages to the Moon, and he said that to conquer a land was one thing, but to be the first ever to set foot there quite another.

But even a King had constraints. For one thing his small ships weren't capable of surviving at sea for more than a few days without putting in to shore. The quiet words of his counsellors persuaded him that the new world of the west would wait for other days. So, with reluctance mixed with anticipation, Alexander agreed to turn back.

The fleet sailed back along the Mediterranean's southern shore, the coast of Africa. The journey was unremarkable, the coast apparently uninhabited.

Bisesa withdrew into herself once more. Her weeks on Alexander's expedition had taken her away from the vivid intensity of her time with the Eye itself, and had given her time to reflect on what she had learned. Now, something of the blankness of both sea and land made the mysteries of the Eye revive in her mind.

Abdikadir, and especially Josh, tried to draw her out of herself. One night, as they sat on the deck, Josh whispered, 'I still don't understand how you *know*. When I look up at the Eye, I *feel* nothing. I am prepared to believe that each of us has an inner sense of others – that minds, lonely bits of

315

spindrift in the great dark ocean of time, have a way of seeking each other out. To me the Eye is a vast and ponderous mystery, and clearly a centre of awesome power – but it is the power of a machine, not a mind.'

Bisesa said, 'It is not a mind, but it is a conduit to minds. They're like shadows at the end of a darkened corridor. But they are *there*.' There were no human words for such perceptions, for, she suspected, no human being had experienced such things before. 'You have to trust me, Josh.'

He wrapped his arms tighter around her. 'I trust you and I believe you. Otherwise I wouldn't be here.'

'You know, sometimes I think all these time-slices we visit are just – bits of a fantasy. Fragments of a dream.'

Abdikadir frowned, his blue eyes bright in the light of the lamps. 'What do you mean by that?'

She struggled to explain her impressions. 'I think in some sense we're *contained* in the Eye.' She retreated to the safety of physics. 'Think of it this way. The fundamental units of our reality—'

'The tiny strings,' Josh said.

'That's right. They aren't really like strings on a violin. There are different ways they can be wrapped around their underlying stratum, their sounding board. Imagine loops of string floating free on the board's surface, and others wrapped right around the board. If you change the dimensions of the stratum – if you make it thicker – the winding energy of the wrapped strings will increase, but the vibrational energy of the loops will decrease. And that will have an effect in the observable universe. If you keep that up long enough, the two dimensions, long and short, exchange places . . . They have an inverse relationship.'

Josh shook his head. 'You've lost me.'

'I think she's telling us,' Abdikadir said, 'that in this model of physics, very large distances and very small are somehow *equivalent*.'

'Yes,' she said. 'That's it. The cosmos and the sub-atom – one is just an inverse of the other, if you look at them the right way.'

'And the Eye—'

'The Eye contains an image of me,' she said, 'just as my retina has on it a projected image of you, Josh. But I think in the case of the Eye the reality of the image of me, and of the world, is more than a mere projection.'

Abdikadir frowned. 'Then the distorted images in the Eye are not just a shadow of our reality. And by manipulating these *images* the Eye is somehow able to control what goes on in the outside world. Perhaps that is how it managed to induce the Discontinuity. Is that what you think?'

'Like voodoo dolls,' Josh said, enraptured by the notion. 'The Eye contains a voodoo world . . . But Abdikadir isn't quite right, is he, Bisesa? The Eye doesn't *do* anything. You have said that the Eye, marvellous as it is, is only a tool. And that you have sensed – presences – beyond the Eye, which control *it*. So the Eye is not some demonic controlling entity. It is merely a – a—'

'A control panel,' she whispered. 'I always knew you were smart, Josh.'

'Ah,' said Abdikadir slowly. 'I start to understand. You believe that you have some access to this control panel. *That you can influence the Eye.* And that is what scares you.'

She could't meet his bright eyes.

Josh said, bewildered, 'But if you can influence the Eye, what have you asked it to do?'

She hid her face. 'To let me go home,' she whispered. 'And I think—'

'What?'

'I think it might.'

The others fell silent, shocked. But she had said it, at last, and she knew now that as soon as this jaunt was over she must confront the Eye once more, challenge it again. Or die trying.

Some days short of Alexandria, the fleet put to shore. This, Alexander's surveyors assured him, was the site of Para-etonium, a city he had once visited, although there was no trace of it now. Eumenes met them here. He said he wished

317

to accompany his King as he retraced the most significant pilgrimage of his life.

Alexander sent out scouts to round up camels, which were laden with water for five days' journey. A small party of no more than a dozen, including Alexander, Eumenes, Josh and Bisesa, with a few close bodyguards, quickly formed up. The Macedonians wrapped themselves up in long Bedouin-style winding cloths: they had been here before, and knew what to expect. The moderns followed their lead.

They set off south, inland from the sea. The journey would last several days. Tracing the border of Egypt and Libya, they followed a chain of eroded hills. As her stiffness wore off, and her muscles and lungs began to respond to the exercise, Bisesa found herself losing her thoughts in the simple physical repetition of the walk. More therapy, she thought dryly. Overnight they slept in tents and their Bedouin wraps. But on the second day they were hit by a sandstorm, a hot blizzard of coarse grit. After that they ventured through a ravine oddly carpeted by seashells, and through landscapes of wind-sculpted rock, and across a gruelling gravel plateau.

At last they reached a small oasis. There were palm trees and even some birds, quail and falcon, preserved in a desolate landscape of salt flats. The place was dominated by a gaunt, ruined citadel, and small shrines stood coyly half-hidden by vegetation among the springs. There were no people here, no sign of habitation, nothing but picturesque ruin.

Alexander stepped forward, shadowed by his guards. He walked past the eroded foundations of vanished buildings, and reached a set of steps which led up to what had once been a temple. Alexander was visibly shaking as he climbed these worn steps. He reached a bare, dusty platform, and knelt down, his head bowed.

Eumenes murmured, 'When we were here this place was ancient, but not ruined. The god Ammon came riding out in his sacred boat, borne aloft by purified bearers, and virgins sang songs of divinity. The King went through to the holiest shrine of all, a tiny room roofed by palm trunks, where he

318

consulted the oracle. He never revealed the questions he asked, not even to me, not even to Hephaistion. And it was here that Alexander realised his divinity.'

Bisesa knew the story. During Alexander's first pilgrimage the Macedonians had identified the ram-headed Libyan god Ammon with the Greek Zeus, and Alexander had learned that Zeus-Ammon was his true father, not King Philip of Macedon. From this point he would take Ammon to his heart for the rest of his life.

The King seemed crushed. Perhaps he had hoped to find that the shrine had somehow survived the Discontinuity, that this place, most sacred of all to him, might have been spared. But it was not so, and he had found nothing here but the dead weight of time.

Bisesa murmured to Eumenes, 'Tell him it wasn't always like this. Tell him that nine centuries later, when this place was part of the Roman Empire, and Christianity was the Empire's official religion, there would still be a group of adherents, here at this oasis, still worshipping Zeus-Ammon, and Alexander himself.'

Eumenes nodded gravely, and in measured tones delivered this news from the future. The King replied, and Eumenes returned to Bisesa. 'He says that even a god cannot conquer time, but nine hundred years should be enough for anybody.'

The party stayed a day at the oasis to recuperate and water the camels, and then returned to the shore.

CHAPTER 42

LAST NIGHT

A week after their return to Babylon, Bisesa announced she believed the Eye of Marduk would send her home.

This was met with general incredulity, even from her closest companions. She sensed that Abdikadir thought this was no more than wishful thinking, that her impressions of the Eye and the entities beyond it might be fantasy – that all of this was no more than she wanted to believe.

Alexander, though, faced her with a simple question. 'Why you?'

'Because I asked it to,' she said simply.

And he thought that over, nodded, and let her go.

Sceptical or not, her companions, modern, British and Macedonian, accepted her sincerity, and supported her preparations for her departure, such as they were. They even accepted the date she announced for going. She still had no proof of any of this, and couldn't even be sure if she was interpreting her inchoate impressions of the Eye correctly. But everyone took her seriously, and she was flattered by that, even if some of them gloated a little about how stupid she was going to look if the Eye let her down.

As the last day approached, Bisesa sat with Josh in the chamber of Marduk, with the looming, silent Eye hanging over them. They clung to each other. They were beyond passion: they had made love in defiance of the Eye's cold glare, but even that could not drive the Eye out of their consciousness. All they wanted now, all they could ask of each other, was comfort.

Josh whispered, 'Do you think they *care* at all about what they have done – the world they have taken apart, those who have died?'

320

'No. Oh, perhaps they have a certain academic interest in such emotions. Nothing beyond that.'

'Then they are less than me. If I see an animal killed, *I* am capable of caring for it, of feeling its pain.'

'Yes,' she said patiently, 'but, Josh, you don't care for the millions of bacteria that die in your gut every second. We aren't bacteria; we are complex, independent, conscious creatures. But *they* are so far above us that we are diminished to nothing.'

'Then why would they send you home?'

'I don't know. Because it amuses them, I suppose.'

He glowered at her. 'What *they* want doesn't matter. Are you sure this is what *you* want, Bisesa? Even if you do go home, *what if Myra doesn't want you?*'

She turned to look at him. His eyes were huge in the lamplight gloom, his skin very smooth, young-looking. 'That's ridiculous.'

'Is it? Bisesa, who are you? Who is *she*? After the Discontinuity, we are all fractured selves that straddle worlds. Perhaps some splinter of you could be given back to some splinter of Myra—'

Resentment exploded in her, as her complicated feelings for both Myra and Josh came bubbling up. 'You don't know what you're talking about.'

He sighed. '*You can't go back*, Bisesa. It would mean nothing. Stay here.' He grabbed her hands. 'We have houses to build, crops to grow – and children to raise. Stay here with me, Bisesa, and have *my* children. This world is no longer some alien artefact; it is our home.'

Suddenly she softened. 'Oh, Josh.' She pulled him to her. 'Dear Josh. I want to stay, believe me I do. But I can't. It's not just Myra. This is an opportunity, Josh. An opportunity they haven't offered to anybody else. Whatever their motives, I have to take it.'

'Why?'

'Because of what I might learn. About why this has happened. About *them*. About what we might do about all this in the future.'

'Ah.' He smiled wistfully. 'I should have known. I can argue with a mother about her love for her child, but I can't stand in the way of a soldier's duty.'

'Oh, Josh—'

'Take me with you.'

She sat back, shocked. 'I wasn't expecting *that*.'

'Bisesa, you are everything to me. I don't want to stay here without you. I want to follow you, wherever you go.'

'But I may be killed,' she said softly.

'If I die by your side I will die happy. What else is life for?'

'Josh, I don't know what to say. All I do is hurt you.'

'No,' he said gently. 'Myra is always there – if not between us, then at your side. I understand that.'

'Well, even so, nobody loved me this way before.'

They embraced again, and were silent for a while.

Then he said, 'You know, they don't have a name.'

'Who?'

'The baleful intelligences who engineered all this. They are not God, or any gods—'

'No,' she said. She closed her eyes. She could feel them even now, like a breeze from the heart of an old, dying wood, dry and rustling and laden with decay. 'They are not gods. They are of this universe – they were born of it, as we were. But they are old – terribly old, old beyond our imagining.'

'They have lived too long.'

'Perhaps.'

'Then that is what we will call them.' He looked up at the Eye, chin jutting, defiant. 'The Firstborn. And may they rot in hell.'

To celebrate Bisesa's peculiar departure, Alexander ordered an immense feast. It lasted three days and three nights. There were athletic contests, horse races, dances and music – and even an immense *battue* in the Mongol style, the tales of which had impressed even Alexander the Great.

On the last night Bisesa and Josh were guests of honour at a lavish banquet in Alexander's commandeered palace. The King himself did her the honour of dressing like Ammon, his father-god, in slippers, horns and purple cloak. It was a violent, noisy, drunken affair, like the ultimate rugby club outing. By three a.m. the booze had polished off poor Josh, who had to be carried out to a bedroom by Alexander's chamberlains.

Illuminated by a single oil lamp, Bisesa, Abdikadir and Casey sat close to each other on expensive couches, a small fire burning in a hearth between them.

Casey was drinking from a tall glass beaker. He held it out to Bisesa. 'Babylonian wine. Better than that Macedonian rotgut. You want some?'

She smiled and passed. 'I think I ought to be sober to-morrow.'

Casey grunted. 'From what I hear of Josh, one of you needs to be.'

Abdikadir said, 'So here we are, the last survivors of the twenty-first century. I can't remember the last time the three of us were alone.'

Casey said, 'Not since the day of the chopper crash.'

'That's how you think of it?' Bisesa asked. 'Not the day the world came apart at the seams, but the day we lost the Bird!'

Casey shrugged. 'I'm a professional. I lost my ship.'

She nodded. 'You're a good man, Casey. Give me that stuff.' She grabbed the beaker from him and took a draught of wine. It was rich, tasting very old, almost stale, the produce of a mature vineyard.

Abdikadir was watching her, his blue eyes bright. 'Josh spoke to me this evening, before he got too drunk to speak at all. He thinks you are keeping back something from him, even now – something about the Eye.'

'I don't always know what to tell him,' she said. 'He's a man of the nineteenth century. Christ, he's so *young*.'

'But he's not a child, Bis,' Casey said. 'Men no older than him died for us facing the Mongols. And you know he is prepared to give up his life for you.'

'I know.'

'So,' Abdikadir said, 'what is it you won't tell him?'

'My worst suspicions.'

'About what?'

'About facts that have been staring us in the face since day one. Guys, our little bit of Afghanistan, and the slab of sky above it that preserved the Soyuz, is all that came through the Discontinuity from our own time. And, hard as we've looked, we've found nothing from any era later than our own. We were the last to be sampled. Doesn't that seem strange to you? Why would a two-million-year history project end with us?'

Abdikadir nodded. 'Ah. *Because we are the last.* After us there is nothing to be sampled. Ours was the last year, the last month – even the last day.'

'I think,' Bisesa said slowly, 'that something terrible must happen on that final day – terrible for humanity, or the world. Maybe that's why we shouldn't worry about time paradoxes. Going back and changing history. Because after us, Earth has run out of history to change . . .'

Abdikadir said, 'And perhaps this answers a question that occurred to me when you described your ideas on spacetime rips. It would surely take a stupendous amount of energy to take spacetime apart like that. Is that what faces the Earth?' He waved his hands. 'Some immense catastrophe: a great outpouring of energy, in the face of which Earth is like a snowflake in a furnace – an energy storm which disrupts space and time itself . . .'

Casey closed his eyes and drank more wine. 'Christ, Bis. I knew you'd bring the mood down.'

'And maybe that's why the sampling happened in the first place,' Abdikadir said.

She hadn't thought it through that far. 'What do you mean?'

'The library is about to burn down. What do you do about it? You run through the galleries, grabbing what you can. Maybe the construction of Mir is an exercise in salvage.'

Casey said, eyes still closed, 'Or looting.'

'What?'

'Maybe these Firstborn aren't just here to record the end.

Maybe they caused it. I bet you hadn't thought of that either, Bis.'

Abdikadir said, 'Why couldn't you tell Josh this?'

'Because he's full of hope. I couldn't crush that.'

They sat in tense, brooding silence for a while. Then they started to talk about their future plans.

Abdikadir said, 'I think Eumenes sees me as a useful tool in his endless quest to distract the King. I've proposed an expedition to the source of the Nile. The Firstborn seem to have preserved fragments of humanity perhaps from the first divergence from the chimps – but *what were the very first?* What quality about those deepest, hairiest ancestors did the Firstborn recognise as human? That's the prize I want to dangle before Alexander.'

'It's a fine ambition,' Bisesa said. Privately, though, she doubted if Alexander would be sold on it. It was Alexander's world-view that was going to shape the near future, and that was a dream of heroes, gods and myths, not a quest for resolving scientific questions. 'I have a feeling you will find a place wherever you go, Abdi.'

He smiled. 'I have always inclined to the Sufi tradition, I think. The inner exploration of faith: where I am doesn't matter.'

'I wish I felt the same,' she said earnestly.

Casey said, 'As for me I don't want to live out my life in a James Watt theme park. I'm trying to kick-start other industries – electricity, even electronics maybe . . .'

'What he means,' Abdikadir said dryly, 'is that he's becoming a schoolteacher.'

Casey squirmed a little, but he tapped his broad cranium. 'Just want to make sure that what's up here doesn't die when I do, so generations of poor saps have to rediscover it all.'

Bisesa squeezed his arm. 'It's okay, Case. I think you'll be a good teacher. I always did think of you as a surrogate father.'

Casey's swearing, in English, Greek and even Mongolian, was impressive.

Bisesa stood. 'Guys, I hate to say it, but I think I should get some sleep.'

With one instinct, they pulled together, and wrapped their arms around each other, heads together, huddling like players in a football game.

Casey said, 'You need a Blue Bomber?'

'I have one . . . One more thing,' Bisesa whispered. 'Let the man-apes go. If I can break out of the cage, so should they.'

Casey said, 'I promise. No goodbyes, Bis.'

'No. No goodbyes.'

Abdikadir said, ' "Why is life given/To be thus wrested from us?" . . .'

Casey grunted. 'Milton. *Paradise Lost*, right? Satan's challenge to God.'

Bisesa said, 'You never cease to amaze me, Case. The Firstborn are no gods.' She grinned coldly. 'But I always admired Satan.'

'Fuck that,' said Casey. 'The Firstborn have to be stopped.'

After a final, long moment, she pulled away, and left them with their wine.

Bisesa sought out Eumenes, and asked permission to leave the banquet.

Eumenes was upright, contained and apparently sober. He said in his stilted, heavily accented English, 'Very well. But, madam, only on condition I am allowed to accompany you for a while.'

With a few guards, they walked up Babylon's ceremonial way. They called at the townhouse commandeered by Captain Grove. Grove embraced her and wished her luck, in his clipped Noel Coward accent. Bisesa and Eumenes walked on, out of the city walls through the Ishtar Gate, and into the tent city of the army beyond.

The night was clear and cold, with the unfamiliar stars and a bony crescent Moon showing through high, yellowish clouds. When Bisesa was recognised she was greeted with cries and waves. The troops and their followers had been given gifts of wine and meat by the King in Bisesa's honour. The whole camp seemed to be awake: the tents glowed from lamps lit inside, and music and laughter rose up like smoke.

'They are all sorry to see you go,' Eumenes murmured.

'I just gave them an excuse for a party.'

'You should not – um, underestimate your contribution. We were all pitched together into this fractured new world. There was great suspicion, even incomprehension, between our various parties, and the three of you from the twenty-first century were the fewest and most isolated of all. But without you to help us, even Alexander's wiles might not have prevailed against the Mongols. We have become an unlikely family.'

'Yes, we have, haven't we? I suppose that says something about enduring qualities of the human spirit.'

'Yes.' He stopped and faced her, and his expression showed the grim anger she had seen in him before. 'And where you are going, as you face an enemy even Alexander could not challenge, you must call on those same qualities again. On behalf of us all.'

A nursing mother, the wife of a soldier, sat on a low stool outside one of the tents, her baby at her breast. The baby's face was a pale disc, like the Moon. The mother saw Bisesa watching, and smiled.

Eumenes said, 'The Babylonian astronomers have decided that the Discontinuity should be considered the start of a new calendar, a new year – indeed, the start of one of their mighty cycles, their Great Years. Everything began afresh that day. And the first babies to be conceived on Mir have already been born. They did not exist in whatever world we came from – *they could not have*, for some of their parents came from different eras – but *their* past is not fractured like ours; they only exist here. I wonder what they will do when they grow up?'

She studied his face, its tanned plains shadowed in the uncertain light. 'You understand so much,' she said.

He grinned, disarmingly. 'As Casey says, like all ancient Greeks I'm smart as a tack, and smug with it. What do you expect?'

They embraced, stiffly. Then they walked back to the city.

CHAPTER 43

THE EYE OF MARDUK

When Bisesa arrived in the Temple of Marduk the following morning, Abdikadir was waiting, and Casey was already working, checking out sensor equipment. They were here for her; she was touched by their faith in her, and reassured by their competence.

The Eye floated impassively, as it always did.

Josh was here. While Bisesa was wearing her flight suit, much patched, Josh wore a rumpled flannel suit and shirt, and, absurdly enough, a tie. But, she thought, they had no idea what they would face today; why not look your best?

But his face was white, and there were deep shadows under his eyes. 'Into infinity with a sore head! At least I can't be made to feel any worse, whatever happens.'

Bisesa felt oddly impatient, irritable. 'Let's get on with it,' she said. 'Here.' She held out a small backpack.

He looked at it dubiously. 'What's in it?'

'Water. Dried rations. Some medical supplies.'

'You think we will need this? Bisesa, we are entering the Eye of Marduk, not hiking across the desert.'

'But she's right,' Abdikadir snapped. 'Why not anticipate what we can?' He took the bag and thrust it at Josh. 'Take it.'

Bisesa said to Josh, 'And if you're going to grouse all the way, I'll leave you behind.'

Josh's pained face crumpled into a smile. 'I'll be good.'

Bisesa looked around. 'I told Eumenes and Grove to keep everybody else away. I'd have preferred them to evacuate the damn city, but I suppose that wasn't practical . . . Is there anything we've forgotten?' She had used the bathroom, cleaned her teeth: simple human actions, but she wondered where, when she would next have time to groom herself. 'Abdi, take care of my phone.'

Abdikadir said gently, 'As I promised. And – one more thing.' He held out two pieces of paper, Babylonian parchment, neatly folded and sealed. 'If you don't mind.'

'From you?'

'Me and Casey. If it's possible – if you can find our families –'

Bisesa took the papers and tucked them inside her jump-suit. 'I'll make sure they get them.'

Casey nodded. Then he called, 'Something's happening.' He adjusted his headset and tapped an electromagnetic sensor lashed up from the guts of the chopper's ruined radio. He glanced up at the Eye. 'I don't see any change in that thing. But the signal's intensifying. It seems somebody is expecting you, Bisesa.'

Bisesa took Josh's hand. 'We'd better take our positions.'

'Where?' A lock of hair on his forehead was ruffled by a breeze.

'Damned if I know,' she said. Fondly she tucked back his hair. But the breeze came again, washing over Josh's face, a breeze that blew in from no apparent source, towards the centre of the chamber.

'It's the Eye,' Abdikadir said. Bits of paper and loose cabling fluttered around him. 'It is breathing in. Bisesa, get ready.'

The breeze had become a wind, flowing towards the centre of the room, strong enough to buffet Bisesa's back. She pulled Josh with her, and stumbled towards the Eye. It hung there as still as ever, returning her own distorted voodoo-doll reflec-tion, but bits of paper and straw flew up and clung to its surface.

Casey threw his headphones aside. 'Shit! There was a shriek – an electromagnetic chirp – it's blown the circuits. Whoever that thing is signalling, it isn't *me* . . .'

'It's time,' Josh said.

So it was, she thought. On some deep level she hadn't believed it herself. But now it was happening. Her stomach fluttered, her heart pounded; she was profoundly grateful for the feel of Josh's strong hand.

'Look up,' Abdikadir said.

For the first time since they had found it, the Eye was changing.

The reflective sheen was still there. But now it oscillated like the surface of a pool of mercury, waves and ripples chasing across its surface.

Then the surface collapsed, like the skin of a suddenly deflated balloon.

Bisesa found herself looking up into a funnel, walled with a silvery gold. She could still see reflections of herself, with Josh at her side, but their images were broken up, as if scattered from the shards of a smashed mirror. The funnel seemed to be directly before her face, but she guessed that if she were to walk around the chamber, or climb above and below the Eye, she would see the same funnel shape, the walls of light drawing in towards its centre.

This was not a funnel, no simple three-dimensional object, but a flaw in her reality.

She looked over her shoulder. The air was full of sparks now, all rushing towards the core of the imploded Eye. Abdikadir was still there, though he seemed to be drawing more distant, and he was oddly blurred: he was clinging to the door frame, and he was on the ground, and he turned away and turned back – not sequentially, but all at the same time, like the frames of a movie reel cut out and reassembled in a random order. 'Go with Allah,' he called. 'Go, go . . .' But his voice was lost on the wind. And then the storm of light grew to a blizzard, and she could see him no more.

The wind tugged at her, nearly knocking her off her feet. She tried to be analytical. She tried to count her breaths. But her thoughts seemed to fragment, the inner sentences she formed breaking into words, and syllables, and letters, jumbling into nonsense. It was the Discontinuity, she thought. It had worked on the scale of a planet, cutting adrift great slabs of landscape. But it had broken into this room, cutting Abdikadir's life into pieces, and now, at last, it was pushing into her own head, for, after all, even her consciousness was embedded in spacetime . . .

She looked into the Eye. The light was streaming into its heart. In these final moments the Eye changed again. The funnel shape opened out into a straight-walled shaft that receded to infinity – but it was a shaft that defied perspective, for its walls did not diminish with distance, but stayed the same apparent size.

It was her last conscious thought before the light washed down over her, filling her, searing away even her sense of her body. Space was gone, time itself suspended, and she became a mote, nothing but an animal's bright, stubborn, mindless soul. But through it all she was aware of Josh's warm hand in hers.

There was only one Eye, though it had many projections into spacetime. And it had many functions.

One of those was to serve as a gate.

The gate opened. The gate closed. In a moment of time too short to be measured, space opened and turned on itself.

Then the Eye vanished. The temple chamber was left empty save for a tangle of ruined electronic gear, and two men with memories of what they had seen and heard, memories they could neither believe nor understand.

Time's Eye

PART SIX

TIME'S EYE

CHAPTER 44

FIRSTBORN

The long wait was ending. On yet another world, intelligence had been born and was escaping from its planetary cradle.

Those who had watched Earth for so long had never been remotely human. But they had once been flesh and blood.

They had been born on a planet of one of the first stars of all, a roaring hydrogen-fat monster, a beacon in a universe still dark. These first ones were vigorous, in a young and energy-fat universe. But planets, the crucibles of life, were scarce, for the heavy elements that comprised them had yet to be manufactured in the hearts of stars. When they looked out across the depths of space, they saw nothing like themselves, no Mind to mirror their own.

The early stars blazed gloriously but died quickly. Their thin debris enriched the pooled gases of the Galaxy, and soon a new generation of long-lived stars would emerge. But to those left stranded between the dying protostars, it was a terrible abandonment.

And as they looked ahead, they saw only a slow darkening, as each generation of stars was built with increasing difficulty from the debris of the last. At last there would come a day when there wasn't enough fuel in the Galaxy to manufacture a single new star, and the last light flickered and died. Even after that it would go on, the clamp of entropy strangling the cosmos and all its processes.

Despite all their powers, they were not beyond the reach of time.

This desolating realisation caused an age of madness. Strange and beautiful empires rose and fell, and terrible wars were fought between beings of metal and of flesh, children of the same forgotten world. The wars expended an unforgivable proportion of the Galaxy's usable energy reserve, and had no resolution but exhaustion.

Saddened but wiser, the survivors began to plan for an inevitable future, an endless future of cold and dark.

They returned to their abandoned machines of war. The ancient machines were directed to a new objective: to the elimination of waste – to cauterisation, if necessary. Their makers saw now that if even a single thread of awareness was to be passed to the furthest future, there must be no unnecessary disturbance, no wasted energy, no ripples in the stream of time.

The machines had been honed by a million years of war. They fulfilled their task perfectly, and would do so for ever. They waited, unchanging, dedicated to a single purpose, as new worlds, and new life, congealed from the rubble of the old.

It was all for the best of intentions. The first ones, born into an empty universe, cherished life above all else. But to preserve life, life must sometimes be destroyed.

CHAPTER 45

THROUGH THE EYE

It wasn't like waking. It was a sudden emergence, a clash of cymbals. Her eyes gaped wide open, and were filled with dazzling light. She dragged deep breaths into her lungs, and scrabbled at the ground, and gasped with the shock of self-hood.

She was on her back. There was something enormously bright above her – the sun, yes, the sun, she was outdoors. Her arms were spread out wide, away from her body, and her fingers were digging into the dirt.

She threw herself over on to her belly. Sensations returned to her legs, arms, chest. Dazzled by the sun, she could barely see.

A plain. Red sand. Eroded hills in the distance. Even the sky looked red, though the sun was high.

Josh was beside her. He was lying on his back, gasping for air, like an ungainly fish stranded on this strange beach. She scrabbled over to him, crawling through loose sand.

'Where are we?' he gasped. 'Is this the twenty-first century?'

'I hope not.' When she tried to speak her throat was dry, scratchy. She pulled her pack off her back and dug out a flask of water. 'Drink this.'

He gulped at the water gratefully. Sweat was already standing out on his brow and soaking into his collar.

She dug her hands into the dirt. It crumbled, pale, lifeless and dry. But something shone in it, fragments that glittered when exposed to the overhead sun. She dug them out and laid them on her palm. They were coin-sized fragments of glass, opaque, their edges ragged. She shook the fragments out of her palm and let them fall to the ground. But when she brushed away more dirt, she found more glass bits everywhere, a layer of the stuff beneath the ground.

Experimentally she pushed herself to her knees, straightened up – her ears rang with dizziness, but she wasn't going to faint – and then, one foot, two, she stood up. Now she could see the landscape better. It was just a plain, a plain of this glass-ridden sand, that marched away to the horizon, where worn hills waited out eternity. She and Josh were at the base of a shallow depression; the land subtly rose all around them to a rim, no more than a few metres high, perhaps a kilometre away.

She was standing in a crater.

A nuke would do this, she thought. The glass fragments could have been formed in the explosion of a small nuclear weapon, bits of concrete and soil fused to glass. If that was so, nothing else was left – if there had been a city here there were no concrete foundations, no bones, not even the ashes of the final fires, only the fragments of nuclear glass. This crater looked old, worn, the bits of glass buried deep. If war had come by here, it must have been long ago.

She wondered if radioactivity lingered. But if the Firstborn had meant her any harm they could have simply killed her; and if not, surely they would protect her from such an elementary hazard.

Her chest ached as she breathed. Was the air thin? Was there too little oxygen, or too much?

Suddenly it got a little darker, though there was no cloud in the ruddy sky. She peered up. There was something wrong with the sun. Its disc was deformed. It looked like a leaf out of which a great bite had been taken.

Josh was standing beside her. 'My God,' he said.

The eclipse progressed quickly. It began to feel colder, and in the last moments Bisesa glimpsed bands of shadow rushing across the eroded ground. She felt her breathing slow, her heart pump more gently. Her body, responding even now to ancient primal rhythms, was reacting to the darkness, readying itself for night.

The darkness reached its greatest depth. There was a moment of profound stillness.

The sun turned to a ring of brightness. The central disc of shadow had a serrated edge, and sunlight twinkled through those irregularities. That disc was surely the Moon, still travelling between Earth and sun, its shadow sliding across the face of the sun. The sun's glare was reduced enough for Bisesa to make out the corona, the sun's higher atmosphere, easily visible as a wispy sculpture around that complex double disc.

But this eclipse was not total. The Moon was not big enough to obscure that glowing face. The fat ring of light in the sky was a baffling, terrifying sight.

'Something's wrong,' Josh murmured.

'Geometry,' she said. 'The Earth-Moon system . . . It changes with time.' As the Moon dragged tides through Earth's ocean, so Earth likewise tugged at the Moon's rocky substrate. Since their formation the twin worlds had slowly separated – only a few centimetres per year, but over enough time that took the Moon ever further from the Earth.

Josh understood the essence of what had happened. 'This is the future. Not the twenty-first century – the very far future . . . Millions of years hence, perhaps.'

She walked around the plain, peering up at the complex sky. 'You're trying to tell us something, aren't you? This desolate, war-shattered ground – where am I, London? New York, Moscow, Beijing? Lahore? And why bring us to this precise place and time to show us an eclipse? Has all this got something to do with the sun?' Hot, dusty, thirsty, disoriented, she was suddenly filled with rage. 'Don't give me special-effect riddles. Talk to me, damn you. *What's going to happen*?'

As if in reply an Eye, at least as large as the Eye of Marduk, snapped into existence above her head. She actually felt the wash of the air it displaced as it forced its way into her reality.

She took Josh's hand. 'Here we go again. Keep your hands inside the car at all times.'

But his eyes were wide; sand clung to his sweat-streaked face. 'Bisesa?'

She understood immediately. *He couldn't see the Eye.* This time it had come for her – her alone, not for Josh.

'No!' She grabbed Josh's arm. 'You can't do this, you cruel bastards!'

Josh understood. 'Bisesa, it's all right.' He touched her chin, turned her face towards him, kissed her mouth. 'We've already come further than I could have dreamed possible. Perhaps our love will live on in some other world, and perhaps when all possibilities are drawn together at the end of time we will be reunited.' He smiled. 'It's enough.'

In the sky the Eye flipped into a funnel shape, and then a corridor in the sky. Already sparks of light were rushing across the plain, gathering around her, hurtling upwards.

She clung to Josh and closed her eyes. *Listen to me. I've done everything you asked. Give me this one thing. Don't leave him here, to die alone. Send him home – send him back to Abdi. This one thing, I beg you . . .*

A hot wind gathered, rushing up from the ground into the mouth of the shining shaft overhead. Something tugged at her, pulling her from Josh's arms. She struggled, but Josh let go.

She was lifted off the ground. She was actually looking down at him.

He was still smiling. 'You are an angel ascending. Goodbye, goodbye . . .' The searing, beautiful light gathered around her again. In the last instant she saw him stagger back into a room crowded with wires and bits of electronic gear, where a dark man rushed forward to catch him.

Thank you.

A clash of cymbals.

CHAPTER 46

GRASPER

With the coming of the morning, Seeker woke with a start, eyes snapping open.

For the first time in five years there was no net sheltering her from the sky. She cried out and curled over her daughter.

She forced open one eye. There was still no net, nothing but bare ground around her, a few scuff marks and tracks. The soldiers had gone. They had taken away the cage.

She was free.

She sat up. Grasper woke up with a grumble and rubbed her eyes. Seeker looked around. The rocky plain swept away, bare of life save for a few tussocks of grass. In the distance, snow-capped mountains loomed over the horizon, blue and floating in the morning mist. Near the base of the mountains she made out a stripe of green. Her old spirit stirred. *Forest*: if they could make it that far, perhaps she would find others like herself.

But the breeze changed, coming from the north, and she tasted ice. She quailed. Suddenly she longed for the smells of cooking, the clattering of machines, the high, gull-like voices of the soldiers. She had spent too long in her cage; she missed it.

Grasper, though, shared none of her mother's hesitation. She knuckle-walked forward, chimp-like, exploring the rocky ground. It seemed rich in texture compared to the swept-bare, stamped-down dirt floor of the cage. Here was a rock that fit neatly in her hand, there a dry reed that folded and bent and twisted with ease.

Clutching the rock, Grasper unfolded her legs and stood upright. She peered across the broken ground towards the mountains, and the ice.

In the north the cold was gathering. The new volcanic island in the Atlantic had deflected the Gulf Stream, the flow of southern water that had kept northern Europe anomalously warm for millennia. The Gulf Stream's loss had already had impacts on agriculture as far south as Babylonia. Now it was going to get worse. This year autumn would come early, and by midwinter massive Arctic superstorms would erupt with fury over the continents, depositing more snow in a few days than would once have been seen in five or ten years.

For two million years before the Discontinuity, the ice had come and gone from its fastnesses at the poles, its complex cycles governed by subtleties of Earth's passage around the sun. This new world, Mir, thrown together from fragments of the old, had at first oscillated unsteadily, but as that first motion damped it was settling down to a new pattern of cycles: a pattern that, in the short term, promoted the spreading of the ice. It would take only a decade for the icecaps to form, a decade more for them to extend as far south as the sites of London, Berlin, Manhattan.

Further ahead, even more drastic changes were to come. Since its formation the planet had been steadily cooling, and the flow of heat from its interior had driven the mantle currents on which the continents rode. Now the Discontinuity had caused disturbances in the deep strange weather of Mir's liquid interior. Eventually a new pattern of currents would settle into place, but for now it was as if a vast lid had been clamped on a boiling pan.

Beneath the hearts of the continents the mantle material had begun to swell and rise. Earth had never been perfectly spherical anyhow. Now Mir was growing bulges, like lumps of mud stuck to the side of a spinning top. In time the crust and upper mantle would shear off the planet's core, and the deformed planet would seek a new stability by shifting the lumps away from the axis of rotation. As the major continents slid to the equator, ocean currents would be altered again, sea levels raised or lowered by hundreds of metres, dramatic climate changes induced.

342

In Mir's long chthonic annealing there would be difficult times for the planet's cargo of life. But people were mobile. The citizens of Chicago were already preparing for a vast migration south. Many humans would survive.

As would the man-apes.

Grasper was not as she had been before her inspection by the Eye. The probing of her body and mind had been meant only to record her capabilities, to note her place in the great spectrum of possibilities that was life on this blue world. But Grasper was very young, and the machinery that had studied her was very old, and no longer quite so perfect as it had once been. The probing had been clumsy. Grasper's half-formed mind had been stirred.

This patched-together world would be dominated for a long time by the humans, there could be no doubt about that. But even they could not defy the ice. On a shifting, dangerous world there was plenty of empty space to explore. Plenty of room for a creature with potential. And there was no particular reason why that potential had to be realised exactly as it had been before. There was room on Mir for something different. Something better, perhaps.

Grasper hefted the heavy stone in her hand, and dimly imagined what might be done with it. She was quite without fear. Now she was master of the world, and she was not quite sure what to do next.

But she would think of something.

CHAPTER 47

RETURN

Bisesa gasped, staggered. She was standing.

Music was playing.

She stared at a wall, which showed the magnified image of an impossibly beautiful young man crooning into an old-fashioned microphone. Impossible, yes; he was a synth star, a distillation of the inchoate longings of sub-teen girls. 'My God, he looks like Alexander the Great.' Bisesa could barely take her eyes off the wall's moving colours, its brightness. She had never realised how drab and dun-coloured Mir had been.

The softwall said, 'Good morning, Bisesa. This is your regular alarm call. Breakfast is waiting downstairs. The news headlines today are—'

'Shut up.' Her voice was a dusty desert croak.

'Of course.' The synthetic boy sang on softly.

She glanced around. This was her bedroom, in her London apartment. It seemed small, cluttered. The bed was big, soft, not slept in.

She walked to the window. Her military-issue boots were heavy on the carpet, and left footprints of crimson dust. The sky was grey, on the cusp of sunrise, and the skyline of London was emerging from the flatness of silhouette.

'Wall.'

'Bisesa?'

'What's the date?'

'Tuesday.'

'The *date*.'

'Ah. The ninth of June, 2037.'

The day after the chopper crash. 'I should be in Afghanistan.'

The softwall coughed. 'I've grown used to your sudden changes of plans, Bisesa. I remember once—'

'Mum?'

The voice was small, sleepy. Bisesa turned.

She was barefoot, her tummy stuck out, fist rubbing at one eye, hair tousled, a barely awake eight-year-old. She was wearing her favourite pyjamas, the ones across which cartoon characters gambolled, even though they were now about two sizes too small for her. 'You didn't say you were coming home.'

Something broke inside Bisesa. She reached out. 'Oh, Myra—'

Myra recoiled. 'You *smell* funny.'

Shocked, Bisesa glanced down at herself. In her orange jumpsuit, scuffed and torn and coated with sweat-soaked sand, she was as out of place in this twenty-first-century flat as if she had been wearing a spacesuit.

She forced a smile. 'I guess I need a shower. Then we'll have breakfast, and I'll tell you all about it . . .'

The light changed, subtly. She turned to the window. There was an Eye over the city, floating like a barrage balloon. She couldn't tell how far away it was, or how big.

And over the rooftops of London, a baleful sun was rising.